T. R. Wilson was born and [...] ough on the edge of the Fe[...] [...] attended the University of East Anglia, and his love of East Anglia – its landscape, people and history – has always been central to his life and work. He submitted his first novel, *Master of Morholm*, at the age of twenty-three, at which time he was a student on the University of East Anglia MA course in Creative Writing, under Malcolm Bradbury and Angela Carter. His MA submission was part of the novel which was later published in 1989 as *Treading on Shadows*. His most recent novel, *Heartsease*, is also available from Headline. He lives with a word processor in a small flat.

A Green Hill Far Away

T. R. Wilson

KNIGHT

Copyright © 1994 T. R. Wilson

The right of T. R. Wilson to be identified as the Author of the
Work has been asserted by her in accordance with the Copyright,
Designs and Patents Act 1988.

The rights to the Knight chess piece reproduced on this book
are the property of Hodder and Stoughton Limited
and it is reproduced with their permission

First published in 1994
by HEADLINE BOOK PUBLISHING

First published in paperback in 1994
by HEADLINE BOOK PUBLISHING

This edition published 1999 by
Knight an imprint of Brockhampton Press

10 9 8 7 6 5 4 3 2 1

ISBN 184186 0379

Phototypeset by Intype, London

Printed and bound in Great Britain by
Mackays of Chatham PLC, Chatham, Kent

Brockhampton Press
20 Bloomsbury Street
London
WC1B 3QA

For Mary-Anne

Infinite passion, and the pain
Of finite hearts that yearn.

ROBERT BROWNING, 'Two in the Campagna'

Part the First

The Shoemaker's Daughter

I

'You see, he wants me to go with him to Cleatham tomorrow, to see the bones.'

'Does he? And shall you go?'

'Well, that's what I wanted to ask you, Lucy. Because I shan't go with him, not unless you come too.'

'Oh, Connie! What on earth would you want me there for?'

'Because I can't go on my own with him! You know who it is goes to see the bones – couples who are walking out. Couples who are courting. That's who.'

'But you *are* walking out with Kit Lightfoot. En't you?'

'We-ell . . . I don't want him to see it that way. He's one of these fresh ones, y'see. And he'll likely think, once we git in Cleatham church crypt, that that's his chance to git fresher than ever. And I wun't entertain it, Lucy. Not that sort of malarkey. I wun't entertain it.'

'But, Connie, what's he going to say when he finds me dragging along o' you like the tail on a donkey? I shan't know where to look!'

The two young women talking thus were part of a swift tide of people pouring forth from the boot-factories of Cottesbridge. The hour was past noon on a Saturday – the time when the whistles blew all across the town to release the shoemaking folk from a working week of some fifty-two hours.

Seeing that multitude of labour hurrying out from little factories built of blankest brick, and moving with a clatter of riveted boots, with a flap of aprons, and with a sort of hungry, unseeing haste down the high gritty causeways which gave to the streets the look of dry river-beds, an observer might have fancied the scene to be the heart of some conurbation of the North, and supposed it to be repeated like a hall of mirrors at all points of the compass. But a view from the high crane doors of one of those factories, a prospect from

3

the iron footbridge arching over the railway line like some grim pergola trained with dismal blooms of gas-lamps, even a glimpse between the close ranks of terraced houses that shouldered and squeezed each other for room – for all the world as if they had grown up together in a thin soil, instead of being planned and built by the mind and hand of man – would have revealed not further plantations of brick and tile, but countryside.

Countryside, too, of great beauty, especially at this moment of the year, which was so early in the summer that hardly any of that season could be said to have gone by, and practically all of it remained for the enjoying. It was not that blighted margin of open space that is often found on the periphery of towns – a sort of country-by-default, which simply hasn't been built on yet – but a landscape with a long history of cultivation, both meadow and arable; a landscape of strong, pungent greens and rich, clayey, clotted browns, more susceptible to the power of the oil-painter than the watercolourist, and then only with a broad technique and much use of the palette-knife. So near was this landscape, that shrubs at the bottom of gardens on the edge of the town, growing under the gas-tarred fences and throwing out shoots on the other side, found themselves living in both town and country at the same moment; and haymakers swung their scythes within earshot of shrill stitching-machines, and peppered the factory windows with pollen. Yet so essentially separate were the two environments, that the same haymakers walking into the town would have appeared as different from the townspeople as wasps in a beehive: not chiefly in build or colouring or dress, though all these would have been conspicuous; but in the lack of a certain nervous, wiry something, visible in all those hurrying forth from the boot-factories, from the old 'crafts' in their white aprons and bowlers and side-whiskers, to the young girls who ran home from work with a skittering of foal-like legs, just as their wealthier coevals ran after hoops and spinning-tops. It was something taut, tense and overdriven that united the variety of faces and figures, old and young, plain and handsome, to be seen in the twice-daily migrations about the streets of Cottesbridge.

It was contrast above all that gave those broad prospects of country their poignant attraction. Viewed from a vantage of gable, timber and thatch, they would have agreeably beguiled the eye. Viewed from Cottesbridge – which was

4

such a concentrated essence of the urban that the very air, smokily flavoured with leather-dust, seemed to be of human manufacture, and supplied to the town by a Works – they had the fascination of a vision.

Familiarity, of course, dulled the impact of even such a contrast as this. Probably for the majority of the townspeople, turned out from the dingy interiors of boot-factories, the glimpses of country were no more than a fleeting impression of pleasantness, a caress on the jaded eyesight. But an observer might have perceived that, for the taller of the two girls making their talkative way across the town bridge, the compulsion of those green fields was keen and persistent. For, even as she held up her end of the conversation, she turned her head about, all unconsciously, to fix with an intense, lingering look the sun-brimming bowl of river valley that came into view from the bridge – rather as a child, though urged on by its mother, will gaze till the last possible moment upon the face of a passing stranger.

'Well, I don't know, Connie,' said the taller girl, at last returning her full attention to her companion, though not without a last backward glance at the perspective of valley now being closed off by a smoky huddle of tanneries. 'I'll come if you want me to; but I shall feel so awk'ud and in the way – and I'm sure Kit will call me all sorts of names under his breath.'

'Well, but you don't have to come on your own, y'know,' said Connie. '*You* could bring a chap, couldn't you? Then you wouldn't feel as if you was just raggle-taggling along.'

'I haven't got a chap,' returned the taller girl.

'No-o,' said Connie judiciously, her gravely considering manner forming a curious contrast with her bland milky face. 'But there's Billy French, in the rough-stuff room – *he'd* go wi' you.'

'Oh, Connie!'

'Or there's Ned Wallis – he's a handsewn-man at Parmenter's: he was the one we saw at last year's Feast, d'you remember? Now *he'd* go with you. I know that for a fact,' Connie said, nodding with her peculiar gruff seriousness. 'Now that I do know. For certain. You wun't convince me otherwise.' Connie was the most ingenuous of girls, and fancied herself the most shrewd.

Her taller companion, Lucy, had meanwhile been shaking her head and laughing a little distressfully. 'No, no, Connie!'

she said. 'I wish you wouldn't go trying to make matches for me. And I don't want these chaps thinking I'll walk out with 'em – it en't fair on 'em.'

'Oh, you don't want to worry about them. *I* don't,' said Connie. 'Chaps always come bouncing back – don't matter what you do to 'em, tek my word for it.' It was Connie's idiosyncrasy likewise to believe herself the sturdiest of sceptics, whereas her heart was in fact permanently affixed to her sleeve, and sustained so much wear and tear that Lucy's share in their friendship consisted in great part of consoling, commiserating, and assuring her that it was not broken. 'Any road, just because you walk out with a chap, it don't mean it's anything . . . *you* know.'

'Well, you *are* a story!' Lucy cried. 'There was you saying you couldn't go to see the bones with Kit Lightfoot, because it would look as if you were serious about him!'

'Never mind me,' Connie said, not at all put out. 'I know what I'm about wi' that gret fool-jabey, don't you worry.' She stole a sideways glance, more wondering than sly, at her companion's face. 'Only you *could* walk out with a chap if you wanted, Lucy, you know you could.'

'Oh! pooh – only for the sake of it: what would be the good of that?' Lucy said absently, pushing back a lock of hair that had escaped her cap.

'Well, it's fun, you know,' said Connie; but Lucy's unmoved expression seeming to deny the validity of this argument, she did not pursue it, only stealing another glance at her friend as if there were much she would like to ask if she only dared.

They went on to Connie's house, whither Lucy had promised to go as soon as they finished work and help Connie alter her Sunday frock. It was near the end of a terrace; adjoining it was a bakehouse, where on Sundays men could be seen bearing away tins of Yorkshire pudding and roast joints, cooked in the baker's oven, and which winter and summer made the party-wall of the Pollards' house as warm to the touch as a hob. Connie being an only child (how often, and how guiltily, Lucy had envied her that!), she had one of the two bedrooms to herself, and there they spread the frock out on the floor to work on it.

'It's all tight in the waist, and gives me a bust like a pub-parlour mantelpiece,' Connie confided in a solemn whisper, 'and if Kit Lightfoot sees me soodling along like that, he'll say to himself, "Hullo! She's a fast one!" and then there'll be no end to it.'

6

'You want to look your best, though,' Lucy said, looking at the dove-grey frock not without a certain wistfulness, 'don't you?'

'Well, I don't want him gitting it into his head that I've made a special effort. Not any more than I'd mek for anybody else. But then I don't want to look the same as when I walked out wi' George Hays last year, because I reckon Kit knows George, and they might compare notes, and then Kit might reckon I'm a loose piece as goes through the chaps one after t'other – d'you see?'

'Mm,' said Lucy, experiencing that baffled sensation she often had when talking to Connie, who seemed to regard life through a mental telescope, which gave a fearful magnification to problems that most people could not even see.

'I don't want to be mistook for one of them horsebuds you see going in the Horse and Jockey, all done up like a dog's dinner,' Connie said. 'There en't one in ten of them as buys their gloves out of wages, that I know for a fact.'

'Oh well, it beats closing boots for a living,' Lucy said, mischievously. Connie's mouth was full of pins, but her eyes sufficiently expressed her shock. 'Anyway,' Lucy went on, pinning up the hem, 'what does it matter what people think?' This was more of an abstract proposition than an argument from experience, as Lucy recognized a moment later, colouring and adding, 'I mean, about what you look like, and all that.'

'All very well to say,' Connie said portentously. 'That's how Alice Wedderburn started, I'll bet . . . Oh! I *knew* there was summat else I had to tell you. About Alice Wedderburn.'

'Not another chap?'

'No. She's still with that ole disgrace with the big house on the Lessington Road. The one with the tennis-court,' Connie added in a whisper, as if that were somehow the most scandalous thing of all. 'No, this is about her mother. Alice Wedderburn's mother's failing, they say – on her last legs; there's been straw down outside her house for the past week, and the doctor don't expect her to last till the Feast. And she's been calling for her daughter, so they say, wanting to see her one last time. And Alice Wedderburn's not been anywhere near her.' Connie bit through cotton thread with a snap, the action giving her mild face a briefly ferocious expression, as if it were Alice Wedderburn that she was savaging. 'Nowhere near her.'

'How do you know this?' said Lucy, realizing at the same

time that that was a pointless question: Connie was just one of those people who collect gossip as a corner collects cobwebs.

'Oh! it's common knowledge. Folk still see Alice Wedderburn all fligged up riding around in a gig with that ole rascal, and looking like the cat that got the cream. Would you credit it? There's nothing as'll drag her back to the Hole, seem'ly – not even her mother laying at death's door – when everybody knows she come from there. Why, I can remember her tekking the cutlery in a paper bag down to the pop-shop of a Monday morning, when she hadn't even a pair of decent boots to her feet . . .'

Connie went on to a brief review of the career of Alice Wedderburn, a tale which was well known in Cottesbridge, but which never lost fascination in the telling. The part of the town known as the Hole, where the tale began, derived its name originally from a slight hollow in which the first cottages stood, in the days when Cottesbridge had been little more than a village; but since then the name had taken on a more evocative meaning. Like others along the valley, the town had grown in a startling spurt, transformed in half a century from a pottering community of hand-shoemakers and smallholders to the thrustful place of boot-factories and gasworks and redbrick chapels that was all Lucy knew; and in consequence it exhibited a certain social uniformity. It had its wealthy men, certainly, for there were fortunes to be made in leather, and those who made them built villas like monstrous gingerbread-houses on the outskirts in emulation of the shoe-barons of Northampton; but in that year of 1899 the great majority of Cottesbridge's twelve thousand souls worked in the boot-factories – of which there was at least one in practically every street – and lived in terraced houses, two-up two-down, squeezed in the narrow margin between poverty and chapel-going respectability. Judged absolutely, there was not far to fall from this hard, pinched, monochrome existence: judged relatively, there was such an enormous metaphysical distance between self-respecting Cottesbridge and the Hole that it must have been a hole indeed before it could have sunk lower in the estimation of those hard-working enough, prudent enough or lucky enough not to live there.

Out of that seething little warren of streets down by the railway; out of that squalid neighbourhood of back-to-backs, and yards, and back-alleys, and lean-tos and privies of such foul character that the trees that had furnished their timber could truly be said to have died and gone to hell; of cramped corner pubs which advertised Harmonic Evenings on their frosted windows, and whose clientele so promoted the cause of harmony amongst themselves that they invariably closed the evening's entertainment by beating out bloody tunes on each other's faces; of pawnbrokers' which were the only shops that would open there; of men lounging and playing at taws in passageways and women hanging out babies' napkins that were like grey fishing-nets; where it was always muddy in winter and dusty in summer, and the burning of scrap-leather on household fires set a greasy slaughterhouse film upon every surface; out of that place which, it seemed, no one ever left except in a plain deal box drawn on a cart, had come Alice Wedderburn, to blaze a trail that scandalized the good people of Cottesbridge, and which they would not have missed seeing, and being able to gossip about, for the world.

Alice Wedderburn was not a beauty: that was what seemed to affront them more than anything. 'Nowt special to look at at all!' the women would say, discussing her latest delinquency. 'I've seen a lot better figures than hern. Who does she reckon she is?' And if the men ventured to say, as they sometimes did, 'Well, I don't hold wi' her carryings-on; but she's got summat about her, I don't know what – just summat unusual,' they were scathingly put down: 'Huh! Hark at him! She wouldn't look at you, my buck – not 'less you got a few thousand pounds you en't told me about – she wouldn't so much as look at yer.' Beauty or not, a string of well-heeled men had looked at her and, in consideration of being permitted to do more than look, had given her the use of their wealth, to the extent that Alice Wedderburn's latest costume, Alice Wedderburn's latest yellow-wheeled buggy, Alice Wedderburn's latest extravagant acquisition from the jeweller's and, most of all, the status of Alice Wedderburn's latest escort, were topics of compulsive interest in Cottesbridge.

The interest, of course, was of that sympathetic kind that chiefly consists in an eager anticipation of the subject's Coming to Grief, which all of Cottesbridge's soberer spirits, communing during Sunday morning chapel parade, were united in agreeing was bound to happen sooner or later – if only because Alice seemed to be enjoying herself so much. She was as yet only in her middle twenties but, as everyone said, that sort of living took its toll – and besides, what those old rakes looked out for was freshness; and so every year that passed surely brought nearer Alice Wedderburn's Fall. Indeed, there were several vinegary old bodies well past their allotted span who were clinging on to life simply in the hope of witnessing that event, and of closing their eyes upon the world at last with the pious satisfaction of knowing that one more mortal was miserable.

Thus it was natural that Cottesbridge should taste this newest morsel of gossip – that Alice Wedderburn's mother was dying, apparently ignored by her scandalous child – with special relish. For Mrs Wedderburn (the 'Mrs' was, it was hinted, a polite fiction) had not climbed with her daughter, but had remained in the Hole, in the same hovel that had seen Alice's growing up and from which, presumably, she had plotted her escape. 'Never been back to see her,' Connie said, 'ever since she first left home to tek up with that leather-factor from Wellingford – the one what had to go abroad to tek the cure, on account of a sorceress in his liver.'

Just occasionally Connie took a wild plunge into uncharted vocabulary, and Lucy had long given up trying to pursue her. 'You'd think she'd pay the fees for a doctor to see her mother, at least,' she said.

'Well, there is a doctor goes to see her, that I know for a fact – though there's nowt he can do,' said Connie. 'So maybe she does that much for her – open her purse. Bad conscience, I reckon. Bad conscience.'

'Yes, I suppose,' Lucy murmured. Though she ruefully admitted to herself that she was as fascinated as anyone else by Alice Wedderburn's career, she felt at that moment a curious sensation of stepping inside the woman's skin, of feeling the oppressiveness of the town's prurience focused upon her like so many pitiless beams of light. On those few occasions when she had seen Alice Wedderburn – usually bowling along in an open carriage, or being handed out of the same by a masher with a diamond tie-pin – she had received an impression of pert arrogance; now she wondered whether there had been defensiveness there too. Ashamed of the poor dying mother she had outgrown! That was a terrible thing, if true, but Lucy could not think of it in quite the same unequivocal terms as Connie, simply because she knew – and wished she did not – the feeling of finding within herself the disfiguring spots of shame in a place where there should have been only love and respect.

The work on the frock was nearly completed when the fragrance of liver and onions began to drift up from below, and a few moments later Connie's mother – a stout, neat, tight-laced woman, like an animated bandbox – called up to ask if Lucy would like to eat with them.

'Oh, thank you, Mrs Pollard, that's nice of you – but I've got some dinner waiting for me at home, so I'd better git off for it,' Lucy said; and she pretended not to see Connie's fleeting look of embarrassment. She was not unused to those looks.

At the street door Connie said, renewing her assault, 'Will you come along of me and Kit tomorrow then, Lucy? Please?'

'Go on then,' Lucy said. 'You'd wittle the britches off a missioner, you would. I'll meet you here, shall I? After chapel?'

Connie beamed her relief. 'On your own?' she said.

'On my own,' Lucy said smiling.

'Well, if you say so,' Connie said; and then, apparently forgetful of the innumerable tears, heart-achings and soul-searchings that the tender passion had cost her, added: 'You don't know what you're missing!'

II

This apparent indifference on the part of Lucy Middleton to an emotion – or, at least, a social convention approximating to it – which occupied Connie Pollard completely, and exerted a similar influence on many of their contemporaries, was perhaps the more surprising in that Lucy was a handsome girl. She was in certain respects a triumph of nature over nurture; for though she had not always eaten well in her nineteen years, and had had to struggle up to adulthood through a variety of inauspicious circumstances, she was well-grown, tall and upright in bearing, with a certain amplitude of figure and generous moulding of limb unusual in the people of the Nene Valley shoe-towns who, when they attained to beauty in either sex, tended to its sparer, more finely drawn aspect. Nor did the work-clothes she wore for her job as a 'closer' in a boot-factory – a cotton drawstring cap and a coarse black apron over an old cloth frock of the plainest, most shapeless cut – entirely negate the richness of her looks. The hair that would not be confined in the cap made up in volume and colour for what it lacked in smoothness of texture; the smudges of dark brown leather-grime threw into relief the extreme fairness of her skin. The soft curve of her jaw and cheekbone, like the crook of an infant's arm, was the more striking in the context of the valley's general sharpness of physiognomy, which too often developed into the gauntness of consumption, the shoemaker's curse; whilst her eyes were of the luminous sort that are not so much fringed as shaded by their lashes, and present an equally beautiful form when closed. Her mouth, mobile and well-shaped, was the feature that counteracted any tendency to statuesque stillness in her looks. There was much natural gaiety lurking in it, but diffidence too: also trouble. If the general impression Lucy Middleton gave was of a bloom-like opulence struggling with conditions that tended to contract

12

and pinch, then the unease about her lips revealed the severity of that struggle. When she smiled at you her eyes reassured, her mouth sought reassurance.

No one, then, could have mistaken Lucy, glowingly human from crown to toe, for an ascetic; hence Connie's puzzlement at her friend's declining to tread so much as a measure in the courtship-dance that went on – none the less lively for strict Methodism, tyrannous factory-whistles, and leather-dust – in Cottesbridge and its sister towns strung out along the valley. But Connie had come closer to the point than she knew when she had said, 'It's fun.' For it was the jigging triviality of the steps that deterred Lucy from making a figure in the dance. Somehow, in her nineteen years' passage through life, she had maintained a bright flame of idealism – a feat which, given the conditions of her bringing-up, was comparable to the carrying of a lighted candle through a gale.

Innocence and experience are generally conceived of as irreconcilable opposites, but in Lucy they were mingled in such a potent and combustive mixture that it seemed unlikely that fate, that irresponsible alchemist, would decline to experiment with it and test its properties. She had been always poor; she had gone to work – hard, demanding work – before her thirteenth birthday; and she was the eldest child of a household the mention of which around Cottesbridge caused raised eyebrows at best and a snigger at worst. The scales had fallen from her eyes at the age of five regarding certain elemental matters which to more privileged girls would for ever remain a sordid mystery. Yet though she knew that the world dealt roughly with her, she did not know that it tended to be quite as unforgiving, in various ways, in spheres different from her own; she had little conception of the long backward ages of mankind in which such as she flowered and quickly withered, like daisies in an illimitable field. When she declined to walk out in Sunday best with any available beau – who considered himself sufficiently eligible because he had a clean collar, because he went to chapel, and because he had asked her – it was not with the disdain of a cynic, but with the passionate inward refusal of an artist who tears up an unsatisfactory sketch. It was not enough; and she did not judge it so by any conceited opinion of her own worth, but simply by the intensity of her inner emotional life. The ardent glance that she always gave to the vistas of green country between the chimney-stacks was an indication of the way Lucy habitually felt and thought. Such was the thrill of longing, as strong as it was unspecific, called forth in her by such sights that, beside it, the prospect of a Sunday stroll in the Gardens on the arm of an anonymous obliger in punishing boots was a nullity.

The streets through which she hurried home were still busy in the early afternoon. A few late shoe-workers were about: a trotting man trundled a handcart of boot-uppers, a couple of finishers with blackened aprons and blacker hands gossiped at yard-gates, a dray bearing a last load of belly-leather made its straining, lurching way up from the station. Along the High Street the shops, which depended on this one short space in the week when the hive-like industry of the town was stilled, were all alive. Barber-saloons, where chapel-going men with hair no longer than the nap on a billiard-table dropped in to 'git theirselves trim for Sundy'; chemists, haunted by women so wrung out by childbearing that there was nothing left in them but a residue of illnesses, and who apparently bought their patent powders and pick-me-ups on the principle that, as they had never worked yet in ten years, the day was surely near when they would; drapers and haberdashers, with young apprentices climbing in and out of the windows to fetch displayed goods, and main-taining a marvellous unconsciousness of their schoolfellows of last year crossing their eyes and pressing their noses white against the panes; butchers, making a great show of their weekend joints, as if they never dealt in such lowly meats as the offal and chipolatas that filled their windows for the rest of the week; fish-shops, with as nautical an exhibition of bloaters, kippers, cockles and whelks as if Cottesbridge were a coastal town, instead of as far from the sea as it was possible to be in England: all crammed into premises that seemed too small for them, as if the town were as parsimonious with space as it was with time, and all topped with upper-storeys faced with terracotta. The only building that stood proud of this low-lying world of squeeze and scramble was the church, remnant of the older Cottesbridge; the great crocketed spire of which heaved itself free to semaphore to the tower, high and solitary likewise, of the church in the neighbouring town of Lessington, and might have been saying to its fellow, 'Do they scurry and toil about your feet there, as they do here? Do you feel the same pulse of fret and trouble – of quivering hope, and disappointment throbbing no less feverishly – beating through your old stones? The very same? Ah – sad, sad!'

No: one other building broke the pattern. At the corner of a narrow turning near the end of the High Street, there was an old house of limestone, with tiny, deep, shuttered windows and low eaves of thatch. The outward bulge of the stone wall, which formed a profile as round as a baby's cheek, looked all the more swaggeringly ample against the prevailing straightness of new brick in Cottesbridge. The place was used as a seedsman's premises now, but Lucy knew from her neighbour Mr Birdsall that it had been a farm once, and that across the street where one of the town's fifty boot-factories reared its featureless façade, there had stood barns and byres, and that plough-teams must once have been turned out to graze where now the sun raised a dismal smell of hot asphalt from a chapel-yard.

The place had always held an attraction for Lucy. Perhaps it was in her blood, for the year was fairly recent in which the shoemaking population of Northamptonshire had outstripped the farming. Or perhaps it was the result of that strong power of fancy that lent to everything that stood outside Cottesbridge's harsh monotony of leather, newness and Methodism a dreamlike vividness in her eyes. Whatever, she could not pass the old farmhouse without slowing her pace, and allowing her fingertips to run along the rough surface of the stones. They seemed to bear the impress of the hands that had laid them, she felt, in a way that bricks never could.

'There you are! I been looking everywhere for you.'

It was her brother, Jim, a sharp-featured, good-looking boy: fourteen years of age, forty in terms of the grimmer sorts of wisdom. From the scorn in his eyes she knew he must have seen her dawdling by the stone wall and running her hand along it.

'Where you bin? Mother's bin going spare. Fit to fly, she is.'

'I went to Connie's after work to help her alter her Sunday frock. I told Mother all about it this morning. Didn't she remember?'

Jim merely lifted his eyes, as if the mere idea of Mrs Middleton remembering anything were not worth discussing. 'Father's not come home,' he said flatly.

'Oh no.' Lucy felt a familiar sinking within her.

'She wants you to go fetch him home,' Jim said, as they hurried along together. 'She tried to mek me go, but I wouldn't.'

15

'Where's he gone?' Lucy said – a pointless question, as Jim's expression showed.

'I went down to the factory, just in case he was still there,' Jim said. 'He'd finished work usual time, all right. Well, I en't going to go looking for him. I don't want a larruping. He can sup hisself underground for all I care.'

A swarm of painful sensations – amongst which were shame, impatience, bitterness, anger, regret, and weariness – closed upon Lucy, the whole forming a complex emotion that was for her uniquely associated with the word 'home'. It was only after a visit to Connie's that she became fully aware of what a sad outrage was done to that word, of all the kindly words in the world, by such associations. The only consolation was that that web of unpleasant feeling contained no strand of contempt, as it all too obviously did in Jim's case, but she was afraid that one day she would look into herself and find it there.

Alma Street: one of many such narrow, working-class streets in Cottesbridge. A little more respectable at the nearer end, where the chapel was; a little less respectable at the far end, which was closed off by 'Kidney' Weston's scrapyard, and where the unmistakably shabbier frontage of the Middletons' house stood out from the terrace like a dirty-necked child on a Sunday school treat. Around the unlit gas-lamp, girls were playing a chanting-game that Lucy herself had played, years ago, in the same pinafores and thick stockings. Her world.

Down the steep back-alley that led to the rear of the terrace went Lucy, followed by her brother. Women anxiously felt the strings of washing flapping in the yards, lest it be necessary to break the fearful taboo on hanging it out on Sunday. At her own back door, Lucy was knocked aside by Sidney and Benjy, her two little brothers, who cannoned out of the house, fighting as they went.

'Here, here, you pair, what's this all about?' Lucy said, separating them by taking a grubby shirt-collar in each hand.

'When we gitting some dinner?' Sidney said, presenting a choked face like a mutinous beetroot. 'I want me dinner.' He aimed a blow at Benjy's small, spiky head.

'We'll none on us git no dinner, way things are going,' their mother said, appearing at the door. 'Sidney, don't go clouting Benjy's head like that, my lamb, you know he don't like it. Go and play.'

The scullery was full of the smell of damp washing that

was piled in a frowsy heap by the mangle, and a flat-iron was warming in the grate. On the brick floor sat Dicky, at three the youngest of the Middleton brood, trying to eat a piece of blacklead. Amongst these domestic properties Mrs Middleton moved in her vague, floating, dreamy way, like a plump ghost that had never frightened anybody, and had been condemned to an eternity of laundry.

'Mother, what's this about Father?' Lucy said. Without being aware of it she had taken the blacklead away from Dicky, wiped his face, and begun to fold and smooth the crumpled washing. 'Don't say he's broke out again – not after last time.'

Mrs Middleton hugged her arms and spoke with a fretful crooning. 'I thought he'd finished with it. He promised me. He made a solemn promise to me. "Clara," he said, with his hand on his heart, and his other hand on the Bible – open at the Acts of the Epistles, or was it Hosier; anyway, the place where the daddy-long-legs got squashed flat – and his other hand in mine. "Clara", he said, "I tek my oath this is the very last time. I shan't break out no more. God strike me dead if I do." I remember it like it was yisd'y.'

'So you should – it weren't that long ago,' muttered Jim, nosing in the bread-bin. 'En't there owt for dinner? I want summat to eat. En't there no bread?'

'Come out o' there,' Mrs Middleton said. 'No call to go scrattin' in there. We'll all sit down to eat civilized. You'll git your dinner civilized wi' the rest on us.' Her pretty, dim eyes, having roamed all round the steamy little room, came to rest at last on Lucy. 'He promised,' she said again. 'What's he want to go and do it for?'

Lucy shook her head.

'Lucy. Be a good gel.' Her mother picked up the flat-iron and held it absently, delicately, like a lady with a little watering-can. 'Go and fetch him home. Fetch him now before he gits too bad. If he comes home now there'll mebbe not be too much harm done. Eh? He'll listen to you.'

'Unless he's too far gone,' said Lucy.

Pangs of loyalty creased her mother's face. 'It's his nature,' she said, and began to press the iron with weak, perfunctory strokes on washing that was still too wet. 'He can't help his nature.' She spoke, habitually, as if consoling a child: the child was herself. 'It can't be helped.'

17

III

There were many pubs for Lucy to try in the search for her father. Cottesbridge, like the other valley towns, was steeped in a fervent Methodism of which temperance was one of the chief tenets; but the strict abstinence of one part of the population was offset by the riotous indulgence of the other. There was something very typical of the valley people in this, of their intense, sinewy, rather bleak character, which had given the region the distinction of producing the last wave of overseas missionaries. If they did not grimly refrain from liquor altogether, they drank themselves blind; if they did not embrace a stifling creed of quietist respectability, they fought each other tooth and nail. A Manichaean duality was in their nature. The dullness that was often to be seen in those mushroom towns along the broad valley was of a seething rather than a sleepy sort; even the thriving shoemaking trade was an affair of dizzy booms and slumps, and bankruptcies and suicides were common in the columns of the local newspapers. The doubleness could even exist in an individual. There was none so sober, so righteous, so judgmental as Lucy's father when he had the Lord in him, none so reckless and uncontrollable when possessed by spirits of a more earthly nature.

Finding her father before the drink swallowed him up completely was, Lucy knew, an urgent necessity. Of course there were other women down their street who sometimes waited, grimly, at the end of ash-paths for husbands waylaid by pubs: it was the stuff of jokes, of apocryphal tales of fire-pokers broken over errant heads in revenge for housekeeping money soaked away at the Clicker's Arms or the Lord Spencer. For Lucy's family the joke was a decidedly off-colour one. The last time Chauncey Middleton had 'broken out' and gone on a binge, eight days had elapsed, in which he was fighting drunk, sentimental drunk, defiant drunk, maudlin drunk, bellowing drunk, silent drunk by turns – but always drunk, drunk, drunk.

She found him at last in the Salutation, a blowsy establishment of skittles and boxing-prints on the walls and crushed-velvet drapes, and pier-glasses that gave back a blurred and foxed reflection, so that you felt you were tipsy as soon as you walked in. The men who gathered here were, in their own eyes at least, of a sporty, rackety character. Many still wore the shoemaker's apron, the *toga virilis* of the valley towns, the varying grime on which was a precise indicator of the wearer's profession in the trade. On their heads they wore hard bowlers set rakishly back on the crown; and at the feet of many of them sat small terriers, which they took rabbiting on Sundays. They were a noisy, swaggering, ribald crowd; but on walking in you had a curious visual impression – formed by the smoky air, the redness of the men's faces, the beads of sweat trickling down them, and their square, stretched mouths as they huffed with soundless laughter – of their all being in tears.

A fat fellow was sitting in the doorway with his leg up against the jamb when Lucy tried to enter, and when she asked him to move he let the leg fall with an emphatic, trotter-like smack, leering at her the while. In truth she hardly noticed him; for her emotion on having to enter this place, the harshly male atmosphere of which was about as congenial to her as the surface of the moon, was all swallowed up in the simple practical imperative of bringing her father out. This was no bad example, in fact, of Lucy's general state of mind as the chief prop of the sagging Middleton household. Necessity pressed so hard upon her that she scarcely had time to feel mortified.

Her father was with a group of men at the great brass-railed bar. It was clear to her experienced eye how much he had had – not a great deal by his standards, but already enough to put the family on short commons for half the coming week. He was in the act of throwing back his head and laughing when he caught sight of her. The laugh froze on his face, and gave way to a frown which betrayed his furious shame at being summoned by his womenfolk in front of his cronies, who were watching with suppressed relish, moustaches rimed with beer-froth above wet, parted lips.

But then – after a moment in which Lucy had seen violence pass across his face like swift cloud-shadow – her father was suddenly beaming, welcoming, the fond father.

'Why, here's Lucy, here's my gel. She's a picture, en't she? En't she a sight to be proud on? What's up then, gel?'

Often her mother would say, especially when the family was suffering as a consequence of his failings, 'Your father were a very handsome man when he were young – the finest-looking man in three towns,' as if this somehow excused much. But Chauncey Middleton at forty-five still bore sufficient traces of those good looks to make him vain of them, and to enable him to patronize men who otherwise had everything that he lacked in temper, dignity and sense. Pityingly he would speak of poor Dusty Rhodes, bald as an egg at thirty, or wonder at how a measly, scraggy specimen like Josh Craddock could have got four children – though these observations never extended to a consideration of how it was that those children were well-fed, well-clothed, and exhibited no bruises. His very fair colouring was not yet obliterated by the bloom of toper's veins starting to flower on his nose and cheeks; and his strong, corn-coloured hair and moustache were almost as luxuriant as in the photograph of him in the front room at home, taken on a club outing twenty years ago, when he had been a handsewn-man and had ramped laughing about the valley as if the world were his. Now he smiled on his daughter with something of the same glad assurance, negligently waving his half-empty glass of beer; but she saw the little sharp furrows around mouth and brow that said, *Don't you show me up.*

'Mother wants you to come home for dinner,' Lucy said in a low voice. Her father's companions were all attention, foxy eyes glinting sidelong from lowered lids.

'Be along home soon,' her father said. 'Need a drop o' wet in this weather. Terrible dry weather, en't it?'

'It is that,' one of the others said, grinning and watching still.

'Shan't be long, tell her,' her father said. It was impossible to tell whether he himself believed in this cheerful casualness. 'Just got to lay the dust.'

He began to turn his shoulder to her. Hating herself, Lucy began to coax. 'But Mother's got summat special in for your dinner,' she said, 'and she don't want it to spoil.' The transparency of this fiction was probably as obvious to the men in the bar as it was to her, given the Middletons' reputation. 'She wants you to come now.'

'All right, for crying out loud! I tell you I'll be home soon! You want me to say it in French?' Her father's voice, which in a good mood was a rich, cakey baritone that gave some clue as to why her mother had been charmed into marrying him, took on that coarse brazen note that Lucy knew and feared; but immediately he tried to modulate to a genial key again. 'Her mother's daughter,' he said, smiling round at his companions, 'wun't tek no for an answer. Women – they'll wittle you while bull's noon if you let 'em, bless their hearts. Wun't they?'

'They will, Chauncey, they will.'

'Just time for another before I git off home, then,' her father said, turning and rapping on the bar.

Lucy saw, with distress tempered by unsurprise, that it was no good. Chauncey Middleton could no more stop after three drinks than the rising sun could stop half-way above the horizon. As far as he was concerned now, she was not there at all.

She was on the point of begging and pleading with him – her pride on this point, again, simply overruled by the thought of the wages filling the publican's pockets instead of the children's stomachs – when something made her stop. As she regarded her father, standing at that bar laughing along with his cronies, a bleak revelation came upon her. Subtly, covertly, they were laughing not with him but at him. Sooner or later they would drop out of the drinking, and watch him go on alone, hoping that old Chauncey Middleton was going to give them a good one and end up fighting his own shadow. He was to them, in fact, a sideshow.

It was a thing she could have perceived, perhaps, long ago: it was a possible that she had, unconsciously. Maybe the family contagion had infected Lucy to the degree that, realistic and practical as she was forced to be, she still had a tendency to see only what she wanted to see, and to block out with fancy-painted screens the uglier features of experience. But the force of that revelation in the bar was too strong. Her father had appeared many things in her eyes, but never, till now, pathetic; and it was indicative of what a depth of warm and natural feeling existed in Lucy, despite a home life which denied and distorted it at every turn, that the chief pain this gave her was on her father's account – for she knew that to appear a laughing-stock was the thing her father would hate most in all the world.

Stung by this, she could bear to look at him no longer. She left him there, and made her hurried way back home, imagining that her errand and its failure were plainly written on her face for every passer-by who cared to look.

She found her mother in the back yard, brandishing the iron carpet-beater like a sword and pointing up at next door's windows.

'It's her again! She urges me to death, that one! I can see you there, peeping and prying through the curtain – don't you think I can't!'

'Mother, come inside,' Lucy said.

Her mother's bottom lip trembled with martyred outrage. 'I shouldn't have to put up with it. She's at it again – peeping and peering and prying and poking.' Emotion made her alliterative. 'Like a plaguey old pig. She drives me scatty. Look down here!' She stamped on the brick path. 'She's bin chucking her mucky old bucket-water over my fence again! She does it a'purpose! I shouldn't have to put up with it!'

Mrs Middleton's feud with her neighbours was a long and complex saga of slights and snubs, mostly imagined. Naturally inquisitive though the local community was, no one in their right mind could have been so compulsively interested in every detail of Mrs Middleton's affairs as she fancied the neighbours to be. She was on continual lookout for affronts to her dignity – an attribute that she perhaps guarded the more vigilantly because she possessed so little of it.

'No call to go tugging on my arm like it's a Christmas cracker, Lucy. She knows I'm speaking nowt but the truth: her with her lodgers. I don't know about where she comes from, but where I come from, lodgers en't generally reckoned to hang their trews over the end of their landlady's bed, but there we are, perhaps I was brought up different . . .'

Only when Lucy had persuaded her to go inside did her mother remember what her errand had been.

'Oh, Lucy, didn't you bring him? I was sure you'd fetch him home. Did you really try, now?'

Lucy knew the tone of hurt reproach, but was not immune to it. 'He was in the Salutation, with a lot of other drinking-men. He – he says he'll be home soon.' She did not look at her mother: they both knew the pubs would detain him until the money ran out. 'Where's the young 'uns? We'd better mek some dinner anyway.'

'Benjy and Sidney and Dicky-bird are out playing . . . I don't know where Jim's gone. Joanna's often late of a Sat'dy . . .' A sort of absent vagueness came over her mother as Lucy looked in the pantry: she hummed a tune and folded and refolded the ironing.

'Haven't we got owt in, Mother?'

'You what say, my petal?' her mother said amiably, twisting a strand of greying hair back into her dishevelled bun. 'Oh, no . . . I kept meaning to go out today, but what with the washing and all . . . I shall have to ask you to step down to Lil Fry's and see if she's got half a loaf to spare. I don't know how it is, there en't a tanner in the house . . .'

'But I give you my money just the other day,' Lucy said.

'So you did, my lamb, but your father wanted some extry – for his baccy, you see. You can't grudge the poor man his baccy, after all, sweating in that factory all week . . .' She patted and primped at the laundry, avoiding Lucy's eyes. 'Tell Lil I'll pay her back Monday.'

Lil Fry lived at the other end of the row, a severe, grim-featured woman of granite correctness, whom not even Mrs Middleton had been able to quarrel with. She listened without comment to Lucy's faltering request, disappeared into her scrubbed and shrine-like kitchen, and returned with half a loaf wrapped in brown paper.

'Tell your mother that's the second time this week,' Lil Fry said. Her face was marked with deep grooves that ran down either side of her unsmiling mouth and snub nose, giving her something of the look of a boxer dog in a pinafore.

'I will,' Lucy said, and felt her cheeks flaming. Lil Fry's gaze was the more lacerating because it was almost neutral; there was no surprise or ire left in it.

Her mother was cheerful as she sliced the bread and spooned the last of the tea into the pot: she was floating on capricious waves of reminiscence about her life before her marriage. She had lived then in Northampton, the metropolis of the shoemaking towns of the Nene Valley, and in comparatively comfortable circumstances. As a little girl Lucy, listening entranced to these oral memoirs, had formed an idea of her mother's background which placed it at the very least in the minor aristocracy; but worldliness growing apace on her, she soon knew that her mother's father had been nothing more than a railway clerk, and the high-water mark of her family's social elevation the possession of a piano in the front room. The presence of this piano was a thread that wove itself into the fabric of all Mrs Middleton's recollections. Just as the piano must have taken up an inordinate amount of room in that parlour, so her mother's anecdotes could never quite lose sight of it, and were liable to bump up against it in the most unlikely manner.

'Bread and scrape again, I'm afraid,' she said, 'but it's wholesome . . . I could have fancied a bit of fish today. My father was a great one for fish. I remember once he brought home a piece of halibut, his favourite that was. Wrapped up in the *Northampton Mercury* with the Prince of Wales having typhoid on the front, I can see it now. And then it vanished. He'd put it down in the kitchen and it just vanished.' She laughed breathlessly, dimpling, as she slapped the bread-and-scrape out on to plates. 'And then we noticed this terrible smell of fish in the parlour. Oh, that place reeked of it. And it turned out our old cat had got hold of the fish and dragged it underneath the armchair where nobody could see it. We couldn't get that smell out for days, it fairly clung, and you know mother was a bit worried for the piano, because a piano's a very delicate sort of instrument, and she was afraid the smell might affect the strings somehow.'

'En't we waiting for father?' said Joanna, Lucy's sister, who had just come in. She was sixteen, and so far had escaped the common fate of the boot-factories, going instead as a day-servant or general drudge to two old spinsters who kept a milliner and haberdasher's in the High Street.

'He's on the sauce again,' said Jim.

'Hush, don't speak that way,' their mother said. 'And where's your collar? Sitting down to table without your collar.'

'It's too hot,' Jim said. 'How long's he going to be on a blinder this time, then? I en't bringing my wage home just to pour down his throat.' Jim had started as a sweater in a boot-factory last year.

'Mother, you know what Jim means,' Lucy said. 'You know how it was last time, when father didn't turn up for work. The foreman give him a warning then. If he misses work again—'

'Ssh!' Her mother made urgent motions of her head towards the children. 'Not with the young 'uns here.' It was significant of Mrs Middleton's peculiar remoteness of mind that she thought of Sidney and Benjy and Dicky, for whom life had been a school of the hardest knocks virtually from the cradle, as tender innocents liable to be blighted by a breath of reality. 'There's nowt wrong with your father's work. You wun't find a better craft in Cottesbridge.'

'But it's different in the factory, Mother,' Lucy said. 'You've got to keep time.'

But time, she knew, did not mean much to her mother; nor had it meant much to her father when he was a younger man and had worked as a hand-shoemaker answerable to no one. She herself could just remember the days when he had done all his work in the 'shop', the little shed at the end of the yard. She could recall toddling down the path to watch him crouched over his last, surrounded by the hemp, the wax, the spools of thread, the awls and sprigs and tacks and files and all the cunning paraphernalia that her small fingers itched to play with; and later, when she was put to bed, hearing the monotonous hammering from the shop going on into the night. That was the time when it was almost a point of honour with the shoemakers not to work on Mondays. The feast of St Monday was sacred to the hangover: the next five days passed in a desperate fury of work with men sometimes falling asleep over their benches in the small hours. But even then, the factories that gave out the hand-work were beginning to move over to machinery, and a tra-dition that linked the medieval and modern ages – and men like Chauncey Middleton with men who had shod the bowmen of Agincourt – was coming to an end. Now the whine and thump of mechanical presses was heard all over the shoe-towns of the valley; whistles called men at regular hours into new factories all built to the same plan, and the back-yard shops had fallen into a desuetude so complete that they might have been part of some Pompeian excavation, petrified for ever with the tools still on the benches.

It was a change that Chauncey Middleton had never quite got used to: not just a change in the way of working, but a transformation of identity. Impatient, despairing, furious with him as Lucy often was – she had indeed known what it was to hate her own father – that did not mean she did not understand him, or that she failed to see in his binges a wistful searching for the glad-handed recklessness of a lost age, when he could break out for a week at a time and go rabbiting and fishing and fighting and there would be no foreman marking his name in a book. She could grant him that – even if, with the hungry faces of the children before

25

her and the familiar unsatisfied feeling in her stomach, she could grant him nothing else.

'En't there any more?' Jim said.

'There's a morsel of cheese,' their mother said. 'But you'd best leave that for your father.' She studied the leaves in her teacup: she was humming again, and her round face brightened with a sudden optimism. 'He'll mebbe be home soon.'

It was late evening before Lucy had completed the various household chores that her mother's limited perseverance had been unequal to, and was able to go upstairs to change at last out of her working clothes. The room, scarcely more than a partitioned cupboard stuck about with pictures she had cut out of illustrated papers, was nearly taken up by the bed she shared with Joanna: Jim, Sidney, Benjy and Dicky slept in beds on the other side of the partition. Lucy washed herself as best she could with jug and basin, and listened without much hope for sounds of her father's return. Her fears about his job, though they could not penetrate her mother's insouciance, were very real. He had been in trouble for absenteeism from Stokes' factory before, and though the trade was buoyant at the moment with plenty of work, eventually an unreliable man would simply not be employed. There was a terrible example in the Hammonds' house across the street. 'Topper' Hammond had gone too far with the booze some years ago, and now the family had sunk as far as it was possible to go without ending up in the Hole, which everyone expected to be their ultimate destination. Ada Hammond, a large pink freckled woman with a goitred neck, wore no shoes, a thing almost unheard of in a town like Cottesbridge where the poorest took a pride in being decently shod. The ever-open front door revealed her puttering about on bare grey feet in a room empty except for some ragged coconut matting, a blackened pan over the fire, and numerous soiled nappies. Topper was an absurdly dapper runt of a man, like a sleek stoat, who sallied out each day in a clean stiff collar in search of work that was never there, and kept himself in rum with gambling and odd jobs. Her father spoke with high disdain of Topper Hammond – but if he were to lose his own job ... Her wages, and the pittance brought home by Jim and Joanna, could never feed, clothe and house eight people.

She lay weary on the bed for a while, but anxiety made

her restless, and at last she went out to the street to get a breath of air and also, secretly, to watch for her father's return. The lamplighter had been by, and Sidney and Benjy were playing soldiers beneath the gas-lamp. The water-cart had passed by earlier too, damping down the dust: most of the water had already dried up but Benjy, with unerring instinct, managed to fall seat-first in the one large puddle remaining.

'Oh, Benjy, git up out o' there,' she said, pulling him to his feet. 'Look – mud all over your britches. You are a mucky arab.'

'Sidney shot me – you have to fall down when you git shot.'

'Well, just git wounded next time. Go on in now – it's time for your bed. You an' all, Sidney.'

She turned to see Mr Birdsall, three doors down, standing outside his house in the circle of the gaslight, smoking his pipe. He smiled and raised his hand.

'Evening, Lucy. It's a mite close, isn't it?'

'Evening, Mr Birdsall. I wish we could have a good storm. That would clear it.'

'You always did like a storm. I remember a terrific one when you were little, and you were standing outside and watching the lightning when all the other children had run indoors.' Mr Birdsall's eyes narrowed humorously. 'And so had I, come to that.'

She had known Mr Birdsall all her life, and knew him by no other name: the Mister was unusual in a neighbourhood where most men were identified by nicknames. Mr Birdsall was a bachelor of forty-five and worked as a clicker, a skilled job that involved cutting out the pieces for shoe-uppers from the leather hides; amongst shoemakers the clickers stood in somewhat the same relation as engine-drivers among railwaymen. Mr Birdsall had the reputation of a 'scholard', from the little glass-fronted case of books in his house, and he was a great lover of music, singing in a men's choir and playing the cornet in Cottesbridge town band. To Lucy he was a kind of unofficial godfather; as his words suggested, he had watched benevolently over her growing up, and it was to Mr Birdsall and his store of books that she owed such glimpses as she had had of a life beyond the confines of necessity – of leather and chapel and bread-and-scrape. He had been her ally, though to no avail, in a brief battle to allow her to stay on at the Board school before the factories claimed her. She liked him enormously: was very fond of his sad, jowly face with its oddly childlike freshness of complexion and blue eyes. He knew perfectly well what her mother and father were like; but if the name of Middleton had become something of a bad joke in the neighbourhood, it was not the least part of Lucy's affection for Mr Birdsall that he always accorded it the greatest respect.

Sensitive as Mr Birdsall was in this regard, he perhaps did not notice Lucy's uncomfortable smile at the mention of the long-ago storm. If there has ever been a young person who positively enjoys being reminded of what he or she was like as a child, Lucy was not the one. Nor, perhaps, was she unusual in regarding someone who was past forty as old, and somehow beyond human joy and woe.

'Shall you be playing in the band tomorrow, Mr Birdsall?' she said.

'All being well.' He glanced down the street, and said with great casualness, which the vigorous puffs of smoke from his pipe belied, 'Father not home yet?'

'No,' she said, 'not yet.'

'Ah.' Mr Birdsall jingled the change in his pockets, neat and stocky, and smoked like a tug-boat. 'Lot of work in town lately. I hear Stokes' have got an Army order.'

'Yes.' It was transparent enough, but she was grateful.

'Whew! It's warm. You know, on a night like this I could just fancy going down to the King's Meadow and doing a spot of fishing. You get a wonderful cool just before the dawn. And then you can watch the sun come up.'

'I never knew you were a fisherman.'

'Don't get the time now. I used to go down to the King's Meadow a lot when I was a boy-chap. You probably wouldn't catch anything there now. Cottesbridge was still a little behind-hand place then. It was only a step out to the fields.'

'I can't picture it without all this here,' said Lucy, looking at the brick perspectives that hemmed them in on all sides, and visited by a longing, almost brutal in its intensity, for the freedom of the fields. Not even Mr Birdsall, who was a close observer of Lucy, saw any outward symptom of the burning wishfulness that was almost as constant with her as her heartbeat: her physical composition, from the heavy crown of hair to the slightly slow, hesitant mezzo register of her voice, was precisely of the sort to disguise it; and she did not reveal it simply because she believed no one else felt it.

'My father worked on a farm, you know,' Mr Birdsall said. 'He never thought much of shoemakers. Wouldn't recognize the valley if he saw it now. Most of the towns this side of Northampton were only villages in his day. It was round about when the French and the Prussians had their war that the trade really took off, I reckon. That's when it changed.'

'Don't you ever wish you'd worked on a farm, or summat like that?'

'Oh, well . . .' Mr Birdsall gave his peculiar smile: not a public smile, but the sort of smile one gives when alone, remembering. 'If wishes were horses . . . It's always been the trade for me. Besides—' He appeared to consider whether to say something or not. 'There's nothing worse than regret, you know. No hellfire that's conjured up in all the chapels of Cottesbridge is worse than regret. Once you let it get a hold on you, you're finished.'

There was feeling in his words, and Lucy was surprised: perhaps this showed, for Mr Birdsall took out his pipe and looking at it said, 'I mean, I'd not say this to everybody, Lucy, but I've worked in the trade for thirty-five years – and I've hated every minute of it.'

There was a startling vehemence in his tone, which had the effect of rousing the vexation that had been smouldering in Lucy since she had seen her father in the Salutation. 'Well, but you go on with it, Mr Birdsall,' she burst out, 'you mek a fist at it, and turn up for work, and don't go mekking a laughing-stock of yourself all over town.'

As soon as it was out she felt she should not have said it, for the loyalty that her father did so little to earn and so much to forfeit still survived in her. But it could not be unsaid now. 'It sounds awful,' she murmured. 'But I'm afraid you know what I mean.'

'Well . . .' Mr Birdsall could not deny it. 'We're none of us perfect, Lucy.'

'Oh, but people do laugh at us, Mr Birdsall – you know they do,' cried she. 'I know I shouldn't mind it, but sometimes . . .' Strange to say, Lucy had never before inter-preted her habitual longing for what might be as a discontent with what was; and now that she did see the connection, she was as shocked at herself as if she had uncovered a great sin. Chapel, with its emphasis on unworthiness, was partly responsible for this; but, more than that, she was a person who was made for happiness, whose instinct was all towards ppiness as a plant gropes towards the light, and to whose nature discontent was not a fruitful medium for growth and change, but a blighting desert. 'I just wish Father hadn't broken out again – that's all,' she concluded softly. 'It don't do him no good.'

'Lucy!' Her mother's voice hailed her. 'Lucy, chicken, come and help me git these little 'uns off to bed.' She came over, sighing and patting her ever-unwinding hair into place. 'Evening, Mr Birdsall. I can't get 'em to settle. It's this weather. There's Sidney and Benjy shrieking about and beating each other with bolsters like two peas in a pod.' Mrs Middleton had no regard for aptness in her use of proverbs, but merely drew from the stock at random. 'Chauncey's broke out again, Mr Birdsall. I thought he'd finished with it. He's been sober as a lord these last two months. You've seen him at chapel. There was prayers every night before supper – you never heard such prayers. Full of scourging and suffering and affliction, it was quite a treat to hear 'em. And now he's gone and scattered himself by the wayside again.'

'I'm sorry to hear that, Mrs Middleton,' Mr Birdsall said. 'Anything I can do?'

'Not unless you can change his nature, Mr Birdsall,' her mother said, with a comfortable sort of resignation. 'It's his nature. I remember my poor father saying to me when I was getting wed, "Clara," he said, "that man's got a volatile nature." I can see him now, leaning on the piano, with his spectacles in his hand – he didn't wear 'em much, on account of his eyes. "A volatile nature," he said.'

'Come on then, Mother,' said Lucy, who had just spotted Nancy Smallbones coming out of her house and making for them like a ball down a skittle-alley. 'We'd best go and see to them little 'uns.'

She was too late. Nancy Smallbones was already at her side, peering sideways up into her mother's face.

'Got trouble, ha' you, gel? Got trouble with his lordship? Not come home yet?'

'I wish I could say no, Nance,' said Mrs Middleton, who was currently at peace with this one of her neighbours, though hostilities might be declared at any moment. 'I wish I could say I en't got trouble, but I'd be a liar.'

'Shame. Shame, that is. And once he gits going, he don't stop, do he? That's the pity of it. Dear oh dear,' Nancy Smallbones said, clucking her tongue, and staring the while at the faces of Lucy, Mrs Middleton, and Mr Birdsall in turn. She was a very little woman, round as a plum duff, with a tight skullcap of curls, and a hump which was less a congenital infirmity than a consequence of her eternally screwing her head to one side, and drawing it back into her shoulders. She had on always a hessian apron, in which she was continually rubbing her hands as if to dry them; and altogether there was a sort of prurient writhe about her, all the more distasteful for her tremendous blandness of manner. No bush-telegraph of gossip had been needed to alert her to the fact that there was trouble with Chauncey Middleton, and bring her scurrying out into the street. She was simply one of those people who are first on the scene at accidents – a sort of carrion crow who fed upon the carcasses of other people's misfortunes.

'And him just got his wages today, I should think?' Mrs Smallbones pursued. 'Ah! That's when they're worst. En't it? Yerss. Even my Arthur, rest him, was tempted sometimes.' The late Mr Smallbones had been a railwayman who, one day, perhaps pondering too deeply on the joys of married life, had fallen under the wheels of the London express. 'Bin in trouble at work for the drink, en't he, afore now?'

'He's a free spirit, that's what it is,' Lucy's mother said. 'But yes, I can't deny it, Nance.'

'Shame, en't it? Yerss. Terrible shame it is.' Nancy Smallbones pressed her face up even closer to Mrs Middleton, as if she were sucking, vampire-like, on her discomfiture.

'We'd better go and see to the little 'uns, Mother,' Lucy said.

'Ah! Little 'uns as well. That's the wust of it. They're always the first to suffer, en't they? Yerss. Tsk-tsk. You're looking a mite peaky yourself, gel. It's a worry, en't it? Dear oh dear,' said Mrs Smallbones, seeming to screw herself up into more dreadful shapes in an effort to get her face up to Lucy's and taste any pain that happened to be going.

'Yes, I'd better be thinking about turning in myself,' said Mr Birdsall, who had looked uncomfortable throughout this.

'Ah!' Mrs Smallbones made a little crabwise scuttle right round him where he stood, popping up on the other side of him. 'You're lucky in some ways, Mr B. Being on your own, I mean. Not being married, I mean. Some folk think it's a mite peculiar, a man of your age not being married, but it's got its advantages, en't it? Yerss. I wouldn't have missed being married to Arthur for anythink, even though he was took from me, but then we're all different.'

Mr Birdsall, with a shortness unusual for him, made his excuses and went inside, and after a few moments Lucy prevailed on her mother to do likewise. Nancy Smallbones, wriggling her body about as if to make sure her venom-sac was not empty, glanced up and down the street for further victims and then, finding none, darted into her house like a trap-door spider.

Peace was soon established in the boys' room. Dicky – Dicky-bird, as her mother fancifully called him – was already asleep, hands clenched and face flushed. He was a sickly infant, and Lucy felt his brow carefully to see if he was running one of his frequent temperatures. Benjy was quiet too, but Sidney, who had his father's barley-coloured hair and expansive manner, was still inclined to play soldiers in the bed until Jim dissuaded him by the fraternal expedient of clouting his head.

Lucy still thought of her little outburst to Mr Birdsall as a vague form of treachery to her own kin; but seeing the large, crowded, patched, underfed family settling unrestfully down for the night, and keeping one ear cocked for sounds of her father's return, she could not prevent the stealthy return of similar thoughts. She had heard Mr Birdsall tell of the days when little boys were given over to chimney sweeps, and the terrible lives they had under their brutal control, until it was stopped by law. But where, she thought now, was the law that could prevent children being delivered into a governance no less irresponsible and harmful, simply by the fact of being born? Into the hands of persons owning no qualifications for such a tremendous trust (beyond the fact that they had accomplished an act performed nightly on the rooftops by the mangiest of alley-cats) were consigned these helpless young souls, who had no court of appeal, no possibility of redress anywhere in the universe into which they had been hauled screaming, and who might well consider themselves lucky if their lot was no worse than a benign, slovenly neglect.

These were harsh thoughts: Lucy realized so, as she caught herself in the act of all but labelling parenthood a crime. It wasn't so bad as that, she told herself as she prepared for bed. Their mother meant well; even their father, though he could lay about him in a bad temper, was by no means the worst of his kind. Still, she had a sense of a layer of illusion

32

detaching itself from her, like the shedding of a last milk tooth.

Joanna, who was kept running up and down stairs all day for the two old spinsters, had already got into bed, her long plait of fair hair carefully laid on the pillow beside her and looking like gold braid in the light cast into the room by the street-lamp. She was sometimes known in the family as 'the Little Lady' on account of her porcelain complexion and something quiet and self-contained about her ways.

'You don't see Father coming, Lucy, I reckon?' Joanna said as Lucy stood near the window in her petticoat gazing out.

'No,' Lucy said. She could see the roofs of the town, their gaslit silhouettes laid one upon the other like appliqué-work; beyond, a richer swathe of darkness that was the country, with at its lip a curious rosy phosphorescence – the iron-ore furnaces that rimmed the escarpment of the valley and combated the night with their radiance until it was extinguished in turn by the dawn.

Joanna sighed and shifted in the bed. 'The Misses Herring had a lady in today for a regatta-hat. Carriage-trade. They don't git a lot of that. She was going down to the Isle of Wight for the summer. It'd be nice to see the sea, wouldn't it? I've never bin to the sea.'

'We'll go one day – we'll go to the sea one day,' Lucy said. She did not know why she said it: did not know why that peculiar conviction entered her voice just then. 'Joanna,' she said after a moment, 'd'you ever wish you'd been born somewhere else?'

'Like the seaside?'

'Perhaps . . . Somewhere where things are different. Or is that – you know, sinful? Proud, and all that?'

'I reckon so. I reckon they used to say summat like that at Sunday school. You're not s'posed to question God's will – where he's put you, how he's made you, and everything. Just give thanks.'

Lucy said nothing. She knew Joanna was quite a firm believer in her unemphatic way. She had been so herself till recent years, indeed, for the touch of the chapel was difficult to elude in Cottesbridge; but nowadays it often seemed to her that there was a good deal of Hobson's choice about the dispensations of the Almighty, and she felt herself drawing away from a deity who required to be so constantly and fulsomely thanked for blessings that were neither constant

33

nor fulsome – like a fiddler demanding applause whether he played or not.

'When Father comes home,' Lucy said, stirring, 'he'll probably sleep late into the morning. Maybe if we're quiet, and leave him sleeping really late, it'll break it up and he won't carry on boozing.'

Joanna nodded. 'It worked once before, I remember.'

'Have you got any money?'

'Only a few coppers.'

'Well, hide 'em anyway. He might be spent out already.'

It did not occur to either of the girls that there was a sad incongruity in their youthful minds being put to these shifts and devices, more fitted to the disenchanted pragmatism of age. After a few more whispered words on how best to deal with their father's current delinquency, Lucy slipped into bed. Though Joanna was soon asleep, Lucy lay wakefully listening for the tramp of heavy feet down the back-alley; but while her thoughts of the morrow were troubled, something lit them from beneath like the glow of the furnaces on the valley-side – the bright knowledge that next day she was going, albeit as chaperone to Connie and Kit, out into the country.

IV

Mr Birdsall did not go straight to bed, but waited until Nancy Smallbones was safely out of the way before strolling out into the street again to smoke his pipe. His eyes, as they often were, were on the Middleton house. Any casual observer at a glance might have correctly judged, like Lucy, that his was a kind face; but they might have seen too – as she through fondness and long familiarity did not – that it was the face of a man who had missed something, perhaps wilfully; had closed and locked certain doors, had chosen to leave certain regions of experience white on the map, and moreover carried the consciousness of his renunciation about with him. Perhaps, too, a glance at his neat, solitary little house with its bookcase and sheet-music would have given the impression not so much that he was content with this, but that he had decided to be.

He stood smoking in abstraction for some time until he noticed Lil Fry standing at her open door across the way, arms folded across her chest and seeing everything in the street whilst appearing to look neutrally before her.

'Evening, Mrs Fry. Hoping for a breath of wind, eh?'

'Evening, Mr Birdsall. Terrible muggy.'

She crossed the street in a stately glide, pausing only to give a glance of appraisal to her scrubbed front doorstep. It was Mrs Fry's boast that she had the cleanest doorstep in Cottesbridge, and her husband was so often warned against the dreadful impiety of treading on it, and was put to so many jumps and capers in getting into the house without polluting the sacred stone, that that doorstep quite ground down and bowed him, and was as much of a burden to him as if he had gone about with it tied round his neck.

Mrs Fry swivelled her lofty gaze significantly in the direction of the Middletons' house.

'Bit o' heavy weather in that quarter, seem'ly,' she said.

'I'm afraid so,' said Mr Birdsall. 'I'm very much afraid so.'

Lil Fry narrowed her eyes, and seemed to be withholding some bitter words about the state of the Middletons' front doorstep.

'Meks you count your blessings,' she rapped out. 'I just thank goodness I've got a reliable man. I just thank heaven my Tom don't touch it.'

Mr Birdsall nodded amiably.

'I'd not pretend my Tom's perfect. But there's never any of that.' She was perhaps pardonably smug on this point, and illustrated it again from several angles. 'You can be sure he'll be home on the dot. Likes his baccy, but no strong liquors. He never plays up like that. No one could accuse him of not tekking care of his family.'

Mr Birdsall mildly murmured that he was sure no one would suggest such a thing.

'Well,' Lil Fry said with a mollified air, 'it's the gel I feel for. She tries hard, that one.'

'Ah, yes! Lucy,' Mr Birdsall said, and sent up clouds of smoke.

'Chauncey Middleton seems to think he can break out every few weeks and no harm done,' Lil Fry said. 'Well, he wants to mind she don't break out one of these days.'

Mr Birdsall looked his surprise.

'Oh! I don't mean on the sauce. Nothink like that.' Mrs Fry shook her head grimly, her severe scraped-back hair seeming to bristle with righteousness. 'But a gel like that, she en't going to keep her head down for ever. Not with red blood in her veins. It en't natural.'

V

The part of England wherein Lucy Middleton had passed virtually the whole of her nineteen years was that tract of borderland between Anglia and Mercia, where the River Nene, on its way from Northampton, twists and gives itself a shake before heading north along the ancient fringes of Rockingham Forest to Peterborough and the Fens.

It is not a large river, but the valley through which it runs, like an artery linking Middle England with the flat acres of the east, is surprisingly ample and broad. Rich grazing meadows, and ploughed land of strong, recalcitrant clay, had long clothed this great shallow bowl; and they continued to do so as the little towns along the river, themselves transformed by the sudden transformation of their shoemaking tradition into a full-scale industry, threw up their redbrick ramparts and traced their banners of factory-smoke on the blue valley air. Three-score miles from the sea, beyond the limit of inland navigation, it was a place that had never had much to do with the wider world. Even the hint of the exotic brought by the boom to the shoe-towns – which could pride themselves, for example, on the knowledge that their products equipped the armies of Imperial Russia – did not touch the countryside between them, which remained much as it had always been: a secretive place of lanes and high hawthorn hedges, of quietly flowing waters and high crocketed spires.

It was towards one of these spires, belonging to the church at Cleatham, that Lucy and her companions, Connie Pollard and Kit Lightfoot, directed their steps the following afternoon. The weather was sultry, the heavy air now and then disturbed by little freshening eddies of breeze which, together with a mottled tint in the sky and a curious, lustreless sheen upon the leaves of the hedgerows, indicated that thunder might be at hand.

'I declare if a big clap of thunder goes off when we're in

that crypt I shall jump a foot in the air,' said Connie. 'I a'most wish I hadn't come now. I don't like ghosty things at the best of times, let alone with all this 'lectric in the air.'

'That's being with me, that is,' said Kit Lightfoot, who was as alert for the slightest possibility of innuendo as a dog hoping for scraps from the table. 'That's where you git that feeling of 'lectric. From walking along of me.'

'Git along. Gas more like it. That's what you're full of – gas. En't he, Lucy?'

'Eh?' absently said Lucy, who was allowing her gaze to dwell on the pastures along the valley-side that in the brassy storm-light appeared a supernatural shade of green.

'Dolly Daydream,' Connie said. 'I hope them clouds don't break. I shall be mortified if it rains on me hat.'

Kit Lightfoot, after a brief mental struggle to extract some trace of *double entendre* from this remark, turned to Lucy. 'You all right? Not tired yet?' he said, as he had said every hundred yards or so of their progress along the Cleatham road. She supposed he was motivated by a vague hope that she would suddenly say yes, and walk home alone.

'No, not tired,' she said.

Kit looked disappointed: then said, taking off his straw boater as if to give her the clearest possible view of him, 'Guess how old I am.'

'Oh! I don't know . . .' Lucy hesitated, tempted to say 'twelve', in consideration of his powers of mind, but knowing that he expected a tribute to his physical development. 'Twenty-six?' she said, choosing the kinder option.

Kit Lightfoot looked vastly satisfied. 'Nineteen last November,' he said, replacing his hat carefully – as if the brilliant light of him might dazzle her, and must be shaded.

'Fancy,' said Lucy. Certainly he was tremendously well-grown: he towered above Lucy, who was not small, and in order to link arms with him Connie was obliged to reach up, hook herself over the crook of his elbow, and be practically carried along like a folded umbrella. He was broad-shouldered too, and his face might have been accounted handsome but for its vacancy, and for a peculiar growth of pimples and bristles round its circumference, suggesting that he made his toilet on the principle that the parts he didn't shave he washed, and vice versa.

'Guess how tall I am,' he said now, with the same air of complacency.

'Six foot three,' said Lucy.

'Oh,' he said crestfallen: apparently she had guessed right. She wondered whether she was supposed to have said four foot ten, to give him the opportunity of triumphantly correcting her; but his dejection was only momentary, and soon he was turning to her again with another poser on his lips, and Lucy supposed he would have gone on inviting her to guess everything about him right down to his shoe-size had not a rumble of thunder sounded like a muffled gong across the valley.

'Oh! God-a-mussey,' said Connie. 'Hark at that. We s'll be caught in it – I knew we would – and me with a great steel pin in me hat!'

'We're nearly there now,' Lucy said. 'See, there's the church spire.'

It was indeed no great distance to the little town of Cleatham, which lay a few miles along the country road to the north of Cottesbridge. It was traditional for swains of the region to take their chosen to see the bones at Cleatham – these being an ancient heap of intermixed human skeletons, stacked in the crypt of the parish church, and happened upon many years ago when two sextons, digging a grave, had suddenly found themselves crashing through the ground into an unsuspected charnel-house. Such a sight offered not only grim novelty but also an opportunity to display manly indifference, and to slip a reassuring arm round the girl's waist when she got the creeps. Lucy had heard that not a few men had got the creeps and been in need of a reassuring arm themselves, but Kit Lightfoot did not appear to consider this possibility as they approached the little town with distant thunder vibrating in the hot air; he was busy erecting vast towers of innuendo on the flimsiest of foundations.

'Jist one finger,' Connie said, 'you lay jist one finger on me, Kit Lightfoot, and I'll go straight home.'

'Oh! Only one finger, eh? So two's all right then, is it? S'pose I was to lay tuthri fingers on you, what then?'

'Man alive, blamed if I can say anything 'ithout being took up wrong! Where was you brung up, a muck-heap?'

'Must have been. That's how I grew so big – like a hollyhock. Nowt wrong wi' big hollyhocks, is they . . .?'

Lucy was content enough to drop back a little behind her companions and let them get on with it, whilst she blissfully took in the sight and scent of the fields, casting her mind occasionally back to her home with something more than the trouble and anxiety that that thought usually cost her. Her father had returned home late last night, in his most expansive mood of liquor. Crashes and a booming song had accompanied his negotiation of the dark back-alley behind the row, culminating in a cordial exchange with their next-door neighbour, 'Fly' Corbett – so named from his nervous habit of rubbing his hands together – who had thrown up his bedroom window to see what all the noise was about.

'I see you there, Chauncey Middleton! You mind my pigeon-house, burn you! Banging and crashing about at this time o' night . . .'

'Fly, my ole shopmate! Fly Corbett, you ole davil, how are you?' her father's voice had answered.

'All right while you come along, singing and banging about . . .'

'Fly, my ole dear, don't you whittle your britches out. You git back in bed along o' Mrs Corbett, her feet'll be gitting cold. All right, Mrs Corbett? I've no doubt you're listening, crouching there behint your old man. You drag him back to bed, gel. He en't much, but he's better than nowt.'

'You're a bad lot, you are, Chauncey Middleton. Do you no harm to git to bed yourself, like most decent folk a' bin two hours since . . .'

'Mag, mag, mag. Goo on. Git on. Start horse-facing. Don't he give you the pip, Mrs Corbett, horse-facing away? Urge you to death, he would. You want to tek the copper-stick to him, that's what. All right, all right—' as there was a sort of muffled explosion from Fly Corbett – 'I'm gooing, I'm gooing. Good night, all! "Farewell and adieu to you fair Spanish ladies . . ." '

The song had continued as her father had entered the house, swelling with his noisy progress up the narrow stairs. For a big man, he was not in fact clumsy at all, even when drunk. He had the shoemaker's high-strung deftness and, despite his spreading flesh, the remains of a certain dapper bodily ease of his own, which when young had made him an enthusiastic dancer. It was just that in liquor his presence, already overbearing and emphatic, seemed to enlarge so that it filled the little house and rebounded from the thin walls.

He had found his way to bed; and in bed he had remained until late that morning, when he had surfaced looking not much the worse for wear. He was in the backyard, perching on the edge of his handcart and taking deep breaths of the sultry air, when Lucy had tackled him.

'Sat'dy night,' he had said unconcernedly. 'Nowt much amiss wi' gitting your jag of a Sat'dy night, is they? Got all Sundy to sweat it out.'

He knew what she was trying to say, but would not acknowledge it. Only the apparent mellowness of his mood encouraged her to press.

'As long as it's just Sat'dy, that's all,' she said.

'Why, I'm here now, en't I?' He shook his head, casting on her a glance at once cheery, admiring, and pitying. 'I don't know. You worry too much, gel. That's your trouble. Git it from your mother, I reckon. She'd wittle a mussel out of its shell, she would.'

She had wanted to be convinced by this breeziness, but she knew him too well. Boldly, she said, 'So you're not going drinking tonight, then?'

He ran a finger along his stiff pale brush of a moustache. 'Why, whoever said I was? Hair and teeth, it's come to summat when a man's got to say sorry for what he en't even done. Who'd be a father, eh?'

He looked humorously downtrodden. However, she knew that ruse too; it was not that but something else that made her feel fleetingly sorry for him at that moment. It was the fact that he was perching on the handcart, or truck as it was called. This truck, a simple two-wheeled but lovingly made affair, was a relic of the days when he had been a hand-shoemaker working from home. It was in the truck that you brought back the boot-uppers that were given out from the factories, and in the truck that you trundled back the finished articles. Once the streets of Cottesbridge had resounded with the grumbling of their wheels, which had thrown out sparks as they bowled down the steepest of the granite alleys. Now, of course, those days were as lost as Lyonesse; but still Lucy's father kept his truck in the yard instead of chopping it up for firewood as others had done. It was as if to get rid of it would be to admit finally that his old life, and his old self, was gone.

So it was that a flash of sympathy, on seeing him jauntily sitting on that truck which was as outmoded as the wooden plough, had almost diverted her. Almost, but not quite.

'I'm only thinking of what the foreman at Stokes' said – last time,' said she.

'Him? Slyving little twopennorth of scrag-end, he is. Frit to spit 'ithout he's told.'

'Father, it don't matter what he is. You got to keep time at the factory, else you'll be out. And if you go on the spree again—'

Her father stamped his boot on the ground. 'Now I wun't be took up like this, Lucy,' he said, his fair colouring turning red in a moment. ''En't it anew that a man wukks all the hours God sends, 'ithout women horse-facing at him? It urges me to death! I'm here, en't I, and I've told you Sat'dy night was my lot – what more do you want?'

The signs of his quicksilver temper were on him, but she persisted. 'How about a promise?' she said.

They gazed at each other a moment – the two strongest wills in the Middleton household meeting in silent opposition.

Then her father shifted his ground: he had been fond of wrestling in his younger days, and had been adept at outmanoeuvring opponents. He burst into a rich, droll, tolerant laugh, and said, 'Promise? Course you got my promise, Lucy. How could I say no to you, wi' your mother's pretty eyes peeping out from them lashes? Need heart of stone to refuse, a man would, that's a fact.' Faced with her adult will, he was simply denying it; he was addressing her as just such a plaintive, ineffectual being as her mother was – a creature to be pandered to, too naïve to bear harsh treatment. 'Now stop wittling. You'll git a crease atween them nice eyebrows one of these days, all the wittling you do.'

Lucy's brow was as yet as smooth as the shell of an egg; but if it had been marked with furrows, she might with justice have said that it was he who had put them there. For the moment, however, she was chiefly concerned with pressing home her point, even though he had tried to blunt it.

'A promise, then, Father,' she said. 'I shan't forget you made me a promise. That's all I wanted to hear.'

He must have heard something clear and downright in her tone, which told him that he could not bluff her; but after a moment's hesitation he chose the easy laugh again. Chauncey Middleton was a bully, but not of the sullen sort who feed on the fear and hate they inspire. He was a bully who thought himself lovable – who, indeed, earnestly craved love the more he dug at its foundations.

Knowing her father as she did, Lucy could not rest easy

with that promise. It was wonderful to be in the country again, to feel the irregularities of grass and earth beneath her feet which never touched a natural surface from week's-end to week's-end; but it could not wholly quieten the anxiety she felt about what her father was up to back home, which formed a droning counterpoint to the tuneful theme of her feelings on walking to Cleatham that afternoon. It was as well she was not superstitious, or the sombre timpani of thunder that pursued them, from the direction of Cottesbridge, might have fallen with a more ominous significance upon her ear.

'Oh no, I shan't go in!' said Connie, as they came to the church of Cleatham, a neat little market-town into which a couple of shoe-factories had insinuated themselves and stood, the most conspicuous wolves that ever donned sheep's clothing, amongst the gabled houses. 'I shouldn't want people gawping at my bones when I'm dead – I should go and haunt 'em if they did.'

'Oh, there's no harm in it, Connie,' said Lucy. 'We shall all be the same then – you wun't be able to tell one of us from t'other.'

'Well, you must both stay close either side of me, case I go off in a swound,' said Connie, slipping her free arm through Lucy's.

'Oh, I shall stay close all right,' said Kit; at the same time darting at Lucy, over Connie's head, such a look as suggested he would not be inconsolable if Lucy were a part of the bone-heap herself.

The church at Cleatham, almost lofty and massy enough in its proportions for a cathedral, was made doubly impressive by the atmospherics; the florid sky throwing into strong relief the great tower, the stonework of which was exposed by the bleach-white palpitations of lightning in moments of supernaturally intense detail. Opening the door, they found the interior so cool that it was as if the thunderstorm had advanced to another stage within, and fat raindrops might have been expected to begin falling from the nave roof.

'Are you frit, Lucy?' Connie whispered.

'No, course not,' Lucy said; though a strong sensation of awe contended with her chapel-bred sensibilities, which told her what a nonsense it was that these thumping great places should be built so that priests could prance about in night-shirts.

43

The verger who acted as guide was a little irascible man with soil under his fingernails and peppermint on his breath. It was while he was unlocking the door that led to the crypt that a young man entered the church and stood irresolutely at a distance from them.

'Come to see the bones?' the verger snapped at him.

'Yes, I – that is, when you like.' He gestured at the three of them. 'You've already got a party, so I'll come back later.'

'Oh no! I aren't doing it all over again just for one,' said the verger. 'I might as well tek you down all four, now. Two-be-two, like the animals in the Ark, that's how I usually tek people. Now, are you coming?'

There was a brief confusion, in which Lucy said she wasn't really bothered about going down, and Connie tugged her arm and said in an anguished whisper that she couldn't leave her now, and the verger got more irritable; the end result of which was that the young man made a fourth in the party. The narrowness of the stone steps leading to the crypt meant that Connie had to let go of Lucy's arm at last, and so Lucy descended at the young man's side, feeling rather awkward, but reassured by a glance at his face that he felt no less so.

'Now then, now then, everybody mind their step. I don't want no broken ankles, with all I got to do,' the verger said, leading the way with an oil-lamp. 'Now, if you'll all gather round me, I'll pint out what you've come to see, and tell you all about it . . .'

'I'm sorry, I didn't mean to barge in on you,' the young man said to Lucy.

'It's all right,' she said.

'Crosspatch, en't he?'

'Now, ahem, if I got everybody's attention . . . The discovery of this here cache of bones dates back a hundred years . . .'

The verger had placed the oil-lamp in a recess in the wall, in such a way that its light fell full upon the stack of human bones that filled one end of the crypt. The lamp-wick guttered in the bad air, which was so stifling and oppressive that the place might have been the very nucleus of the thunderstorm developing without; but it was sufficient to show as much as anyone could care to see of the conglomeration of limbs and skulls – an undifferentiated mass of extinguished humanity, pure, white and stark.

But to Lucy it was not the disorder that was terrible, and

made her shrink back in spite of herself: it was the neatness of the stack, reminiscent of bolts of cloth on a draper's shelf. Connie was clinging to Kit's arm, and both were exhibiting the sort of fascinated horror that the prating verger plainly expected of his visitors – like the not unpleasurable creeps caused by a ghost story or a waxwork. Lucy's emotion was of a different sort. She certainly did not fear those skeletons leaping to life – indeed it was precisely the opposite presentiment that chilled her. She was not the first mortal reared in the certainties of faith to have been suddenly faced with the old question, *Can these dry bones live?*, and to have found her heart answering *No*; but seldom can the bleak revelation have been so concretely presented, and to a nature so intensely disposed to hope and aspiration. She did not gasp or shiver, but a cosmic terror possessed her. That all those human lives, the very shortest and quietest of which comprised a whole universe of thought, feeling and experience, should in the end be reducible to this, seemed to her an outrage unsurpassable – except by the ultimate outrage, that the creatures upon whom this doom was placed were given also the intellect, nerves and heart to comprehend it. On the surface of her mind the belief of her chapel upbringing struggled to assert itself, but at a deeper level the collapse was complete. Though she formed no conscious conclusion, if there was a Mover behind such a state of affairs, he felt Lucy's heartfelt curse breathe upon him at that moment.

A glance at Connie and Kit convinced her that they were not shaken as she was; but when she shyly turned her eyes to the unknown young man, she saw that he was no less affected by the sight, though in a different way. He was standing a little apart from the others, his arms folded across his breast, his head slightly lowered as he gazed at the bone-heap, his feet planted apart: curiously, in that airless vault, his posture recalled that of a man standing steadfastly in the blast of a gale. Was it the force of a similar revelation to Lucy's that he was standing so stubbornly against? Certainly his whole expression was one of violent rejection – the expression of someone listening to the expounding of an evil doctrine.

The verger had very soon told the tale of the discovery of the cache, and was taking the oil-lamp from its sconce even as the last words were on his lips; and presently they were emerging again into the body of the church, where a flash of lightning made a ghastly effect at the stained-glass windows.

'Oh! Man alive, I'm as jumpy as a flea now, what wi' bones and storms,' cried Connie. 'Kit Lightfoot, what'd you want to bring me on a jaunt like this for? And you needn't keep limbing me about like that – I don't want to learn Cornish-wrestling, thank you very much.'

'Why, you weren't so fussy down there,' said the sparkling Kit. 'You was all but shinning up me like a drainpipe . . .'

A wrangle ensued, which Lucy was called upon to referee, and she did not see the young man slip away. When they left the church they found the sky a yet weirder colour, and ripples of thunder still disturbing the sluggish air, but it looked as if the storm might finally break further down the valley. Connie and Kit's quarrel persisted as they made their desultory way down the High Street of the little town, the couple arguing the merits of going to find a tea-shop with a laborious circular inconsequence peculiar to lovers, and so Lucy, suspecting that her presence was contributing to the strain, and a little weary of the bickering, suggested that she go off for a while by herself. The river was near at hand, and attractive to her; and so they parted with an agreement to meet outside the church in an hour.

Lucy found a path that led through the flood-meadows to the river. Her plan of blissfully beguiling the time by walking its green banks, however, was thrown into jeopardy by the weather, which gave indications that the threatened storm was not going to pass on but break in full violence overhead. All at once the temperature had dropped, and cool little cross-winds were at large; stray blossoms and twigs sprang suddenly and vertically in the air with the look of sentient beings, and the peal of thunder that at last boomed out seemed not so much to originate from the sky as to travel with a titanic shiver through the earth at her feet.

The raindrops, at first few enough to count, became in a matter of seconds a tremendous perpendicular drumming of water. Lucy's first thought was to run back to the shelter of the church, but the feelings she had experienced there made it an unappealing refuge. An old stone water-mill, plainly disused, stood beside the river a short distance ahead of her; and so, ducking her head and lifting up her skirts, she ran towards it.

For a moment, as she came to the path by the mill-pond, its surface pitted and seething with the downpour, she thought she would be unable to get inside: the windows were boarded and she could see no door. A moorhen lurched across the pond with forlorn flaps as she hurried past weed-green sluices round to the back of the building. Then, through her dripping hair, she saw a doorway, with gaping holes in the jamb where the door had rotted off its hinges, and she darted inside.

A yeasty smell of damp was within; ragged beards of moss hung from the stone wall of the entrance passage. Unpinning her hat and stroking back her heavy wet hair, Lucy went further in. The place had obviously been abandoned for a long time; her boots made powdery prints on the mouldy floorboards, and the decayed ceilings above her head had in places completely fallen through to reveal rafters and upward perspectives into the storey above. But one room that she came to still bore marks of its former occupiers – outlines of picture-frames on the sweating plaster of the walls, circular smudges on the ceiling where oil-lamps must have burned, a fireplace with a few rusty fire-irons and, on the hearth, startling her, sat a small frog, as smooth, shapely and shiny as a creature of ceramic, which gave a single fluty warble when she bent to look at it, but declined to move.

Outside the thunder was making ripping and tearing noises, as if great bundles of ponderous sound were being rent open, and the rain was falling with a deep sizzle on the pond and the mill-race. Feeling the primitive delight of having found shelter, Lucy explored further, and came upon a spiral staircase; its iron steps seemed quite sound, so she lightly ascended. The upper space into which she emerged was partly taken up by the disused and rusted mill machinery, but there was a narrow landing, and the boards seeming tolerably secure underfoot, she proceeded along it with feline curiosity.

Practicality had been forced on Lucy – as the only adult in the Middleton household with more than a notional sense of responsibility – but it was impossible that she should entirely escape the family fecklessness, and its concomitant belief that the ill-will of the universe must surely be limited rather than infinite. She had accordingly a strong willingness to take risks, which as a child had made her, in spite of herself, the Boadicea of her playmates, who had hung back in awe as she had rescued the trapped mouse from the tor-menting hands of boys, or run through the shadow-teeming

47

alley of the worst repute in the Hole. Thus, when she came to the threshold of a large room in which the floor had almost completely fallen away, leaving only a naked beam that bestrode the empty space to the further wall like a bridge, she was seized by an impulse to walk across it.

Looking down as she tentatively set her foot upon the narrow timber, she saw a dramatic perspective of the storey below – the mill, as was usual with buildings of its type, being built to a lofty scale, and the bare brick floor almost twenty feet beneath her. Undaunted, she began the crossing in the fashion of a tightrope-walker, arms outspread to maintain her balance, eyes fixed on the opposite wall rather than on the yawning space below. She was nearly across when a whipcrack of thunder startled her: she wobbled, and for several moments the image of plunging to the brick floor below was vividly present to her mind before she regained her balance.

Completing the crossing, she held on to the rough stone of the farther wall, looking back along the beam. As if expressing the thought that was in her mind, a voice spoke from below her.

'Now you've to get back.'

Looking down she saw, standing in the room below, the same young man who had accompanied them into the church crypt. The realization that her freakish act of daring had been witnessed caused her cheeks to burn for an instant; but there was nothing of mockery in his manner, and he seemed rather to observe her proceeding with a grave interest. As she hesitated, however, he said, 'Does it put you off, me here? Shall I go out of the way?'

'No . . . I don't know . . . you needn't,' said she and, to overcome the awkwardness of the moment, she turned about and recrossed the beam as swiftly and easily as if she were walking upon a pavement.

There was nothing for it but to go downstairs, though she was a little embarrassed again, the walking of the beam being a variant of her habit of straying into a dream-world, like the way she ran her hands along the stone of the old farmhouse in Cottesbridge High Street. The consciousness of being alone with a strange man, which would have sent Connie into a prodigious flutter, was but dimly developed in her; for that mutual experience in the church crypt, though they had barely exchanged a word, seemed to her to have established

48

a relation between herself and the stranger that a more conventional introduction could hardly have effected.

He was waiting for her at the foot of the stairs, and as soon as she appeared he said with the same tone of intense interest, 'Weren't you frit of falling?'

'I should have been, I suppose,' she answered honestly. 'But I just wasn't thinking.'

The tumult of the storm filled the short silence that ensued.

'Hark at that rain,' the young man said. 'Lucky we found this place.'

'Oh, you must have got caught in it!' she said, seeing now that the jacket he carried over his shoulder was dripping.

'I am a bit wet,' he said absently. 'En't you with your friends?'

'They're in the town.'

'Courting, I reckon.'

She nodded.

'No fun playing gooseberry. What did you think of the bones?'

'I thought they were terrible,' she vehemently answered, with a refiring of the emotion she had suffered in the crypt. 'I wish I hadn't seen that place. At least – no, I don't mean that. I'm glad I did, in a way.'

'*I'm* glad I saw it,' he said decisively. 'It meks life more precious, don't it? Meks you think what a sin it would be to waste it.'

Without either of them initiating it, they had begun to wander from room to room of the mill. The intermingled footprints that they left on the mildewed floorboards in their aimless progress gave the appearance of a couple's having chosen that unlikely spot to dance in.

'I wonder what became of the people who lived here,' she said.

'There's not much water in the mill-race. Maybe the river got too low and the mill wasn't worth working any more.'

They paused before a window from which the boards had fallen away in decay, revealing a view, between doddered willows, of the far valley-side drenched in summer rain.

'How would you like to live in a house like that?' he said, pointing. The house, a solitary gabled manor, stood on the crest of the escarpment, and in the shimmer of the rain seemed to float free of the earth.

'How do you know I don't?' she said, though with sad humour rather than tartness, for everything about her from her accent to her clothes marked her as one of the shoemaking folk.

The young man smiled. 'Cottesbridge? Me too. Moved over from Wellingford a few months since. I work at Whiting's.'

'Oh! My neighbour works there. Mr Birdsall.'

'I know the name. Clicker, en't he? I'm in the rat-pit myself. Finisher.'

Automatically Lucy looked at the young man's hands, for finishers' black stained so deeply that some men in the trade gave up the effort to wash it off, and were permanently swarthy to the wrist. But the young man's hands were very white, except for tiny traces of the dye around the cuticles.

'Carbolic soap,' he said, observing the direction of her gaze, and lifting his hands up. 'I git through pounds and pounds of it. Sometimes I think, this time I'm not going to git 'em clean, and I scrub and scrub until they're sore. The day I can't git 'em clean, I shall—'

He broke off as a violent explosion of lightning and thunder together clove the sky directly in front of the mill, causing them both to flinch back involuntarily. Recovering themselves, they shakily laughed.

'You'll do what?' she said.

'Oh!' He shrugged. 'That day won't come. I s'll have got out by then.'

'Where to?'

He abstractedly regarded the view of the valley. 'That house on the hill, maybe. Somewhere different. Somewhere things go better.'

' "And there shall be no more death, neither sorrow, nor crying, neither shall there be any more pain: for the former things are passed away",' said Lucy. She smiled uncomfortably at his look. 'That was the text at chapel this morning.'

The young man shook his head. 'No. I en't waiting while I'm dead for it. I don't know whether there is a heaven or not, but it's going to be a poor joke if it all turns out to be a story . . . Now look here!' With touching awkwardness he stuffed his hands in his pockets. 'You did feel it too, didn't you? Down in that crypt? I thought you did, else I wouldn't have said that about heaven and all; but if you're chapel—'

'I felt it,' she said. 'Oh, yes, I felt it. It was like . . . like

50

being shown a picture of your own grave.'

He nodded. 'That's what it was like. And I thought: I shan't look. I've seed it now, fair enough, and I know now what's behint everything, and how there's a mistake, a botch somewhere, that the preacher can't explain no matter what he says. But I shan't look again. Not ever. Not till I'm made to. Whatever there is to be had, it's here below, and I shan't forget that.'

'It's the only way, I reckon,' said Lucy.

Somehow this conversation did not strike her as morbid, and neither did the young man appear to have any consciousness of it as such. For though Lucy's emotion was very real, the body through which it throbbed was young – as significantly distant from the dry bones in the crypt as a living tree is from the lump of coal formed by the decay of its primeval ancestors; and the invincible vitality of it could no more be stifled by lugubrious thoughts than the sun can be extinguished by a passing cloud. What was more, she was for the first time finding her own feelings echoed by another mortal, the circumstance which, above all others, charges experience with meaning; and the young man who talked with her of these things did so with a peculiar liveliness, spirit and emphasis, the very opposite of melancholy. While the two of them spoke of death, life asserted itself insistently from their every pore.

'Is that what you want, then, here below?' she said, indicating the view. 'The house on the hill?'

'It'd be nice,' he said. 'Hark at me. Nice. It'd be wonderful – you should see my digs. Only that's not a thing to set your heart on, is it? Not jist a house, and a carpet on the floor and all that – nice, like I say, but that only goes so far. I mean, what happens when you look round at your house and your carpet and them dangly things a-hanging off your chairs – what they called . . .?'

'Valances,' she said smiling.

'Valances, that's it – I mean, once you've looked round at it all, and run the feather duster over it, then what? But then,' he said, beginning to pace with his eyes bent, considering, on the floor, 'I don't mean to sound like one of them creeping-Jesus items who's always saying how they're happy wi' what they've got and wouldn't want no more and all that. Course I want more. Only it's got to be – special: d'you see what I mean?'

He turned to her in perplexed appeal. As he talked he had an air of being argumentative, but not in a disputatious way; the words simply came tumbling out as if contrary propositions were continually occurring to him. In the same way there was a restlessness about his movements, which his physique prevented from becoming clumsiness: he was a lightly built man, with the typical valley wiriness about his arms and shoulders. He was not particularly tall, but his slenderness lent him height, and he had the athlete's long legs and high rib-cage which seem to have been commoner in the ancient world than in modern times. The beauty of his face was also of a sort to commend itself to an age which valued expression above ruggedness in the male of the species: clean-shaven and pale, its dominating feature was a pair of deeply set grey eyes, fixed and preoccupied in their gaze, and shadowed by a strongly marked brow that might have given a grim and baleful look to an older man, but which youth presented as intensity and decision. His nose and mouth were finely and sparely made, the lips making up in mobility for what they lacked in firmness: his black hair, cut short at the nape, grew thick and strong at the front, and was pushed back either side of his forehead in a rough parting. His dress, whilst not shabby, was certainly a little eccentric for the valley Sabbath, of which best clothes were as indispensable a part as chapel-going and Yorkshire pudding: he had a cap instead of a hard hat, his striped shirt was clean but he wore no collar, and on his feet he had only plain riveted boots, mired with walking. A flower in the buttonhole of the jacket he carried was his only concession to Sunday formality. Altogether his appearance, speech and gestures suggested a man whose feelings were strong, but were mixed up with his ideas, so that neither of them gave him ease.

Lucy, whose own tendency was to think through her skin, was far from finding this uncongenial; but she was all at once taken with a sudden shyness of him, and said inconsequently, 'There's a little frog in the next room – come and see him.' On their repairing to the spot, however, they found that the frog had disappeared. They continued their exploration down a passage that neither had tried yet, and came to a door that opened almost directly on the mill-pond. The thunder was reduced now to a few bass stutterings in the distance, but the rain still poured, and at the edge of the pond the most scrawny and bedraggled old heron in creation stood patiently enduring it.

'Look at that poor old hernshaw,' Lucy said.

Almost at the same moment the heron darted its head down into the lily-pads, and came up with a squirming frog in its bill. Lucy shuddered as the bird convulsively swallowed its meal, and said, 'I hope it's not the frog I saw ... but then it's still some other poor little frog gitting ate; and I felt sorry for the old hernshaw, too!' With a rueful smile, she allowed her glance to meet the young man's. He was looking at her intently.

'What's your name?' he said.

'Lucy.'

'I'm Matt.' As if this simple exchange of information had suddenly destroyed his equilibrium, he hurriedly blurted, not looking at her, 'What gurt fool-jabeys them friends of yours were mekking of themselves, carrying on in that church!' She tended to agree, but already he had caught himself up and, colouring, was saying, 'Nice thing to say, that Matt, very nice indeed, knock down a person's friends to her face, that's charming—'

'They're courting,' she interposed, to put an end to his embarrassment, 'and it seems to be a rule that when you're courting you have to twitter and act daft. I don't know why.'

'Oh, it's what people expect! If a couple tek a shine to each other, the whull world and his wife expect to see the business through, step by step, in public. I sometimes wonder folk don't mek 'em wear a sandwich-board, saying they're courting and when they expect to git wed and everything about 'em. What a lot of flapdoodle!'

'And after all, it's nobody's business but their own.'

'This is jist it, you see – what folk can't stand, what urges 'em to death beyond everything, is people doing summat different,' he said with energy. 'If you don't do as other people do, they'll hate you as much as if you'd done 'em a bad turn. Now why do they feel like that?'

'Perhaps because their parents did. And so it goes on and on, with nobody ever breaking out of it and thinking for theirselves.'

'Well, maybe I'm in luck there. I got no kin. You got kin in Cottesbridge?'

Her gnawing anxiety over her father, she realized now, had left her: it came back as soon as she noticed its absence. 'Yes, I got kin,' she said. 'We're Middletons.' But the expected look did not materialize on the young man's face at her mention of the name: of course, she remembered, he was a newcomer to the town. 'En't you got kin where you come from? Over Wellingford?'

'None as I know on,' he said. 'Father did a bunk, and mother died. I got nobody, and it suits me. Just got a room in Bright Street. Walls so thin you can hear him next door turn over in his bed. I shan't stop there long. I shall git out soon.'

There was such a poignant mingling of vulnerable hope and downright determination in the way he said this that all the pressure of Lucy's own longing seemed to rise in her. 'I wish I didn't have to go back to Cottesbridge,' she murmured. 'I wish I could stay always in the country!'

'Ah, it's rare beautiful,' he said. 'Look there where the sun's coming through. And en't that a rainbow? One of them faint ones – there one second, gone the next.'

In silence they regarded the clearing of the storm across the valley. In one choked quarter of the sky the rain could still be seen sweeping down, but at the opposite extremity crystal pillars of sunlight descended from zenith to horizon, so that a fine day and a wet day were presented simultaneously to their sight. Momently the sombre shadow was peeled from the valley-side as the clouds retreated, the river-meadows reclaiming their emerald colour to such luminous effect that it scarcely seemed possible they were clothed in so humble a material as grass, and the sheep thereon might have been pasturing on spun glass. The two observers, who were so still and quiet that each beat of an eyelash was a matter for awareness, were curiously both joined to and severed from the scene that impressed them so deeply. Only a couple of generations separated them from a world in which this rural spaciousness had been the natural habitat and workplace of their kind, and its unchanging rhythms still lapped at their town-lives like the sea around island shores; yet the twain were as remote from the production of the bread, meat and milk they consumed and the wool they wore as any Mayfair *grande dame* who breathed coal-smoke instead of air and thought that ditches dug themselves. These young souls were permanently estranged from a fund of rustic tradition, folklore, pastime, and custom, which in their grandparents' time had permeated the valley; but the raw little towns in which they lived, pickled in an aspic of puritanical Methodism, had yet to fill the gap with a native urban culture of their own. Thus they achingly invested the countryside with a significance purely personal; and so it was perhaps not merely in an optical sense – the rainwashed air magnifying the distant prospect – that the beautiful fields seemed nearer to them than they really were.

'I wonder,' said Lucy, in a muted tone, half-shyness, half-rapture, 'I wonder if Cottesbridge will keep on growing, and the other towns too – Kettenham and Wellingford and Bishop's Burton and Saunds and all of 'em – so that one day they'll all be joined together, and all this country will be lost underneath the pavements.'

It seemed a cruel prospect, but a distant one, as the whole valley-side came into the sunlight; and nearer at hand, moor-hens left the shelter of the rusted mill-wheel, and resumed their bustling about the surface of the mill-pond, which the strong beams revealed to be teeming with specks of life. Nature took up, in fact, its interrupted business, with the coolest indifference to the watchers, and no sign that it was touched by any vibrations of momentousness emanating from the site of their meeting. While the silence between them deepened to a terrible eloquence, rainwater dripped and beaded from the paddles of the mill-wheel, fish rose with a liquid flap to the green skin of the pond, gnats whined, birds piped up, and the last resigned utterance of thunder faded down the valley. The passing storm that had been fate's instrument in bringing the twain together was to the animal and vegetable world just that – a passing storm – with no larger repercussions than a little more water in the river, and a few more worms groping about on the earth's surface.

Lucy, owning no watch, was unsure how much time had elapsed since she had parted with Connie and Kit. Thinking of the fuss Connie was likely to make if she were late, she said, 'I'd better get back to my friends – they'll be waiting. Well, one of them will, anyway.'

He smiled. 'He en't keen on you tagging along, then? Bit hard on you, that.'

'Oh, I don't mind! Connie just wants me around. I can still . . . think my own thoughts, you know.'

'Ah, that's just what they can't tek away from you, you see!' he said with his sudden impetuosity of expression. 'They can't touch it. They can mek you toe the line, and be just like them in every partick'ler – right-thinking and God-fearing and dickey-wearing and as dead as the Sunday joint – but they can't put their wagging fingers inside your head!

You must know that feeling of – sorry, you are in the trade, en't you?'

'Closer, at Parmenter's.'

'Well, you'll know that feeling of shutting out all the factory noise round you, all the grease and the smell of the gas and the thumping of the presses, and just going through a door in your mind where nobody can follow you – don't you?' A shade of anxiety crossed his face, as if he feared he had been foolish.

'I know it,' she said. 'And when I step through the door, what's on the other side is something like that.' She pointed to the sunlit scene outside. 'Oh, yes, I'm always stepping through that door. And not just in the factory . . .' She thought of her father again: it was her turn to feel she had said too much, and she moved hurriedly away from the open door. 'I've really got to get back,' she said. 'Connie and Kit'll be falling out over me else.'

His smile was sad. 'Courting couples,' he said. 'Gi' you the pip, don't they? Catch me gitting mixed up in that flapdoodle.'

'Some of us have got more sense,' she said.

He hesitated, leaning backwards against the door-jamb in his loose-limbed way, one leg propped up against the wall. He was one of those men, Lucy thought, who would always appear to be slightly outgrowing his clothes at wrist and ankle. 'You'll be all right, will you? D'you want me to walk wi' you down to the town?'

'Oh no, it's all right,' she answered, 'and anyhow, Connie and Kit will think . . . oh, you know, if they see us coming along, they'll think . . .'

'Course – course they will. Didn't think. Sorry.'

'Daft, en't it?'

She made her way to the hallway by which she had entered.

'Reckon I'll stay around here for a bit,' he said. 'I'll mebbe see you about, eh?'

'Oh yes,' she said. 'Cottesbridge en't that big, after all.'

But neither was it so very small, she thought with a curious empty feeling as she left him; and it was not until she was walking away from the mill through the wet grass that she realized that neither of them had said goodbye.

Lucy loved to be alone: working with a score of other girls in the closing-shop, and living in a house which in point of privacy compared unfavourably with a pigeon-loft, it was the richest luxury she knew. But walking the meadow-path back to Cleatham, her solitude struck with an alien chill upon her, as if she were experiencing it for the first time, and she found that she was unexpectedly glad to see Connie and Kit waiting for her by the lych-gate of the church.

Lucy found her friends in good spirits, Kit in particular making much of his discovery that, with his hat on, he was as tall as the roof of the lych-gate – the latter presumably having been constructed at a period when people were smaller, or less stupid. The couple had had some tea in the parlour of a little inn in the town, where Kit had excelled himself in so many amorous sallies to Connie that he felt compelled to repeat them all to Lucy, the most scintillating of these epigrams being to the effect that the sugar in the bowl was sweet, but it wasn't half as sweet as he was on Connie, so there.

Connie, however, became concerned that Lucy had had no tea herself and must be parched, and was soon earnestly proposing that they go back to the inn so that Lucy could have a cup.

'No, no, Connie, I'm all right, really,' Lucy said. 'What say we start for home now?' The mention of a bar-parlour had strengthened her disquiet about her father, and she was anxious to get home and reassure herself that the binge had not been resumed.

Accordingly, they set out on the country road back to Cottesbridge, which was pitted with puddles from the storm, so that they picked a path between fragments of reflected blue sky. Kit was so boisterous and familiar in his attentions as they went along that Connie complained it was like being with an octopus; and though Lucy usually was the most tolerant of girls, and wouldn't have minded this a bit, she found herself growing impatient of her companions, and in a state of grumpiness that she could not account for.

They had not gone far when they were overtaken by a two-horse open waggon, with 'Caldwell Ironmongers' painted on the backboard; and the little whiskered old man who was driving, pulling up the horses, turned to address them.

'You gooing Cottesbridge way? You can jump up and ride, if you've the mind. If you en't preachy about travelling a-wheel of a Sundy, that is. Old Caldwell was iffy-butty 'bout me fetching her back from the wheelwright's on the Sabbath, as it smacks o' business, but he wants her at the shop fust thing in the morning, and so he squared it with his conscience somehow. Marvellous what wriggly shapes a man's conscience can tek on, when it's a matter as touches his pockets.'

The three were glad enough of the lift, and soon scrambled into the bed of the waggon, Kit taking advantage of the situation to curl an arm about Connie's waist in case, as he said, she fell out – an eventuality which the temperate pace of the vehicle and Connie's undeniably low centre of gravity rendered highly unlikely. Lucy, settling herself opposite the intertwined pair, was pensive. She wished, as she had been unconsciously wishing all the time, that she could have talked more with the young man in the mill: there had been such a grateful feeling of release in the experience, and of discovering things that she thought only she knew. If only he were here with her now! She wouldn't care, then, how slow the shaggy-footed carthorses were in getting them to Cottesbridge. But that would have been no good; the circumstances would only have turned the two of them into just such another courting couple as Connie and Kit: constrained to talk only of trivialities, forced to be eternally together when each might have wished for a space to be alone, and exposed to the scrutiny of a world whose cynically grinning expectations seemed designed to deny whatever was unique in their relation, and reduce it to a combination of sentiment and reflex, of cooing and rut.

No, she didn't want any part of that. All the same, it was no fun being the third party to Connie and Kit's whisperings and slappings, and she was about to clamber forward to sit beside the driver of the waggon and talk to him, when her ears caught the sound of her name being called.

It was the young man from the mill, who was fifty yards down the road behind them, and running hard in pursuit of the waggon. The vehicle was hardly outstripping him for speed, but he was almost at the end of his breath, and the gap between them ceased to narrow when he was within calling distance.

'Will you – will you meet me?' he cried, slowing to a trot, one hand clutched to his side.

'When?' Lucy called back, leaning over the backboard.

'Say Sundy – the Gardens.'

'I – yes. Yes, I will.'

'Three o'clock?'

'Yes!'

He came to an exhausted halt in the middle of the road, and waved a hand as the waggon carried her away from him. 'Sundy!' he called, his voice faint now with distance.

She waved back, until a bend in the road obliterated his figure from her sight. Only then did she turn to face Connie and Kit, who were regarding her with open mouths – or in Kit's case a mouth more open than usual.

'Well! you're a deep one,' Connie said; and then, adopting that confidential feminine whisper which is only slightly louder than normal speech: 'D'you mean to say you're going to be walking out with him Sundy?'

'Well – no,' said Lucy. 'Not necessarily.' And she thought, with a rebellious protest rising alongside the excitement: *It's different. It won't be like that. This is different.*

VI

'Lucy, my poppet, come and try the promise box,' her mother called when Lucy entered the house. 'It's bin telling us such things, I don't know what to mek of it!'

Lucy went through to the front room, which was used only on Sundays, and contained a table covered with a cloth of funereal velvet, a tea-service remarkable for the way no two items in it bore the slightest resemblance to each other, and a framed print of Christ feeding the five thousand, in colours. Her mother and Joanna, in Sunday pinafores, were seated at the table with the promise box open before them.

'Did you git caught in that storm, my lamb? You look as dry as toast any road,' her mother said. 'It come down in buckets here, didn't it, Jo? And lightninged like anything. I had to turn the mirror round and put the cutlery away. I remember when I lived at home mother always used to cover the piano with a hoss-blanket when there was a storm, on account of the wires.'

'Where's Father?' said Lucy.

'Back a-bed,' said Mrs Middleton. 'His head was still mizzy-mozzy, poor man, and it was best laid atween the sheets a while, specially with this weather.'

Lucy exhaled a small breath that she did not know she had been holding in, and at her mother's urging sat down at the table to try the promise box.

This was a small casket, common in chapel households, containing biblical texts inscribed on tiny pieces of paper like miniature scrolls, which were lifted out at random with a pair of tweezers. Though intended as an aid to devotion, and a prompter of religious thoughts and resolutions, it was not unusual for the promise box to be treated rather in the manner of a parlour-game with a fortune-telling element.

'Now look at the one I got fust, Lucy, and see what you mek out of it,' Mrs Middleton said. ' "Wizards that peep, and that mutter." Isaiah eight, nineteen. Well, it's scripture, so I'm sure it must be full of all sorts of things, but I'm blamed if I know what. The only one who does any peeping and muttering around here is her next door – ' she lurched backward in her chair to bang at the party wall – 'though Lord knows she does anew of that. Nivry day goes by 'ithout her peeping and muttering, in fact, so mebbe that's what it's all about. I don't know about wizards, but she's a witch if ever I saw one. Nosy neighbours, that's what it must mean. En't there something in scripture about moving your neighbour's landmark? She's always chucking her mucky bucketwater over my fence, which comes pretty close to it. Well! What a deal of instruction there is in these texes when you prop'ly put your mind to 'em, to be sure!' Having interpreted the text thus to her satisfaction, Mrs Middleton pushed the casket over to Lucy. 'You have a go, Lucy. Tek and have a go.'

Lucy drew out a text with the tweezers and unrolled it.

' "The fathers have eaten sour grapes, and the children's teeth are set on edge",' she read out. 'Ezekiel, chapter eighteen, verse two.'

'Well! There's another odd one,' said Mrs Middleton. 'Mebbe it means mothers, on account of the mother's milk. I know when I was nussing Dicky-bird, I could never eat hungins or horse-radish, for he'd be sure to taste it, and turn his face away and wrinkle his nubbies up till he looked like a little old man.'

Lucy regarded the promise box as no more than a piece of harmless fun – though truth to tell she was a little disappointed that no text had been forthcoming which might have had some bearing on her meeting with the young man Matt, and on the fact, still scarcely believable to herself, that she was going to meet him next Sunday. And so she gave no further thought to the text she had drawn, until a few minutes later when, getting up to start preparing tea, she called upstairs to ask if her father wanted any.

There was no reply. She climbed the stairs to knock at the bedroom door, her mind still dreamily running on the events of the afternoon, and the misgivings did not strike her until she lifted her hand to knock, and found the door ajar.

She pushed it open. The room was empty, the bed roughly made, her father's tin watch gone from its little stand on the night-table, and his hard bowler from its peg on the back of the door.

'But he can't have gone out 'ithout us knowing, my petal,' her mother fluttered when Lucy came hurrying down with her news. 'We've been sat here all afternoon, en't we, Jo?'

'Well – we did go out for a while, Mother,' Joanna faltered, meeting Lucy's eyes with a solemn expression.

'Oh!' Mrs Middleton nervously twined back her straying hair. 'What am I thinking on . . . Course, we stepped over to Nance Smallbones' to borrow a pennorth o' butter for we teas – and so we had to stay and chew the fat a space, you know what Nance is like, she'll mag while bull's noon if you let her . . .' Mrs Middleton tapped her own nose with the tweezers, and balefully regarded Lucy like a reprimanded child. 'But I'm sure he wouldn't have gone out, not with his head the way it was . . . Are you quite sure he's not there, Lucy? Mebbe he's . . .' Mrs Middleton appeared to consider the possibility of her husband's hiding under the bed, and reluctantly reject it. 'No – well, he's mebbe just slipped out for some fresh air, now the storm's cleared . . .'

Lucy turned away from her mother's helplessly hopeful expression to gaze out of the front parlour window. What money did he have left after last night? Where could he have got enough to renew the binge? Alongside her anxious vexation was another feeling – a sort of guilt: somehow this ominous turn of events appeared to her as a punishment for her allowing herself to become lost in dreams and fancies conjured up by her meeting with the young man Matt.

She found Mr Birdsall at home and preparing his solitary high tea. The watercress-seller had just been by, and Mr Birdsall came to the door with his hands full of dripping green cress, picked from the iron-rich local streams.

'Not trouble, I hope, Lucy?' he said when she asked if he had seen her father.

'I don't know . . . Mr Birdsall, you haven't lent him any money, have you?'

'Now, you know I wouldn't do that. Not in the way you mean.' He paused. 'I did see him earlier, though. When I came back from the band concert. He was just going into the Hammonds' house.'

Her father paying a call on Topper Hammond – runt of runts, of whom he was always so dismissive? From anyone else but Mr Birdsall she would not have believed it. She thanked him and went on down the street to the Hammonds' house.

The front door, as usual, stood open. The window was so opaque with dirt that this was probably to admit light, but still the interior of the room was so dark that the naked infants crawling on the floor appeared as whitish glimmers like fish at the bottom of a pool. As Lucy tapped on the door-jamb and peered into the dimness, another blob of dingy phosphorescence resolved itself into Ada Hammond, who was sitting on a stool, barefoot as usual, and giving suck to her youngest child from a breast like a tremendous grey udder.

'Come in or goo out then, gel,' Ada said in her thick suety voice. 'One or t'other.'

'It's all right, Mrs Hammond. I was just wondering if you'd seen Father today.'

'He come round this afternoon. Didn't he, Topper?'

Lucy's eyes, adjusting now to the light, made out the diminutive figure of Topper Hammond, seated in the corner with his customary fastidious air of having nothing to do with the chaos around him. He licked a finger to smooth down his little moustache and turn the page of his newspaper. 'Stopped in for tuthri minutes,' he squeaked. 'Anythink the matter?'

'You . . .' Lucy hesitated, but it must be said. 'You didn't happen to lend him any money, did you, Mr Hammond?'

'Matter of fact, I did lend him a few bob. Just as a favour between shopmates, like,' Topper Hammond said, very lordly and negligent: he had so little opportunity to be so that he was making the most of it. 'I'm a bit flush at the moment, as it happens—'

'Had a winner,' put in Ada with a yeasty chuckle. 'Fust one he's picked in weeks that weren't a carthoss.'

Carefully ignoring this, Topper loftily went on, 'Yis, it's a shame if you can't help a friend in need. Mind you, I shall want it back, you know, soon as pay-day comes. You tell him that from me, gel.'

Lucy murmured her thanks and walked blindly away from the door. It was no worse, she told herself, it was no worse than borrowing from anybody else; but her heart would not be convinced. To borrow from Topper Hammond!

It might have been better if she could have been hardened like her brother Jim, who would merely have raised a scornful eyebrow at the news. But she felt the injury to her father's pride as if it were her own – felt it, if truth were told, perhaps more than he did. Knowing quite well that he brought his humiliation on himself, she still ardently wished that she could spare him it.

And all his easy assurances to her that morning – his promise – had been worthless! That hurt too; but she mustn't think of that. The cold fact was that he had got hold of money, that he had gone to turn it into drink, and that he had to be at Stokes' factory for work early in the morning. The shrieks of her little brothers playing round the gas-lamp down the street were a forcible reminder that it was more than just her father's livelihood that was at stake.

Well, she would go and make tea for them; and then tonight she would sit up and wait for her father's return, no matter how long it took. And when he came back she would have to play the termagant daughter: make him drink pints of strong tea, make him swill his head under the tap in the yard, sit up all night herself so long as she could be sure to rouse him in good time for work in the morning.

As she returned to the house she was visited by the thought of the mill and the young man – Matt. It was significant of the impression he had made on her that she could not pronounce his name, even mentally, with composure: it is with the names of those to whom we are indifferent that we make most free. The thought presented itself to her mind as something precarious and precious, like the glimpses of country between the roofs of the town. But she put it away, for now. Iron necessity beckoned her, and the thought of him must at all costs be kept separate from it. She seemed with that one meeting to have entered a new world of feeling; and she knew with a curious urgency that that world and this must never be allowed to meet.

VII

Lucy woke with a start.

What was that noise that had roused her? She knew it. A long horrible grinding . . .

Fly Corbett opening the door of his pigeon-house, that was it. He always went to talk to his birds first thing in the morning. The door was warped and always made that scranching noise—

The morning! All at once the reality of her situation broke in on her. She sat up with a cry. She had wrapped herself in a shawl and sat up in the bedroom chair by the window, intending to wait thus until her father came home; but somehow she had fallen asleep, and must have slept the night through.

She sprang up, ignoring the protest of an aching neck. Joanna was asleep in the bed. The room was full of sunlight.

Could she really have slept through the noise of her father's coming in? But he could be quiet when he wanted to. Especially if he knew that a promise had been broken and she would be on the watch . . .

Cursing herself, she rapped on the door of her parents' bedroom. Her mother at last gave a sleepy groan, and Lucy opened the door.

'Morning, my petal. Whatever's the time? I was all in a funny dream, it was that queer. I was living in a cottage with a lot of little fishes who all kept singing saucy songs . . .'

Her mother blinked amiably at her from the bed. There was a motionless mound under the bedclothes beside her.

'Oh, Mother, when did Father get in? I—' Lucy stopped as she saw the trail of hastily abandoned clothes leading across the floor, the pipe spilling its dregs of tobacco, the empty bottle smashed where it had fallen.

It was a quarter of an hour's work to rouse him sufficiently to open his bleared eyes and swear at them. Cold water, hot tea, and entreaties went no further than to make his curses slightly more articulate. It was difficult to tell whether he was still blind drunk, or blind with the hangover: it really made no difference. As her father turned from them and buried his heavy tousled head in the pillow, Lucy knew that he would be fit for nothing till noon at the least.

'Oh, Mother, look at him! He'll miss work again, and you know what that means . . . If only I hadn't fallen asleep! I meant to stay up till he got in.'

'Well, I never heard him come in, but then I've always been a deep sleeper,' said Mrs Middleton, regarding her snoring husband with doleful resignation. 'I remember when I was living at home, Father used to say, "She'd sleep through doomsday, that gel!" It didn't even wake me when he practised on the piano of a morning, rattling through "Begone Dull Care" just like another Shopping, or Ruby Stein. Well! We'd best get the others out of their beds, even if we can't shift him.'

'But what are we going to do, Mother? What will they say at Stokes' when he doesn't turn up?'

'You or Jim will just have to go and say he's sick. And he *is* sick, poor man – look at him. Oh! I know,' she hastily added at a flash from Lucy's eyes, 'I know he shouldn't have done it, but it's his nature.'

'I'll go to Stokes' myself,' Lucy said. 'And say he's took badly.'

She did not relish the prospect; but she considered herself partly to blame for falling asleep: a nonsense, perhaps, but she could not reason herself out of it. Accordingly she set out earlier than usual for work, breakfastless, so that she could call in at Stokes' first and attempt to plead her father's cause. She was further fortified by the recollection that today was the day the rent-collector made his rounds.

The shoe-factories of Cottesbridge were all as alike as the bricks of which they were built; only size distinguished Stokes', for it was one of the town's larger concerns, and its late proprietor, Mr Edward Stokes, had been one of its most prosperous citizens. The three-storey building had the standard opaque windows, the standard flight of steps up to the door, the standard asphalt yard sanded with leather-dust and, within, the standard smell of gas and grease and the feverish juddering clatter of presses and sewing-machines as if the whole edifice had the ague. Lucy knew the foreman, and caught him at the bottom of the wooden staircase leading to the first-floor offices.

'Sick? Sick? Drunk more like. On a blinder more like,' the foreman said hotly. He gave an irritable shrug and gestured to the door. 'You'd best git off to your own wukk, gel. Unless you want to lose your job like your father.'

'Oh – please, wait a minute, he'll be here on time tomorrow, I promise—'

'*You* promise, gel,' the foreman said. 'And if it was you who had to do the keeping of it, I might feel better about it. But it en't you. It's Chauncey Middleton, and I've had about as much trouble from him as I can tek. If it en't the cheek and the sauce, it's the other kind of sauce. I told him last time if it happened again he'd be out on his ear. He can't say he weren't warned. He can come here tomorrer if he likes – there wun't be any wukk for him. You can tell him that, gel, if he's in any fit state to listen to you.'

'Oh, but please . . .' The foreman was already half-way up the stairs: she darted after him and seized his arm. 'Mebbe he's deserved it, I don't know, but it won't be just him as'll suffer, it'll be the little 'uns as well—'

'Don't you think I've not got little 'uns of me own at home?' the foreman said, shaking off her hand. 'And don't you think I'd rather go soaking meself in booze than wukk in here all day to keep 'em fed? Only I don't, see. That's what meks me mad. That's what urges me to death—'

'What's going on, Shepherd?'

The voice was that of a man who had come out of the little matchwood office above, and was standing at the top of the stairs looking down at them.

'Oh! Mr Stokes, I beg your pardon – it's nothing, it's just Middleton's daughter, come to say he won't be in to work today.'

'Why's that?' said the man, addressing himself to Lucy rather than the foreman.

Young Mr Stokes, Lucy thought: she had heard that old Edward Stokes' son was running the business now, though she had never seen him. As she hesitated over her answer, her mind made a thumbnail sketch of the figure at the top of the stairs: thirty-odd, soberly dressed, small hands, heavy-lidded eyes, thinning hair, neat ears that made her think of some tidy and inoffensive domestic animal.

'He's sick, Mr Stokes,' she said, fixing his eyes with her

own. The lie was a lie: no point in blushing or being furtive about it.

'Hm. Haven't we had trouble from this quarter before, Shepherd?'

'Any amount of it, Mr Stokes,' said the foreman. 'Just what I was telling her. And that he'd been warned last time—'

'He'll be here in good time tomorrow, I promise,' Lucy interposed. 'And I promise it won't happen no more. I promise you, Mr Stokes.' She did not know why she addressed her appeal so personally to him, except that she seemed to see something temperate in the proprietor's look, despite his extreme punctiliousness of bearing – and, of course, it was her last hope. The rashness of the promise did not for the moment trouble her: our tongues are always ready to make out a cheque that the bank of our actions may not be able to honour.

'Talk,' the foreman said. 'All talk. Talk don't work leather—'

'He'll be here tomorrow,' Lucy said. 'And every day after that. Give him another chance, and I promise you won't regret it.'

Young Mr Stokes felt absently for his watch in the pocket of his dove-grey waistcoat. 'Middleton is a good workman, I think, Shepherd?'

'When he's here,' said the foreman grudgingly.

'Well, as we have a firm promise that there will be no more of it, I think another chance is in order. As long as this is the very last time. I don't wish to put anyone out of work, but of course you understand, Miss Middleton, that I can't afford to employ people who only choose to come in when they feel like it.'

Young Mr Stokes' voice, despite its clipped formality, had also a certain feline softness: it reminded Lucy of the soft padding of cat's feet. Yet it was quite audible over the noise of machinery.

'Yes,' she said, 'I understand.'

'Very well. Shepherd, will you bring me Saturday's invoices?'

Mr Stokes turned back into the office. The foreman glowered at Lucy a moment and then shrugged. 'Well, it's up to your dad now.'

Lucy had to run to her own place of work in order not to be late; but there was time for a flush of relief at the success

68

of her enterprise. During the course of her arduous morning in the closing-shop, however, it was succeeded by anxiety. She had given her word: would her father honour it? Or was he at that moment surfacing from the groggy depths of his hangover to a renewed thirst? She was so preoccupied with this that she could hardly give an ear to Connie's probings for information about the young man she was to meet on Sunday – and besides, he was not to be thought of here. That was something different. This was earthly life, that was salvation.

She hurried home at dinner-time to find her father dressed, if not exactly up and about. He was sitting on the edge of the bed and trying to get his hands still enough to comb his hair.

'Ah, you're a good gel, Lucy,' he said, when she told him she had been to the factory to make his excuses. 'Beggar me if I didn't think I'd be fit for wukk this morning, if a bit seedy mebbe. I reckon I must have had a drop of bad stuff last night.'

'It's your last chance, mind you, Father,' Lucy said.

'Life's full of last chances, gel,' he said, with a weak twinkle. 'You'll find that out. Old Sheepy Shepherd was on his high hoss, was he?'

'It weren't him as said it. It was young Mr Stokes.'

'Well, I'll be dalled! You saw that little squab, did you? Not much of a chip off the old block, he en't.'

'Yes, I saw him. And I gin him my promise that you'd keep time, and not break out any more.'

Chauncey Middleton stared, his full red lips agape, and a flush crept over his pallor. 'The davil you did! What? My own daughter, gooing and mekking promises to a little Sundy suit full o' milk-and-water like him . . .'

'He seemed quite nice,' Lucy said. 'And it don't matter what he's like, Father. He's let you have another chance, and I gin him my word that you'd be at work tomorrow.'

'I wun't have it! My own daughter, having to beg and plead with the likes of him. God alive, what's it come to . . .'

She saw then that he was touched in his weakest place – what he would call his pride, and others might call his vanity; and she was quick to seize the advantage it gave her. 'I know,' she said, 'but it don't matter – it's done now; and as long as you keep my promise, there's no harm done, is there? As long as you keep my word.'

'I'll keep it, don't you worry.' Her father began shakily to comb his hair, as if he were ready to sally out to work that very moment. 'I'll show that tight-laced little poll-parrot what Middletons are made on. I suppose he reckons to mek a liar out of my daughter, does he? We'll see. We'll see about that.'

VIII

It was touch and go, but to work her father did take himself the next morning, on time; and the next day, and succeeding days. Self-regard had achieved what a regard for the welfare of his dependants should have effected; and though he was crotchety and unapproachable for the rest of the week, no doubt in the knowledge that the fruits of the labour he was undertaking were only going to fill the gap left by the reckless spending of his binge, it was the settled ill-temper of sobriety rather than the explosiveness of liquor.

A sort of martyred righteousness characterized his relations with Lucy that week. Saying nothing, he yet said plainly: 'See what I do for you!' as if by some rash promise she had committed him to the Labours of Hercules. She was well accustomed, however, to the manipulative side of her father's domineering nature, which would readily try to coax submission to its will if bullying failed to produce it. She rested content with her success as far as it went; and if motes of trouble danced in the beams of the future, arising from the certainty that her father must one day be tempted to break out again, they were obscured by the near approach of the Sunday when she was to meet Matt in the Gardens.

Throughout the week she wondered whether she might meet him by chance about the streets of Cottesbridge. Earnestly wishing to see him, still she felt an almost superstitious dread of doing so before the appointed time – deriving, perhaps, from the already fixed determination in her mind that he represented something quite separate from the workaday world. But though in the course of her walks to and from the factory she was continually looking out of the corner of her eye lest one of the hurrying white-aproned forms be his, no chance encounter occurred, and on Sunday afternoon she arrived at the Gardens in a state of unspotted expectation almost painful in its purity.

Amenities were the lowest of priorities to Cottesbridge, thrumming between its two poles of industry and chapel. The Gardens were a recent and not very extensive concession to the alien concept of relaxation; some formal parterres and lawns, rhododendron bushes that in their sticky painted greenness looked as near to artificial creations as it was possible for vegetation to look, a few park benches bearing the names of their donors, and a small bandstand comprised the whole of their extent. But they were popular, and the day being bright and hot, the small green space was so thronged with people that it was only possible to move about the gravel paths at a sedate shuffle, and bottlenecks were continually forming at which complete strangers were forced to stand squeezed together in unnatural intimacy, and could think of nothing except to stare terribly at each other until they were able to move on; whilst children released from Sunday school – where the twin miseries of their lives, religion and education, came together to such wonderfully inspiring effect – ran like goaded beasts through a forest of stiff-trousered legs and pleated skirts.

How on earth will I find him? was Lucy's first thought on arriving here; a thought touched at first with amusement, as she pictured the two of them toiling separately about the rhododendron maze the whole afternoon, but succeeded by a mild panic. 'What if he can't find me, and goes home?' she murmured distressfully to herself; and her relief on seeing him hailing her from a short distance along the path was such that they might have been searching for each other from opposite ends of the earth.

'Thought I shouldn't find you,' he said, as little calm as she. 'I should have said the bandstand or the keeper's house or something.'

'There wasn't much time, was there? I thought you'd do yourself a mischief chasing after that cart.'

'Very near did, I reckon.'

She was a little surprised, at first, to see that in place of the eccentrically comfortable costume of last week he wore the constricting serge suit of the valley Sunday; but after a moment she acknowledged that she was in like case herself, dressed as she was in her straw hat and best high-necked frock with velvet edging. For such a meeting, in such a place, there was really no alternative; and with this realization some of the glow seemed to fade from the occasion.

It faded further when he offered her his arm, and she took

72

it, and they began to promenade round the Gardens. Not the proximity to him – the feel of him, fresh-washed scent of him, closeness of his shaven face and soft-haired nape – not these were responsible for the sense of bathos: no, they were fomenting in her the unknown and frightening tumult that had been inwardly gathering all week. It was the very reduction of all this significance to the ritual of walking out, the pouring of such unruly material into a standard vessel, a set of public forms and gestures, that caused the sense of disappointment.

She did not know if what he was feeling was something similar: certainly there was about him a stiffness and circumspection quite foreign to the eager, limber figure she remembered from the deserted mill. They walked, and were silent; they could think of nothing to say to each other. 'I could talk to him, talk to him for ever, if we were somewhere else – but not here!' she thought, desponding.

However, this was no way to think if the afternoon was not to be a disaster. (What, indeed, *was* she hoping from it?) Forcing a brightness into her tone, she said, 'It's nice here, en't it? Only I wish there weren't *quite* so many people about.'

'I wish there were none!' he rejoined with a sudden gloomy ferocity. 'None in the world at all – except you and me!' And he directed a grim glance at two parasol-swishing maidens who passed him giggling.

Lucy could not forbear smiling. 'You don't mean that, I'm sure,' she said.

He rested his glare on her a moment; then his face too broke up into a smile.

'Mebbe not,' said he. 'But it's not as nice as our mill, is it?'

'Oh no,' she said warmly.

'It'd be nice to go back there some time.'

She assented; and felt the silence creeping up again.

'What – what sort of week have you had?' said Matt. 'Since we met?'

'Oh, it's been . . .' A peculiar constriction closed Lucy's throat, and she found the rows of bright flower-beds within her view swirling in futile patterns like those that form on closed eyelids before sleep. 'Nothing,' she said, with a sort of wretched luxuriousness of confession. 'Nothing, it's been nothing, it's just been nothing since then . . .'

'Me too,' he said vehemently, 'it's been like that for me too. I wondered . . .'

The silence that ensued was of an entirely different sort:

73

different too the contact between their linked arms which, while gingerly in the extreme, was now not so from shyness, but rather as if the friction might produce some tremendous combustion. An observer looking at the twain in passing might indeed have supposed them to be in a state of profound unhappiness. As the paroxysm of grief and the paroxysm of laughter are often indistinguishable, so when we happen upon a pair of lovers in a lighted doorway and receive their baleful, tragic stare, it is difficult to tell whether we have intruded upon the terrible end of the affair or some moment of soul-thrilling avowal. Certainly the promenaders in the Cottesbridge Gardens that Sunday afternoon could hardly have supposed, from the demeanour of the young couple who passed in their midst, that a great upsurge of joy was there.

For Lucy joy was a less accurate term than a sort of wild wonder. If she had examined her emotional creed, she would have seen there a fervent belief in the instantaneous revelation as the agent of great life-changes, rather than the stealthy infiltration of new sympathies, yet it was still a shock to her to find her heart seized, uprooted, transplanted so quickly and completely. As for the formula, 'But I hardly know him!' that truth seemed rather to reinforce the marvellous inevitability of the transformation than to challenge it.

With an apologetic laugh, she said, 'I don't know your last name.'

'Doughty. Matthew Mark Doughty. Mother was a bit biblical-like. I might have been Zebedee Zachariah if she'd had her way. That's one good thing Father did, anyway.'

'Don't you know where he is?'

'Father? No. He slipped off with a carpet-bag one night soon as I was old enough to earn. Nobody missed him 'cept the men he owed money to.'

'En't you got brothers or sisters?'

'Nobody. I got nobody.' He laughed. 'Don't look like that. It suits me.'

'Oh, yes . . .' The idea was not without attraction, viewed objectively; but the cocooning experience of a large family, oppressive as it often was, still meant that she could not contemplate so naked a solitude without a certain chill.

'Phew, I feel like an organ-grinder's monkey in this suit,' he said. 'I didn't know what to do. You've got to flig up for a place like this, en't you? And yet I thought, it meks it look like we're . . . well . . .'

'Walking out,' said she. 'All the things we said last week we couldn't abide. It's funny, en't it? And here we are like summat off the top of a wedding-cake.'

'Oh well, it's nothing to do with anyone else, what we choose to do, is it?'

'Nobody else's business at all.'

They had come to the open space before the bandstand, and over the sea of hats she could just see Mr Birdsall among the musicians. The presence of that figure, as familiar a part of her world since childhood as Alma Street itself, intensified the strangeness of what was happening to her. There was nothing of the serenade in the oom-pah-pah rhythms of *The Thieving Magpie* overture, but music of all kinds affected Lucy powerfully, and from that moment forth the melody fixed itself in her mind fused with an association that would never leave it.

Inevitably, Mr Birdsall's was not the only familiar face to Lucy, who had lived her whole life in the town. How-dos, nods and smiles were given and received on all sides; and on all sides too there was an unabashed interest in her companion.

'They're all having a good gline at you, I'm afraid,' she said in an undertone to Matt. 'I'm sorry!'

'I do feel a bit like the Bearded Lady at Wellingford Feast last year,' he said cheerfully. 'Queer sight, she was. The beard was real all right, but I don't reckon there was any more of the lady about her than the pink frock amounted to. I reckon it was jist a chap with a couple of Norfolk biffins down his shirt . . . Why, they've seen you walk out with a fellow before, en't they?'

'Not me!' she laughed.

He gave her a look that was both admiring and flatteringly sceptical.

'No,' she said. 'I could never be bothered with it. It's like we were saying last week – you have to act so daft, and mek sheep's eyes, and giggle and carry on so. Oh, that meks me sound like such a hard ole dolly!'

'I don't think so. T'other way round surely. They're the hard ones,' he said in his decisive way. 'En't they? Playing a chap like he was a fish on a line.'

'And then you have to say a lot of teasy things you don't mean. I can't understand that. Where's the sense in talking if you don't say what you mean?'

'I knew you weren't like that,' he said in a tone of perfect confidence. 'Soon as I saw you. Walking acrosst that beam in the mill.'

'Oh, don't,' she said, embarrassed at the memory. 'I shall—'

'What? Blush?' He looked inquiringly into her face. 'No: not you. You en't that sort either – thank God for it!'

She returned his look frankly. Somehow it did not seem odd to be gazing into this young man's face, on so short an acquaintance, with as little reserve as if she were regarding her own face in the mirror; yet she was obscurely aware of the development's significance. The animal speaks with its whole body, but much of human expression, and hence individual personality, has become concentrated in the small area between the hairline and the neck; and when two faces meet closely without dissembling there is an exposure and intimacy to which the uncovering of bodies can be but a supplement.

The greetings had all hitherto been for Lucy, rather than Matt the newcomer in Cottesbridge, and so she was surprised when they were interrupted by a voice calling his name.

'Well, shopmate, and what sort o' hand's life dealing you lately? Not a bad 'un by the looks of things. Oncommon lucky by the looks of things.'

The young man shaking Matt's hand with a touch of mockery, and including them both in a wry, speculative glance, was a comical, snub-nosed, red-haired fellow, slender as a stoat, with a pink mouth that moved in loose, india-rubbery fashion when he talked. He was shabbily dressed but for a large nosegay in his buttonhole, which he likewise seemed to invest with mockery; and, as he stood regarding the two of them with ironical wrinklings of his pale eyebrows, his feet planted jauntily apart, he was continually making those fine adjustments of balance which indicate a drink or two taken.

'How do, Luther,' Matt said. 'How's yourself?'

'Fair to mid, me bucko, fair to mid. Not that this here chapel-suit brigade don't give me the screaming hab-dabs, but then each to his own they say. Mind you—' he made a motion of falling back in surprise— 'burn me if you en't all the dand yourself this fine afternoon! Whatever's behint that, I ask meself?' Again he glanced from Matt to Lucy, with the pert conscious look of a cat upon a shelf about to break something. 'Introduce, then, shopmate. Got to mind we manners on a Sundy, en't we?'

'This is Luther Benson,' Matt said with an exasperated smile. 'He works in the rat-pit wi' me. This is Lucy Middleton.'

'*Used* to work, he means,' Luther said, lifting the bowler slightly from the back of his head like the lid of a tankard. 'Luther Benson and Whiting's boot-factory have parted due to irrecon-cilable differences. Rumours that Luther Benson dropped various hints to the foreman of the said works, to the effect that his old woman was having more than her scuttle filled by the coalman while he was at work, are totally 'ithout foundation. Wait a minute! Middleton – relation of Chauncey Middleton?'

'That's my father,' Lucy said, and wished she could say it with more ease.

'Know him,' Luther said, closing one eye as if taking aim at a target. 'Just to share a glass or three with, mind you. Man alive, us three, we're gitting on like house on fire, en't we? Shame to break it up, really, but I got to see a chap about summat, and as for you two – well, you want rid, don't you? I en't daft. You're thinking, Luther, stop horse-facing and leave us be. And so I shall. Only there's one snag, and blame me if I know how to put it!'

There was abundant good humour in the grin he gave them; but though Lucy could not help smiling a little in return, there was something about the mobility of his face that was disconcerting. Matt's mobility of expression reflected his mercurial thought – his mental life seeming to proceed at a faster rate than the average, as the heartbeat of a bird outstrips ours. With Luther Benson, she could not escape the feeling that his expression would always change as soon as your back was turned.

'Now, if it was just my ole stepmother – God bless her, and tek her to him as soon as he likes – badgering me for a bit o' rent, I wouldn't ask. If it was just me boot-soles wore down so much I'm walking on me corns – shoeless in *this* town, now en't that a scandal? – I wouldn't ask. But down Gas Street there's an awkud ole blank-blank, ladies present, who's took it into his head that he wants paying back a trifling sum as he once lent me, and that any reasonable man would be glad to call a gift, and add to his credit in heaven – but any road, he en't reasonable, and he keeps mentioning some friends of his who seem to be in the fisticuffs line, and promising to introduce me to 'em. Now that's very nice of

him, but you know me, I'm shy: I don't tek to being introduced to new folks, and if it's all the same to him I'd rather
go 'ithout the pleasure—'

'Here,' Matt said, with the same air of amused annoyance,
'I can give you two bob, but that's your lot.'

'Funny! Damn funny how life turns out, en't it, Miss
Middleton? That sum's ex-actly what's needed to keep these
here pugilistic gents from demanding the honour of my
acquaintance, seem'ly. Who says there en't a Providence
behint it all?'

Pocketing the two shillings, and lifting the tankard lid
again, Luther Benson gave them both a winked farewell and
disappeared into the crowd.

Matt threw Lucy a sidelong look, half smiling. 'What's that
proverb? Summat about a fool and his money?'

'Is that true about the chap threatening him?'

'Probably. But he'd still ask if it wasn't. I don't know, he's
a hard man to say no to, somehow; and besides, he lives in
the Hole, and things are grim there, en't they? He was a
good shopmate to me when I fust come to live here, not
knowing anybody.'

Lucy soon had reason to wish that she knew no one in
Cottesbridge, for scarcely had Luther Benson left them than
the towering figure of Kit Lightfoot came in sight, with
Connie clinging alongside. They were spotted and cornered
in an instant. The usual introductions were made – Connie
meanwhile managing mutely to express to Lucy, with every
inch of her plump body, the single expletive 'WELL . . .!' in
large capitals. Kit Lightfoot, with that look of glazed affront
often seen in young men when called upon to meet their
contemporaries, jabbed Matt with a short series of questions.
'You in the trade, then? What work? What fact'ry? Where
you from?' And, having pinned the stranger down, like a
specimen butterfly, to his satisfaction, he proceeded to an
account of how he had mended a gas-bracket at Connie's
house that morning.

'Only took him a minute,' Connie confirmed. 'Would have
took Father while bull's noon to do it. He'd have had to
climb on a chair, to start with, but Kit just reached up as
easy as you like. Ever so clever like that, he is.' Kit meanwhile
basked quite unabashed in Connie's adoring glance: like most
men in his situation, he regarded his sweetheart's love not as
a gift to be received with humility, but as the appropriate

tribute paid to undeniable worth.

'Well, any road! Now we can all walk along together,' said Connie, taking charge of the other three, all bigger than she, like a tugboat. There was nothing for it but to surrender. Kit, pleased with himself, condescendingly invited Matt to guess how old he was – Matt wearing an expression that could only be described as thoughtful; whilst Connie plied Lucy with whispered questions: 'How old is he? Has he got kin here? You took him home yet? When you having him to tea?'

Lucy was dismayed to find what had seemed so mysterious and unique being so rapidly assimilated into the standard courtship pattern. It was all so calculating and purposeful! Yet at the same time she felt guilty at wishing Connie and Kit gone; and silently posed herself the question: 'After all, why should it be so different for you?' only to receive the protesting answer: 'It *is* different – it just is!'

Dismay, indeed, was her portion for the rest of the afternoon, in which they were forced to circulate as a foursome. Matt was friendly, but she was sure he must be secretly annoyed; and when it was time to go home for tea, and the party could at last break up, she was hot, tired and irritable.

Thankfully, her route home lay in a different direction from that of Connie and Kit; and from that of Matt, too, but he took her arm without a word and walked with her.

For some minutes she could not speak; but at last she burst out with a sort of cross despair, 'Well, that was no good, was it?'

'No,' he said. 'No, it wasn't.'

He met her eyes, and burst out laughing.

'Oh well!' she said, laughing too, though still smarting a little. 'I know they meant well, and they are my friends, and it seems awful to wish they weren't there, but . . .'

'I know. It's not just that, though, is it? It's that whole business of parading round, and having to be – now what did you call it? – like summat off the top of a wedding-cake. Oh! I wish I'd been born a savage, Lucy. Don't you? A Red Indian or summat. I dare say wigwams are a bit on the draughty side, and you're liable to git pine-needles in your britches, but even so – think o' the freedom! But mebbe it's not like that. Mebbe Hiawatha had to tek Minnehaha home to meet his folks, and sit there handing round the buffalo scones with his best feathers on.'

79

Still laughing, but still disappointed, she said, 'Let's not go there again, Matt. I mean – at least, I mean, if we go anywhere.' She stopped and faced him. 'I mean, what *are* we doing?'

'Walking out,' he said. 'In the eyes of other folks, anyway. En't we?'

She nodded.

'And do you want to? You see—' he chuckled nervously, shrugging – 'I haven't really asked you, have I?'

'You didn't need to,' said she, feeling her heart give a curious emphatic thump right in the middle of the sentence.

Stammering a little, though his eyes on her face were eloquent enough, Matt said, 'So – in the eyes of other folks we're walking out or courting or whatever . . . and they can see it like that if they like. But we know it's . . . summat between us. It's . . . different.'

He took her hand: she squeezed his tightly.

'Run with me,' he said.

'Eh?'

'Run. Fast. Now. If ever you feel bad, troubled-like, then run. It's summat I've always done – it works.'

She grinned at him.

'Come on then,' she said.

They ran, with linked hands, down the steep streets; and were watched with amazement by the sober-suited towns-people, who could not decide whether the twain were running to, or away from something.

'Matt,' Lucy said softly to herself as she lay in bed that night, the regular sigh of Joanna's breathing beside her. 'Matthew Mark Doughty.'

She needed to say the name: had indeed an absurd wish to write it down.

The silliest of besotted schoolgirl routines, she told herself; but if that was the form this new sensation must take, then so be it. A revolution was occurring within her. She had not so much despised love as looked with perplexity on the triviality of its manifestations: now she glowed with the extra fervour of the convert.

The need for love to be new, special, turned from no previously used mould, was no less central to her belief: she had not abandoned it; rather, her demanding criterion seemed all of a sudden to have been met. It must be so: this convulsive overthrow of her emotional being could surely not have been repeated in a million breasts, and begun a million commonplace unions!

She looked at the tin clock by the bed, and stole softly to the window which overlooked the street. When they had parted this afternoon, Matt had proposed to walk down her street before the lamps were put out that night, and look up at her window.

'Why? Because I can't wait to see you again. I just got no patience, never have had. Mek meself lukewarm pots of tea because I can't wait for the kettle to boil . . . It'll be like being with you, sort of.'

She did not know whether she was a patient person or not – her own self had suddenly taken on mysterious dimensions – but certainly she did not feel patient now.

She peered down the street. The night was cool, and one of the insidious mists to which the low-lying valley town was prone had settled, so that the row of gas-lamps seemed not so much to shed their circles of light as to hug them to themselves like bright shawls against the damp air. Though she had laughed at Matt's fancy of seeking out her window, still she had been moved, and she had told him how to find it; but now, looking at the mist-muffled street with its twin rows of identical houses, she experienced a spasm of panic.

'They're all the same!' said she to herself, pressing her burning face to the glass. 'He'll never find it – how can he? We're all the same – all just the same!'

In the peculiar horror this thought caused her there was something of the same dread presentiment that had come upon her in the church crypt at Cleatham; but it had barely lasted a few moments when a figure stepped into the haze of light around the nearest gas-lamp. It was Matt. Looking up at the window, he raised his hand in solemn salute and kept it there. Whether he could see her against the darkened bedroom she could not tell, but flooded with relief, as if some catastrophe had been averted, she spread her own hand palm outwards against the glass, and mouthed his name. Thus they stayed until the lamplighter came along with his pole and hook, extinguishing the lamps one by one; and by staring at Matt as if he were a madman, sent him at last reluctantly away.

IX

They would not court in the accepted way; they were adamant about that. Those who make a religion of love seldom find a tolerant church, and can be quite as dogmatic as the orthodoxy they reject.

Cottesbridge offered discouraging conditions for a great love, but for these two natures nothing else would do. Romeo had to scale a balcony to Juliet and brave the swords of her kinfolk, the love of Abelard for Héloïse contended with the jealous proscriptions of the Church, and the breadth of the Hellespont separated the yearning hearts of Hero and Leander. But what were these obstacles compared to the web of small clinging conventions, habits and restrictions which the town wove about Lucy and Matt, and which made them feel as though they were falling in love inside a glass case, with pointers and magnifying glasses on all sides? The town was brisk, hard-nosed and prosaic, and as uncongenial to romance as an ice-cap to a vineyard.

Would they have been better in a great city, perhaps, or in an empty, spacious countryside, Lucy wondered sometimes? But that was to ignore the old conundrum of character and destiny, nature and nurture. The intense capacity for longing which both Lucy and Matt possessed, and which when they were together acted like the two poles of an electrical current, was not a product of environment – it was just the way they were; the fact that each had never before found someone who thought that way was evidence of that. On the other hand, circumstance had sharpened the blade that nature had furnished, and brought it to its present sharpness: not merely the imprisoning streets of the town, but the ways of the Middleton family had been landmarks on Lucy's mental horizon, and helped create her peculiar personal mixture of practicality and idealism, not to mention her hunger for escape. An ardent soul struggling against oppressive conditions: this she was, certainly; but she herself recognized that, just as she was part of this narrow world, it was part of her.

It was much the same with Matt, as she came to learn from his story. But whereas hers had been a restlessness of mind, he was a physical gadfly. Wellingford, his previous home, was not his birthplace: he had gone from town to town about the valley, seeking a better opening, a more promising chance in life. Even as he told her these things, he was seldom at rest. He might lie quite easeful on the grass, but one crossed foot would be nervously swinging, one eyebrow going up and down in flickerings of irony or perplexity as he talked.

'It's there, somewhere,' he said. 'The better place. The real start of things. You jist have to keep looking, and not lose hope of finding it. Once you give up, you're like them – the ones you see walking along with the dead look in their eyes and their coats hanging on 'em like you hang a coat on a peg.'

'I remember Mr Birdsall saying something the other week about there's nothing worse than regret, and how he'd been in the trade for thirty-odd years, and hated it every minute,' said Lucy.

'There you are,' Matt said. 'Look at him. That's how you end up.'

'I like Mr Birdsall,' Lucy said, pricked by loyalty.

'Oh, he's a nice chap, right enough. But is he happy? Hasn't he just given up?'

Lucy thought. Mr Birdsall unhappy? She had never thought of him as such, but truth to tell she had never genuinely thought about his happiness at all – like most of us, who tend to consider another person's well-being less vitally important than their contribution to our own. But she felt that from now on she would look on his little glass-fronted case of books and his sheet-music, which hitherto had seemed to her emblematic of enviable content, with a different eye.

Restlessness also characterized Matt's ideas. His head was always full of them, but they changed rapidly. He seemed to have gone through his young life picking up, examining and rejecting propositions. As a youth he had been, as he said, very creeping-Jesus. 'Swallowed it all with mother's milk, I suppose. Knew gret chunks of the Bible like I know my own

83

name. Mother said she could see me as a preacher on the circuit, or even a missioner – we were living in Kettenham then, where a lot of missioners had gone out to Africa and such to pester the heathens. It even appealed to me, but I reckon it was jist the idea of seeing these far-off places that I took to. But it was poor old Mother who made me see things different. Look at her: she slaved for the old man for twenty years, then he done a bunk and left her 'ithout so much as a ta-ta. Then she got sick and lay there gitting thinner till she was like a broomstick in a bed. I knew most of the Bible, but I couldn't find nothing in it that made any sense of that.'

It was in the country that they talked thus; the country, so tantalizingly near, so crucially different from the town that offered them nothing but claustrophobic frustration. On Saturday afternoons and Sundays they fled together out of Cottesbridge as if the town had the plague. The valley was very beautiful in the hot summer, with its countless brooks and streams, its juicy river-meadows, its hawthorn-clad lanes that seemed to wind and meander for the very pleasure of it, and then came all of a sudden upon the blind back of a stone farmhouse, as if that were the very last place they had meant to lead to. In the early Sunday morning (Lucy had stopped chapel-going, though for some time it had been only her body and not her spirit that she had taken to the pine pews) they explored damp, shadowy spinneys, where the existence of fairies seemed a dull fancy compared with the strange realities of nature: unearthly butterfly-orchis, moss of such richness that the lean trees on which it grew might more feasibly have been the parasites upon its garish luxuriousness, fungi flourishing upon stumps in great lobed masses like grotesquely coloured cabbages, and long straight grass that the wind never touched, so charged with dew that to walk through it was like wading through a ford. They walked field-paths, between the ripening wheat and barley that from a distance presented such a silky appearance but seen closely was like cruel sharp bamboo as it sprang from the strong clay land. Thirsty in the heat, they called at little farmhouses to buy a drink of buttermilk, taking it in turns to drink from the iron pan while the sun glared dryly upon the cobblestones of the yard. They paused by brooks to take off their boots and stockings and dabble their tired feet in the water, gasping and laughing, for it always seemed as cold as an Alpine stream even when the stones upon the banks were like bricks straight from the kiln.

Once Lucy had trouble undoing her bootlaces, and Matt had already bathed his feet before she had untangled them. Looking up at him stepping out of the water on to the bank, she gave a cry.

'Oh! God, Matt!'

His slender bare feet and calves were streaming with blood – covered with blood. The blank, uncomprehending way he gazed at her convinced her that he had hurt himself badly; she recalled a man at her father's factory who had mangled his hand in a leather-press and who had exhibited just that sort of serene indifference before collapsing.

'Look – your feet, look . . .' She had dropped to her knees beside him, and was just steeling herself for whatever horrors an examination would reveal, when he gave a shout of laughter.

'Oh! fire me, what a mucky mess!' he chuckled, sitting down and rubbing his feet upon the grass. 'I forgot it was rusty round about here . . .' He looked at her, and his laughter faded. 'It's the iron – the ironstone in the streams, it meks the water run red sometimes. En't you seed that before?'

She could not speak. Probably she had seen it before: the rust-coloured iron deposits were common in the valley; but somehow she had not thought of that when she saw the redness pouring from Matt's skin. The terrible conviction of bad dreams, in which hideous harms come to our loved ones while we impotently look on, had possessed her at that moment, and she felt too much of a fool to feel relief.

'Did you think it was blood?' he said. His tone was surprised, but he was not laughing now. He knelt beside her and placed his hands on her upper arms. 'Oh, Lucy, my lovely, it's all right. Everything's all right.'

They had kissed and embraced but seldom as yet: perhaps solely through shyness, perhaps because they did not trust themselves. Now she threw her arms around his neck, and put her face against his.

'You'll always be careful, won't you?' she said. 'Promise me you'll always be careful.'

'Course I will. I got to keep myself safe for you, en't I?'

She laughed, but she did not like that place, the place she now thought of as the bloody brook, and they did not go there again.

The country absorbed them, and the grimy little town of factory-whistles seemed a world away. Matt's passion for it was as great as her own: all his free time since moving to Cottesbridge had been spent in long tramps about the valley, and he knew many spots and by-ways that were unfamiliar to her. And yet everyone they met in the country knew him for a shoemaker. With his wiriness, his pallor, his rapid speech, with the roving light in his eyes and the coiled-spring quality of his movements, he took the town with him wherever he went; the very things that Lucy found so attractive about him were as urban as gaslight.

Sometimes, if money allowed, they took food with them into the country and frugally picnicked, and once or twice they had a rowing-boat on the river; but in the main their amusements were each other. It was enough; and Lucy was far too happy to wonder whether this exclusive concentration, in which one beloved person took on the dimensions of a whole world, gave a forced hothouse cultivation to something that might have been better growing up more slowly and naturally.

However, even had they consented to a conventional Cottesbridge courtship, little would have been offered them in the way of mutual recreation. Courtship in the town was a thing to be got over. That couples might wish, for example, to dance with each other – and that by doing so they were not necessarily sinking into moral delinquency – would never have occurred to the town's stern Methodist conscience, which baulked at any form of entertainment beyond the sacred concert – a dismal evening affair, at which choral societies publicly exhumed the dullest and dustiest cantatas and oratorios, like musical grave-robbers. The traditional rural amusements, pagan survivals many of them, had disappeared under the blanket of brick and the frown of chapel; and the raw towns had evolved no culture of their own to replace them. It was small wonder that courtship was regarded as merely the briefest prelude to the practical business of marriage.

They were not alone in the country, of course. There were no factory-whistles, but the call to work was quite as insistent. One hot Saturday afternoon they came upon an old gnarled man mowing a hayfield, with his old gnarled wife raking and turning the hay. Lucy and Matt offered to help. Some poorer folk of the valley towns still went out to the fields to glean after harvest, but for most of Lucy and Matt's generation farmwork was a lost art. Matt took up the scythe and Lucy the rake with a will, and by the end of the afternoon they had become a little more handy; but Lucy could not help wondering whether that was a sardonic glint in the old man's eye when they said goodbye at last.

'Phew, I feel like I've done a week's work in one afternoon,' Matt said. 'Mind you, it's a different sort of tired feeling from when you come out the factory . . . What about us having a farm of our own one day, eh? Now wouldn't that be a life worth living?'

'We'd have to be a bit quicker at the work than that, I reckon,' Lucy laughed, glancing back at the lamentably small area of field they had mowed.

'Oh! I reckon we did all right, you know,' Matt said. 'We were new to it, after all. It's the sort of thing you pick up. I reckon we could mek a go of that sort of life, Lucy.'

'Course we could.' His optimism was infectious; and if sometimes he seemed to believe what he wanted to believe, against the evidence of his senses, she preferred to see it as impatient idealism rather than wrong-headedness. The cavilling valley fatalism that saw only obstacles and difficulties ahead, that darkly added to every plan the invocation, 'If we're spared' or, 'All being well' or, 'God willing', was something that her heart had long been in mutiny against. She feared, indeed, that she had not quite escaped its taint herself, and that that was why she could not quite follow Matt on his wildest flights of imagination, and found herself with one foot firmly on the ground even when she earnestly wanted to take wing too.

Matt Doughty was a dreamer, but not of the sort who finds in dreams consolation for the disappointments of the everyday. His dreams gave him no peace. He was not one whom the material world passes by; he was good at his trade, as was testified by the fact that he had been able to go from town to town, factory to factory, and always be sure of a job: he had a quick eye and deft, sinewy hands, a craft's hands as Lucy's father would have have said. He was indifferent to his immediate circumstances, not with an ascetic's holiness, but because he was looking to better things. Lucy was full of curiosity about his digs, wishing to picture him in the place that he called home, but he could not find much to say about them.

'Oh, it's a dingy sort of place, I suppose. The old woman lets all the rooms to chaps like me. I've got a bed, and a few bits and pieces of my own, books and such. I shan't be there long, anyway.'

He seemed indeed to regard so much of his life as temporary that she wondered aloud, half jokingly, but with a pounding heart, whether she herself fitted that description. 'Mebbe there's been a girl in every town in the valley,' she said, 'like sailors with a girl in every port.'

He was more startled than hurt. 'You think that?' he said. 'If only you knew the truth of it. Kettenham, Lessington, Wellingford – I've been the peculiarest, solitariest chap in every one. Aye, and liked it that way. Lucy, you know what I said about the real start of things? That's what you are to me. A better place, a better job, a better way o' living – they're all what's to come. But I've found the one that meks 'em all worthwhile. That's fixed, perfect, for ever. That's you.'

She was warm at the words, though a little guilty at having sought them, at having demanded a reassurance that his every look and touch amply conveyed; for as a lover he was as ardent and unreserved as in everything. It was impossible even to imagine him flirting, given his hearty contempt, stronger even than her own, for the small change of experience. 'Let your yea be yea; and your nay, nay' was one biblical precept that Matt Doughty still stuck by – and, like Lucy, he would parch rather than consent to sip at half measures.

In fact, during those summer days in the country – the only days that counted to Lucy, who during the working week only lived in the sense that a tuber can be said to live – they did not consider the future at all, except in Matt's visionary terms, which was a different matter. They put aside the question of where they stood as a – dread word to them – couple; they put aside the question of where this loving idyll would lead. For one thing, the mundanities of engagement would surely cast the blight of convention over what was to them private, unique, rapt, and sacrosanct; and for another, the very fact of their love seemed to render such cold projections irrelevant. From the cradle, song and story had drummed Love into their ears: Love the magician, Love the conqueror, Love the all-powerful and all-sufficient. Like most recipes, it is improved by a pinch of salt; and there are some who decline to taste it altogether, however seasoned, and do not seem any the less happy for it. But on these two intense and impressionable natures, both accustomed to developing their thoughts and feelings in solitude, the gospel of Love had had a profound effect. They believed that, rather than offering incidental pleasures and consolations to a human existence that is fundamentally intractable, Love solved problems: that it was a key, and a master-key at that.

They kept their romance separate, a thing unto itself. Matt, of course, had no family with which to discuss it, but there was no pressing reason why Lucy should not mention it at home. Growing up in the Middleton household was such a matter of being left to your own devices, and struggling through life under your own steam, that there could hardly be any indignation at her keeping quiet – she could have taken the veil without anyone at home noticing. And yet she didn't want to mention it, did not want them to meet him.

She scrutinized herself closely: was this shame, shame for her own family? Terrible, if so; but surely it was not. The Middletons might be a bad joke in Cottesbridge, but if Matt should think the less of her for that, then he was not worth loving – and nor was she, if it was shame she felt. Besides, Matt had been frank about his own background: his father had not surprised anyone by his finally running out – he had always been an idler, skulking between pop-shop and pub, and his mother had not matched her piety with good sense. No, it was not shame. But still Lucy felt the simple impossibility of saying to her parents 'I'm walking out with a chap, his name's Matt Doughty, would you like to meet him?' The love belonged to her – it was the first precious thing, indeed, that she had ever had. It was too fierce, proud and uplifted to be brought into contact with the compromised, impure, and unsatisfactory everyday.

She was blissful, exploring each newly revealed facet of this young man. 'The quick and the dead' was a phrase that she remembered hearing in chapel. She liked that word quick: she knew it meant living, but it suggested something more to her, something sharper, more vibrant. It was everything that was actively opposed to death. Matt was quick in that way. He made her laugh: he made her see things differently; he made her, occasionally, infuriated with his wayward disregard of the possible. He made her feel quick herself.

'Did you ever think, we spend a third of we lives asleep?' he said. 'All that time wasted, lost for ever, all the things you could have been doing instead of snoring away under a pile o' blankets!'

'But if you were all groggy from lack of sleep, then you

wouldn't be able to do them other things,' she said, smiling, for she enjoyed watching him reason his way past objections.

'Ah, that's only because we're *used* to that much sleep. We think we can't do with less, but it's jist habit really. I been trying to train meself to tek half an hour less every week, so's I'll have more time. I got a book from Charlie, him as has got the room next to me – one of these teaching books. It shows you how to do book-keeping. Charlie says he never found the time to work through it, but if I can mek the time by cutting down on my sleep, then I reckon I can learn it in a couple o' months, easy as swallowing pibbles.'

'Book-keeping?'

'Useful stuff. When I get my own little leather-factor's business, say, I shall be able to do the books myself. Oh, I know that seems a pipe-dream! But look at John Philip Meredith: richest man in Wellingford, three factories, thousands of pairs on the books. He started out with a lock-up shed and a few bundles of third-grade box-calf. He had luck, all right. But I want to be ready to meet my luck when it comes. Any road, when we're together at last – in that house on the hill, or sim'lar – why, d'you think I'm going to waste *that* time sleeping?'

Perfect love . . . such a thing can hardly exist between imperfect creatures. The extravagance of Matt's ideas, the touches of volatile impatience in his temper – these were simply part of himself, as much as his thick hair which grew in a double crown, or the little dent under his chin where he had fallen from a home-made swing as a child. No, what sometimes troubled Lucy, and cast a shadow across those sunlit days, was his friendship with Luther Benson.

One Sunday they stopped at a little country pub along the Cleatham road, with a shelf fixed to the outer windowsill for off-licence sales. Here they stood and refreshed themselves by sharing a mug of beer, and were just about to go on their way when a voice detached itself from the hubbub within.

'Matt! Is that Matt Doughty I see out there?'

Luther Benson came weaving out of the pub parlour, glass in hand, long limbs making rubbery, boneless shapes as he embraced Matt with tipsy affection and swept off his hat to Lucy.

'It meks a man want to change his ways,' he said. 'It meks a man want to stop thinking the worst of people, and not believing nothing, to see you pair. Who says romance is dead, and all the finer things of life have been trod in the mud? "Folks is grown hard," they say. "They got no heart, no soul, no poetry, no faith, and no morals." I've heard 'em say it! I've even agreed with 'em. Not next time, though. I shall stand up and say "Wash out yer mouth. There's a pair of star-crossed lovebuds, so help me, name of Matt Doughty and Lucy Middleton, inquire as above, who are a living contradiction to your words." But I meanter say,' he added, taking Matt by the waistcoat-button, 'suppose there's a wedding? Who's to be your groomsman? Not your old shopmate, Luther Benson, who's borrowed money off you jist like you was his own brother?'

'You gret fool-jabey,' Matt said. 'I can jist see *you* all got up in a chapel-suit and behaving yourself.'

'You see how it is, Miss Middleton! – lovely as a rose if I might say so, don't mind it from me, I'm just like your court jester of the olden days – you see how it is? Give a dog a bad name and all that. Jist like when I was a little 'un, and I went and picked some flowers out of the vicar's garden. Would they believe it was because I liked flowers, and couldn't resist tekking a few of the blighters for myself, to sniff to my heart's content? Oh no! It was because I was a little thieving hound. But there, I don't expect no better, even from the friend of my bosom. What do you think, Miss Middleton? Gin a chance to turn out respectable, don't you reckon I'd mek a proper fist at it?'

'I suppose it depends whether you want to,' Lucy said.

'Matt, tek her away from me. I'm frit on her. She sees right through me, jist like one of them new machines what look through your guts, and can see what you've had for dinner.' He winked at Lucy. 'But there, what's it signify? Luther Benson's past saving anyway. If there's anythink that could save me, and give me a bit of tone, and a bit of heart, it'd be hanging around you two – but I won't do it. I en't partial to the taste of gooseberry, and I'll bet it fair sets your teeth on edge. Besides, there's a fellow in there who owes me a drink. Now *he's* a bad 'un if you like – such a regular out-and-outer, that even I'm ashamed of accepting a drink off such a fellow. But there – he owes me it, and if I go and let him off his obligation, wun't that just be encouraging his tendency to vice, and mekking him think that debts don't have to be paid? Fact is, I've got a moral duty to tek that drink off him, and I shan't shirk me moral duty a moment

longer. Cheer-oo!' Luther turned away and came back all in
one movement. 'Half a minute, though. What about next
Sat'dy, Matt? You thought about that? You're not going to
let an old shopmate down, I reckon?'

'I don't know,' Matt said. 'I'll let you know, Luther.'

Luther winked again at Lucy, patting Matt's shoulder.
'He's a diament, that's what he is. But of course you know
that, don't you, Miss Middleton? Course you do.'

'He's going poaching again,' Matt said to Lucy as they
went on their way. 'Wants me to go along of him.'

She was not greatly surprised. In years gone by it had been
common for shoemakers to go poaching on the estates of the
valley; her father often boasted of the nocturnal expeditions
he had made in his young days. But it was common too,
nowadays, for the poachers to be caught and hauled to the
police court.

'Shall you go?' she said.

'Depends. I don't care about tekking a bit of game off Lord
Whatsname – they've got plenty to spare. But the trouble with
Luther is, he likes to tek risks, and sometimes the game en't
worth the candle.'

She held her peace, but she was troubled. She trusted
Matt, but she did not trust Luther Benson. That he should
seek to recruit Matt to poaching expeditions merely confirmed a mistrust that seemed to originate in her very bones.
There was something about the way he chummily touched
and cuffed Matt that she disliked. It reminded her of the way
an adult will handle a doll or a toy, with a sketchy parody of
affection but no real interest.

Still, she tried not to pay too much heed to this. Newcomer
as she was to the ways of love, some instinct told her that a
genuine liking for your lover's friends was the rarest of rare
birds, though she did not go so far as to perceive that it was
not only uncommon, it was unnatural; for with friends we are
ourselves, whereas with a lover – sincerity notwithstanding –
we inevitably adopt a persona.

Besides, as they often said, what there was between them
was nobody's business but their own. But in that watchful
community an affair that was not actively a secret, as theirs
was not, was sure to be observed and noted. Returning home
one smouldering midsummer evening, Lucy was ambushed
in the street by Nancy Smallbones, who materialized so suddenly beside her that she seemed to come up through a

trapdoor like a devil in a pantomime.

'Evening, evening, gel. Hot en't it? Yerss. Sticky-seat weather my Arthur used to call it. Wherever you sit you feel like a babby with a full clout. Puts you off gitting on wi' things, don't it? Yerss. Not that it seems to bother you, gel, always scratting about like a flea in a colander lately, en't you? Walking out, so I hear, that's nice that is, not before time some might say but not me; wait while you're ready I say, always have. Find the right one, eh? Yerss. Never had a cross word wi' my Arthur, twenty years from the wedding to the day they picked him off the railway line with a long stick, God rest him. This young man of yourn, he's got a name, I suppose?'

'Yes,' Lucy said with a glacial smile, 'he's got a name.'

Mrs Smallbones gave a frightful writhe, and thrust her face up to Lucy's, as if she would suck her secrets out from her very lips. 'Not a Cottesbridge man, so a little bird told me. Got kin here, has he, perhaps, I wonder?'

Lucy said no.

'Oh! Fancy. Well well. Still, he'll likely have kin be marriage before long, who knows, eh? Yerss. Nice that is. Course, I'm all behind-hand. No doubt your mam and dad have met him lots of times. I said to meself, Lucy Middleton's not the sort to go sneaking behint their backs, I don't care what anybody says.' Mrs Smallbones, smiling, made a sort of snap with her teeth, as if she were gobbling down a tasty morsel of discomfiture.

Lucy made her excuses and escaped into the house. She found, however, that Nancy Smallbones had been there before her.

'Well, Lucy, what a black horse you are, and no mistake!' her mother said, abandoning the peas she had been shelling and jumping up. 'Here's me never guessing you had a beau, and you keeping as quiet as a church mouse about it! Dicky, my treasure, don't eat them peas, they won't agree with you. Well, is it true then? Nance Smallbones seemed to know all about it, but then she's a gossipy sort of woman, always got her nose in her neighbours' business, and I wouldn't tek her word for gospel. I don't know why I'm so onlucky in my neighbours, but then it was the same when I was living at home – that was a very choice neighbourhood, but you still got wrong uns. I remember like it was yesterday the time my father gin a proper dressing-down to the man next door, who'd come complaining and wanting him to stop playing the piano, on account of his Staffordshire was whelping in the potting-shed.'

'Oh – it's nothing, Mother,' said Lucy, taking up the basin of peas. Now why had she said that? It was very far from nothing: in fact, everything.

'Come to think of it, you have been a bit faraway like lately, and forever off on your travels, but then you always were a bit like that,' her mother said, disregarding her. 'Git it from your father, I reckon. Well? What's his name? He must be in the trade, I should think. You must bring him here for tea Sundy. Does he like radishes? My poor father could never tek radishes, they used to bring him up in gret weals all across his back, and he couldn't play the piano for wanting to get his hand round and scratch 'em.'

Her father coming in at that moment, Lucy's mother extracted herself from the thicket of reminiscence, and told him the news.

'Lucy's walking out with a chap, Chauncey – would you credit it? Nivry word did she breathe about it all this time! I was just telling her, she must bring him here for tea, so's we can all have a good look at him.'

'Aye, aye, bring him,' said her father, who was in his most genial and twinkling mood. 'Let's have a look at the fellow. In the trade, is he?'

'Yes – he's a finisher at Whiting's,' Lucy said, with a sort of oppressed happiness. 'His name's Matt Doughty. He come here from Wellingford.'

'Not a bad little place, Whiting's,' said her father. 'Aye, we'll have him to tea this Sundy. Well, well, our little Lucy! Don't seem five ticks of a donkey's tail while she was in pinafores with her hair all down her back like a yard of pump-water. Are we gitting old, Mother?'

'Git along. *You* don't look no different from when we were courting ourselves,' Mrs Middleton said, dimpling.

'Well, mebbe I en't worn so badly,' Chauncey said, with a modestly beaming consciousness of his wife's admiration. 'You know, I saw the young Stokes sprig going clippety-clip up to the offices today . . .' In his good mood he omitted to give Lucy the usual reproachful glance in reference to that promise she had made to Mr Stokes on his behalf. 'And it just struck me what a poor slip of a thing he is. Have to stand twice to throw a shadow. Least, he en't much compared with old Edward Stokes – masterpiece of a man he was. He could be a Tartar all right, but you knew where you were with him. Broad as a water-butt acrosst the chest, voice like an organ with all the stops out. And yet here's this cold fish of a son of his, with his mincing "Good mornings" like he can't open his mouth properly, and looking ten years older than thirty. Sad thing to see! Thank the Lord *I'm* reared such a fine-looking brood.' As he spoke he gave a jovial cuff to Jim, who had just come in – the boy responding with a scowl, as if he longed to point out that their father's part in their rearing had chiefly consisted of blows of a less playful kind.

Going upstairs to change, Lucy sat down on the bed and tried to put her feelings in order.

It was nice, it was good, it was gratifying, surely, that they wanted to meet Matt, even if it meant the ritual of Sunday tea. It had to come, anyway. Why then did she feel as if something had been stolen from her?

Her reflections were interrupted by Joanna, who came breathless from work full of news.

'Lucy, you ought to hear the latest about that Alice Wedderburn!' she said, pulling off her cap and fumbling with her apron-strings.

'Here, I'll do that. Well, what is it? Another admirer?'

'Oh! no. You know Alice Wedderburn's mother's mortal sick? They don't know how she's held on so long, poor woman, unless it was through hoping to see her daughter one last time. Well, she has. Somebody was telling the Misses Herring all about it, and I was cleaning the big window inside so I heard. The doctor didn't give Mrs Wedderburn another twenty-four hours, seem'ly, and the message must have gone to Alice, because all of a sudden this morning she was seed riding into the Hole in a gig – imagine, a carriage in the Hole! There was all these mucky street-arabs chasing after it and pointing, and people coming out of their houses to look. And she stopped outside her mother's little old falling-down house, and got down, and told the driver to go away, and she went into the house, all wickedly dressed with her nose in the air, and she en't come out since, so they reckon.'

Joanna turned her shining face to her sister's; then said, as if a little ashamed of her excitement, 'Terrible, isn't it?'

'Good God, en't there nothing you can do in this town without being watched by everybody?' Lucy said. 'What Alice Wedderburn must have been feeling, with everybody's eyes on her like that, I can't think.' It was not the first time she had experienced an obscure sympathy with the scandalous woman, and was the sharper for her present feeling of being observed and trespassed upon.

'Oh, I know. But still, to turn up right at the end like that, after ignoring her all them years . . .' Joanna sat down on the bed in her ladylike way. 'I don't know whether she was in time or not. How will she bear going back to living in sin, after seeing something like that? Though perhaps she won't. Perhaps it'll change her. I'm ashamed of talking about her so, but I can't help thinking about it!' Joanna was tender-hearted, and all at once her large eyes solemnly filled. 'Oh, Lucy, I can't bear to think of anybody close to me dying, even though I know we all meet again afterwards.'

Lucy hid her own private doubts on that last point, and patted her sister's hand. 'Nobody's going to die,' she said, realizing at the same moment that her statement was the complete opposite of truth. 'Any road, did Mother tell you I'm to have a chap here for tea on Sunday?'

'Oh yes! I'm that glad for you, Lucy. I *thought* you must be falling for somebody – in the night sometimes when you're asleep you get hold of my hand in the bed, and then let it go as if it weren't the one you wanted.'

'I never do!' laughed Lucy, with a curious internal prickling.

'He's coming this Sunday? Well, we'd better make sure things are . . . ready,' Joanna said.

Lucy understood without the need for Joanna to say more. She meant that they had better make sure that there was food in the house, that their father stayed off the booze, that their mother did not get into a slanging-match with the neighbours, that Sidney did not fall out of the bedroom window, that Dicky-bird did not appear naked from the waist down . . . 'Yes,' Lucy said, 'we'd better make sure.'

Matt here! How strange it would be. Of course, she would be proud to introduce him; but still she wished they might have gone on as they were for a little while.

That evening Lucy's mother, having talked indefatigably all through tea, found herself not surprisingly suffering from indigestion, and asked Lucy to go down to the chemist's in the High Street for one of his emetic powders. 'He usually stays open while this time,' she said, 'and there en't a better thing for the acid than them powders he meks up. I can bear it now, but once I git laid flat in bed tonight I shall burn like a stove.'

Lucy's errand did not take long. Returning by the Station Road, she lingered a moment to watch the Northampton train depart, scattering sparks on the mild blue night air. A dreaminess came over her as she wondered what Matt was doing at that moment, and when they would go on a train together, and what their destination would be; and she found that she had been idly gazing for some minutes at a cloaked figure standing in the middle of the high iron footbridge that crossed the railway line.

Was it a figure? From the way it leaned right over the guard-rail of the footbridge, at a drooping angle, it might almost have been a bundle of clothes propped there.

Then all at once she was sure. The figure moved – a woman's figure: it sprang lightly up so that it was sitting on the guard-rail, somewhat as a woman rides side-saddle.

Lucy reacted instinctively, and she was half-way up the steps of the footbridge before she wondered whether intervention might do more harm than good. But the young woman perched upon the guard-rail did not seem to hear her approach. She wore a full cape with a high collar, and her hat was veiled: her face was averted, and she seemed to be gazing down at the rails below with fascination. One daintily booted foot, dangling, swung with a jittery motion while all the rest of her was motionless, and for a curious instant Lucy was reminded of Matt's restless tics.

She was still hesitating as to whether to speak and what to say when the woman abruptly turned her head. The lamp on the girder behind Lucy shone through the veil full upon a pale, fine-boned, narrow-eyed face; a face she had seen before, but usually in a carriage driven by a doting escort: the face of Alice Wedderburn.

The white lips trembled a moment, and then Alice Wedderburn said sharply, 'What do you want?'

'Nothing,' Lucy faltered. 'I just wondered if . . . You're Alice Wedderburn, aren't you?'

'You seem to know me, but I don't know you,' the woman said, pulling her cape about her, and turning her face back to the contemplation of the dark gaping space below her.

'I'm Lucy Middleton.'

A faint shrill hooting in the distance indicated the approach of the London express. Alice Wedderburn seemed to flinch a little at the sound.

'Well?' she said after a moment, presenting the pale scornful face again. 'So you're Lucy Middleton. I don't know any Lucy Middleton, so I don't know why you're standing there like a spare part.'

The voice was a cool, throaty one, oddly compelling to the ear; the articulation was precise, but Lucy could hear the accents of the Hole breaking through it.

'I just thought you might want somebody to – talk to,' Lucy said.

'Even supposing I did,' Alice Wedderburn said with a fretful motion of her gloved hands, 'why on earth should it be you?'

'Oh, because I'm here, I suppose,' Lucy said. She was feeling her way blindly through the talk, certain only that she was in the presence of a great crisis, and that to turn away would be – she could think of no better word – a sin.

'Because you're here,' the woman said. 'Well, you can easily remedy that, Lucy Middleton. And I wish you would.'

There was another shriek down the line, and a humming became audible in the rails below. With a desperate plunge, Lucy said, 'I was very sorry to hear about Mrs Wedderburn.'

'Sorry to hear what?' Alice said, not looking at her, her voice almost bored.

'About her being ill.'

The narrow eyes – Lucy could see now that they were green – turned to her again. They were quite dry, but far from clear. It was like looking at two fresh bruises.

'She isn't ill,' Alice Wedderburn said. 'She's dead.'

'Oh . . . Oh, I'm so sorry.'

'Why? You didn't know her, did you?'

'No.'

'Hm. You surprise me. You seem to know all my business.'

There was no point in being anything but frank. 'Everybody knows,' Lucy said.

'Do they? And what does "everybody" have to say about it?'

Lucy cleared her throat. 'Miss Wedderburn . . . it isn't safe up there.'

'I know. What do people say?'

The lights of the oncoming express were now visible, and a few hot smuts were borne on the light wind and touched

Lucy's face. 'Oh, you know what people are like,' she said lamely.

'What do they say?' repeated Alice. She shifted her position slightly on the rail, and the dangling foot twitched more violently. 'Not nice things?'

Suddenly Lucy found herself speaking firmly and fluently, as if some outside force were guiding her. 'It doesn't matter what they say. Nobody has any right to judge you – you know that. Nobody can know what it's like to be inside your skin – same with me, same with anybody.' The girders of the footbridge were beginning to vibrate with the roaring advance of the express. Lucy took a careful step closer. 'Only you know the truth of things. All I know is you've had a great grief, and you're not thinking straight—'

'Don't come near me!' the woman said, seeing Lucy's stealthy approach.

The express thundered towards the footbridge, a black fiery commotion making the world shake. There were several long seconds of confusion; dense clouds of steam enveloped the twain on the bridge; Lucy thought she saw an irresolute movement from the figure perched on the rail, lunged forward, and somehow had hold of Alice's arm in a tight grip.

'No,' Lucy was crying over the noise of the express as it hurtled beneath them, 'no, no, no . . .'

The steam and smuts billowed, faded, cleared. The express pounded away into the distance. Alice Wedderburn was still hunched over the guard-rail. Her head drooped, and shook a little; and Lucy saw that her eyes were squeezed shut, and were dropping tears into the emptiness below.

Lucy relaxed her grip a little, turned it into a caress. 'Come down,' she said. 'Please – come down.'

Alice continued to shake with silent sobs, head bowed; but at last she stirred, and stiffly climbed down from the rail, leaning on Lucy for support.

'You shouldn't be alone tonight,' Lucy said.

'Shouldn't I?' Alice Wedderburn took out a fine lace handkerchief and, throwing back her veil, wiped her face with it. She managed to lift her chin with the old arrogant look – more piteous than any tears, it seemed to Lucy. 'If ever there was a night when I should be alone, it's this night . . . And I am alone. I couldn't be more alone if I were cast away on a desert island, a thousand miles from the nearest human face.' As if fearing to sound pathetic, she threw Lucy a sharp look, the bones of her face very prominent in the lamplight, and then put down her veil. 'It isn't the fact that she's dead, you know,' she said harshly. 'I don't cry for that. She was sick and in pain and it was a release; and we all have to die. Today, tomorrow, next year, it's just a matter of dates. But the thing is, she was proud of me. She'd kept things – my first long frock, a dance card, a note my first beau sent me ... She'd lived it all herself, alone, in that house, happy for me and – and proud. That's what makes me ... Do you understand?' Her eyes seemed to beseech Lucy for just a moment, then she shook her head. 'Of course you can't. Forget what I said.'

'I still say you shouldn't be alone tonight,' Lucy said gently.

'No? Who should I be with then?'

'Someone who loves you. That's all that matters, after all, en't it?'

A wry shadow crossed Alice's face. 'How old are you, Lucy?'

'Nearly twenty. But I don't see—'

'No. Forget I said that too.' Suddenly, with an almost pettish movement, Alice took hold of Lucy's arm and briefly hugged her to her. 'Don't worry,' she said, drawing quickly away, 'I don't have to be alone. Not for a single moment if I don't want. As for the love bit—' She broke off, frowning down at her sleeve. 'What's – it's caught . . .'

A button on her sleeve had got caught fast in a thread at Lucy's waistband. For some moments it proved impossible to extricate, as if the two of them had somehow become fastened to each other for ever. At length, however, the thread broke; and now Alice, becoming very brisk, put away her handkerchief. 'You'd better go,' she said.

Lucy hesitated. 'Where will you—'

'Oh, don't worry! I shan't stay here – you can watch me go if you like. You go that way, and I'll go this.'

'All right,' Lucy said. 'You go home before the owls get you.'

It was a common local phrase, casually said; but Alice Wedderburn looked seriously at her a moment and said, 'Watch out they don't get you, Lucy.' Then she straightened, turned, and walked smartly away, and Lucy presently heard her footsteps descending the bridge on the other side. Taking the other way herself, she stopped to look across the railway tracks. The woman in the cloak and veil could be seen walking away in the direction that led between coal-heaps and warehouses towards the streets of the Hole; but though Lucy waited for some gesture of goodbye, Alice Wedderburn did not look back.

Lucy made her way home, wondering greatly, but with one certain settled knowledge upon her. She could say nothing of this meeting, not even to Matt. No bond of confidence had been enjoined, but still she recognized that she bore a great trust.

New insights had come from that strange meeting: henceforth she would look differently upon any new tales of Alice Wedderburn's doings. At the time she had simply acted with sympathetic instinct; she could not foresee a time when she would be brought to a deeper understanding of the anguish that had flared upon the iron footbridge that night, and know its bitter secrets for her own.

X

Matt came to Sunday tea. He readily agreed, and was pleased to be asked, and Lucy said it would be nice; and they smiled ruefully at each other, and admitted that this was exactly the sort of thing that they had tried to avoid.

'Not that we can, of course,' he said. 'It's only natural your folks should want to see what sort of a chap you're gitting tied up with. Whether I'm reliable, and honest, and all that.'

Lucy's upbringing in the Middleton household had been such that marriage to the most improvident slave-driving wastrel could only have been a step upward; but she suppressed such disloyal thoughts. 'You mustn't mind if they have a good look at you, and want to know all about you and how much you earn and such,' she said. 'Like you say, it's only natural.'

'Course it is. Any road, we got to think of hard practical things sooner or later, en't we?'

'I suppose so,' she said, without enthusiasm: the whole of her life had been made up of hard practical things, and she thought of her time with Matt as the glowing exception.

'You don't sound so sure.' He studied her. 'That don't mean you en't sure about things in the long run, does it? I mean, you and me, together, for always?'

'No!' Unaccountably she was trembling. 'You shouldn't tek me up like that, Matt. That isn't what I meant at all. I – just like things the way they are now.'

'Well, so do I . . . I just wish life wouldn't jog-trot along so, and never git along when you flick the whip!' he savagely burst out. 'How much I earn – now there's a joke. Precious little, and precious little it'll stay unless I can break through into summat better. It urges me to death sometimes, to think of the time that's a-wasting.'

'We're young yet,' she said. 'I just wish the world would . . . leave us alone for a bit.'

102

'Well, it en't going to. That en't the way it wags. You have to tek it on, and fight it and throw it to git any good from it. And I will, too! We're going to have that house on the hill, Lucy.'

'Oh, but that's starting from the wrong end! It's enough if we can manage to be together,' she said.

'But don't you see . . . Oh, never mind.'

They looked at each other unhappily. This was the nearest they had yet come to quarrelling; and it seemed to be the very introduction of practicalities into their romance that triggered it. Fleetingly Lucy wondered whether their love shared that other quality of very fine things: brittleness.

Yet the happiness of being with Matt soon reasserted itself, and made these reflections seem mere gloomy self-communings – even more so when Sunday came, and Matt made his appearance at the house in Alma Street. Joanna and herself had made sure of furnishing a good weighty Cottesbridge high-tea, from celery to curd-tarts, and had succeeded in keeping the younger boys from demolishing the food before time. Her mother was all girlish pleasure at having a visitor – an event made infrequent by her habit of attributing slights and persecutions to virtually everyone she knew. Most importantly, her father was sober, and on the pleasant rather than the righteous chapel-going side, his occasional religious revivals being almost as fearful to contemplate as his binges. Jovially beaming, rich-voiced, spruce and handsome, he appeared that afternoon as the man he ought to have been, and might easily have been but for a crucial conjunction of circumstance and temper. Lucy was proud of Matt when he came in with his bright looks and frank manner; finding herself proud of her father too, she reproached herself for being surprised at the fact.

There was no accommodating that family, plus guest, round the modest table. Lucy's parents, herself and Matt, Joanna and Jim were all that could be squeezed in, with Benjy, Sidney and Dicky-bird taking their victuals on their laps, and running out to play as soon as they were replete.

'That's not a habit I'd want to encourage 'em in, Matthew,' Mrs Middleton said. 'It's not the way to be well brung up. When I was a girl in Northampton, you were never allowed to leave the table while your elders had finished, and you had to sit there and listen to 'em chomping even if you couldn't eat another mouthful, and a very good rule it is too

– but there, they're such lively boys, they'd only be pulling at the tablecloth or some such larks if we made 'em stay, or putting salt in your tea like they did when we had a preacher off the circuit come calling once, and when he tasted it he used such language as you wouldn't believe – they say he went off as a missioner in Africa later, and all I can say is, if he used such expressions to the natives when he tried to convert 'em, then they were better off as they were, sticking tea-plates in their lips and praying to crocodiles.'

'How was the trade in Wellingford, then, Matt?' said Chauncey.

'Holding up pretty well,' said Matt. 'The wage-rate's better in Cottesbridge, but they say it's best in Kettenham. Hard to keep track of it.'

'Ah! it's a funny up-and-down trade, right enough,' Chauncey said, grasping celery in his big golden-haired fist. 'I reckon it's set fair for now, though. More army orders coming in soon, I shouldn't wonder. We shan't see years like I knew when I was a bwoy-chap. Hard winters you'd see men waiting wi' they trucks outside the old fact'ries at four in the morning, just in hope of gitting tuthri pairs to mek up. I've done it meself. Weeks at a time living on bread and scrape, and consumption tekking off somebody from every family in the valley, seem'ly. I en't in favour of the whole trade going over to machines and in-work like it has, because you don't git the craft like you used to: your skiving-machines and slugging-machines can't turn a boot like a pair of hands that knows the ways o' leather, and never will; but at least we don't git winters like that any more . . . But look here! What a secretive pair you've been! Lucy never gin us any idea that she was walking out with a chap. I expected you to have two heads at least, the way she havered about bringing you round! And yet he seems quite normal, don't he, Clara?'

'Oh, it was the same when we were courting, Chauncey!' Mrs Middleton said, coyly nibbling radishes. 'I remember when I fust met you, and Mother thought I had the green-sickness on account of I wouldn't say nothing except Pardon, and I couldn't hear Father play "Champagne Charlie Is My Name" on the piano 'ithout bursting into tears; and she made me lay in bed with a hot brick under my feet, and never guessed the truth till she found that rose you give me under the bolster, wi' the thorns all mekking holes in the pillow-case.'

Lucy, exchanging a covert smile with Matt across the table, felt both happy and sad. It was strange to see him sitting there, so handsome with his quick, alert look, against the so-familiar frowsty background – rather as if one of the many dreams she had dreamed in this house had left the confines of her head and materialized, genie-like, before her. She was proud: imagine Kit Lightfoot sitting there, staring lumpishly about him! And yet wasn't the sheer romance of Matt diminished by this easy inclusion of him, this talk of courting? It made him seem ordinary, and that was the very last word she associated with him.

But these were bad thoughts. It was all going swimmingly, and she should be grateful.

'. . . Course, house-rents have gone up a lot since I was a bwoy-chap,' her father was saying. 'That's what meks the biggest hole in a man's wage—' He was interrupted by a sharp rapping at the back door, and frowned. 'Now who's that bothering us of a Sundy afternoon? If that's Nance Smallbones come prying, I shall tell her where to go . . .'

Mrs Middleton came back from answering the door with a perplexed look. 'It's Topper Hammond,' she said. 'Says he wants to see you urgent . . .'

Topper Hammond was suddenly in the room. His narrow rabbit jaws worked nervously as he stood in his shiny Sunday suit avoiding everybody's eyes.

'Topper, my old shopmate, can't you see we got company for tea?' Chauncey said.

'I can't help that,' Topper said, his eyes still evasively travelling as if he were watching the progress of a fly round the room. 'I come to ask you for that money you owe me.'

Chauncey's frown deepened. 'Funny time to come asking for it, en't it?'

Topper dabbed perspiration from his little moustache. He looked like a shady jockey. There was a desperate, blinking, quivering sort of determination about him, however: Lucy wondered if the mountainous Ada had been firing him up. 'I don't care if it's a funny time. Any time's a funny time, seem'ly. I asked you last week, I asked you yist'dy; I've asked you a score o' times. Now I want that money I lent you.'

'And you'll git it, burn you! But not when you come barging in on a man's Sundy tea, you wun't!' said Chancey, reddening. 'You'll git it when I'm ready!'

Topper's Adam's-apple dipped below his stiff collar and

came gulping up again. 'All right then,' he said. 'If you wun't pay your debt, I shall jist have to tek some security while you do.'

'Security? What the davil do you mean?' said Chauncey; but already Topper had scuttled out of the room.

The window, giving on to the yard, showed what Topper meant. There Chauncey kept his redundant truck, and Topper was grasping it by the handles and pulling it away.

With a bellow, Chauncey sprang up from the table and ran outside. It was all visible, and audible, from the window. Chauncey grasped the other end of the truck; Topper kept a grim hold of the handles: a mulish tug-of-war ensued while they shouted at each other.

'Fair's fair, Chauncey Middleton! A man what's owed a debt's entitled to tek some security! I've seen bailiffs do it!'

'I don't give a bugger for your fancy ideas! You tek my truck and I'll burn you, Topper Hammond!'

'You'll git your truck back when I git my money back. I en't looking for a stack-up. I only want what's right!'

'You want! You'll git my hand acrosst your ears, that's what you'll git, if you don't tek your paws off my truck . . .'

Next door Fly Corbett's window flew up. 'What the davil's all this horse-facing of a Sundy? Can't folk eat their tea in peace 'ithout you gitting over your collar and kicking up a racket, Chauncey Middleton?'

'You stick your nosy face back where it come from, Fly Corbett!' roared Chauncey. 'It en't no business o' yourn . . .'

The quarrel became a three-way affair. Joanna and Jim went on with their tea, well accustomed to such affrays, and not so accustomed to a well-stocked table that they could afford to neglect it. Mrs Middleton, meanwhile, managing to look smiling, absent, troubled and untroubled all at once, hummed a tune and asked Matt if he wanted another cup of tea. Matt was doing a good job of appearing unconscious of the fracas; but what he must surely be conscious of, thought Lucy miserably, was the absurdity of it. Quarrelling was endemic in the yards and back-alleys of Cottesbridge, but never could there have been a more ridiculous row than this, in which two grown men fought over a truck – fought and yelled and swore over something that had been a useless anachronism for a decade. The squalid scene engraved itself on her mind, a perfect vignette of folly.

We must escape was the thought that repeated itself insistently in her head as the row spluttered to the end of all rows, with glares, trouser-dustings, and finger-pointings, and with Topper Hammond relinquishing the truck with a promise to be back tomorrow; *we must escape* was the towering imperative that overshadowed them both as she met Matt's eyes across the table, and knew that this world and the world she had found in him must never be combined.

XI

All the towns of the valley had their Feast in the summer.
Cottesbridge Feast fell in August, just as wheat-harvesting
was beginning in the fields within sight of the town. This was
one local custom that the anonymity of redbrick and chapel
had not suppressed. For a whole weekend the town, normally
so dourly harassed and businesslike, gave itself over to con-
viviality, and something very like a Christmas spirit reigned
in the baking harvest heat. The fair came to town, and on
Saturday night turned the market-place into a pleasure-
ground. The pubs were crammed to the sills, meek men who
all year round were strictly Temperance becoming roarers,
and the hardened drinkers challenging each other to tremendous carouses; and on Feast Sunday the little terraced houses
sweltered with cooking and with the press of relatives gathered within, until they were like great boiling pots themselves,
and seemed about to throw off their roofs with a blast of
steam.

For Matt and Lucy it was an eagerly awaited occasion. A
slightly tense note had entered their relation of late, born not
out of any dissatisfaction with each other, but out of their
increasing dissatisfaction with their circumstances. Stern
reminders that the world at large was deeply unsympathetic
to an ardent and uncompromising love seemed always to be
presenting themselves. One such came from Connie Pollard
and Kit Lightfoot, whom they bumped into as they were
making their escape to the country one Saturday afternoon,
and who announced to them their engagement.

'Course it's a bit secret as yet,' Connie confided. 'We'd not
tell everybody. We reckon to make it formal-like on Feast
Sunday. But we're letting special friends know.'

'Oh, Connie, congratulations!' Lucy said. 'You thought
about when you gitting married?'

'Oh, we'll see – we'll see!' beamed Connie. 'It en't a thing to rush into, and you got to think of all the preparations, and how you're going to manage and everything. Course, I don't need to tell you pair that! But there's one lucky thing – we shall be able to live wi' Mother and Father for a start-off, while we save a bit.'

'Be all right if there's any gas-brackets wants mending,' said Kit, who could hardly speak for smirking.

'Yes, congratulations,' Matt said. 'That's fine news.'

Lucy and Matt went on their way, in slightly downcast spirits that neither would admit to. Nor did they mention the impossibility of their living with Lucy's family, which the Sunday-tea débâcle had only painted in more lurid colours, and the equal impossibility of making a home in Matt's bachelor digs. They did not need to mention these things: each knew the other was thinking of them.

In a drowsy copse-hollow, where grass-seed and aphids thickened the air to a green haze, Matt pressed Lucy to him, kissing her long and insistently and between whiles gently holding her face in his slender hands to look with a sort of concentrated candour into her eyes.

'This is my love for you, Lucy,' he said. 'This is my love . . . Everything . . . yet I wish it was more – I wish it was enough.'

'It is enough, Matt,' she said. 'Oh, it is.'

He regarded her with tender perplexity, restive. 'Life en't long enough,' he said. 'Life en't half long enough. Not the way we have to live it.'

The skin beneath his eyes was dusky: he was missing sleep, she knew, labouring away at trying to learn book-keeping. She kissed his face. 'It will be,' she said. 'It will be.'

The week before the Feast was one of intense heat. The closing-shop where Lucy worked, chill and damp in winter, became a stifling kiln, and the sewing-machines as hot to the touch as a boiling kettle. Yet Lucy was indifferent to the weather, or, at least, was vaguely surprised when other people sighed and commented on it, for she had reached that emotional pitch whereby external circumstances seemed simply part of her own inner landscape, and the blazing sun no more than an element of her own feelings. At work, at home, alone or in company, she thought of Matt, and grew as impatient as he with the slow material grind in which their love for each other had somehow to find a place. It was a thing so momentous, so important! Its importance, indeed, was magnified by perverse whispers to the contrary that occasionally stole over her, and which seemed to emanate from her experience in the crypt at Cleatham. 'Not important at all,' said a whisper, as one day she watched a fly, grown bold and deliberate in the heat, crawling across the tablecloth at home. 'Just insects on a table-top, that's all we are – crawling and groping.' Her heart was violent in its protest at this, and she looked longingly to the Feast, when she and Matt could be together as much as they liked; when the grim industry of the town would be stilled and its proprieties waived in a general junketing; when they could seize and claim the time and put those whispers to flight.

It was a time for dressing-up. Lucy's best frock was a fixture that would have to remain so for years, and was besides too heavy for this weather; but Joanna sometimes brought home from the milliners' such bits and pieces as the Misses Herring could not sell and which they gave to the servant-girl with a great show of magnanimity. With these Lucy contrived a new trimming to her hat, a lace front to her blouse, and new buttons to her tight-waisted jacket, and felt she made a decent enough show when Matt called to take her to the fair on the Saturday evening of the Feast.

'Ah! You look a treat, a rare treat,' he said absently, and absently he greeted her family, who were to walk up to the fair later. She did not understand why he was so abstracted until they were on their way to the market hill, when he suddenly stopped and, digging his hand in his pocket, drew out a little box.

'I was going to wait,' he said, 'but I can't any longer. I shall have to see what you think.'

The box contained a brooch of jet. As she wonderingly took it out, he stood with the anxious burdened look of men when presenting items of personal adornment to women.

'I don't know,' he said, 'I'm not very good . . .'

'You're very bad!' she said. 'Spending your money on me like this!'

'Oh, that,' he said, laughing and relieved. 'Will it suit, though? I thought so – with your colouring . . .'

She was afflicted with one of the sudden unaccountable shynesses of him that could visit her even in their most passionate moments, and could not speak for a moment.

'You don't have to wear it,' he stammered, misinterpreting her silence, 'you know – if it—'

'I shall,' she said. 'I shan't put it on now. Later.' She met his eyes. 'You can put it on for me.'

All of Cottesbridge, it seemed, was out of doors in the humid evening, and there was a great good-humoured crush at the fairground. Something light-headed, almost childlike, came over the townspeople amongst the lamps and the Dutch pipe-organs, the steam-roundabouts and shooting-galleries, the smells of gingerbread and spit-rock. Their mouths, normally so tight and pinched as if they were absorbed in an eternal mental calculation of how to make ends meet, opened wide and loose and laughing, and instead of the phlegmatic nods with which they usually greeted their friends and neighbours, they hailed each other with noisy delight as if they had not met for years. In the enveloping crowd, with convention off the reins, Lucy and Matt could laugh and kiss just as if they were alone, and Lucy could not remember feeling so happy.

'It's the best time of the year, the Feast,' she said. 'I've always loved the Feast.' And in a warm rush of feeling she added in Matt's ear: 'And you too. I love you, and I feel as if I always have – and I always will.'

Outside a refreshment tent they bumped, literally, into Luther Benson. Cottesbridge would not unbend so far as to allow liquor to be sold at the fair, so it must have been the bottle sticking out of his jacket pocket that accounted for his condition, which was not so much foxed as foxy. There was a sharp, tipsy glitter in his eyes, and a subtle smile on his pouted lips, and altogether he had never looked more good-humouredly knowing and crafty: Lucy felt a strange conviction that he could see out of the back of his head.

'I'll tell you what it is,' he said without preamble, placing his fingertips on their shoulders, and moving them on. 'It's a scandal. There's folk paying twopence to see a fat lady in a booth – blamed if I know why, you can see my stepmother for nothing, and I'd pay any price you care to mention *not* to see her any more, but any road – there's folk paying out money to see peep-shows, and to see a chap eat wine-glasses, and to see an old swizzler with a crystal ball; and yet they can see you pair, the handsomest sight in three towns, absolutely free, gratis and for nowt! Now does that seem fair? Not to Luther Benson it don't. I'd hand over a shilling here and now, just for the pleasure of seeing your faces, and call it cheap at the price, if it weren't that me money's tied up, like, and not to be got at.'

'Mebbe we should set up in a booth,' Matt laughed.

'Go on,' Luther said. 'You can fleer. You can laugh. I'm used to it, being a funny carroty-headed sort of fellow, as nobody's ever going to look at with a gently throbbing heart. You don't happen to know any carroty-headed gals, a bit short-sighted mebbe, who'd tek a chance on me, d'you, Miss Middleton?'

'It en't just how you look, Luther,' Lucy said with a slight smile. 'It's what's inside that counts.'

'What's inside, eh? Well, let's see. There's a slice of veal-and-ham pie, there's some cockles and vinegar, and on account of them being rich foods, and needing soothing, there's a quantity of intoxicating liquor took as a medicine.' Luther cocked his head at her, his expression a singular compound of cunning and innocence. 'Oh, but I don't think it's the stommick you're referring to, Miss Middleton, is it? I reckon we're talking about hearts here. Trouble is, hearts are such tender articles, a bit like that soft place atop of a baby's head, that really if you're going to git anywheres in this vale of tears and knocks, it's best that they git hardened pretty early on. Now look!' Luther dropped his voice. 'There's a shining instance of what I mean – her ladyship herself – see her?'

Ahead of them, moving amongst the crowd with seeming disdain, was Alice Wedderburn, leaning on the arm of a ruddy-faced middle-aged gentleman in boater and flannels. Though no one stared directly, heads turned in her wake, and cheerful faces froze in a look of speculation – sharpened, Lucy guessed, by the fact that she was not in mourning but in a bright costume with puffed silk sleeves and a gorgeously scalloped blouse-front. Lucy regarded the pale, indolent face with a sharp pang of memory, and confused understanding.

'Now en't that a perfect illustration?' Luther said. 'Now we're both from the Hole, me and her. Why, I can remember her as a little 'un walking down our street in a frock you could put your hand through, and her hair like a nits' outing; and now look at her, and look at me, if you can bear it! Now what's she got that I haven't?' He chuckled softly. 'You don't have to answer that, Miss Middleton. But I know one thing. It en't her heart that old codger's interested in. It en't her heart he's hoping to git access to, when he hangs her with jewels like a Christmas tree.'

Alice Wedderburn and her escort drawing close to them,

112

Luther fell silent. Lucy hoped that Alice would not see her, since it might upset the woman; but Alice looking lethargically about her as she passed, her eyes happened to meet Lucy's, and consciousness sparked instantly in them. All at once their intense greenness, which a moment before might have been taken for grey, seemed to stand out. Perhaps only Lucy saw the fractional hesitation: she appeared on the verge of speaking, but seeing that Lucy had companions, Alice averted her face and went on her way.

Stirred by a peculiar and profound sadness, Lucy did not for a few seconds attend to what Luther was saying. Then she gathered that he was inviting them to come to the boxing-booth.

'This is between you and me, y'understand, but there's a young chap from Saunds due to fight in a few minutes who's – well, let's say he's come to an agreement wi' me and some friends of mine that he won't tire everybody's patience by pummelling away while bull's noon, but hit the deck in the second round, and he won't be over-partickler about whether he's been hit or not when he goes down. We've all got bets on the other fellow, you see, so it all comes out neat. Now what say you come along, and mek a bet yourselves?'

'It'd be funny if the other fellow had took a backhander to go down in the first round, wouldn't it?' Matt said.

Luther turned to Lucy in aghast appeal. 'What can you do with him, Miss Middleton? Did you ever hear such a cynical view of human nature? Ah well, if you wun't be persuaded, I'll love you and leave you. Only pausing to remind you, Matt me old shopmate, about next Friday night.'

'Poaching again?' Lucy said to Matt after Luther had gone.

''Fraid so. Gitting so he can't think of nothing else.'

'I don't like you to go, Matt,' she said. 'I don't like thinking of the risk.'

'Oh, the gamekeepers seem to be a slow old lot nowadays.'

'Maybe, but . . .' All at once she stopped: she did not want to think about these things, gnawing shadowy things, on this night of all nights of the year. 'Oh never mind!' she said.

Luther Benson might have been unreliable on some things, but he had not been far from the truth when he had called them as handsome a couple as were to be seen there that night. Lucy was not one of those women whose looks blossom in trouble; hers was no glacial beauty. Happiness, warmth, companionship were her element, and called forth the uncomplicated gaiety in her as they called forth the blood to her cheek and the rich laugh, her father's laugh, to her throat; whilst Matt was most handsome when most alive. Arm in arm, laughing and teasing, trying their hand at the coconut-shies and hoop-las and shooting-galleries and laughing even harder because they were no good at any of them, they had the time of their lives because they were not conscious of time passing at all; and with the warm sky above the fair deepening to indigo, and the steam from the organs and roundabouts softening the lamp-glow and throwing a nimbus about every head, it was possible to feel that they moved in an uplifted sphere, transformed and immortal.

It was when they were at a shooting-gallery, and Matt was doggedly having one last attempt to get a shot on target, that Lucy was surprised to hear a voice saying, 'Miss Middleton, isn't it? Good evening to you.'

It was young Mr Radford Stokes, proprietor of her father's factory, tipping his hat to her. There was a young woman on his arm, small-featured and neat like himself. Overcoming her surprise, Lucy stammered, 'Mr Stokes – hello.'

'This is my sister Georgina. Miss Middleton's father is one of our men, my dear. Well, a good Feast turn-out, isn't it?'

'Yes,' Lucy got out, and then, feeling she ought to say something – anything – more: 'It's good weather for it – some years it rains and it spoils it so.'

'Yes, indeed. Well – ' Radford Stokes tipped his hat again – 'I hope you enjoy Feast Sunday, Miss Middleton. Good evening.'

'Wasn't that Stokes?' Matt said when they had moved on.

'Yes,' Lucy said. 'En't it funny to see him here? Mind you, his father always used to come to the fair on Feast Saturday, but then it seemed more natural with him.' Old Edward Stokes had been a well-known figure in the town, and was always to be seen, a great bewhiskered bear of a man, stumping about the fairground and giving brisk greetings to his employees; but the friendly paternalism sat much less easily on his dapper, formal son, who looked uncomfortable amongst the whelk-eating revellers. But at least, Lucy thought, Radford Stokes was making the effort too; and she thought, not for the first time, that her father's strictures on the young man were surely unfair.

Sooner or later it was inevitable that they should run into Connie and Kit. Connie was bubbling over with the fact of their being officially engaged, rather to the annoyance of Kit, who wanted to give a blow-by-blow account of his success at the hoop-la. 'It's on account of my long arms, see,' he said when he finally claimed their attention. 'My arms are so long I could pretty well reach out and slip the ring over the prize, like that.' He mimed this compelling feat several times, to make sure they had got the point, in the process nearly clouting several people in the face. 'Like that. See? Long arms, see. I don't know anyone who's got longer arms than what I have. Can you name anyone? I bet you can't.'

'I was going to suggest an orang-outang,' Matt whispered to Lucy when they made their escape, 'but that didn't seem a fair sort of comparison. Not fair on the orang-outang, any road.'

Laughing, they decided to slip away from the fair for a while, taking an old footpath that led down from the market hill and out of the town to the river meadows. A summer moon of delicate rose-pink had risen and lit their way, drawing a precise silverpoint shadow for every last straw of stubble, and evincing that strange wasteful mania for detail in nature, which will lovingly paint the brindles upon a calf it means to kill at birth. The ground was dry and warm, and the two soon threw themselves down to kiss and embrace as if prompted by some audible signal.

At length they sat up and Matt drew out the jet brooch. His fingers trembled slightly as he fastened it at the high neck of her blouse, and she heard him draw in breath as he pricked himself.

'Is it deep?' she said. 'Let me see.'

She took his hand in her own. A small bead of blood, looking as black as the jet brooch in the moonlight, hung from the tip of his forefinger. 'It'll be all right,' she said, and pressed her mouth to it, the coppery taste of blood touching her tongue.

'Lucy,' he said thickly, 'it got me thinking, them pair going on about their engagement . . . What about us? Will you . . .?'

'Yes,' she said. 'Yes.'

'Only I don't want it to be that way,' he said. 'You know – all formal, just for the sake of other folk. D'you see?'

'It's our engagement,' she said. 'This is our – what d'you call it? – a ritual. Here, away from everybody. With the moon like a witness.'

'Sealed in blood,' he said smiling faintly. 'For ever and ever.'

'For ever and ever.' She felt a terrible solemnity that at the same time was suffused with joy. The noise of the fair was an ineffably distant hubbub, a sound on the edge of the world. His arms went round her again, and she looked up into his face. 'I've never been so happy,' she said. 'I've never been so happy as tonight.'

'Only the start, Lucy,' he said urgently. 'You'll see – I promise you – we'll mek such a life together as nobody ever had. I promise you!'

When they rose and walked on it was with no clear direction in mind; they moved somewhat like sleepwalkers, arms twined about each other. Little by little they became idly absorbed in trying to trace the location of a cricket's chirp which, wherever they went, always seemed to be a little further on, and in this way they came to the lip of an ironstone quarry. Many such had been dug along the valley in recent years, tearing open meadows and sometimes leaving old farmhouses peeping over into their depths. This one seemed to have been recently exhausted, but the trestle bridges that crossed it were still intact. Matt put a cautious foot on the first. It was composed of single planks, which the moonlight attenuated to the thinnest of threads stretched across the dark, sheer drop.

'It's sound,' Matt said. 'D'you dare? Like that beam in the mill?'

'All right,' said she; and they began to walk across the plank bridge, which creaked and bent beneath them.

But they had not gone far when Lucy found she could not move. It was not so much fear of falling that paralysed her; somehow her eyes became hypnotically fixed on the empty darkness below. The quarry was dry, but she seemed to see it as a fathomlessly deep pool, waiting with a black and evil patience to suck her down. She blinked blindly around, rooted to the spot, and could not see Matt.

'Matt! Matt, where are you? Matt—' she cried, with panic clutching at her chest. She seemed to be stranded alone, in the middle of yawning space, with nowhere to go but down. 'Matt—'

'Here, here,' he said, his hand grasping her arm firmly: he had gone further across the bridge, and came hurrying back. 'What's wrong? What's the matter, my lovely?'

'Oh, Matt, I – I thought I'd lost you,' she stuttered, as he helped her back to safe ground. 'It was all dark, so dark down there, and I seemed to be falling down into it . . .'

'You haven't lost me,' he said, holding her. 'I'm here.'

'It was silly, I know,' she said, already ashamed of her curious weakness. 'But I couldn't help it . . . That blackness down there – it was like the place where I would be, if ever I lost you.'

'Oh Lucy!' he said, holding her tightly, 'that's a place you'll never go. I promise you. Never in our two lives, my Lucy.'

She buried her lips in his neck, and again she could not speak for happiness.

XII

Chauncey Middleton did not accompany the rest of his family to the fair that night: he arranged to meet them there later. He had been blissfully drunk every Feast Saturday of his life, and he did not intend this to be an exception. So he spent the first part of the evening drinking mightily in the crowded pubs of Cottesbridge, while Mrs Middleton took the young ones to the fair. It was only when he felt that he had drunk enough – not as much as he could hold, but enough to make his footsteps feel as light and elastic as they had been when he was young – that he left the beery fug of the Clicker's Arms and walked up to the fairground.

As he walked he felt that he should have had just one more, for the fresh air seemed to take the edge off his intoxication, leaving it frustratingly just short of that euphoria he craved; but he had promised the little 'uns he would be there, and he could always go back to the pubs later.

He found his family after an irritating search; but presently he was cheery again as he showed off his prowess at the coconut-shies and shooting-galleries to the admiration of Sidney and Benjy. His elevated mood increased when a shopmate tipped him off about a ginger-beer tent where bottles of more potent character were being sold under the counter. With one of these snugly in his pocket he felt fine: the spring in his step became more pronounced, and he could not help thinking how much prettier his wife was than most of the old haybags he saw around him, how much more handsome his children than the other mealy brats, how much he had to be proud of.

It was in this mood that he turned to see Radford Stokes, his employer, with a little mincing woman on his arm. His sister, Chauncey supposed at once, for he didn't reckon the young Stokes sprig would have much to offer women.

'Ah, evening, Middleton,' Radford Stokes said. 'Quite a lively occasion, isn't it?'

'How do, Mr Stokes,' Chauncey said, his manner determinedly offhand, for he wasn't going to have his family see him tug his forelock to such a runt as this.

'We ran into your daughter earlier,' Radford Stokes said urbanely, tipping his hat towards Mrs Middleton. 'Um, Lucy, isn't it?'

'That's the name,' Chauncey said, cutting his wife off. There was something about young Stokes talking familiarly about Lucy that obscurely annoyed him, though for the moment the fumes of liquor concealed the reason why. Then he remembered. He remembered that through Lucy he was under an obligation to this man, was forced to keep a promise of good conduct made in her name: this little dand whom he could break over his knee! The fury rose swiftly in his head, but it had something of euphoria about it too.

'Very pleasant girl,' young Mr Stokes was saying, 'as, er, indeed, are all your children, I see. You must be very proud of them.'

'Ah! She's a good gel, Lucy,' Chauncey said, and he did not notice how loud his voice had become. 'Only trouble is, she goes mekking promises for folk 'ithout their leave.'

'Ah?' Radford Stokes blandly raised an eyebrow. 'Well, I believe that's all sorted out now, Middleton, and we needn't talk about it any more.'

'Talk about it?' Chauncey made a sweeping gesture with his arm, but kept his balance. He was all right: he felt fine, never better. 'Who ever talked about it? Not me. It was all done behint my back. All at once I found I was on some bloody promise of good behaviour, like I was some bloody kid at a Sunday school. And all over nothing!'

'Well, it was over your job, you know, Middleton,' Radford Stokes said, in his mild, unemphatic voice. 'Hardly nothing.'

'Job.' Chauncey spat the word out. He felt himself lifting, big and joyous, like a beached boat being raised up by the tide, his tongue moving with wonderful fluency. 'And I'm supposed to be grateful for it. Why, I can recall a time when I made better boots than your fact'ry on my last at home, and wi' no foreman breathing down my neck either. So why should I be grateful for your job? You can keep it. You can keep your job. I got my pride. Where's the pride in working for such a dried-up little slyver as you, eh?'

Radford Stokes pursed his lips slightly: he wore no more expression than if he were listening to a polite suggestion, though his sister had turned crimson, and Mrs Middleton was frantically tugging at Chauncey's sleeve. 'Well, if that's the way you feel about it,' Mr Stokes said in the same unconcerned way.

'Ah! I do! I do!'

'Chauncey!' Mrs Middleton hissed, shaking his arm.

'Well, what's to do, woman?' he said turning on her. 'Don't you like to see your man stand up for hisself?'

'Say you're sorry!' Mrs Middleton was roused to an unaccustomed assertiveness, while the face of Joanna at her side was white and solemn. 'For God's sake, say you're sorry!'

It was too late, however, even had Chauncey had any intention of saying sorry, for Mr Stokes and his sister had turned away without another word and disappeared into the crowd.

XIII

With a heavy heart and a faltering tread, Lucy crossed the Lessington Road to the house of Mr Radford Stokes.

It was Feast Sunday, and after the showiest, happiest morning church-parade of the year, the people of Cottesbridge had disappeared into their houses for the great eating-fest that was the high point of the weekend. But no holiday spirit reigned in the Middleton household. Lucy had parted with Matt late last night, and had returned home, walking on air, to be greeted by the tragical faces of her mother and Joanna, and to hear the news of her father's latest, most disastrous lapse.

That he had undone the work she had performed on his behalf; that he had seemed to do so with a perverse, swaggering resentment of the promise she had made to Mr Stokes, almost as an insult to her; these things not only pained but angered her. Her first swift thought, indeed, had been, 'He's done it – let him mend it himself, if he can. I'm finished with him!' But it was not merely herself that was involved. Her young and vulnerable siblings were the ones who would suffer most from the likely consequences of her father's action, and they must be protected, even if it meant such a swallowing of pride that she would be almost choked. Her mother was too foolish, Joanna too diffident, Jim too young to take a hand in repairing the damage – if reparable it was. It was up to Lucy. She accepted it, but for the first time she inwardly murmured mutiny. For the first time she tasted bitterness and contempt as she regarded the mess her father had made.

Her father had not returned home all night – not an uncommon occurrence for Feast Saturday, when drink flowed till all hours and men slept it off wherever they could lay their heads, but a discouraging indication that he felt no remorse for what he had done at the fair, and did not consider it a thing to be undone at all costs. Privately Lucy doubted that it could be remedied; but even as her mother was tear-fully and tentatively suggesting that a personal appeal from her to young Mr Stokes might yet save Chauncey's job, Lucy had decided to do just that. The Stokes' house was well known: she would go there, apologize on her father's behalf, and ask Mr Stokes to give him a second – or rather third – chance.

She felt, besides, a certain responsibility to Mr Stokes, when it was she who had made that promise of good behaviour. She would have felt shabby if she had not at least faced him. Yet even though she did in a marginal sense know Radford Stokes, and had received nothing but politeness from him, she felt a trepidation on going to see him that she was sure she would not have felt had it been his father, old Edward Stokes, that she had to appeal to. Old Mr Stokes, though a fire-eater, had been much closer to his workmen – had, indeed, come from their class himself – and while he would undoubtedly have exploded in wrath at being spoken to in that way by Chauncey Middleton, he would have had an instinctive understanding of the excesses of the Feast. Emotional ties had linked him with the men who laboured for his wages. Young Mr Stokes, Lucy perceived, was of a different stamp. He had always been separate from the working people. He was cooler – and, she somehow feared, more pitiless. She could not imagine a sentimental attach-ment to the shoemaker's beery, two-fisted traditions figuring in Radford Stokes' assessment of her father's case.

But, he must be faced. The one thing she must not allow herself to do as she went on her errand was dwell on Matt, on the enchanted time they had spent together last night. Such a headlong fall from those heights to these depths suggested a wry malignancy on the part of fate, an inbuilt tendency for things to go cruelly, mockingly awry, that threatened her fundamental optimism; and she set her face against it. She would not believe that such sick jesting was the way the world habitually dealt with the mortals brought into it.

Lessington Road, a broad thoroughfare leading out of the town, was not Cottesbridge as she knew it. Here were no cobblestones, no alleys, no hurrying shoemakers: indeed, such was the space and greenness that it appeared to her as more country than town. The Stokes' house stood well apart from its neighbours and well back from the road, behind tall box-hedges, with a gravel carriage-drive at the side. To her sensibilities, most responsive to the curves and crannies of old stone, it did not appear greatly handsome: it was less than twenty years old, of bright red brick, and in design a fairly subdued example of shoe-baron villa-Gothic. With its corner cupolas, many-shaped windows dotted with panes of stained glass, and its strawberries-and-cream contrast of brick and clean white paint, it had the clumsy, vivid look of something drawn by a talented child. Yet it was weighty too, weighty with money; each of its heavy square bay windows appeared more solid and substantial a construction than the entire house in which Lucy and her family lived.

In the drive she hesitated. Should she use the side entrance, the place for tradesmen and servants? The struggle was short: it was Mr Stokes she had come to see, after all, not the cook; and she would keep a little of her pride by her, if only as a talisman.

Besides, she told herself as she knocked, she had on her best clothes. Put on in so different, so hopeful a mood yesterday! – but she mustn't think of that.

She should, she supposed, have expected a maid: people who lived in houses like this didn't answer the door themselves; but so strictly confined was her experience to the two-up two-down uniformity of shoemaking Cottesbridge that the sight of the starched apron and cap, not to mention the starched expression on the maid's face, took her aback. She stammered out her request to see Mr Stokes, and found herself left waiting in the hall, and staring at some monstrous jars of palm and fern that looked big enough to hide Ali Baba and all his forty thieves in.

She had not heard Radford Stokes' approach: he was as quiet in his movements as her father was emphatic.

'Oh! Mr Stokes,' she said. 'I'm sorry to come bothering you like this, but could I have a word with you?'

'Of course.' His dress and manner were as formal as ever; randomly she noticed that he favoured dove-grey waistcoats. 'Perhaps you'll come into the study.'

He paused to open a door and say 'Excuse me, Georgina. I shan't be a moment.' Through the gap Lucy glimpsed his sister, seated on a sofa with another lady who seemed to crane her neck to see what was going on; then the door was closed and she was being ushered into a study. She had time only to notice the extreme neatness and order of the desk with its files and papers before she blurted out, 'Mr Stokes, I've heard what happened last night at the fair – with you and my father – and I've come to say I'm sorry.'

Radford Stokes stood by the window, his hands behind his back, his face mild and neutral as he looked at her, his voice as always pleasant and uneager as he said, 'Well, thank you for that – but where is your father now? Why has he not come himself?'

It was a pointed question, for all its gentleness of tone; she had to admit that he had seen straight to the heart of the matter.

'Exactly,' he said as she was silent. 'He's still, I gather, out on the spree. You see my drift, Miss Middleton. It's very good of you to seek to apologize, but it really isn't up to you. If your father wished to make amends, he would not be where he is now. And where he will be tomorrow, I suspect. That is what concerns me. His behaviour towards me isn't important; what's important is that I have reliable employees. And really, as far as I'm concerned, your father has only stated openly what his continual unreliability and absenteeism have long suggested: that he doesn't want his job at my factory. And, as I'm sure you're aware, there are many men who do.'

Lucy became aware of the slow tick of a clock somewhere in the room, the only sound to be heard: a heavy Sunday silence of respectability swathed the house. She tried to piece together her thoughts. Mr Stokes' unemotional discourse seemed to have left none of her carefully rehearsed persuasions intact.

'I'm – I'm not going to say he deserves another chance,' she got out. 'I know he's already had that. I haven't got any good reasons, Mr Stokes, except to say that we're a big family, with young children, and Father needs the work for their sakes – but I know you can say he should have thought of that himself . . . I just wanted to say I was sorry, because it was me who made that promise to you, and the things he said were terrible . . .' Joanna had repeated their father's insulting diatribe to Lucy very faithfully, and she blushed now at mentioning it, with Radford Stokes standing a few feet from her. But no colour rose to his even complexion, and the smooth hand that went up to stroke his silky moustache was perfectly steady. 'All I can do is ask you to tek him back,' she concluded, desperately. 'I can't even mek any promises, not now. All I can do is ask, and that's what I'm doing.'

Mr Stokes turned to the window, where a squirrel had appeared in full view on the lawn and was making its way across in a series of sinuous, weightless hops. 'Our squirrels are getting bolder and bolder,' he said. 'They even come into the conservatory now.' For an incredulous and angry moment Lucy thought she was simply being dismissed; but then he turned again with a thoughtful frown and said, 'Well, Miss Middleton, I'm forced to repeat that the answer lies not in your hands but in your father's, though again I appreciate your coming. Now just suppose . . .' He hesitated. 'Just suppose I was prepared to overlook your father's outburst. Then the rest would depend on him. It would depend on his turning up for work promptly tomorrow. I would expect him to come to see me before beginning work. Now all this—'

'He'll do it,' Lucy said urgently. 'I'll mek him do it.' As he seemed to regard her a little doubtfully she hurried on, 'I know – I know I said I couldn't mek any more promises. And I'm not, really. But can I tell him – can I at least tell him that if he comes to work prompt tomorrow, and says he's sorry, then there's a chance he could have his job back? Can I do that?'

Her appeal was agitated, and for the first time Radford Stokes looked less than calm himself. He paced for a few moments, his eyes on the floor, then spoke decisively. 'It is an absolute condition, Miss Middleton – an absolute condition that he is at work on the dot tomorrow morning. If not, then I tell Shepherd to replace him immediately. If he does come, then I dare say we can work something out.'

'Oh, thank you, Mr Stokes – that's all I ask.'

He smiled. It was a melancholy smile, but still it gave a remarkably boyish aspect to his sober face. 'Perhaps you'd better wait and see before thanking me,' he said. 'But then I'm told I'm a dreadful pessimist. I don't think I am, but then I don't suppose anybody believes they are an optimist or a pessimist – everybody believes that he's a realist, and is the only one to see things as they truly are.'

The flash of personality, sparking out from the shadowy formality and reserve, was curiously fascinating; but before Lucy could reply there was a tap at the door, and the lady she had seen sitting on the sofa with Radford's sister put her head into the room.

'Radford, when are you – oh!' The lady counterfeited

tremendous surprise on seeing Lucy, which also gave her the opportunity for a good look at her. 'I'm sorry, I didn't know you still had anyone with you. We rather thought you must have drifted off and got absorbed in some accounts or something.' The lady, who was fair, buxom, heavy-lidded, and thirty, smiled with her mouth all the time she was speaking.

'Just coming,' Mr Stokes said, ringing the bell, and to Lucy, 'Well, if you will tell your father I'll see him at the factory tomorrow morning, Miss Middleton . . .'

'I will,' Lucy said. 'Thank you very much.'

The unknown lady showed no great inclination to get out of the doorway, until the maid appeared behind her to show Lucy out. Lucy was too preoccupied with the important business on hand to pay her much attention; but she did wonder in passing who she could be. If there were some romantic relation between her and Radford, she thought, it did not reflect credit on his taste and judgement, and for that very reason she could not believe it.

Feast Sunday being an occasion that not even the indolence and improvidence of the senior Middletons could ignore, there was roast pork and green peas that day. Matt, having no family of his own, was invited to join them, but the master of the house had not appeared by the time the dinner was ready, and they were constrained to eat without him, the young ones casting longing eyes at the portion that was saved for their father's return. Mrs Middleton was sanguine, however: Lucy had squared it all with Chauncey's employer, so there was nothing to worry about.

Such was her mother's feeble grasp of the situation. Lucy told Matt the real facts of the case when they went out walking after dinner, and added that she thought she ought to go round the pubs and search for him.

'No country for us today then?' he said bleakly.

'I'm sorry, Matt. You don't have to come with me . . .'

'Oh, of course I'll come! It don't matter.'

They made the rounds of the pubs of Cottesbridge – in the town's black-and-white way they all seemed to be directly opposite a chapel, as if to hammer home a stark choice between perdition and salvation – but they had no luck. It seemed likely that Chauncey, as in his old handsewn days, had extended the binge to one of the neighbouring towns, Lessington or Kettenham or Bishop's Burton; it was not unknown for such rovings to culminate in grand inter-town brawls, a 'good stack-up' being considered the perfect end to a spree. It was now early evening, and beginning to spit with that desultory summer rain that can be more muggy and clammy than heat. They stood in Lucy's street beneath the gas-lamp, lingering out a dissatisfied goodbye. They were not going to quarrel, but a quarrel was somewhere in the air near them, an unachieved fact like next week.

'Well, there goes Feast Sunday,' Matt said, pulling down his cap.

'I'm sorry, Matt,' said she.

'It en't your fault. That's just what urges me to death – the way none of this is your fault, and it's you who's having to suffer for it! Having to go crawling to old Stokes, having to spend your one free time of the week traipsing from pub to pub: what sort of life's that? You can't go on forever propping your father up. If he can't stand on his own let him fall, I say.'

'That's easy for you to say. You en't got family. You en't got brothers and sisters.'

'Well, thank God for it. To see the mess folks get into, and expect other folks to get 'em out of, it's enough to mek a man thank his lucky stars he's all alone.'

He spoke with the hasty wildness he often showed in disappointment, and which meant nothing; but she was in that mood in which we are disposed to be hurt by anything people say. They regarded each other through the tickling rain, with aching legs and aching hearts. Then, with the same impetuosity that made him impatient, Matt threw his arms round her, hugging her to him so completely that he lifted her feet slightly off the ground.

'Very nice, Matt,' he said against her hair. 'Git mardy and mek things wuss for the gel, very nice that. Got about as much tack as a sow in farrer ... I just wish I could put you in my pocket and tek you somewhere where it'd all be all right!'

'You do,' she said. 'You do when you hold me like this.'

A paroxysm of curtain-twitching in Nancy Smallbones' house indicated that their long kiss was observed.

'If he don't come home tonight,' Matt said at last, 'and if he don't turn up for work tomorrow—'

She put her fingers to his lips. 'Don't say it, Matt,' she said. 'We'll just have to wait and see.'

127

'I know . . . There seems to be a lot of waiting-and-seeing in life, don't they? I wonder if we ever get to the seeing part!'

She waited. All night long she waited, not dozing this time, even though Joanna offered to relieve her for a while. A dawn sky of nacreous beauty was brightening above the slate roofs, and getting itself besmirched with the smoke of fires already being stoked for wash-day, when Chauncey Middleton came crashing into the house.

He was worse than she had ever seen him. The lineaments of the wreck he would surely become were visible on his florid face, obscuring the joviality like a hooligan scribble across a fair drawing. The stairs were beyond him, and he could only loll in his armchair, stertorously blowing, nodding, and startling himself awake with rasping snores.

Lucy stood regarding him. Joanna and Jim had come down in stockinged feet, and watched at a distance: Joanna very grave, Jim wearing the expression of someone detecting a lie and disgusted at himself for ever believing it.

'What shall we do?' Joanna said.

Lucy did not answer, but walked out of the room to the scullery. She took a bucket, filled it with water from the tap in the yard, brought it brimming back, and tipped the whole lot over her father.

It roused him – roused him enough to half rise dripping from the chair and feebly raise a fist to her; but he was too far gone even to hit out, and sank back again, cursing. Thinking she might at least have cleared the fumes from his understanding, she knelt down and began carefully, firmly explaining that his job depended on his turning up for work that morning.

She had not got very far when she realized that her father was laughing – a deep, subterranean laugh, welling up and shaking his body, but with no real mirth in it; and all at once he cut her off. 'Stokes! Radford piss-emmet Stokes!' he bellowed, his face staring into hers. 'Radford Stokes can go and poke hisself, if he can even manage that. D'you think I want a job from him? Little tyke's not half a man. Disgrace meself wukking for him. Tell him so, gel, as you're so thick with him – tell him so! He wun't see me in his piss-emmet factory no more!'

Lucy rose to her feet, and stood looking down at her father for some moments. Then she turned and went upstairs, and began getting ready for work.

She would call in at Stokes' factory on her way, but she knew that nothing she could say there would be any use. The die was cast, and already she was looking apprehensively into a future in which her father was without work, with his reputation preceding him at each new application.

What would such a future be like? The impossibility of her leaving home now, and thus depriving the family of her wage in the hard times to come, was the thing that above all hammered itself into her consciousness; but almost as strong was the angry disdain with which she thought of her father's boozy sneers at Radford Stokes. *Little tyke's not half a man*, he had pronounced as he wallowed like a hog in a sty; and Lucy knew that she had turned a terrible corner in her feelings about the family from which she had sprung as she tied on her apron and mentally asserted: *Twice the man you are, Father. Twice the man.*

XIV

'So that one's gone too far at last, seem'ly,' Lil Fry said to
Mr Birdsall one evening a week after the Feast, as they stood
on the corner watching the gas-lamps being lit. She jerked her
head at the Middleton house, her face a study in resolutely
choosing not to say any more.

'Yes,' said Mr Birdsall, 'yes, I'm afraid so.'

'Well, I'm not the woman to say I told you so. I keep my
opinions to meself, always have. But I will say this. When I
heard I weren't surprised. Not a bit. The only surprise was
that it never happened sooner. And what's to come of 'em
now – gret family like that 'ithout the man of the house in
wukk? That's what I'd want to know, if I was the sort to pry.
But it en't my business.'

'Well, I've asked around at Whiting's, in case there's a man
wanted,' Mr Birdsall said, 'but I'm afraid there's nothing
going. At least, not for – well, not for . . .'

'Not for an unreliable man,' Lil Fry said. 'I'll say it for
you, Mr Birdsall. I call a spade a spade, always have . . . And
there's an example for you, while we're on the subjick,' she
added, seeming to see out of the back of her iron-grey head
the figure of Topper Hammond skulking by, the nap on his
ancient masher suit so shiny he might have been clad in satin.
'You've only got to look at the state of their doorstep. And
that's the way the Middletons'll go, Mr Birdsall. I wouldn't
say it if it weren't plain truth.'

'I wish I could have been more help,' Mr Birdsall said
sadly. 'I wish I could have done something – perhaps a word
at the right time . . .'

'Course, you've always had a bit of an interest in that
quarter, en't you, Mr B?' said Nancy Smallbones, who had
suddenly materialized out of the ether, and who now sociably
interposed her hump between them. 'Only fatherly-like, I
know. Nice that is, en't it? Yerss. Mind you, not much you

130

can do with folks like that, is there? No. Man o'passions, that's his trouble. Shame. Tsk-tsk. And the gel not long been walking out with a chap as well. Meks it awk'ud for her. She'll be half keeping the lot of 'em now. Poor gel. She must be suffering.' Mrs Smallbones focused her gaze intently on the Middleton house, as if she might get at the suffering that way, and relish its flavour.

'Well, I've always said it – people shouldn't have children when they can't support 'em. When me and my Tom were starting out we waited. We waited while we were settled,' said Lil Fry, and looked so grim that it seemed likely that her husband would have been quite content to have waited for ever.

'Ah, I'm glad we only had the one before my Arthur went under the ingin, and was took from me,' said Mrs Smallbones. 'It's hard for a widder-woman if she's got a lot of children. It was hard anew for me, jist thinking of my Arthur all spread out over the railway line. Took the best part of a day to clean the ingin wheels, they reckon, and that was with hosepipes. But then children are a blessing an' all, en't they, Lil? Yerss. Course, that's something you've missed out on, en't it, Mr B? No children to carry your name on and look after you when you're old and on your own. Shame, en't it? Yerss. Still, too late now, en't it? I suppose you're used to it.'

Mr Birdsall shifted as Mrs Smallbones' mouth came uncomfortably close to his ear. 'Yes, well,' he said, 'we're perhaps putting too dark a complexion on things, you know. Chauncey Middleton's a good craft, and good crafts are always wanted; and maybe if he can sort himself out a bit, then . . . who knows.'

Lil Fry made her back even straighter and her lips even tighter, as if to say *she* knew; whilst Mrs Smallbones, wriggling ecstatically, said, 'Oh! yerss, we must hope so – we must hope everythink'll be all right,' expressing so clearly, in every gloating writhe and twist of her body, that what she hoped for was the exact opposite, that Mr Birdsall broke the good manners of a lifetime, and walked off in disgust.

131

XV

Lucy's father showed no remorse, but it would have been surprising to her if he had. He was one of those men who resort to such blustering defiance rather than admit they were wrong that they end up believing in their own bravado. Best thing he had ever done, he said; he should have got out of Stokes' long before, it was a poor place nowadays. That it was one of the most thriving concerns in Cottesbridge, that he had thrown up a job that most shoemakers would have given their eye-teeth for, that he had done so in a way that set against him a black mark visible to every prospective employer, that he was having no luck in finding another job – these facts were mere motes in the fierce beam of his egotism.

He picked up a little casual work, helping with the harvest in the fields outside the town; but though he came home with his fair skin red from the sun and full of rodomontade about how the farmers had praised his work and wished all their hands were such strong lusty fellows, even he knew that this could be no more than a stop-gap. He was a shoemaker, and his household needed a shoemaker's wages.

In the meantime it was Lucy's wages, and the minimal amounts brought home by Jim and Joanna, that kept the family going; and what kept Lucy going was Matt, and the bright green prospect of hope beyond the dark foreground of necessity that their love represented. If the prospect had receded, its details grown fainter, that only made her yearn more hungrily towards it, and seek it in a more complete redemption. At night she slept with her arms crossed about herself, as if hugging the thought of Matt to her.

She had sometimes to be content with the thought rather than the reality; for as summer gave way to autumn, cold and wet days began to nibble away at the time they could spend with each other in the country – and that did not leave them much leeway. With scarcely enough to feed the family, there could be no invitations to Sunday teas; and besides, as the workless weeks went by, her father became like a snappish, pent-up dog about the house, with guests the first to be savaged.

No, her home was out of the question, and Matt's digs equally so, with a landlady of rigid views who tended to throw her lodgers' possessions out of the window at the first sign of female company. Then, one October day, when everyone at Lucy's factory had been talking of the outbreak of war with the Boers of South Africa, and Connie Pollard had been reasoned out of a confused impression that the foe was a peculiar tusked race who lived on free oranges, Matt met her as she came out of work and gave her some news that came like rain in a drought.

'The old dragon's going away for a couple of days,' he said, eyes shining. 'Her sister in Northampton's broke her ankle.'

'Oh! Has she?' Lucy was smiling, then laughing. 'Sorry, I'm not laughing at that.'

He was laughing too. 'Monday she's coming back,' he said. 'We can be together Sundy. I'll square it wi' the others in the house so they won't snitch. We can have a slap-up tea, just on our own, just as we like. We can have all day. Can you come?'

'Yes' seemed a feeble enough word for the affirmative thrill that went through her. Strange as it was to think of, she had never been alone in a room with Matt since their first meeting at the derelict mill.

The days till Sunday crawled by, filled with talk about the far-off war: Lucy's father claimed loudly that, if he were a few years younger, he'd take the shilling and go out there to give them what-for himself; while Mr Birdsall, who was a strong Liberal and venerated the memory of Mr Gladstone, murmured that he saw no good coming of it. As far as Lucy was concerned it might have been a war fought on the moon. The war for survival was what concerned her – and, most of all, the wonderful and complete respite from it that this Sunday offered.

The house where Matt lodged backed right on to the railway, and soot, she found when she arrived on Sunday, featured prominently in its interior decoration, coating even the banister so that you arrived upstairs with a black hand. 'Have to be quiet when we go past this next door,' Matt whispered to her on the landing. 'That's Knocker White's room. He's behint with the rent, and a crafty old cuss, and I wouldn't put it past him to go tattling tales to git on the right side of the old dragon. I've squared it wi' the others. Now, here we are.'

The room was very small – it must have been for Lucy to have thought so, for she had spent all her life in small rooms where even one other person formed an obstruction. It was dingy enough too, but she examined it with great interest, having tried to picture it for so long, and being in that state of love in which even the most trifling physical accoutrements of the lover take on a thrilling significance. Here were his few books, his shaving-brush and hair-brush, the bundle of papers on which he was struggling with his book-keeping course, and his narrow iron bed, on which was set, as the only available surface, a tray loaded with tea-things.

'There's a mirror here,' he said as she took off her hat, 'in case you want to look at yourself and – everything.'

'No, I'm all right,' she said.

They laughed together, nervously, at this odd little formality, and Matt said, 'As if you needed that, looking like you do. Oh! I've tried to picture you in here, time after time – you standing there, looking like that. I can't hardly believed it's happened.'

They kissed, and she sank on to his knee, on the only chair in the room; but as ominous creakings suggested that this was unwise, they uncomfortably got up. The tea of potted meat and pickles and bread-and-butter was there, and taking up a lot of room, and so Matt suggested that they eat it; and Lucy agreed, though she felt oddly awkward and shy and as a result not at all hungry.

A fire had to be lit in order to boil a kettle for tea: the resulting smoke necessitated opening the window, which brought in smuts from the railway, and inevitably some of this got on to the food, further diminishing Lucy's appetite, though she did not like to admit as much to Matt when he had gone to such trouble.

'Are you sure that's all right?' he said more than once: he perching on the bed, she sitting in the chair. 'Don't eat it if not.'

'No, no, it's all right,' she said, trying to balance her cup on her knee, whilst a train thundered and shrieked at the window.

Matt took the used tea-things downstairs, and while he was gone she reproached herself for her awkwardness, whilst at the same time feeling that the walls of the tiny room were oppressively closing in on her. Then she was startled by a knock at the door.

'Oh! Beg pardon. Thought Matt was here.' The young man craning round the door gave her a look of frank curiosity. 'I'm Charlie, by the way. Room next door.'

'Oh! Yes, he mentioned you.'

'Did he?' Charlie showed no disposition to do anything more than look at her round the door, until Matt appeared behind him.

'Now then, Charlie, what's to do?' he said frowning.

'Ah, Matt. Just saying hello to your guest here. Sorry, didn't catch the name . . .?'

'Lucy,' she said.

'What is it, Charlie?' Matt said impatiently.

'Eh? Oh! Well – bit of a ticklish matter, shopmate, but I won't beat about the bush. Couldn't see your way to helping me out with another bob or two, could you, while pay-day? I wouldn't ask, only—'

'Yes, all right,' Matt said, fumbling in his pocket. 'Here.'

'Ah, you're a gem. Gem, en't he? Ah well, I'll git out of your road.'

'Sorry,' Matt said when he had gone. 'There's no harm in him, but he's got a nose like a broom-handle. Now then, what would—'

A knock sounded at the door again. Cursing, Matt yanked it open.

'Only me again,' Charlie said. 'Couldn't lend me a pinch or two of tea could you? I wouldn't ask, only—'

'Here. Tek it.' Matt thrust the tea-tin at him and bundled him out of the room, closing the door with a bang. He sat down on the bed with a stormy expression.

Normally she could lift him out of such black troughs with one smile; but today she felt peculiarly unequal to it, and she said hurriedly, 'How are you going on with your book-keeping?'

'Eh? Oh – I'm gitting along, slowly. It's 'nation complicated . . . Would you like to have a look?'

'Oh, yes.'

It was difficult for her to understand, and difficult for him to explain: she was not in truth greatly interested, but found herself pretending to be, and he too went over it with a sort of dogged blankness, as if he didn't know why he was doing it. They were both pretty relieved to have done with it; but a worse silence ensued, which they filled with such painful spurts of chat as made it seem impossible that on their days in the country they had each talked until their mouths were so dry they had to scoop up brook-water to refresh them.

Then there was the sound of the front door, and Matt leaped up as if electrified. 'Don't say that's the old dragon come back,' he said, and went softly out to the landing to look over the banisters; but it was a false alarm, merely one of his fellow lodgers.

'Would you like some more tea?' he said.

'You gave it to Charlie,' she pointed out.

'So I did.' He reflected, his elbows on his knees. 'Mind you, I could ask for it back.'

'No, I'm all right, really.'

'Right you are. Would you – would you like to go out for a walk?'

'Oh, that'd be nice!' she said with relief.

They made ready to go out, brushing against each other in the cramped room; but for the first time there was ease and affection in their contact. Lucy looked at Matt pushing back his strong unoiled crop of hair. Her love for him was like a great stone at her heart; but here, in this place designed only for necessity, in this web of trivial and entangling circumstances, she could not properly express it, and neither it seemed could he. It was not a great matter, she tried to tell herself; but it seemed so, for they had anticipated so much of this afternoon.

Certainly this was not the first time in human affairs that the longed-for event has failed to live up to expectations. Perhaps there is something in the very sight of our excited preparations that prompts the Spirit of Irony to descend, and scatter disappointment like wet sawdust; or perhaps there is some minor deity called the Spirit of the Sense of Occasion, who in the capricious way of spirits declines to come when called, and only pops up when least expected. The unforgettable meeting, the significant moment, the heart-swelling revelation, seldom occur against the appropriate backdrop and with all the right upholstery in place, and we are quite as likely to realize that we have fallen in love – or out of it – when we are tying our shoelaces as when we are gazing at the moon. But theirs was such a circumscribed life, and offered so few such opportunities, that the anti-climax struck them with the force of tragedy.

Perhaps they should have laughed; but laughter implies detachment, the very last attribute that these troubled young souls possessed. Once they were out in the fresh air, they were able at least to be more natural with one another, and to manage a mutual smile when Matt said, 'Well – that was a corker of an afternoon wasn't it?' But his mood was dark – how dark became plain when they stood on the bridge over the river, and he suddenly said, regarding the town: 'You've heard of the Great Fire of London, I reckon? Must have been a terrible thing . . . And yet there's times when I want to do the same with this town: set fire to the place, and watch it burn!'

XVI

That harsh and desperate note that had entered their two lives became more prominent as autumn deepened, and the gaunt shades of the material fell across their path. It was no use trying not to discuss the practical aspect of their affair, for that was to retreat into a dream-world; but whenever they did, prickly difficulties seemed to hedge them in, and made them fractious.

That tremendous piece of wisdom to the effect that money isn't everything, so often trotted out by those who have plenty of it, was never more searchingly exposed than by Matt and Lucy's situation. Two ugly facts governed it: she could not leave home, and he had no money to spare; and they worried and gnawed at these facts until they were sick of them. There was no possibility of their marrying yet – and that 'yet' seemed to stretch from everlasting to everlasting.

It was frustrating, and Lucy occasionally felt bitterness – but she was not bitter. Perhaps this was because of the streak of irresponsible Middleton optimism; but more than that she was a person who was instinctively appreciative; her nature was such that, of a fortunate circumstance and an unfortunate circumstance occurring in the same day, the fortunate would always make the deepest impression on its surface. This was not because of any conscious tendency on her part to look on the bright side; she was simply sensitive to small stimuli, so that merely the fact of meeting Matt, of having loving words together, acted upon her like sunlight upon a plant.

With Matt it was different. The part only made him more eager for the whole. He had been born, as he freely admitted, with ants in his britches. For him resignation was death – death the arch-enemy, as had been expressed in his defiant face the first time she saw him in the crypt at Cleatham. 'We got to steal a march on death every day of our lives,' he once

138

said, 'and every day that we let the pot go off the boil, and just don't bother about nothing, we give the old swine a bit of ground.' And he seemed to draw no clear line between apathetic resignation and quiet patience.

Doggedness was his answer. His eyes now often had the bright, unfocused look of someone who has stayed up too long, and moved into a second wakefulness. His determination had a sort of uplifted savagery. 'We'll manage it somehow,' he said. 'And not ten years from now neither. We will be together, Lucy – on our own terms an' all – I swear we will! This jog-trot way of living can't go on.'

She knew he was still going poaching with Luther Benson; but she did not realize how well known this was until one evening when she went out to call Sidney, Benjy and Dickybird to their beds, and Mr Birdsall beckoned to her from his front doorstep.

'Have you got a minute, Lucy?'

She ushered the boys in and went over. Mr Birdsall smiled, but looked curiously ill at ease. 'Come on inside,' he said. 'Bit nippy, and so's Mrs Smallbones if she sees any conversation going on without her.'

She went into his clean little parlour, with its smell of pipe-smoke and portrait-engraving of Gladstone and single armchair with his shape impressed into the seat. She knew that he had been exerting himself greatly trying to find another job for her father – his standing as a skilled clicker meant that he would be listened to with respect – and it occurred to Lucy with a flash of hope that he might have been successful at last.

His manner, however, did not suggest good news. He fiddled with some spills on the mantelshelf and then said in a rush, 'You perhaps won't like me for saying what I've got to say, Lucy, but I'm going to do it anyway, because – well, because I think I should, and because I've known you all your life, and what's more I know your – I know Matt too. Not so well, maybe, but we often pass the time of day both working at Whiting's, and I like him, and so – that's why.' He turned his melancholy blue eyes on her and waggled his jowls in another attempt at a smile. 'Don't look so worried. I dare say it doesn't amount to much really, but – I suppose you know a young chap called Luther Benson?'

'He's a friend of Matt's.'

'Well, that's just it, you see. I don't think he is,' Mr Birdsall said in his considering way. 'Not a true friend to him, I mean. For one thing . . . You see, I don't know how to go on. I may be telling you old news, even leaving aside the fact that I'm being interfering.'

'I know he's been poaching with Luther Benson,' Lucy said. 'And I wish he wouldn't – but I can't stop him.'

Mr Birdsall nodded. 'I wish he wouldn't too. Oh, I know these young chaps do it, but from what I hear it's becoming a bit too much of a habit.' He frowned and snapped a spill in two. 'There was me calling Nance Smallbones for being a gossip, and here I am doing the same. But I get to hear a lot of things and usually I can sort the true from the nonsense. And I'm pretty sure that Matt's sailing a deal too close to the wind with this chap. Benson's been in trouble with the law before, it seems, and for more than poaching. Now he's a clever fellow, that's the trouble. I wouldn't put it past him to try and get Matt involved in something more serious than poaching . . .'

'Why? Has he?' Lucy cried. 'Mr Birdsall, what do you know?'

'That's just it, Lucy. I *don't* know,' Mr Birdsall said unhappily. 'That's what made me hesitate about saying all this to you. It's bad enough interfering, but interfering on the basis of nothing more than hearsay . . . All I know is that Matt's been very thick with Benson lately, and one or two of his shopmates have noticed, and are a mite worried about it. One of them said to me, "That Luther Benson's got such sticky fingers it's a wonder he can get them out of his pockets." Now I know Matt's no fool. But neither's Luther Benson, that's the trouble with him. Once get involved with a character like that . . . well, mud sticks. That's all I've got to say – and now I've said it, it seems like a deal of hot air. I just wanted to warn you, and then you could find out the truth of it however you think best, but I see it's not that easy. I'm sorry, Lucy – I've been chewing over whether to say anything these past three days, and now—'

'No – no, it's all right, Mr Birdsall,' Lucy said. She did not know what to think. All he had said tallied exactly with her own mistrust of Luther Benson, and she was glad to have that mistrust reinforced; but what she could not believe was that Matt could be involved in anything – anything at all – which he would not tell her about. He had never made any secret of the poaching.

'You're not . . . offended, Lucy?' Mr Birdsall said. 'It's all right – if you are, I won't be, if you see what I mean.'

'No, no, not at all,' said she. It was not that which was making her hurry out, but the urgent need to be alone, to think it through – and, after that, the still more urgent need to speak to Matt.

If only those we love could like each other, and not divide our hearts! Lucy tried to raise with Matt the question of her mistrust of Luther Benson, and its being echoed by Mr Birdsall; and found that mistrust echoed in turn by Matt, this time with Mr Birdsall as its object.

'Why, whatever meks old Birdsall think he can go poking and prying into my business?' Matt said. 'What have I ever done to him?'

'It's not like that,' Lucy said, showing that remarkable forbearance that women through the ages have shown to men getting on high horses. 'He likes you, and he's always been like a sort of godfather to me – and so he's sort of watching out for us, that's all.'

'Is he?' Matt looked sceptical. 'Or is he watching out for you?'

'I *think* I know what you mean,' said Lucy. 'And I don't like it.'

'Oh! I wouldn't blame him if he was,' Matt said. 'How could I? He'd only be feeling what I feel. It's when he pretends just to be doing this out of the goodness of his heart that I get a bit suspicious . . . Mebbe I'm being unfair.'

'Yes, you are.' That Mr Birdsall might be less than impartial in his attitude towards her came as a new and disquieting idea; but loyalty to him was her prime concern. 'Matt, he en't a gossip. He wouldn't say it unless—'

'Unless he'd heard some daft rumour, and thought to stir things up between you and me with it. That's just what urges me to death about this town! Fingers forever pointing at you, everybody trying to bring you into line. You can't breathe, can't move.'

'There's no truth in these rumours, then? Oh, Matt, I know about the poaching, and I've never pretended to like it, because of the risks . . . But you wouldn't let Luther get you mixed up in anything else, would you? Just out of friendship?'

'Lucy, you've heard of giving a dog a bad name, en't you?

Because that's what's happening with Luther. Mebbe he en't perfect nor nowhere near it; but he en't going to get no better while nobody's willing to give him the benefit of the doubt. And as for the poaching... You know how much game fetches?'

'I know you can get chucked in goal for selling it!'

'But Lucy, don't you see – I got to tek every chance I can get. How else are we ever going to get to that house on the hill? And as for Mr Birdsall – well, I'm sorry for what I said about him.'

But he resented and mistrusted Mr Birdsall's interference; it was written all over him; and there was division between them on the subject, real division too deep for a quarrel. Trust is pure and absolute; one grain of suspicion taints the whole. Lucy saw that the mere mention of Luther Benson on her side, and Mr Birdsall on his, would always be accompanied by a certain doubt and unease.

'We must just love one another.' She repeated this phrase like an incantation, when she was apart from him. 'Then it will be all right.' Perhaps a certain confusion was revealed, in this dual image of love as something all-powerful and yet needing to be continually buttressed and safeguarded, but she did not see it. Nor did she guess how soon events would overtake them, and prove her incantation to be only so many empty words.

XVII

She was hurrying back to the factory after her dinner one day when she was surprised to see Mr Birdsall waiting at the gates for her.

'Thank goodness I caught you, Lucy,' he said. 'I must be quick, I've got to get back to Whiting's. Bit of bad news from there, I'm afraid . . .'

'Matt,' Lucy said. 'There's been an accident—'

'No, no. Nothing like that. But he's in trouble, Lucy. Him and that Luther Benson. Silly, daft boy, why did he do it? Thieving, Lucy. Or it looks that way. Somebody's been creaming off bits and bobs of warehouse stock from Whiting's – the odd box of eyelets or sprigs, odd rolls of hessian, pieces of kid. And Benson's been keeping the same stuff in an old barge-house down by the river and selling it off. It looks as if it's Matt who's been taking the stuff.'

'Not Matt,' Lucy said. 'No, not Matt.' So said her lips, at any rate; she was not sure what her mind was thinking. As often happens at such times of crisis, her surroundings were imprinted in weird detail upon her eyes, so that every bar on the gates, every iridescent colour on the breast of the pigeon fluttering down to the yard would remain with her as an emblem of this moment.

'Just what I said,' Mr Birdsall said hastily. 'But I'm afraid it looks bad for him. I think they've been watching him for a while. Now look here, Lucy. They've still got him up on the carpet at Whiting's now, and I must get back there. I'm doing my best to pin as much of it on Luther Benson as possible – they've not tracked him down yet, it's my belief he's done a bunk. I've known old Josh Whiting for twenty-five years, and I reckon he trusts me and will listen to me. So maybe I can – well – persuade them not to be too hard on Matt.'

'Too hard? What do you mean, Mr Birdsall . . .?'

'I mean maybe they'll just throw him out on his ear, and not go to the police.' Mr Birdsall was solemn. 'I'm afraid that's as much as we can hope, Lucy.'

Lucy swallowed and nodded, trying to shut out new grim visions of the future; trying to shut out too the bright visions that they had had, and which now seemed swallowed up in the night.

'I must go now,' Mr Birdsall said. 'When you finish work, come to my house. With luck, you'll not be the only one there.'

'Oh, Mr Birdsall, thank you – can you . . .?'

'If he's free. I'll bring him to my house. If he's free . . .'

Lucy's afternoon at work passed in a daze of conjecture. What was happening now, at Whiting's? What was going to happen? Her mind was one beating mass of questions, and only occasionally was it shot through with an identifiable emotion. Anxiety was one such; but there was another, a lurid streak like a splash of blood. It was outrage; wild, furious outrage at what Matt had done.

When the factory-whistle blew at last, her legs were trembling so much that she thought they would never get her to Mr Birdsall's door. But they did, slowly; and Mr Birdsall was waiting for her on the step.

'He's here,' he said. 'All sorted. I think we got it all sorted.'

Lucy followed him inside.

Matt was in the parlour. He was still wearing his finisher's apron. He was standing, as if too proud to sit – standing in almost exactly the way he had stood in the crypt at Cleatham, head forward, braced and defiant against a bitter knowledge. His eyes kindled when he saw Lucy, but somehow the effect of this was remote, as if they were facing each other across a wide and unbridged gulf.

'Oh, Matt,' she said softly.

'Well, well,' said Mr Birdsall, who had disappeared for a moment into the kitchen, 'put the door on the latch, will you, when you go?'

Lucy blinked at him. 'Where are you going?'

With the faintest of smiles, Mr Birdsall lifted the fishing-rod he held. 'Down to the King's Meadow,' he said. 'Never fancied a spot of fishing so much in my life.'

He left them: Lucy was still too stunned to be thankful. She groped blindly to a chair and leaned her hands upon the back of it.

'What happened?' she said.

'I got the sack.' His tone was colourless.

'Nothing – nothing more?'

'It's enough, en't it?' he said sharply; and something seemed to give a gasp of death in the little room. It was not love, but it was surely understanding.

'Oh, Matt,' she said, 'I've been thinking – imagining all sorts of things . . . You going off to the police court . . .'

'It was a near thing,' he said. 'It was a damn near thing . . . Mr Birdsall spoke up for me. I don't know what he said, but it seemed to tip the balance. They said they wouldn't prosecute, and I was to count myself very lucky . . . Not that it meks much odds, now.'

'What?'

'Well, I'm finished, en't I?' With a sudden clawing movement he snatched off his blackened apron and threw it on the floor. 'I'm beaten. This bloody town's beaten me. What chance have I got now? I might just as well be in jug. Nobody's going to give me a job after this. Not in Cottesbridge. Probably not in the whole damn valley. So I'm finished.'

You should have thought of that before you started stealing. Lucy did not say the words, but it was enough that she thought them. She tried to grasp a last trailing thread of calm. 'What about Luther?' she said.

'Oh . . .' Matt sighed. 'Should have known he wouldn't be around when things got hot. He must have got wind of them being on to us, somehow. Whiting's tried to chase him up today, and it turned out he'd slipped away, 'ithout even a word to his stepmother. No one's got any idea where he's gone. I suppose I should have expected it: he never pretended to be anybody's hero.'

Lucy looked down at her hands. 'This afternoon – I was even hoping – hoping it might be a mistake, that it would turn out that you . . .'

'That I didn't do it?' He shook his head. 'No, it's true enough. Whatever else you think of me now, I wouldn't lie to you, Lucy.'

'You *have* lied to me, Matt!' she cried. The spasms of purest, deadliest hate we ever feel are for those with whom we are in love; and she felt such now. 'You hid all this from me! That's lying just the same. All this time . . . How long was it going on?'

'Not long,' he said. 'Lucy, it wasn't a matter of hiding it

145

from you. I knew how you felt about the poaching, the risks and all—'

'You knew, but you still did it, and you still did this mad thing,' she said passionately. 'You went ahead, and chucked everything in the dust, all our chance of a future together . . .' She could not go on: the image of her father rose up before her. Matt had seemed everything that her father was not; but here was this same wilful destruction of what was already precarious. For she knew that Matt did not exaggerate when he said that he was finished in Cottesbridge. The boot-manufacturers were a close-knit breed; even without prosecution, Matt would be known amongst them for a thief.

'You really don't understand, do you?' Matt said. He was white and still, but not cold; he spoke with the gutteral intensity of molten heat. 'You really don't understand, and I've got to spell it out for you, seem'ly. What anyone with real love in their heart would see straight off. Why I did it.'

She was breathing as hard as if she had been running. 'Tell me, then,' she said.

He uttered a half laugh, shaking his head, and his voice was cracked as he said, 'For you. *For you*, for God's sake. En't that obvious? You think I'd run that sort of risk just for the fun of it? Yes, everything was at stake when I agreed to do it, when Luther talked me into it. I don't deny that. But I had everything to win as well. You. Us. A chance of having some sort of life together, now while we're young, 'stead of waiting while we've got one tooth between us and have to crawl to the workhouse on sticks. Look at my stinking little hole of a room! Look at that house of yourn, all stacked to the rafters with folk. Look at what I earn. Not much hope there, is they? And then Luther comes up with an idea to mek some money at last, to break out of the circle, get off the bloody treadmill. Why, I'd have been a fool not to tek the risk!'

If he thought he was convincing her – and there was no doubting he believed what he said – then he was sadly mistaken. The monstrousness of it seemed to grow upon her as he spoke. *Everything* – he had rashly endangered everything, without so much as a word to her. Was *that* valuing her, cherishing her? It did not seem so to her: far from it.

'You know you're lucky not to be in court,' she breathed. 'You've only Mr Birdsall to thank . . . and after those things you said about him! Oh, you should be ashamed!'

146

'I might have known you'd tek his part,' Matt said. It was the sort of empty remark that is thrown back at such times, as a child will toss a stone, but that is likely to do quite as much damage as blows deliberately aimed.

'We're in his house,' Lucy said, trembling.

'Aye! Always in somebody else's house! Always mekking do, always mekking the best of it, tucked away in corners and meant to be thankful for the mouldy ole crusts of life we're allowed to eat! Well, that wun't do for me, Lucy, and I thought it wouldn't do for you. I thought you felt like I did. I was wrong, seem'ly.'

Hurt and anger were both within her, but tied into such a tortuous knot at her heart that she could not disentangle them. 'You reckoned I'd be flattered,' she thickly said, 'that you did this ... foolish, ridiculous thing for me. For us, so you reckon.' She shook her head. 'Well, you don't know me, then, Matt.'

'Prob'ly not. Starting to look that way. I thought you loved me. I thought so because you said so, and if you said something then I believed it. Funny doings, eh? One person in the world I thought would understand don't – or don't want to. And like I say, seems like there's something missing there. Something like love.'

There were tears in Lucy's eyes, but she did not want them: her mood was not a melting one. 'I've lived for twenty years with a man who goes and meks a noose for his own neck and then expects to be loved for it,' she said. 'And look at him! Mortaring round after odd jobs, while folk laugh behint their hands. And look where you are now. Things might have been hard for us, but they could never have been as hopeless as you've made 'em now!'

'Well,' he said, and his lips were pale, 'it don't seem as if the two of us have got much future, any road, does it? When a chap does his best for a gal, trying to mek his way so's they can be together, and all she can do is sneer, he begins to see her a bit different-like. Begins to wonder if she means summat different from him when she says the word love.'

'I think I do,' Lucy said bitterly. 'I don't think we mean the same thing at all. Not if this is supposed to be love.'

They stared at each other – such a terrible pain-filled stare as must pass between enemy soldiers who, face to face, just as they might in peacetime meet in the street, know they must kill each other.

'I thought you'd stand by me, Lucy,' Matt said at last.

'If you thought that,' she said quietly, 'why did you keep it a secret from me?'

He did not answer. He lowered his eyes, then bent and scooped up his apron where he had dropped it. 'Well,' he said, 'don't reckon I'll be needing this any more.'

'What are you going to do?'

His eyes lit with the old stubborn fire. 'Something,' he said. 'I'll find something. And if it's not in Cottesbridge, then good riddance to Cottesbridge. There's nothing to keep me here – is there?'

It was her turn to be unable to look at him. 'That's for you to say,' she said.

'I think we've both answered that question,' he said. He hacked out a harsh breath, as if all the disgust and bitterness of the moment had infected the very air of the little parlour, and walked past her to the door. Their sleeves brushed together: it was the last contact between them. Lucy did not turn to watch him go.

XVIII

A letter came for Lucy a week later.

Lucy
    I'm leaving Cottesbridge. I know a chap whos takeing the shilling and I am going to as well. I'm finished here and like I said good riddance to the place. You get to go to places in the army, maybe it will be South Africa what with these Boers and all or maybe somewere else I don't know but it will be a new start. I dont know why I'm writeing this to you but I thought I should tell you any road. Good luck

Matt

XIX

Disaster which comes out of the blue is really no worse than the disaster which one sees in retrospect to have been inevitable. And so Lucy came to see the collapse of her romance with Matt. The very feverishness of it now seemed to have been building, not to a happy consummation, but to a painful death.

Such a perception seems to suggest resignation, acceptance of the end. It was not so. Lucy was silent, but within she keened and howled.

The idealism, the refusal to settle for second best which had brought them together was the reason why that parting in Mr Birdsall's parlour was so final. The poisonous fog of bitterness was too thick for any gestures of reconciliation. Indeed, it scarcely occurred to Lucy that the attempt would be worthwhile – knowing Matt, and knowing herself. Something had been lost, and no amount of talking could recover it. Each felt the other had failed them, crucially: neither could accept a love so compromised.

And yet the tragedy was that so much love remained – locked up, powerless, but abundant. She knew it was so when she received Matt's letter; she knew it was so from her own reaction to it, which was a shock so powerful that for most of the day she was numb. Yet when she came to terms with the news, she saw that too as almost inevitable, knowing Matt as she did. His chances of making a living in the shoe-making trade of the valley were wrecked, and so he was making the cleanest of clean breaks: she would have expected nothing less of his impetuous and absolute character. There were many new recruits to the army with the South African war, and for a man in trouble at home it was not an unnatural choice, especially a man so little inclined to sit on his hands as Matt Doughty. No, she was shocked because she deeply loved him still and he was disappearing from her world, possibly into danger; but the love she still bore him was a disabled love that could not stand on its feet. Perhaps in the end it would sicken and die: it showed no sign of doing so yet, and was a burden to her.

What was she to do? Go on, of course. The iron fetters of necessity that had bound her since childhood did not fall magically away just because the romance that had transformed her life was over. If anything they were tightening all the time, as her father's hunt for work proved fruitless and winter drew on. She must carry this great weight of anguished feeling at the same time as she carried the struggling household along, working in the closing-shop and working in the home that her father, prowling in irksome inactivity, was making more intolerable than ever.

What was she to do? Remember, and reflect on what might have been if things had turned out differently . . . But such reflections, luckily perhaps for her state of mind, did not lead far. The more she studied every aspect of their situation, the less could she discern any alternative path that they might have taken. The barriers of circumstance, that they thought love alone would give them the power blithely to leap, had proved too high. Will was not enough. It was a hard lesson for her to learn, for it negated much of what she believed in her very bones.

What was she to do? Look upon the clattering sewing-machines, the sleeves of boot-uppers with their grotesquely lolling tongues, the toiling black-aproned forms of her shopmates; look upon the heaps of washing that forever festooned her mother's kitchen, look upon the darns that formed almost the whole of her little brothers' clothes, look upon the bread and scrape slapped out for tea again; look upon all these things just as she had looked during the time of love, but with such a sadly altered consciousness that the things themselves seemed to have taken on a fiendish new life of their own, and to mock her with more and more dismal and hopeless shapes, saying, 'You needn't think that we shall be just the same as we ever were now that Matt's gone. Oh no. While you were dreaming that idle dream with him, we went to the bad terribly: we got worse and worse!'

That Matt was really gone was confirmed for her by Mr Birdsall: one of his shopmates at Whiting's had gone with him to the recruiting station, and had since heard by letter that he had joined the Northamptonshires. Lucy wanted to know no more; and whenever conversation touched on the war, she turned her head away and shut out the sound.

For some time she could not bear to go out into the country: its associations were too poignant. When she finally did so, one mild Saturday afternoon in early December, it was with the idea of making herself confront once and for all the pain that might be lurking there, and conquer it; especially as it might be her last chance before the cold weather set in.

In the end, however, the rush of recollection was too much, and she could only wander the leafless lanes and the iron-hard field-paths and let the memories assault her as they would. It was a bruising experience – possibly purging too; all she knew, when she came to a favourite spot on the escarpment looking down on the valley, was that at some point in the afternoon her tears had dried, and a pensive mood, in which neither past nor future seemed to have more than a notional existence compared with the still moment, had somehow possessed her.

The view, which opened out from a tangled spinney with the dramatic suddenness of parted curtains, revealed the bowl-like aspect of the valley at its most pronounced. The sun in the winter afternoon sky was arrestingly large, and appeared like something beaten flat from dull metal; the only colour in the bare fields was the tinge of iron that reddened the soil here and there, whilst the river in the distance was the coldest of gleams between dun banks. Nearer at hand she saw a flock of starlings descending to feed on a field, and noticed the curious way they went about it. They did not settle all at once, but hung in the air in a whirring mass, and then bird by bird began to funnel downwards from the centre of the flock to the earth, the visual effect being like that of milk pouring from a jug.

It was as she was watching this that a voice hailed her, and she turned to see her father, in cap and muffler and stout boots, making his way up the path towards her. He often went tramping in the country of late: partly to look for odd jobs about the farms, partly from boredom; but was he also revisiting memories, she now wondered – memories of his free-and-easy youth?

That she was not far from the truth was borne out when he spoke, gesturing at the hard-ribbed valley laid out before them.

'Used to be our world once, Lucy. Oh, it belongs to the landowners and the farmers right enough, but we could tek it when we wanted it. Nowadays it's like there's bars round the town, and gates what they shut when you go back to it; but then it seemed to be all one. You could feel the fields calling you when you was sitting at your last in the shop behint the yard, and you knew that as soon as you'd sweated to git your pairs done, you could git out there to 'em. You felt so free, it seemed like nothing short o' steel ropes could tie you down . . .' He smiled ruefully. 'Hark at me. Like an old codger horse-facing about the good old days . . . How's yourself, then, gel? Not been out so much lately, I reckon.'

That she was no longer walking out with Matt had soon become plain to the rest of her family, and she was so little accustomed to any interest being taken in her affairs by them that she had not thought it worth mentioning. Now she coloured a little, and said confusedly, 'No, it's . . . well, the weather en't been up to much.'

Chauncey nodded, and then pointed into the distance, where the details of the scene were becoming clotted with early mist. 'See them woods there? Gret oak tree there – must have been old in Noll Crom'ell's time. When I was a bwoy-chap I used to measure myself by that tree, carving a notch where my head come up to and then my name next to it. Every year I went back to the tree, and saw how much I'd growed, till I was a man and weren't going to grow no more, and then I stopped going. Well, I went back to that old oak tree t'other week, jist for old times' sake, and stood up against the last of them notches I'd cut into the bark. And burn me, I didn't come up to it no more.' He smiled, but his voice had dropped, and his eyes were hooded and sombre. 'I'd shrunk, Lucy. How d'you count for that? They reckon we do, as we git older, and that's plain enough when you see a little shrivelled up old man all bent double . . . But I never knew I was gitting smaller. I never felt it. And I suppose it's like growing – it only goes one way; and if I go back again next year, I dare say I shall be smaller still. That's a thing to think on, en't it?'

'There's an easy answer to that, Father,' said she.

'What's that?'

'Chop down the tree.'

He laughed then, the broad booming laugh that must have rung out across these fields when he was young and did not believe he would ever be anything else. 'Be nice if we could change the past that easy,' he said. 'But it don't wukk that way.'

They walked home together, and through the shades of her own melancholy and loss there came to Lucy, fleetingly, the light of understanding, if not sympathy. For Chauncey Middleton too had found that life would not be moulded according to his will, and that that recalcitrant material tore and gouged the hands that tried to shape it.

She had learnt something else too, that afternoon. Matt was gone. Shades of him might linger about this countryside, but he was not here; he was not going to come striding up the field-path towards her. That was gone, and love was gone. This was a different world, and somehow she must find a way to live in it.

XX

It was shortly before Christmas, with the weather turning stern and bitter, that one of Dicky-bird's almost continual minor illnesses developed into something more serious.

Chauncey Middleton had found temporary work on a building site in neighbouring Lessington. It meant a long walk to work in the winter's morning, but it also meant that there was more money in the house, and they were able to pay the fees for the doctor. He diagnosed a bronchial infection such as Dicky-bird had often suffered before; but the child's condition then took a turn for the worse, and the doctor announced that he had pneumonia.

Lucy remembered the time that followed as a time of curious quietness. Partly this was because snow had begun to fall and drift, hushing the sound of horse-drawn traffic and seeming even to muffle the factory-whistles. Partly it was because even the rackety Middleton household responded to the gravity of the occasion. Benjy and Sidney were solemn as they came on tiptoe to peer into the sickroom; Mrs Middleton's flow of anecdote dried up as she sat by the bedside and feebly exhorted Dicky-bird to buck up; whilst Chauncey was terribly chastened. He was one of those boisterous men in whom illness produces something awed, cumbrous, and stricken. His own bull-like constitution had survived even the abuses he had inflicted upon it, and the rest of his children enjoyed rude health, which was just as well given the insufficiency of food and coals that came into his house. Now an almost superstitious dread stiffened him as he stood by his youngest child's bed and watched the ebbing of the strength that he himself possessed in such abundance.

'What d'you reckon?' he would say to Lucy, time and time again, when she brought down the basin for fresh water. 'What d'you reckon? Is he looking any better? Is he perking up, d'you reckon?' and always she did not know how to

155

answer. She had sat up with Dicky-bird virtually the whole time she was not at work, and he looked as if he were fading before her eyes.

Mr Birdsall came to tap softly at the door and ask after the child. 'Now have you got enough on your fires?' he said. 'Only I've got a whole sack of coals only just started, and you're more than welcome.'

'Thank you, Mr Birdsall,' Lucy said, 'you're very kind, but we're all right just now.'

'As long as you're sure. Terrible bitter weather,' he said, stamping clumps of snow off his boots. 'If only we'd have a thaw, that might help the lad.'

'Thaw, that's what you want, yerss,' said Nancy Smallbones, appearing out of the whirling flakes like some malevolent snow-spirit. 'Small chance of that, though, I'm afraid. Looks like we're set for a good 'un, don't it? Yerss. I don't like the look of they clouds building up. Sort of winters we used to have when I was a gal, you'd remember them, Mr B., being a fair age yourself. Somebody going consumptive in every second house in the row, and the ground so 'nation hard they couldn't git a spade in to bury 'em. Not that it mattered so much with the cold like it was: they weren't about to go off. Still, you never know, do you? No. He might pick up. Mind you, he always had a bit of a graveyard look about him, didn't he? Yerss. Dear dear. Tsk-tsk. Shame—' She had time for no more, for Mr Birdsall, with a last sympathetic nod to Lucy, had trotted off into the snow, and Lucy had shut the door on her; but Mrs Smallbones, not a whit put out, wriggled her hump round and almost seemed to do a little jig in the snow as she hopped back to her house, as if she were having the time of her life.

Snow continued to fall all that night, transforming Cottesbridge, making absurd pillowy places of granite yards and turning dismal chapels into fanciful wedding-cakes, and when the doctor came in the morning, there was a thick white crust on the ulster he wore. Lucy followed him up the narrow stairs with dread at her heart: Dicky had been spectrally quiet all night.

The doctor was a long time examining him. Then he lifted his grizzled eyebrows, which looked yellow against his coating of snow, and looked round at Lucy and her parents.

'I do believe we shall raise this fellow yet,' he said. 'He's over the worst.'

156

Lucy's father, standing in the doorway, stared and stared. He placed his hands against the door-jambs, as if he would push the house down, Samson-like, in the explosive wonder of relief. 'He's better...' he breathed. 'You mean – he's better!'

'He needs care yet a while,' the doctor said, with a hushing motion. 'I'll say he's better when he's on his feet and running around plaguing you. But his temperature's down and he's breathing easier, and he's past the crisis.'

It was true. Lucy passed the day at work in an agony of suspense, lest the doctor be wrong and there was a relapse; but when she ran home at dinner-time, Dicky was sleeping peacefully, and by the evening he was sitting up in bed and chattering. Chauncey could hardly sit still.

'I couldn't bear to have lost him, Lucy,' he confided, coming into the kitchen where she was making tea. 'I couldn't bear it... But it just shows, don't it? He's a Middleton. He's got that toughness there, inside, when it comes down to it. Thank God!' His smile was beatific.

Dicky's improvement, with the amazing resilience of youth, continued apace the next day; and when the doctor came in the evening he announced that he would need to make no more visits. 'You know where I am if you need me,' he said, getting ready to go, 'but I don't anticipate it. Just follow my instructions, and don't let him overtax his strength, for he'll think he's better than he is.'

Chauncey was trying to press money on the doctor over and above his fee. 'Goo on,' he said, 'tek a drink on me – tek a drink for Christmas.'

The doctor refused, saying with a slightly ironical look that he never touched it, and was gone.

Chauncey, however, could not settle. The house was not big enough to contain his expansive mood. Everything was all right; everything was splendid. He had a fine family, all complete, and he could not stop cuffing and chaffing them. And at last he went to the door and looked out at the street. There had been another snowfall earlier, tidily smoothing over the churned footprints and the brown taint of leather-dust, but none was falling now; and the whole street, sparkling in the gaslight and roofed with heavy sky, had that look of snowscapes of not being quite out-of-doors, but some enchanted environment in between.

'Well,' Chauncey said, 'if the doctor won't tek a drop of

wet for me, I reckon I'll nip out and tek one meself. Oh – '
he grinned as he saw Lucy's eyes on him – 'don't you worry,
there'll be none of that. I've learnt that lesson. A glass or
two to say thank the Lord for blessings, that's all I'm talking about.'

'Well, I'm sure there can't be no harm in that,' Mrs
Middleton said beaming. 'I'd tek one myself if I thought I
could swallow it, but I never have been able to, not even
when I was a girl at home, and they tried to put brandy to
my lips when I went off in a swound on account of coming
in and seeing the piano-tuner with his head and shoulders in
the back of the instrument, and thinking it was a burglar
looking for valuables.'

'No,' said Lucy, as her mother cast a glance towards her,
'there can't be any harm in that.' Her own relief was such
that she could not find it in her heart to be severe; and he
did seem to have learnt his lesson.

XXI

The cold weather, Chaucey found, had not kept his cronies from the pubs. There they were as of old, gathered around the bar of the Salutation, which in the low gaslight had the glitter of a palace; and there as of old was the genial beery welcome, the laughter and the tales and the jokes enfolding him and embracing him once more. He had felt a little chary of facing them since he had lost his job, for he believed in holding his head up high; but now he wondered why he had hesitated. He was Chauncey Middleton, wasn't he? – the best craft, and the best-looking man of his age in three towns; and at home he had a fine healthy family, who would grow up and be a credit to him. As for losing his job at Stokes', he brazened it out. It was a matter of pride: Radford Stokes expected him to crawl, and he wouldn't crawl for any man, let alone such a runt as that. He had done the only thing possible to a man of spirit. He was pleased to see how they understood him. 'Aye, Chauncey, you're in the right of it,' they said. 'Aye, we always thought it must have been summat like that, didn't we, shopmates?' And he made them roar with sly jokes against Radford Stokes, while he felt the drink coursing wonderfully through his veins.

And then he was making a night of it. They had moved on from the Salutation to the Clicker's Arms and then to the Locomotive, and it was in his mind to say hello to every pub in Cottesbridge and let them know Chauncey Middleton was back. Of course he had to be up early tomorrow, to be at the building site . . . but then it was only a temporary job, wasn't it? And it occurred to him now that he was worrying altogether too much about this job business. He was a good craft, he could easily find another job, especially come spring when the trade would lift up. And besides, didn't beer give you strength? His old father used to leave his last and go haymaking in the summer, and he always took half a dozen

bottles of beer into the field with him. He said you worked
better with beer. Fine days they must have been, fine times!

The night was bitterly cold, but they scarcely noticed it as
they swung from pub to pub, linking arms and singing 'Rol-
ling Round the Town'. Someone made a snowball and stuck
it in Kidney Weston's bowler hat, and he took it badly. Kidney
Weston was always one to get over his collar, but they soon
calmed him down with another drink. There must be no
fighting tonight, Chauncey thought: it was a night of
celebration.

'One more pub,' Chauncey heard his mouth saying. 'Mek
a night of it, eh?'

One or two of the fellows cried off, saying they had had
enough, and started to skulk away home. It was disappoint-
ing; but others stayed with him, and they crashed into the
Tanner's Arms, down at the end of the town by the river.
Chauncey stood drinks. He was nearly spent, but what did
it matter? The doctor was paid, and everything was all right.

The Tanner's Arms was a dreary sort of place, and presently he was suggesting they go on. But this time it seemed
no one was with him. 'We've done the town pretty well,
Chauncey,' one said; and another came back from looking
out of doors, and said it was snowing again.

'Snowing? Snow never hurt anybody! Any road, it's warmer
with the snow falling – didn't you ever notice that?' Chauncey
cried.

'Where d'you reckon to go, then, Chauncey?'

'The Letter B,' Chauncey said, banging down his empty
glass. 'The Letter B's the place. Now who's wi' me?'

The Letter B was a roomy old pub on the road between
Cottesbridge and Lessington. The landlord served strong
stuff, and wasn't particular about what hours he served it. It
was a prince of pubs, Chauncey said. But gradually it was
borne in on him that his shopmates weren't the men he
thought they were. They shook their heads and shuffled their
feet and looked out of the windows, and said they'd had
enough.

'We're for home, Chauncey. No fun tramping out all the
way to the Letter B on a night like this. Tek another drink
here, if it's another drink you want.'

'Why, I reckon you'd best stick to milk-and-water, if this
is the stuff you're made on!' Chauncey bellowed. 'When I
was a bwoy-chap, my father used to carry a spree on all the

way to Northampton! One more pub—' he felt his balance
go a bit, and smartly regained it – 'one more pub, that's
all I'm saying! Man alive, in the old days nobody looked all
sheepish and pardon-my-fan when a fellow said "One more
pub". Why, they took it as a challenge!'

'Ah, do as you like, Chauncey. I'm for home.'

Disbelieving, he followed them outside. He staggered a
little in the street, because with the snow it was difficult to
tell where the causeway ended and the road began; and when
he had righted himself he saw the others moving off down
into the town.

'Goo on, then!' he cried after them. 'Run off home to your
wives – and I hope they break a brace o' broom-handles over
your heads! I'll have your drinks for you! I've still got my
pride, my sonnies!'

His voice made soft dull echoes around the snowy town,
and when they died away he noticed how silent it was. Not
a soul to be seen: hardly even any chimney-smoke rising in
the whitening air. It was like the castle in the fairy-tale, with
everyone asleep and all life suspended.

He turned his back on it. Well, *he* was awake if no one else
was, and he was going on to one more pub. He struck out
on to the Lessington road.

The snow was falling faster now, and got in his eyes, and
soon he was walking blind; but he could not tell whether
that was the stinging of the snow or just blind drunkenness.
Because he *was* pretty drunk now, that he knew. It was always
when you drank in the fresh air that it hit you just how much
you'd had! He uttered a short laugh, and feathery crystals
got into his mouth. Never mind. He was going to have one
more. That was the golden rule – always have one more! He
tried to say it out loud, but his lips were so cold that only a
burble came out. That made him laugh too in a light-headed
way. He swung his body about to try and see where he was.
There were blackish streaks to the right that must be fence-
posts, so he supposed he was well out of the town now and
passing the ploughed fields; but all else was whiteness, silent
and harsh. In turning himself about again he lost his balance, and fell in the snow.

It was like a cushion – it didn't hurt to fall in at all. He
gave another frozen chuckle and struggled to his feet. Now
which way was he facing? His head was spinning a bit.

It must be this way – yes, there were his footprints leading back . . . Or should he, in fact, retrace them and go home? But no: it was a matter of pride, like he said. He might be shrinking, as that oak tree showed, but he was damned if he was ready for the fireside and slippers yet. One more drink. One more drink would set him up for the walk back home. It couldn't be far to the Letter B now.

The snow made squeaking, scrunching noises under his boots. The sound, and the sugary glitter that danced before his aching eyes, lulled him until he half felt he was in a trance. The trouble with this stuff was it was damned fagging to walk on – his legs felt like lead, and his breath was short. If he could pause a minute, he would feel better. Then he could go on to the next pub and that last drink.

The snow hid a rough depression in the road, and Chauncey's feet stumbled in it. With a curious, slow, weightless feeling he toppled, and landed in the thick drifted snow at the roadside. It felt like sliding into cold, downy blankets, and he found he was comfortable and did not want to get up again. A little rest, a little rest here until his head stopped spinning, and then he would be on his way. Just close his eyes against that terrible sparkling, just for a minute, and he would be all right. Just for a minute.

XXII

It was the potman from the Letter B public house, setting out for Cottesbridge on an errand early next morning, who found the body in the drifted snow by the road. Chauncey Middleton, still looking large and powerful in death, was brought back to Cottesbridge on a cart: the examining doctor pronounced that he had died of exposure. He had fallen in the snow just a hundred yards from the Letter B – which, as it happened, had closed early that evening, on the assumption that no one would turn out to it on such a night.

XXIII

Chauncey, when he was in work, had belonged to a burial-club; and so for the funeral there was, for once in the family's history, enough money.

The house in Alma Street seemed fearfully quiet without him. For some time Mrs Middleton was stunned. The husband who had been so decidedly mixed a blessing to her – and had often made her lot an even harder one than was inevitable, given her deficiencies of understanding and character – was desperately missed. A rotten prop, it seemed, was better than none at all; and she drifted about the house more vague, inconsequential and helpless than ever. The younger children had the sturdiness of youth on their side, and Jim as usual kept his own counsel; but Joanna, tender-hearted in the extreme, took it very badly and as a result Lucy had to do everything during the ensuing weeks. But it was an obligation for which she was obscurely grateful, for grinding work took the edges off her own grief, and at least partly prevented her from chewing over a feeling of guilt about her father's death. For after the many nights when she had sat up waiting for his return, that night she had gone to bed and slept blissfully through till morning – tired from nursing Dicky, relieved at his recovery, and trusting that this time surely her father would be moderate in his drinking. It was pointless and agonizing to think, 'If only . . .', but still she could not help thinking it.

Fortunately Mrs Middleton's habitual optimism, which had seldom been anything but a bane to her and her family, reasserted itself and rescued her. 'Well, my dears,' she said, gathering her children round her, Sidney and Benjy meanwhile taking the opportunity of this proximity to punch each other, 'I've still got you. You've got to count your blessings at a time like this, and buck up, else you're likely to have a face as long as a house for ever more. I remember my poor father saying that, when mother upset her bath all over the floor, on account of a mouse hiding in the towel, and the water all went through the floorboards and got into the piano. Sidney, my lamb, don't pull Benjy's nose like that. Yes, I've still got you, my dears, and you're my blessings; and though I can't hardly bear to think of my Chauncey not seeing you grow up, and be a credit to him, I shall see it, and that's what meks me feel it's worth carrying on.'

Lucy kissed her mother; and could not help thinking, as she looked at the large family gathered round her black-clad figure, 'Yes, mother, but how are they going to grow, on our money? I know it's hard to think of such things now – but how are we going to manage?'

XXIV

'Well, Mr Birdsall, it'll not be much of a Christmas in that quarter,' said Lil Fry, nodding at the Middletons' house. 'My Tom's got cousins over on the fen, name o' Langtoft, who always send us a couple of chickens this time of year, and I shall pass one of 'em on to that family; but of course, it won't help 'em in the long run.'

'A very kind thought, very kind, Mrs Fry,' said Mr Birdsall. 'But, as you say, it's the future that's the problem.'

'The future?' said Mrs Fry, who was one of those people who sound most argumentative when they are most in agreement. 'Of course it is. And shall I tell you how it'll be, Mr Birdsall? That gel will go on wearing herself to a shade, scratting about trying to support the whole issue of 'em, and end up going into a consumption. You've only got to look at her now. Broke it off with her young man an' all, so I hear. She'll go into a decline, jist you wait, and then where will they be? She wants someone to tek her out of it, that's what she wants.'

'Yes,' said Mr Birdsall, 'I dare say you're right, Mrs Fry.'

Presently he said good evening and went into his house. He had a pair of kippers ready for his tea by his frying-pan, but he thought he would wait a while and cook them later. He glanced around his little parlour. Everything was just as he liked it: a good fire going, his pipe and tobacco by his chair, the sheet-music for a new piece the town band was learning open on the music-stand, his book marked with a spill where he had left off reading.

Should he, after all, have his tea now? That was the trouble with him: he could never make up his mind.

No, he would leave it a while. He sighed and sat down with his book, turning his chair about slightly, as if he were turning his back on something.

XXV

The cold weather relented just before Christmas, only to
turn into short dank days of slush and pervasive mists that
chilled to the bone as piercingly as any frost. Neighbours had
helped the Middletons to the ingredients of a Christmas
pudding, even Nancy Smallbones coming round with a hand-
ful of raisins in the pocket of her apron, which she handed
over with a covert, smiling gesture as if she had put a curse
upon them. Lucy was stirring the pudding in the kitchen on
Saturday afternoon, while Sidney, Benjy and Dicky waited
impatiently round her skirts to be allowed to stir and make
a wish.

Her mother was next door gossiping with Mrs Corbett,
with whom she was currently at peace: their voices could be
heard intermittently through the party wall. Lucy worked the
spoon listlessly: it was difficult to muster any enthusiasm for
this task which she usually enjoyed. The events of the last
couple of months seemed to have caught up with her, leaving
her wretchedly tired and low-spirited; and the absence of
sunlight in the dark days seemed further to lower her vitality,
so that she almost felt she wanted to curl up somewhere like
some dormant grub, and be free for a while of the burden
of consciousness.

A knock sounded at the front door. 'Go see who it is,
Sidney,' Lucy said, 'and then you can have your stir and your
wish.' It momentarily occurred to her that it was strange
to hear a knock at the front door, when everyone in the
neighbourhood used the back; but she thought no more of
it, and went on with her stirring until Sidney reappeared,
bringing in his wake Mr Radford Stokes.

'Miss Middleton, I do beg your pardon if I'm intruding,'
Mr Stokes said, his hat in his hand. 'Should I call at
another time?'

Lucy, in a great flurry, said not at all; and was occupied

for some confused seconds in wiping her floury hands, taking off her apron, and trying to convey to the children by means of nudges that they were not to stare, so that she hardly had time to wonder what had brought him here.

'Sidney, go fetch a chair for Mr Stokes,' she said. 'No, wait . . . Perhaps you'd like to come into the parlour, Mr Stokes? I'm afraid Mother en't in just now . . .'

'No, please, don't let let me disturb you, especially at such a seasonal task,' Radford Stokes said. 'The pudding smells very good . . . I really came to offer my condolences to you and your family on your sad loss.'

'Oh . . . thank you.'

'I'm afraid I'm rather behind-hand, for which I have no excuses, except that I was so busy I did not hear the sad news until my sister informed me of it just the other day. And we were both agreed that – well, that the very least I owed you was a visit, particularly as I can't help but feel some indirect responsibility for what happened.'

Lucy, taking his hat and searching for a clean space to put it down, looked her puzzlement.

'Well,' Radford said, with an uncomfortable smile at the gaping face of Dicky, who seemed fascinated by his jewelled tie-pin, 'the fact is, it was in my employ that your late father lost his job; and I can't help feeling that, if he had not done so – if I had given him another chance, in short – then things might not have turned out so unhappily. The loss of a job, I know, entails loss of self-respect, and hence a man takes rather less care of himself, and – but I'm sorry, I'm afraid I'm touching a sore spot. But Georgina and I were agreed that I ought to call and put the case to you as we saw it—'

'No, really, Mr Stokes,' Lucy said. 'That's very kind of you, but I don't think you should feel like that. What happened to Father was . . . just one of those terrible things.'

'They are rather many, aren't they?' Radford said gently. 'I'm more sorry than I can say, Miss Middleton. I just could not stop thinking of that Feast Sunday when you came to my house, and wondering whether, if I had adopted a more forgiving spirit then—'

'But you did, Mr Stokes,' Lucy said. 'You did.'

'Well.' Radford patted Dicky's head. 'It's good of you to say so. I won't harp on it any longer. I just wished to convey our condolences; and my sister is anxious to know whether there is anything we can do for you in this difficult time.'

'Thank you,' Lucy said, surprised and touched, but not knowing quite what to say. 'It's very kind of you – and your sister – but we're all right, really.'

'Certainly, certainly.' Radford, perhaps having found Dicky's head rather sticky, put his hands behind his back. 'But if there is anything at all we can do for you or Mrs Middleton – will you give her my respects? – then don't hesitate to say. Especially as the festive season is upon us . . . Well. I'll leave you to your preparations. I hope the pudding is as good as it smells – I'm sure it will be.'

'We're going to stir it, and have a wish,' announced Benjy.

'Are you indeed?' Radford said. 'And what shall you wish for, I wonder?'

'A box of tin soldiers,' said Benjy, who had war fever, and nightly massacred the Boers beneath the gas-lamps in the street.

'You wun't git what you wish for if you tell it!' Sidney crowed.

'Well, you told me yourn! You said you was going to wish for a trumpet what blows!'

'Shh, shh,' said Lucy, 'you mustn't wish for daft things what you won't get.'

'Oh, I always do,' Radford Stokes said. 'That's what wishes are for.'

With some idea that she had been awkward and unwelcoming, Lucy said suddenly, 'Would you like to take a stir, Mr Stokes? For luck?'

'Yes, I will. Why not?' said Radford after a moment, smiling. He put back his white starched cuffs carefully and turned the spoon a few times about the bowl, his face gravely considering, the faces of the boys just as grave as they watched him.

'What'd you wish for?' Benjy breathed when he had done.

'If it comes true,' Radford said, 'I'll let you know. Well, Miss Middleton, I must – Aren't you going to have a turn?'

'Oh! I wished earlier,' said Lucy, smiling faintly.

'Of course.' Radford picked up his hat: Lucy saw with alarm that it had a little flour on it. 'Well, I'm sorry I missed your mother. Do ask her to accept my condolences, and please don't forget what I said.'

Lucy saw him to the door, and said goodbye; and watched him pick his way down the slushy street with his brisk, neat gait. It occurred to her that he was not really a physically small man at all, as her father had always scoffingly claimed; but he was economically made and economical in his movements, as if he chose to present as little of himself to the world as possible.

Her mother was deeply disappointed to have missed their visitor, and immediately swore renewed enmity to Mrs Corbett as the cause of it; but she decided that Radford Stokes had done no more than he should have done.

'So he should feel responsible, I reckon,' she said in an injured tone. 'Why, it was him giving poor Chauncey the sack that started it all!'

'But it was Father who give the job up, Mother,' Lucy said. 'He could have – Oh, never mind.' She felt that she was being disloyal to her father's memory, though she knew it was the truth. That was the trouble with memories, she thought: they demanded loyalty but could not give it back. The thought led on, as most thoughts did, to Matt; and as always, she wondered what he was doing now. And she wondered, too, how long she would go on doing so. Would she go on thinking of him all her life, until his image in her mind was as confused and unreal as was her mother's of her dead father?

On Christmas Eve a large hamper was delivered to the Middleton house. Inside were a box of tin soldiers, a toy bugle, a rubber ball, some sugar mice, and a smoked ham, together with a note on which was written in a neat hand, *With the compliments of the season, from Radford and Georgina Stokes.*

This was largesse such as the Middleton household had never known; and even as Mrs Middleton was exclaiming over it, Lucy found herself saying, 'But, Mother, we can't accept this.'

'Well, I don't see why not, my petal,' Mrs Middleton said, holding a sugar mouse in each hand and making them rub noses. 'After all, there's such a thing as accepting a gift gracefully – that's what my poor father used to say. And he practised what he preached as well, even when his great-aunt sent him a stuffed parakeet in a glass case what all the feathers had fallen out of on account of the goods-train jumping the points at Rugby; and he still insisted on putting it on top of the piano where everybody could see it, and it give the cat fits.'

170

'But we don't hardly know them,' Lucy said, her mouth watering at the smell of the ham in spite of herself. 'And besides – well, it's a bit like charity, en't it?' She knew, of course, that it was rather late in the day for the Middletons to be standing on their pride; but it was the idea of Radford Stokes in particular thinking of them as a 'deserving case' that she did not like – she couldn't say why.

'Oh, I don't see that, my lamb! After all, young Mr Stokes has been to see us, en't he? A sort of social call. That meks it different – not like tekking stuff off strangers. Oh, if only poor Chauncey was here! He dearly liked a mossel of ham.'

Lucy held her peace; and came to think that there was, after all, something in what her mother said. The gifts were accepted and enjoyed; but it seemed to her more than ever important that some proper acknowledgement of them should be made. After consulting with Mr Birdsall on the right way to go about it, and borrowing from him a dictionary so that she should not betray herself with bad spelling, she wrote a letter to Mr Stokes and his sister thanking them, and adding her hopes that they had had a happy Christmas. A polite note came in return, penned this time by Miss Stokes, and that seemed to close the affair; and so began the new year, and the old struggle to make ends meet.

The struggle did not get any easier. They were in arrears with the rent, and Monday, the day when the collector came round, became an occasion of dread. Mrs Middleton's managing abilities had not improved since her husband's death: she was, if anything, more unworldly and lackadaisical than ever. To make things worse, the boot-factory where Jim worked a channel-closing machine for thirteen shillings a week went on short time, further reducing the family's income. Often when Lucy sat up late at night with Joanna, trying to work out how they could manage till the end of the week, she felt close to despair; and she found herself growing irritable and snappish in her weariness, as if her patience were being drawn out like soldering-wire.

It was especially difficult at work, for Connie Pollard was full of plans for her coming marriage to Kit Lightfoot and, not being the subtlest of spirits, often forgot how differently her friend was situated.

'We're doing the front bedroom up nicely,' she said. 'Kit's ever so handy like that. That'll be like our little place, until we've saved a bit. Course, we shall rub elbows with Mother and Father a bit, that's only to be expected, and no doubt we shall fall out now and then – but that don't matter when you're in love, does it? Love gits you through a lot of things.'

'Love!' cried Lucy, unable to control herself any more. 'Love! It en't love that matters – it's money! Love don't put food on the table, love don't pay the rent-man – it's money that does that! Such a lot of bloody daft fiddle-faddle talked about love, it urges me to death!'

She had never spoken thus to Connie, who was an easily hurt girl, and whose round eyes filled with tears in a moment; and she quickly apologized, bitterly reproaching herself. The inward reproaches lasted all day, and not only because she had been rude to Connie: she could not help comparing the crabbed creed that she had so violently expressed with the devout romanticism that had possessed her just six months ago. Of course, she told herself, she had spoken in bad temper: she surely didn't believe what she had said, not in her heart.

But it was hard not to detect the lees of cynical disillusion at the bottom of her present colourless, apathetic mood. It was hard not to feel that life was a sorry business, and that those who tried to think otherwise were deluding themselves. Matt, with his vibrant aspirations that ended in petty crime, disgrace and flight, her father with his bombast and bravado ploughing to his stubborn, pointless death in the snow. And all the time the real business of life was the loaf that would not go round, the clothes that could not be patched any more, the fires that with their meagre fuel of smoking scrap-leather scarcely stopped the boys' teeth from chattering in their heads.

And then, in early February, when the winter seemed to have stiffened simply into a snowless, rainless petrifaction of the stark grey air, Dicky, who had been in abounding health since his recovery from pneumonia, fell ill again. It seemed to be a return of his bronchial trouble, but it prostrated him so completely, and his skin began suddenly to look so waxen, that Lucy was deeply alarmed. The doctor, she felt, should be summoned, but there was no money in the house to pay him; and as it was early evening, there was no chance of taking something to the pop-shop.

'The chemist,' said Mrs Middleton. 'He'll give us summat to ease the poor lad, if we tell him the symptoms, and he'll give credit if you ask him as a special favour. Make haste, Lucy, before he closes.'

Lucy needed no urging. She ran at full speed down to the High Street, the bitter air so raw upon her face that she felt as if her skin were lacerated with a hundred paper-cuts. Most of the High Street was in darkness, only the Temperance Hotel exhibiting a sickly gaslight at its frosted windows; and when she came to the chemist's she found the blinds drawn there too, and no sign of life within.

She hammered at the door for some time, but she knew it was no good. The chemist was one of the few tradesmen who did not live over the shop, and her knocks roused only the elderly woman who rented the upper rooms, and who flung up her window to cry, 'Stop all that 'nation banging, burn you! He en't here – he's gone home!' before slamming it down again.

Lucy's hands, gloveless, were already stinging with the cold, and the knocking had set up such a pain in her knuckles that she wanted to weep; and all of a sudden she was weeping. Utterly at her wits' end, weary beyond endurance, and made childlike by cold and anxiety she leaned against the doorway and gave herself over to noisy tears.

Presently she became aware that a man and a woman on the other side of the street had stopped, and were regarding her curiously. Hastily she scrubbed at her cheeks, wishing them away; but they continued their scrutiny, and then the man called with sudden recognition, 'Miss Middleton!'

It was Radford Stokes and his sister, arm in arm and warmly wrapped up. They came across to Lucy, their faces full of concern, and though she tried to recover herself, the mere fact of a sympathetic presence sent her into helpless sobs again. She was for some time so incoherent that Radford and his sister were obliged to talk over her head.

'Whatever can be the matter?' Radford was saying. 'And what can she be doing out here alone at this time?'

'Whatever it is, she's chilled to the bone,' said his sister, touching Lucy's arm. 'She'll be ill.'

At last Lucy managed to explain her errand; and Radford, inquiring after Dicky's symptoms, said that he ought to be seen by a doctor.

'We can't – we can't afford it just now, I'm afraid,' Lucy stammered, forced to make the one admission she wanted to keep secret.

173

A glance passed between Radford and his sister. 'Well,' Georgina said, 'one thing is certain, you're going to be ill yourself if you're not careful. I think you should come home with us, and get warm.'

'Yes,' Radford said, 'yes, certainly you must do that, Miss Middleton. Come, it's not far.'

'But there's Dicky, the medicine,' Lucy said.

'Don't trouble about that,' Radford said. 'We'll sort that out.'

She was in such a lowered state that she was glad to relinquish her responsibility, and simply let them take charge of her. Each giving her an arm, they guided her to their house in its tree-lined street, talking on either side of her in their almost identical muted, pleasant voices, like the cooing of two precise pigeons.

They gave her a seat in a neat parlour, where the heat from a well-laid fire made her sting and gasp again. While Radford went away, his sister plied Lucy with hot tea and little murmured questions.

'This is very kind of you,' Lucy said with difficulty. 'I – feel such a fool.'

'Oh no! Not at all. Not at all,' Georgina Stokes said, smiling timidly. She was not a young lady of the cool and officious sort, and that helped put Lucy at her ease. Nor was she very young – about twenty-eight; but her manner was that of a girl of Lucy's age or less, and a girl too who had very little experience of the world. Her face was of what Lucy's mother called the old-fashioned sort: delicate and very pale, with large, vulnerable eyes and translucent eyelids, and a grave look about her mouth, the upper lip of which projected slightly over the lower. She had Radford's air of not taking up very much room, of being physically self-effacing, but without that careful consciousness with which he seemed to invest every movement.

'I mustn't stay long,' Lucy said. 'Mother will be worried, and there's Dicky . . .'

'I believe Radford's gone to see about that,' Georgina said. 'Drink your tea.'

Lucy's eyes fell on the piano in the corner of the room, with sheet-music open on the stand, and for want of something else to say she asked, 'Is it you who plays, Miss Stokes?'

'Oh yes!' Georgina said, with a deep blush. 'At least I – I like to pretend I can, you know . . . Are you fond of music?'

'I love it,' Lucy said, 'but I'm afraid I don't really know anything about it.'

'Oh, it's the easiest thing in the world to learn about,' Georgina said with a sort of bashful excitement. 'At least, it isn't, but it's such a joy learning, I'm sure you would—'

'Well, here we are!'

Georgina was cut off by the entrance of the lady whom Lucy had seen on her previous visit to the Stokes' house, and who now came in with much the same expression of devouring interest as she had shown on the previous occasion, keeping her eyes fixed on Lucy while she adroitly negotiated a path round the heavy furniture of the parlour.

'Oh! Dinah,' said the lady, giving herself a tap on the wrist. 'This is just like you, butting in where you're not wanted. I'm a terrible old thing for that, aren't I, Georgina? I am.'

'Not at all, Dinah,' Georgina said. 'This is Miss Middleton – her little brother's ill, and Radford's going to help. This is my companion, Miss Threadgold.'

'Oh dear, I'm hopeless around illness, I am!' said Miss Threadgold, seating herself with a sinuous movement, and comfortably smiling. 'I was no good at all when Radford had the influenza, do you remember, Georgina? I just turn quite to jelly, no use to anyone.' She laughed a long, low, contented laugh, revealing small moist teeth. 'The little boy'll be all right, I'm sure. Children bounce back, don't they?'

'I'm sure he'll be all right,' Georgina said, 'though his condition does sound rather worrying.'

'No, children are strong, you know. They're stronger than adults, really,' said Dinah Threadgold, absently stroking her own white soft neck with two fingers. 'I don't care what anybody says, I'm sorry. They're stronger because they're young. Isn't that so, Miss . . . Oh! Dinah, you're terrible – you and your memory for names, honestly!'

'Middleton,' said Lucy.

'I used to know some Middletons at Oundle,' Miss Threadgold said, lazily smiling all the time. 'I don't suppose they . . . Oh! Dinah, of course they wouldn't, don't be silly. Georgina, my dear, I hope you didn't take cold out there. You did wrap up well, didn't you? Because I know what you're like.' She swivelled her smile back at Lucy. 'Some people just will not take care of themselves, will they? Radford's another one. Now you know he works too hard, Georgina, and it's not good for him. It's not my business, I know, but I speak my mind, I'm sorry, I always have, I don't care what anybody says.'

'He does work very hard,' Georgina said, 'but I think it's what he likes.'

'Oh! I don't deny that. There's no doubt about that. Even I can see that,' Miss Threadgold said, with the comfortable laugh again. 'But is it good for him? He takes so much on himself. He absolutely *burns* the midnight *oil*, you know.' She produced this phrase as if it were some felicitous and new-minted expression that she had just thought up. 'I don't pretend to have any influence, Georgina, you know that. All I do is speak my mind. When it's people I care very much about, I speak my mind, I'm afraid. That's the way I am, I'm sorry.'

'You're always very solicitous for our welfare, Dinah,' Georgina said in her subdued way, 'and we do appreciate it.'

'Oh, it's not appreciation I look for, my dear! You've got me quite wrong there,' chuckled Miss Threadgold. 'It's just the way I'm made. When I see people I'm fond of taking too much on themselves, I just speak out. I can't help it, I'm sorry.'

Radford came in just then. 'Well, Miss Middleton, how are you feeling now?'

'Much better, thank you, Mr Stokes,' Lucy said. 'And I really ought to be getting home . . .'

'Certainly, certainly, if you feel up to it. I shall accompany you.'

'No, really you needn't—'

'It's no trouble, I assure you. And as for your little brother, I've taken the liberty of sending a servant to my own physician, with a message asking him to go to your house immediately.'

Lucy did not know what to say: she could only stammer out her thanks, whilst Miss Threadgold, who had begun stroking her own rounded arm, regarded her with such an intensification of interest that Lucy seemed to feel it on her skin like the heat of the fire.

Once she and Radford Stokes were outside and on their way, Lucy tried again to thank him, but he brushed this off.

'Not at all. As I mentioned to you at Christmas, I couldn't help feeling a certain responsibility to your family, after the – unfortunate matter of your father; and I'm glad to be able to make amends in some way. My physician, Dr Munro, is

176

very good. I have the greatest faith in him.'

'As soon as we're able,' Lucy said, 'we'll pay his fees. As soon as . . .'

'If you wish it,' Radford said. 'We'll worry about that when the little boy's better.'

The doctor was already there when they got to Alma Street. Radford, at Lucy's urging, came in and waited for the diagnosis.

It was serious: Dr Munro, a thin vinegary Scot, suspected the onset of a pleurisy; but, he added, with proper care and treatment he had good hopes of the patient's recovery. He gave his detailed instructions to Lucy, as her mother was too much fluttered both by anxiety and by the unexpected intervention of Mr Stokes to do much more than nod at everything that was said and twiddle her unwinding hair; and Lucy being occupied in this, she did not see Radford take his leave. It was not until the doctor had gone, and the house had returned to something like calm, that Joanna said to Lucy, 'Mr Stokes said to say goodbye, Lucy; and he said if it was quite convenient, he'd call in again to see how Dicky's going along.'

'Well, he seems a very nice man. Though poor Chauncey, God rest him, couldn't tek to him, and no wonder the way he was treated,' Mrs Middleton said. 'But then it's no wonder little Dicky-bird softened his heart. I don't know the heart that child couldn't soften, bless his socks, and especially Mr Stokes not being a married man and having none of his own, even wi' that gret big house . . . What's it like in there, Lucy? I can't help but wonder.'

'Oh . . .' Lucy was exhausted, in mind as in body, and could not think for a moment what to say. 'Well . . . there's a piano.'

'I knew it!' said Mrs Middleton, and looked happier than she had for months.

XXVI

Dicky's recovery was slow and halting. His was a vulnerable constitution, Dr Munro said: in favourable conditions he would be well enough, but cold, inadequate food, and winter infections would always strike hard at him.

Radford Stokes called regularly to inquire after Dicky's progress. While her mother continued to regard his intervention as no more than Chauncey's memory demanded, Lucy's gratitude to him was deep, and she still wished to pay back the money that Dr Munro's fees were costing. Yet they were so poor that she could see no way of doing so in the near future – except one. She still had the jet brooch that Matt had given her, wrapped in tissue paper and hidden under her pillow. It was a thing she could seldom bear to look at, so painful were its associations; but even more painful was the thought of taking it to the pop-shop. Yet her sense of obligation was uncomfortable too.

It was eased, however, by her beginning to look on Radford Stokes as more of a friend than a benefactor. They had been peculiarly linked since she had first met him on the matchwood stairs of his factory, and now he timed his calls at the Middleton house to coincide with those times when Lucy was home. At first she merely gave him the latest report on Dicky's progress; gradually he began to stay longer, and to sit a while in the front room (Mrs Middleton insisted that he be accorded this honour) and talk with Lucy.

She found herself looking forward to these chats. Partly it was from a simple sense of curiosity, as his reserve began ever so slightly to diminish, and she gained glimpses of the man behind the fastidiously polite exterior. Partly it was because he represented something new in her view, outside the daily round of crushing, defeating struggle. But more than that, she liked him. He was different from the men she had known. His cool, measured voice; the scrupulous self-

178

containment of his movements; the quick, penetrating but uninquisitive look of his brown eyes; the trimmed and smooth hair and moustache and clean, well-manicured hands that appeared as evidence not of vanity but of a typical desire to make himself as unobtrusive and easy on the eye as possible; all these made his presence a sort of uninsistent pleasure, like the air of a mild September that communicates a well-being so subtle that one is scarcely aware of it, or the realization that a niggling bodily pain has finally gone. From her limited experience, Lucy associated the masculine with the mercurial, the uncontrolled, the passionate, the volatile: in her father this had been infuriating, in Matt exciting, but in both it had taken a heavy toll on her peace of mind, and left her feeling that she had had enough of bravado for a lifetime. There was none of this in Radford Stokes, and in her emotionally bruised state his bland mildness acted like a balm.

Perhaps the sympathetic interest thus sparked in her would not have been fanned to any brighter flame had not her physical circumstances continued to be so discouraging. But greyness was now so predominant in Lucy's life that the patch of colour formed by Radford Stokes took on a glowing prominence. The lengthening of the days did not seem like a herald of winter's end, but merely a prolongation into the empty evenings of its cold, featureless stare. Jim was still on short time, and Dicky was getting better only slowly; and Dr Munro's words suggested that this would not be the last time he was so laid up, given their poverty. The love that had seemed to open broad avenues of hopeful futurity to Lucy was gone, and the manner of its going had left behind a sour flavour of disillusion, and a sense of having invested a precious stock of emotion in a speculative bubble. In this lowered, disenchanted and barren mood, she found Radford Stokes stealing into her life.

That was how it began, she afterwards remembered: with stealthy, almost imperceptible shifts in their relation, with infinitesimally growing frankness in their talk, with his staying a little longer each time, with chance meetings in the street protracted rather beyond the casual greetings of acquaintances. But it still did not fully appear to her that a line had been crossed, and that a generalized benevolence had given way to a personal interest in her. Her self-esteem was low, for one thing; for another, she regarded Radford Stokes as

179

such an entirely self-possessed person that the idea of anyone making a deep impression upon him – let alone Lucy Middleton, the daughter of his late employee – seemed faintly absurd. What was more, there was nothing dramatic about the transformation, and her experience with Matt had conditioned her to a view of the feelings painted in the brightest colours, and with the boldest strokes.

Even when Radford, in the first milder days of March, diffidently asked her if she would like to walk in the Gardens with him and his sister on Sunday, she somehow did not allow herself to perceive this as anything beyond normal civility. And yet she must have known it was otherwise; for when the day came and she walked in the Gardens alone with Radford, she was not in the least surprised at his sister's absence, and nor did she believe his explanation that Georgina was a little indisposed.

It was time to think seriously about this. But she could not at first do so, simply because she was extraordinarily touched. She was touched that this man, who seemed so quietly invulnerable, had felt he had to go to these lengths, and to adopt this subterfuge, just for the privilege of walking round the Gardens with her on his arm; that he had so little confidence in his own attractions, and so humble a consciousness of hers, that he supposed she would have refused him such a simple thing. The contrast with the Kit Lightfoots of the world, with their brash go-in-and-win attitude to that mass of potential conquests which they thought of as womankind, scarcely needed remarking.

Would she, then, have refused if he had asked her straight out to walk with him in the Gardens – an unambiguous statement of intent, as the glances they received that Sunday showed? This was one of the questions to which she would have to address herself. And yet it did not seem a difficult or pressing question: her mind simply acquiesced as she posed it. To walk with Radford thus was, above all, undemanding: no heart-wringings, no cataclysmic upheavals in her emotions were caused by it and, as far she could see, none would be caused by their continuing what had been begun today to its logical end. Indeed, she felt more peaceful than she had for months. Why then refuse?

If Lucy sensed evasion in this conclusion – evasion of something terrible and crucial – she lacked the will and energy to overcome it. Radford had made his intentions plain in the subtlest, quietest of ways: it was that very subtlety and quietness, indeed, that prevented her from being more astonished at the revelation. Like darkness in a room at evening, it had come on unnoticed until it was an achieved fact. The only strong feeling she could identify in herself was gratitude at this manner of proceeding, for it required no more demonstrativeness from her.

One thing was clear without her needing to ask: this was a new experience for Radford. He said as much, with difficulty, when she asked him how the factory was prospering.

'Demand seems to be rising again,' he said. 'We have an army order – one of the more fortunate consequences of the war. I don't know how long it will take to settle it – rather longer than the newspapers claim, I fancy. The trouble with such a boom is that slump tends to follow. That seems to have been the pattern of the trade right since my father's early years. Of course we have other destabilizing factors. The absence of a fixed wage-rate, for example; that accounts for the significant variations even between the towns of this small valley . . . Forgive me. This is dry talk for Sunday afternoon. The trouble is, I – well, the trouble is, Miss Middleton, I don't know how to . . . You see, since my father died I have been wholly occupied with the works; it is not too much to say that the factory has been my life, and I have had little time or – or inclination, at least not till now, to enjoy the society of – to enjoy such society as yours.' He took out a carefully folded handkerchief and dabbed his brow: mere awkwardness and discomfort seemed to afflict him like actual pain. 'My life has been so bound up with business, that I – I don't quite know how to go on; so please bear with me if—'

'It's all right,' Lucy said gently. 'You don't have to be sorry for anything. I'm afraid I'm not very good company myself.'

'Oh, on the contrary,' Radford said in his punctilious way; and then, with more feeling, 'With you I feel more at ease than – well, as I said, I've lived a bachelor life of constant work and, except for my sister and her companion, I am not accustomed to feminine society. But with you I feel . . . I feel . . .'

'I'm glad,' she said quickly, and gave his arm a squeeze. She did this to relieve him of the discomfort that was like pain, to help him out of difficulty. She was indeed glad, and flattered; but she acted chiefly because it seemed a pity that he, normally so composed, should be put out on her account, rather as one pities a dignified animal made to do tricks. It was with something of the same idea of smoothing a passage that she said, 'And you must call me Lucy.'

The signs of spring in the Gardens were not many. A few crocuses adorned the flower-beds, fighting their way up from the hard soil for all the world as if they were things of tempered steel instead of tender growths that would break at a touch; the buds on the trees were so tentative that they suggested evanescent phenomena like dew or raindrops, rather than the beginning of a process which would culminate in great solid volumes of green. But just now Lucy, normally so responsive to such things, wanted no theatrical displays from Nature to cheat her heart with hollow foreshadowings of great hopes. The beauty of sun on leaves, the summer-scented earth, the blue-tinged prospect of meadows – these things had formed the background of her romance with Matt and, like everything connected with that experience, she mistrusted them. They had lied. Whatever was happening between herself and Radford, it seemed to Lucy right and desirable that Nature should make no eloquent commentary upon it.

Whatever was happening between herself and Radford . . . And what was that? The answer became unequivocal at the end of that Sunday, when he walked her home and asked her if she would meet him again next Sunday. They were walking out together. No need to rebel against such a constrictingly formal classification, as she and Matt had done: with Radford the courtship was the Simon-Pure Cottesbridge article, conforming to the town's ways exactly.

At least, if one disregarded the disparity between their backgrounds; and in the shoemaking towns, all new, all grown up from humble beginnings, such distinctions were not as great as they might have been elsewhere. There were rich people here, but with none of them was the money more than a couple of generations old: Radford's father, Edward Stokes, of whom he spoke often and with strong respect, had started out with a back-yard shop, and it was doubtful whether the woman he had married, who had died when Radford and Georgina were infants, had come from any higher sphere than did Lucy. The latter was, indeed, a little surprised that Radford should apparently overlook her background, simply because he was so thoroughly respectable himself. But then it was plainly true that he had never been involved with a woman before, and plainly true also that there was something in her that he genuinely responded to, that brought him some way out of his stiff, correct shell and enticed him into taking steps that, as he confessed, he had never taken before. Certainly there were any number of middle-class girls that he could have married had he chosen.

No, status presented no great obstacle – if marriage was Radford Stokes' object. And the mere fact of his so deliberately embarking on so unprecedented a course was sufficient proof that it was, even leaving aside what she knew of his extreme correctness of character. He was hardly the man for dalliance; and that was why, when he asked to see her again next week, and she agreed, Lucy had a good deal of hard thinking to do.

And Lucy did think, deeply. How could it be otherwise? The implications of what was so swiftly, so startlingly and yet so quietly happening to her filled her mind as she worked at the sewing-machine, as she put the children to bed, as she lay wakeful in bed herself. Her thoughts were like butterflies, which momentarily settled only to flutter onward again. She did not know Radford well, but then she thought she had known Matt well, and look what had happened. By walking out with Radford she was not keeping faith with Matt, but then what faith was there to keep when their affair had ended in bitterness, when Matt was gone God alone knew where, and when the memory of him was merely a burden to her? She could not with honesty claim that she loved Radford, but then she had loved Matt, and look what pain that had brought. And that was a love almost at first sight, a love like a lightning-bolt: who knew what time would bring, in this case? And besides, did she really want love? Was it not another word for destruction?

Her thoughts, indeed, took the form of questions more often than not. Her thoughts about Radford himself were no more conclusive: she found she could not fix him in her mind as anything more substantial than a pleasant voice, an attentive manner, a spruce and comely cleanliness; a general impression of something in her life that was not rackety, threadbare, hopeless, and oblivious of her existence. And she was in no more decisive a state when the next Sunday came, aside from realizing that she had been mildly looking forward to the day without being aware of it.

And again there was something soothing to her in his very reticence, his refraining from the romantic gesture. Again they picked their way across gentle stepping-stones of conversation, about Dicky's health, about Georgina, about the town and the valley and the coming spring; and presently, again, Radford was apologetic for not being more loverlike. And yet that was the very thing that she liked: any ardent avowals would have been like pressure upon a bruise.

'The trouble is,' he was saying again, 'you see, the trouble is – I must be frank with you, Lucy; I really must ask you whether I . . . Well, as I told you, I have got into the habit of regarding myself as a perennial bachelor, and so I am rather unsure of the proper way to proceed – and so I must ask you whether I am leading you in a direction you do not care to go, and which you are too polite to protest about.'

'No, Radford,' she said. 'You're not.'

It was said, before she had time to wonder why she had said it. And again she saw that she had spoken out of a simple wish to help him out of his halting confusion, to show him the tactful consideration that he had shown her.

Their next stepping-stone was more momentous: in the lee of a birch tree he kissed her for the first time. Yet somehow it did not seem momentous to her. The kiss was like an unurgent development of his general attentiveness, rather than a crossing of boundaries. As he kissed her he held her hands in his as lightly and formally as if they were about to dance in a ballroom.

'I must confess something,' he said, trembling slightly. 'Last week . . . when I said that Georgina couldn't come because she was unwell . . . I'm afraid I wasn't telling the truth. She was quite well. I just . . .'

'I know,' Lucy said smiling, touched again. 'I knew then.'

'Did you?' Radford seemed quite startled. 'Good heavens . . . Well, I must apologize. For misleading you in that way, I mean. It seems rather underhand and I haven't been quite easy in my mind about it.'

She smiled again, and was about to say that all was fair in love and war; but something held her back.

So it had begun: so it continued. And yet she still had no real sense of something moving onward to an inevitable conclusion, even as she found herself agreeing to go to tea at his house next week. It was all very well to keep telling herself that she must think seriously, but the serious business of life, as it had long been, was survival. And in the event, it was the intolerable pressure of poverty which confronted her with the question that the gentle progress of her relation with Radford, so unexacting and dreamlike, had failed to pose.

The larder being more than usually bare when Lucy got home after work one day, she sallied out again in search of something affordable for their teas, Benjy going with her. A bakehouse sold her a stale loaf – the baker's cart omitted the Middleton household from its rounds now, so infrequent was their payment – and from a greengrocer who was just shutting up shop she bought some odds and ends of dilapidated vegetables that would make a meatless stew. That was the money gone; and she was just about to turn for home when she saw that Benjy had wandered away a little and was staring in at the window of a confectioner's.

She watched him, and her heart ached. It was not that he clamoured for the sweet things in the window, the sugar sticks and butterscotch and liquorice – far from it: he simply regarded them with a dull, hopeless fascination, as a prisoner might look out of the window of a cell he knows he will never leave. Such utter resignation in one so young, even over so trivial a matter, struck Lucy as a terrible thing; and she hastily hugged the boy, and said she would race him home.

They had run themselves out of breath, and were just turning into Alma Street, when a figure darted out from the alley behind the row and stopped them.

'Now then, gel – I don't like having to do this, in the street and all, but there's no help for it. And don't you go telling me I ought to go see your mother – it's no good talking to her and you know it – might as well talk to the wall.'

It was the rent-collector, a little harried peppery man whose voice had become permanently raised from shouting at tenants hiding behind drawn curtains. He stood blocking their way and wagging a stubby finger in Lucy's face.

'Now you know your arrears is gitting chronic – don't pretend you don't – and I want to know what you're going to do about it. Because if you don't start paying up you'll find your furniture in the street one of these fine mornings, d'you hear? That en't me talking – that's my superiors – but it's me who's got to do the job and I'm telling you, d'you hear?'

His sudden appearance, his fierce manner, and the expression on Lucy's face – for this encounter came like the last turn of the rack of trouble on which she was stretched – had the effect of startling Benjy into terror. The little boy burst into tears, clutching at Lucy's skirts.

'You didn't have to frighten the child! What sort of man are you?' returned Lucy stormily, in her wrath unconsciously growing tall and imposing. 'It's all right, Benjy. Don't tek any notice of him.'

'Ah – but it's not all right, see,' the rent-collector said, persevering, though he appeared in some fear that Lucy might fell him with a blow. 'And somebody in your house had better tek notice. Else there'll be another sort of notice. A notice to quit, see?'

Lucy opened her empty purse and brandished it in his face. 'There,' she cried, 'tek what you want, because that's all there is.'

'Never mind that. I shall be round Monday – Monday morning – so you'd better look sharp.'

'Oh, go and boil your head!' Lucy called after his hurriedly departing figure.

But only she knew that this was mere bluster: only she knew how completely at an end her resources were. She went indoors, and began to clean and chop the vegetables, giving half an ear meanwhile to her mother's complaints about Mrs Corbett's latest transgressions; but in her mind she had come to a black and empty place, with nowhere to go but down, just as when she had stood in frozen panic above the abandoned quarry on Feast Saturday.

But one neat prosaic figure appeared to her out of this blackness, offering a white manicured hand to pull her to safety; and so she found that the question she had been evading had been answered for her.

XXVII

The garden behind Radford Stokes' house was large, with a long, sloping, well-rolled lawn leading down to an iron pergola and a pond, and beyond that the river. Here Radford and Lucy walked after tea that Sunday.

It had not been a comfortable meal, but then Lucy had not expected it to be so. Radford's social manners were more polite than easy; Georgina Stokes seemed to wish to be kind, but something of the same muffling and enwrapment of gentility that gave her at twenty-eight the look of a fragile girl afflicted her conversation; whilst her companion Miss Threadgold was only too happy to fill the gaps with indolently smiling inquisitiveness, and drawling remarks that seemed expressly designed to exclude Lucy altogether.

But then Lucy knew that this was to some extent foreign territory to her: she had taken that into account in making her decision, and accepted it. And when Radford, after talking at length about the garden and the flowers that there would be in summer and the liability of the lower parts to flooding and the heron that sometimes came up from the river to raid the pond – when he had exhausted all these things, and with a characteristic little sharp clearing of the throat began to talk of marriage, Lucy had her answer ready.

For she had come to a conclusion which her heart had always resisted – that there was no escape after all. The green land beyond the roofs was not to be reached. She and Matt had failed to reach it, together or apart. There was no escape, except the sort that they had despised – the sort of escape that marriage to Radford Stokes offered. Her ill-tempered words to Connie came back to her. At the time she had not wanted to believe that this was what she really thought, but the sheer pressure of events had proved that ruthless creed true.

But then, after all, what was so bad about it? In choosing

her, Radford was acting from his own free will. It was flattering that he should decide she was the one for whom he would forsake his bachelorhood: whatever he had found in her to lead him to such a decision she couldn't think; but so it was, why quibble about it? She would be making him happy, and as for herself . . . Well, she was almost sure that what she felt for him was not love, but then love was a god that had played her false, and she would worship at its shrine no more. She liked and respected Radford, and she had already decided that she would keep her side of the bargain by being a good wife to him, and schooling herself to fit in with the new world that she would enter. If that was not a reasonable basis for a marriage, what was?

And while she went again over these thoughts, forged in the flat despair of the past week when the position at home had become purely intolerable, Radford pieced out his proposal, going carefully over it point by point as if he were reviewing a business proposition.

'Lucy – this may seem terribly premature; but I'm afraid I'm not experienced in these matters, and so I must simply plunge ahead . . . Besides, I have felt for some time – indeed, ever since I saw you coping so admirably with the unfortunate circumstances at home, I have felt a warm interest in you . . .'

There was the crux of the matter: the unfortunate circumstances at home. A simple escape from those, such as she might have achieved by throwing herself in the river, would have been no escape at all. It was the never-ending anxiety for the welfare of her unwieldy family that she was desperate to be relieved of; and marriage to Radford Stokes would do that. She would be the wife of a well-off manufacturer: the money at her disposal, not to mention what she knew would be Radford's punctilious concern for his new in-laws, would mean security, at a stroke, for ever, for the household in Alma Street. The children, even Dicky, would stand a good chance of growing up into healthy adults. Marriage to Radford would, in fact, solve everything. It was such a simple thing to do – and it would bring all the trouble to an end!

'. . . I believe there is nothing in my circumstances, personal and material, that is not known to you, Lucy. I am thirty years old: this house, and the factory, are entirely my property; I have no family beyond Georgina, whom you know. So, those are the facts of the case. But if there is anything else you would like to ask of me before I go on to

– to the question I have it in mind to ask . . .'

She let her glance fall on the house with its red brick and its conservatory and its little turret-like excrescences. It was not the house on the hill that she and Matt had dreamed about, it was altogether too solid and respectable for that; but only a fool, she thought, would turn down an opportunity to live in it.

And what would Matt have said? That she was selling herself, selling herself to comfort and convention, in just the way they had always despised? But it didn't matter what Matt would have said. Matt was gone, and everything associated with him was gone. Those lofty, rarefied, too-holy ideals that they had nurtured between them had died with a cache of pilfered warehouse stock, with a bitter clash of words dwindling into a bitter silence in Mr Birdsall's parlour, with the funeral of a man who believed that his vain self-will could overcome the elements, with doctor's bills and meals of rotten vegetables and a rent-collector dogging her heels like a bowler-hatted Fury. Farewell to them, then: the narrow tenets of comfort and convention could surely do no worse.

Radford had taken her hand in his. She noticed, in the thin sunshine, how very clear his skin was, and how scrupulously clean-shaven: even the dots where the beard would come were barely visible. But on his smooth brow there was a faint sheen of perspiration. This evidence of nervousness moved her more than anything he had said, but he suddenly put up his handkerchief to dab at it, frowning, as if he resented his body thus betraying him.

'Lucy,' he resumed, 'it must be clear to you that I want to ask you whether – whether you will consider becoming my wife.'

Everything solved, at a stroke! She kept that thought before her as she answered. She kept hold of that thought, because it helped to quell the curious feeling that came over her – a feeling as if she were strangling something with her bare hands.

'Yes, Radford,' she said. 'I will.'

Part the Second

The Blind Fiddler

I

They were married in August, just after the Feast.

At the wedding, which took place in Cottesbridge church, the disparity between the backgrounds of bride and groom was made public for the first and last time. On one side of the church were Georgina Stokes, Miss Threadgold, and one or two connections of the Stokes family: Radford did not seem to have many friends. On the other side were Lucy's large family and friends and neighbours, all looking about them with the disdainful unease of chapel-goers. This would be the only occasion on which the two worlds would have to meet – except, of course, in the persons of Radford and Lucy. Soon she would begin a new life quite separate from her old one. And besides, Radford's influence had already made itself felt amongst the Middletons. The house-rent, which to them had posed such intractable problems, was made up out of Radford's pocket with supreme ease. He had helped Jim to a better job, and was looking to do the same for Joanna. Dicky, under the regular supervision of Radford's physician Dr Munro, was in better health than he had ever been in his life. Like Lucy, they all had new clothes. It was astonishing to them, and quite unremarkable to Radford. The power of money to solve life's problems had always been known to him, and he took it for granted.

' "First it was ordained for the procreation of children . . . Secondly, it was ordained for a remedy against sin . . ." '

The solemnity of the marriage service was something Lucy had not reckoned with, and it took her by surprise. Or rather, her own reaction to it took her by surprise. She had become accustomed to coolly regarding the pronouncements of organized religion as so many lofty abstractions; more than that, the whole of her courtship with Radford had been pitched in so low a key that these serious ideas seemed like a cannon-shot introduced into a minuet.

And yet, momentarily awed as she was, somehow her emotions remained essentially untouched. It was simply difficult for her to feel with conviction that this was Lucy Middleton standing at this altar. For Lucy, body and spirit had always been one; now she was aware of the beginning of a dissociation between the two. Where once her mental life and what she experienced through her senses had been inseparable, now her mind seemed to stand at a distance from what was happening to her, until she could almost fancy it hovering about the roof-bosses of the church, looking dispassionately down upon her body having the ring placed upon its finger.

And yet everything about this occasion – not least the man she was marrying – was so resoundingly normal and prosaic that she supposed that what she was feeling, or failing to feel, was normal too; and that until now her inner life must have been abnormal in its intensity, like an overwound watch or a rapid heartbeat. This mild absent inexcitation was, instead, how it should be. This was how it should be, because other people seemed to think so; and though formerly that argument would have been the very last in the world to have convinced her, it did so now simply because the alternative – the passionate individualism that scorned second-best – was all entangled with painful memories of Matt. And she had consciously decided to leave all that behind her as she embarked on her new selfhood, to cut adrift that wrack of dreams and betrayal and let it float away to oblivion.

There was an open carriage to take them back to the house in Lessington Road after the service, but the reception was not a large affair. Radford liked things quiet, and Georgina was shy in company, becoming pink and breathless and having to rely on Dinah Threadgold to rescue her from embarrassment with her serenely drawling platitudes. A maid circulated with sherry, and there were toasts. The house, Lucy noticed for the first time, seemed full of the slow ticking of clocks; and there was one in particular that had something dragging and yeasty about its tick, very like the voice of someone who needs to clear their throat, and which she found she could not stop listening to. The clocks were audible because something of the sedate and muffled atmosphere infected the wedding party. They talked in low voices: unison silences fell occasionally upon them, and a cough or the clink of a glass seemed to rend the heavy air like a shout.

For Lucy the occasion was exactly like a dream – all the separate elements of one's life randomly thrown together in unlikely proximity. Her mother making timid sorties into anecdote, and hurrying out again when anyone seemed to listen to her; Connie Pollard, soon to be married herself, gazing fixedly at Lucy as if she longed to catch her eye, and blushing like a blown coal whenever she did; Mr Birdsall, looking oddly worn and troubled beneath his avuncular good humour; Radford, very sleek and dapper in his wedding clothes, with his unvarying air of polite interest in whomever he spoke with, well-groomed head slightly on one side as he listened. All gathered together, with the great masses of flowers and the dress she wore, rustling and shifting like some live thing, to add the crowning touch of unreality. She would not have been in the least surprised if some spectacular dream-twist – a bull crashing through the window, or the Queen arriving on a bicycle – had rounded off the reception.

But no such strangeness happened, and presently she was going upstairs and, attended by a maid, changing into her going-away costume; though that was strange enough, for the room in which she undressed, and which bore no more impress of her personality than a hotel bedchamber, was to be hers, just as this whole solemn clock-ticking house was to be her home. And yet even this thought did not do much more than skim her consciousness, perhaps because everything seemed to be out of her hands. The momentum that had so stealthily begun the day Radford had called to find her stirring the Christmas pudding – or perhaps even earlier than that – was now at its peak, and she needed to do nothing but let herself be carried along by it. Even the act of coming upstairs to put on her going-away costume, a tailor-made affair with gigot sleeves and a gored skirt chosen and bought for her by Radford, had scarcely involved any decision on her part. A smooth timetable simply seemed to establish itself around Radford and everyone connected with him.

And so they were presently being driven in the gig to the station, under a hot August sun that threw such precise shadows that the feather in her hat was reproduced in silhouette on the baking road right down to the slightest filament. Georgina had been tearful in her farewells.

'We haven't often been apart since my father's death, and she is not of a robust disposition,' Radford said. 'Fortunately she has Dinah, and will not be alone.' He looked unruffled in the heat, and rather handsome. Lucy found herself laying her hand upon his, but the gloves they both wore made of the act something empty and formal.

They took the train to Shipden, on the north Norfolk coast, an old fishing town that had become quite an exclusive resort. The duration of the rail journey was the longest time that she and Radford had spent alone together. She said something of this to him.

'So it is. So it is,' said he. 'I hadn't thought of that.'

'Oh, look how forward the harvest is here! It must be because we're going through the fens – they've barely started on the wheat at home,' she said. This sudden change of subject was due to a memory that had surfaced in her – a memory of Matt, and how they would have relished such a time on their own, and how they would have used it. She had schooled herself, these past months, to banish all such memories, but now she saw that she must be vigilant against their return. Matt had once said they couldn't reach inside your head (there – there was another memory!) and touch what was in your mind; but even so, she felt that she owed it to Radford not to harbour such thoughts, even though he would never know about them. That was surely part of the contract. For while she could not pretend that her marriage to Radford was a love-match, she was determined that it should, by its own lights, be successful, complete, and not compromised by any reservations on her part. Lucy's nature was such that no other arrangement would have been tolerable to her.

So, her answer to those treacherous memories was to abruptly change the subject, and also to show the affection she felt towards him. Gloveless now, she impulsively seized his smooth pleasant hands and squeezed them, inclining her face for a kiss. For a moment he seemed startled, and it was as if his quietly observant brown eyes, widening, saw an unaccountable stranger in the young woman eagerly leaning towards him across the railway carriage; then, recovering himself, he kissed her lips, patting her hand and then drawing back and smiling, rather as if this were a simple repetition of the prescribed kiss that had concluded the marriage service.

'What about some tea?' he said. 'Or perhaps we could have some iced lemonade, if they have it. I'll go and see if the dining-car's very full, shall I?'

He was shy: again she was touched by this, and wished

somehow to convey to him that she was no more sure of herself than he. But this did not seem the place to make the attempt, and they talked of neutral matters until their arrival at Shipden.

She had never seen the sea before. The beauty of it smote her like a blow as the brake took them down into the little town from the station, the bay appearing in a great swatch of blue between the grand hotels that overlooked the promenade.

'Oh! Radford, it's so lovely,' she cried. 'And the cliffs too – I didn't realize the cliffs would be so high. And the woods – oh! Let's go down to the sea straight away, shall we?'

'I think we should unpack first, my dear, and get settled in,' he said with a slight smile.

'Oh – yes, of course. It's just that – well, it sounds silly, but I've never seen the sea. I didn't know it would be so beautiful.'

'Shipden is a fine spot,' Radford said. 'My father used to come here. It's rather busy nowadays, but still very select.'

The Hotel Metropole was vast and new, like a prodigious stuccoed chateau set down upon that shingled Anglian shore. It overshadowed the ancient flint church, by no means small, and so entirely dwarfed the few surviving fishermen's cottages that two races of widely differing stature – two species even – might more feasibly have inhabited such contrasting environments than mortals made from the same vulnerable clay. Within the hotel all was ponderous luxury – which is a different thing from comfort. Lucy felt far from easy in such surroundings, but was determined not to show it to Radford, in the same loyal spirit that made her determined to suppress the memories of the past. She had married him, and this was his world, and she must start as she meant to go on.

So she made no comment on the oppressive sumptuousness of their bedroom, with its marble-topped washstand, brocade drapes, carpet that gave like dry sand underfoot, and unnaturally high bed with a silken canopy that gave it more of the look of an altar than a place to sleep in; and presently they descended again in the hydraulic lift, attended by a boy who reminded Lucy of an organ-grinder's monkey, and who seemed to leer horribly as he accepted Radford's tip.

She felt much happier outside the hotel. 'The air tastes so different,' she said as they walked down the esplanade. 'At home, in the valley, the air seems so heavy sometimes, especially in the summer.'

'Shipden has been much recommended for convalescents, I believe,' Radford said. 'My father came here often in his last year.'

'I wish I could have known him,' Lucy said.

'Yes, it is a great pity. My dear, you must say when you're tired. I tend to forget . . .'

'Oh no,' she said quickly, 'I'm not tired at all! Let's walk on. It's so nice to hear the sea.'

It was too early for the gas-lamps, the sun quivering yet on the verge of the sea and irradiating the scene with the most delicate of coppery tints. Small crab-boats were drawn up on the beach, the fishermen amongst them looking like little shining figures of bronze in the dusk light; whilst the woods that crowned the cliffs on the left were a thick volume of darkness, all colour and form obliterated, as if inland full night were already in place. The light wind was from the sea, and the presence of that great murmurous expanse, so foreign to her valley-bred nature, filled Lucy with so haunting an excitement that she seemed to be waking at last from the long pointless dream that had been her wedding day; the blood moving in her veins again, her physicality reasserting itself.

They came upon a curio shop still open, with a trestle full of miscellaneous objects set out before the window. Lucy, whose surroundings had always been so utilitarian, was fascinated by such things. 'Oh, look, Radford, isn't that a funny little thing?' she said, holding up a jovial pottery frog. 'The way he looks all pleased with himself.'

'Good heavens,' Radford said, turning the frog over to see its base. 'Made in Germany. As if we can't make such things ourselves. Well, my dear, it will be time for dinner soon. Perhaps we should make our way back.'

The necessity of changing again for dinner made Lucy think with perplexity that well-off people seemed to spend half their lives getting in and out of clothes; but presently this thought was swallowed up in her wonder at the sight of herself in her evening frock, which she had never put on since the fitting. It was cut low in the bodice, and the expanse of bare neck and throat and arms that the dressing-room mirror showed her seemed especially startling against the weighty respectability of the hotel. A faint flush crept across Lucy's skin. A married woman, that was what she was; there would be many such, in similar gowns, in the dining-room downstairs. Yet somehow she had the curious feeling of being an imposter.

'You look charming, my dear,' Radford said when he gave
her his arm to take her down. 'Absolutely charming.' In fact,
little as she knew it, she looked a good deal more than that.
The second glances that came her way in the great palm-
filled dining-room were variously glances of tribute and envy,
rather than, as she thought, of amused perception that she
had worked for her living in a shoe-factory. The dress, with
its puffed, filmy sleeves, tight waist and flowing skirt, could
hardly have suited her more: it brought out the fullness and
opulence in her looks which the years of struggle had constrained, transfigured the slight earthiness, refined the young
gaiety. The self-consciousness that was mingled with the
pleasure of wearing the dress manifested itself as no more
than a glow about her skin and a quick, unquiet glance in
her eyes, eyes so deceptively sleepy-looking that more than
one person in the room started upon seeing their gleam
sparking out from beneath the heavy lashes.

She had never had wine before: from its appearance she
expected a bland sweetness, and she was surprised at the way
it fired and warmed her. Radford too seemed struck by the
fine figure she made, and proud: he was all kind, unobtrusive
attentiveness over dinner, making sure she had everything as
she wanted it, smoothing over her small mistakes. When the
meal was over they listened for a while to the playing of
the piano trio. Indifferently enough played, this was yet music
of a kind that Lucy had seldom encountered and loved to
hear; and after one piece she said excitedly to Radford, 'Oh,
that was a lovely one! What was it, do you know?'

'I'm not sure. I rather fancy it's Schubert. Georgina would
know. She's the great one for music.'

'I'd love to learn to play. Even just a little bit. Do you think
Georgina would teach me?'

He smiled. 'I'm sure she would be happy to. It would be
a nice occupation for you, dear, because of course, I'm afraid,
the works will take me away from you quite a lot of the time.'

'Yes,' she said. 'Never mind.' For a moment the thought
of Radford's house, of her living in it for ever as his wife,
broke in upon her, and her emotion was one almost of bewilderment, as if she had looked around and found herself
walking in a strange landscape with no idea of how she had
got there. But it was quickly succeeded by a happier feeling.
That, after all, was still in the future: it was something that
had to be negotiated. This was holiday, special and exciting
and full of new experience, and she was growing more

responsive to it by the minute; the sleepwalking sensation of the earlier part of the day was gone.

She went upstairs ahead of Radford, who remained in order to smoke a cigarette. She was glad of the opportunity to be alone for a little while, to gather her thoughts, and perhaps discover just what they were, but she soon found the opportunity more troubling than pleasing. When she was with Radford, the fact of her marriage seemed more capable of assimilation: solitude left her a prey to all sorts of uncomfortable questionings, especially in this hotel bedroom, where all the fittings met her eye with a smug, enigmatic look, as if they were in possession of secrets that she knew nothing of.

Should she undress and get into bed? For the first time that day the timetable of events seemed vague and uncertain. She sat for a while in the wicker chair, listening to the sounds of the hotel and trying to separate from them the sound of the sea; then she abruptly got up, turned down the gas until the room was in discreet half shadow, undressed and put on her nightdress, and slipped into the great bed.

She did not know how long she had lain there staring wakefully about the room before Radford came up. He seemed to think she was asleep from the way he padded about, so she spoke.

'Hello, Radford.'

'Hello, my dear,' he said after a moment, coming over to the bed. He bent and touched her hand outside the counterpane. 'Is it . . .' He cleared his throat. 'Is the bed comfortable?'

'It's very soft,' she said. The subdued light showed her little of his face, just faint glints from his eyes, the outline of his cheek: a rather boyishly rounded cheek, in fact, though this only came into prominence when he smiled.

'Are you warm enough?' he said. 'The night's turning a little chilly. I wonder whether we should have had a fire.'

'It's warm in bed,' she said.

Before relinquishing her hand he kissed it. It was not a thing he had done before, and as a gesture it was very unlike him, the least spontaneous of men. The brush of his trim, silky moustache on the fine skin of the back of her hand was curiously pleasant.

He went into the adjoining dressing-room, and presently came back in his dressing-gown. Again she was touched, as when he had first haltingly kissed her in the Gardens, by the sight of him thus homely and informal – all that invulnerable self-sufficiency abandoned for her sake. It was with this mildly moved, mildly tender feeling that she reached out her arms to hold him when he put out the gas and took off his dressing-gown and got into bed.

She had never supposed him to be anything but a shy person; and though she was sometimes a little shy of him, she knew that in the physical sense she was not a shy person. And so, though quite as inexperienced as he, she allowed her instinctive warmth to lead them: she gave him her tongue and moved her body against his. He kept very still, his mouth stiffly fixed on hers, but at length his hand came up and tentatively touched her breasts. The feeling of this was exciting to her, and she pressed his hand more firmly to her and then found herself lifting her nightdress up to her neck.

Still he lay very awkward and tense, and when her fingers touched the soft nape of his neck she found the muscles there like taut rope. The responsiveness of her nature, however, carried her forward, and when he tremblingly placed his hand between her thighs he found her wet. His hand sprang convulsively back as if he had touched fire, and his face drew away from hers. She kissed him again, and guided his hand back: he moved it stiffly around, but still he seemed to shrink from her wetness.

She felt that she ought perhaps to say words of love, but she and Radford had never spoken in that way, and somehow even this silent intimacy seemed easier than that. It was with a sudden desperate clumsiness that he shifted and moved on top of her. She touched him to guide him towards her: she could feel his short breath upon her cheek, but his face was half averted. And then she realized that he was not excited – less and less so, in fact, as her fingers touched him.

Very soon he rolled away from her. They lay side by side. Her eyes had become accustomed to the darkness, which now revealed itself to be incomplete, a slice of moonlight coming through a chink in the curtains and silvering the edges of the furniture, which seemed to step forward from the shadows with an evil wink, like emboldened goblins.

At last she placed her hand over his, intending to squeeze it, though what the squeeze was meant to convey she was unsure. His hand twitched – was it a shrinking at her touch? – before allowing her to take it.

'Are you very tired, dear?' she said after a while. The sound of a human voice seemed as weird and conspicuous against the silence of that room as it would have been on the moon.

'Yes,' he said. 'Yes, I am. Are you?'

She nodded, unable to trust her constricted throat with more words. Finally he leaned over and kissed her cheek.

'Good night, my dear,' he said, turning over on his side.

At last she quietly pulled down her nightdress and turned over too. But she did not sleep for a long time. She lay listening, trying again to pick out the sound of the sea from the background of trifling noises about her; and the dawn was almost at hand before she realized that she could not hear the sea at all.

II

It was the fourth day of Lucy and Radford's honeymoon. The weather had continued fine and warm, and they had made several excursions along the coast and to beauty spots in the wooded country inland. They had visited the Winter Gardens in Shipden, and each evening walked along the esplanade.

On this evening Lucy expressed a wish to go down to the beach. Radford, as ever, was very respectful of her wishes, and they strolled for some time on the flats, until the sun was a flaring ember about to be doused in the sea. It is beautiful here, Lucy thought; and though Radford several times commented on the time, she was absorbed.

The pools left behind by the retreating tide especially tempted her. She had collected a few shells, but skirts and boots made this difficult.

'Well . . . I don't know,' Radford said, when she proposed taking off her boots and stockings to wade into a pool. 'It's getting rather near dinner . . .'

'There's no one about to see,' she said, interpreting his glance over his shoulder. 'I won't be a moment.'

He submitted and, leaning against the groyne and shedding her boots and stockings with her own limber grace, Lucy stepped into the little pool. It was deeper than she had thought; and when she came out, clutching her shell trophies, she found that not only were her skirts sopping wet, but her feet and calves were caked with mud.

'Oh dear! Now I'm a regular mess,' she said, and could not help laughing. The sensation of the cold water on her bare legs had startled and then refreshed her, leaving her feeling light and exalted.

'My God,' Radford said, looking down at her legs with distaste, 'they're filthy – filthy!' He pronounced the word with a sort of wince.

'Oh – it's only mud,' said she, her laughter fading at his expression. 'I'll wash them in the sea.'

'You'll be wetter than ever then,' Radford said, 'and probably catch cold . . .' With a sharp frown he looked about him. 'You simply can't go back to the hotel like that, and I don't see anywhere we can go . . .'

'What about there?' Just up the beach, and overlooking the sea wall, there stood an old and rather run-down inn: the words 'The Crab Pot' could just be read on its weathered signboard.

'Hardly the place for . . . well, I suppose we must,' Radford said. He gave her his arm and, carrying her boots and stockings, and still trying to contain her laughter, she squelched up to the little inn.

Within there were only a few fishermen, who regarded them with stolid unsurprise through the pipe-smoke which filled the bar-parlour, and which must have filled it every evening for scores of years, for it had formed tarry deposits on the low beams, and rendered the interior as black as a coal-hole. The landlady listened sympathetically to Lucy's predicament, and was inclined to chuckle at it too. 'Come you in hare, dair,' she said, opening a door to an inner room. 'There's a bit of a fire, and we'll soon fix you up.'

The landlady brought a bowl of water and a towel, and presently Lucy was clean and dry.

'Would you like a drop of something while you're hare, to set you up?' the landlady said. 'Mebbe some tea, if nothing stronger.'

'Oh yes! Radford – what do you think?' said Lucy, who found the inn a more easeful place than the hotel.

'We really ought to be getting back for dinner,' said Radford, standing at a distance. 'Thank you very much for your help.'

As they left the inn, Radford wiped his hands on his handkerchief. 'Good heavens,' he said, 'the filth in that place.'

He washed himself even more thoroughly than usual before dinner; only then did he seem fully composed again. For her part Lucy was still infected by the light-heartedness that had come over her on the beach. They had wine again at dinner, and she drank several glasses of it, humming under her breath to the music of the piano trio; and after dinner, feeling luxurious, she decided to have a bath. The gleaming fittings and abundant hot water of the hotel eclipsed for her all its other conveniences; how she would have loved this, coming home weary and grimed from the day in the closing-shop!

This reminder of the hardship she had left behind, and the pleasures that her new world offered her, reinforced her sanguine mood. Looking back over the last few days, she felt that the dark pit which she had seen yawning in the centre of her life, and into which she had stared during the sleepless, loveless nights, was surely the product of a hasty imagination – or at least, was capable of being bridged. Yes, it could surely be bridged.

Radford was still downstairs in the smoking-room: he stayed there every night for the same length of time. When she heard him come up she was sitting before the dressing-room fire, wrapped in a robe. The contentment of wine and food and bathing had induced in her a sensuous lassitude, and her voice was thick as she called out her husband's name.

When he entered the dressing-room she had slipped the robe off and was sitting naked.

'I had such a lovely bath,' she said. 'Come and give me a kiss.'

Radford, after one startled glance, had averted his eyes. He stood irresolutely in the doorway, his hand going up to his moustache in a gesture she had already begun to recognize in him: a quick patting self-reassurance. Then, with his conscious briskness, he walked over to her and, face still averted, picked up the dropped robe.

'You ought to cover yourself up,' he said. 'You'll take cold.'

She took the robe from his hand but did not put it on. 'All right. But give me a kiss first,' she said.

He bent to dab his lips on hers, his hand resting on her bare shoulder. She took it and moved it to her breast.

'For heaven's sake,' he said, jerking back with an irritable laugh, 'it's rather early for that sort of thing, isn't it?'

'I don't think so,' she said gently. 'I don't think it's too early. Radford—'

His glance strayed to her nakedness again: cheeks flushing, he swung his eyes away as if from a deformity. 'Well,' he said shortly, turning and going into the bedroom, 'some of us think differently about these things.'

She was still sitting as if paralysed in the same position when she heard him undressing. She heard the creak of the bed, and then silence.

At last she covered herself up; but sat on for some time,

watching the embers of the fire die away to ashes.

After breakfast the next day, with Radford occupied in writing letters, she decided to go for a walk alone. Her steps soon took her down to the Crab Pot Inn: it was the place that had given her the kindliest feeling of her honeymoon, and she wanted to thank the landlady for her help yesterday.

It was another fine, bright day. The landlady was pleased to see her, and pressed her to sit at the little table that stood before the inn door and have some tea. Lucy complied, for though she did not particularly want the tea, the friendliness was very welcome, and she had a splendid view of the sea, which was a deep, calm blue rare on this harsh coast, and hinted at its power only with the white and concentrated wavelets that broke busily upon the beach, like the indolent drumming of a giant's fingers. At length she became aware that she was not alone. Seated on the bench on the other side of the doorway was a very aged fisherman, whom she had not observed because of his perfect stillness, and his gnarled and weathered appearance which made him appear almost a constituent of the old flint wall against which he leaned, and who with Anglian reticence had refrained from speaking to her. Catching her eye, however, he gave her good morning, and asked her how she did.

'First visit to Shipden?' said he.

'Yes – it's the first time I've been to the sea.'

'Is it now?' The old man, whose grizzled beard was so thick that getting his pipe into his mouth was rather a matter of hit and miss, considered. 'Well, thass a thing I can't imagine, being born in sight of it like I was; but then I've never been inland so far as the shires, so I suppose that come out the same. Thass rare calm today: you probably wouldn't see that so blue again if you came back every summer for a score of years.'

'The sea wall's very thick,' Lucy said. 'It must get very rough sometimes.'

'Tain't a kind coast,' the fisherman said. 'They called it the Devil's Mouth in the old sailing days, and thass took a lot of good men in my time. There was an ole chap who kept this very inn when I was a lad – name of Skeels. He'd been as good a sailor as the coast ever knew in his younger days, but one day the sea had changed its tune all of a sudden the way that it dew, and broke his boat and broke his back into the bargain. Never think it to look at it now, would you? But then thass done worse than that in its time. Shipden, this Shipden we're a-sitting in, was inland once. Queer to think on, ain't it? Hundreds of years ago there were two parishes to the town, and this was the inland one. The other one, fronting the sea – well, thass out there somewhere under the waves. It was took by the sea. And so this Shipden found itself shunted for'ard like, and on the coast all of a sudden.' Lucy's eyes must have widened, for the old man went on, 'Oh! don't you worry, mawther. The sea's not going to creep up and take this Shipden as well, not yet, anyways. That might do in a few hundred years' time, for all I know, but then neither you nor me are gooing to be around to worry about it then, so where's the difference?'

Certainly, she said, that was the only way to look at it; but what had impressed itself most forcibly on her mind, and remained imprinted there when she walked back to the hotel, was the image of the old town disappearing under the sea. Had it been a sudden cataclysm? Or a gradual process, houses being successively abandoned before the encroaching tide? Either way, it haunted her.

She tried to say something of the story to Radford later that day, when they took a hired gig to a beauty spot up the coast; but he was dismissive.

'Oh, I should think he was only spinning you a yarn, my dear. You know what these people are like if you encourage them. He would probably have got on to sea-serpents if you'd let him.'

Perhaps it was so. But the image would not leave her; and when she lay wakeful in bed that night, with Radford sleeping an immeasurable few inches away from her side, she thought of it still, even fancying that she could hear the ghostly voices of the old townspeople calling to her from beneath the waves. And as her eyes picked out the shape of her bridal bouquet on the bedside table, beginning now to wither, she could not help feeling that she was in the wrong place; that it would be better for her if she were not in this Shipden, but in the old Shipden under the sea.

III

Radford Stokes and his young bride returned to Cottesbridge at the beginning of September to begin their married life. Everyone agreed how well they looked, and what a handsome couple they made. There was no one to whom Lucy could confide the small, crucial, and to her devastating fact that the marriage had not properly begun at all, and showed no signs that it would ever do so.

Lucy's reaction to the strange lacuna at the heart of her marriage ranged from puzzlement to desolation. It was simply not a thing she could shrug off; she could not call the great ally scepticism to her aid. The culture in which she was raised was a secretive and often prudish one, but it was also terribly earnest and in its way impassioned: there was little about life that it did not take with the utmost seriousness. So even had she known Lord Chesterfield's Enlightenment dismissal of the sexual act – that the pleasure is momentary, the price exorbitant, and the posture ridiculous – its thought would have been alien to her, and not the comfort it might have been to her great-great-grandmother. Poor Lucy felt above all that there must be something wrong with her; felt with rather less conviction that there must be something wrong with Radford; and did not think there was anything wrong with her culture for trying to attach an aesthetic, an ethic and a freight of emotion to something which was merely an aspect of humankind's animal inheritance, and was never intended to bear such a burden of significance.

But of course it was impossible that she should not feel pained and bewildered. For one thing, there was her nature, which was warm and physical. That very warmth and physicality she now began to mistrust, as if it were some weakness that might betray her. But more than that, there was the circumstance of the marriage itself. A love-match that had foundered in the marriage bed would have been a terrible

208

thing, but some purity of intention could have been salvaged from the wreck; heart would surely have compensated for body, in some degree. But this was a marriage which she had entered into as a desperate escape from poverty; and that it should turn out to be unconsummated only threw the mercenary aspect of it into stronger relief in her anguished mind.

For Lucy had sincerely resolved that her marriage to Radford Stokes would not be a sham, as people looking at their respective situations might easily have labelled it. If it was not a great romance – and she felt she had had enough of those – then at least she had hoped to elevate it by a redeeming tenderness and affection, and to fulfil the terms of the contract fully and wholeheartedly. But her honeymoon had been devoid of all intimate expression beyond the formal courtesies that had characterized Radford's courtship and in that dreadful absence, it had already begun to seem to her a mockery to pretend that her marriage was anything but a material arrangement.

And of none of this could she say a word, least of all to Radford. The reserve, the urbanity, the lack of disturbing intensity that had made him so soothing a companion were the very things that precluded her speaking out frankly to him. And any tentative inclination to do so on her part was further complicated by the fact that in everyday matters he was as unfailingly solicitous and attentive to her welfare as he had ever been; and by the fact that every stitch she wore, every crumb she ate, and most importantly every new comfort that her family enjoyed, was entirely owing to Radford. The barely formed buds of grievance within her were nipped by her sense that, in any protest, she would be arguing from a position of acute disadvantage.

A dispassionate observer, hearing this, might have contended that it was nonsense to be thus oppressed and silenced by gratitude, but such an observer, Lucy might have replied, did not know Radford.

They did not know, as she soon began to know, how his impeccable courtesy and consideration made any expression of discontent seem the carping of a fretful child – made it seem, in short, in bad taste. They did not know the way his imperturbable routine wove slight but unbreakable threads about her, enmeshing her in a tremendous normality. They did not know with what authority he invested everything about his ordered life, so that it quickly began to seem that it was she who was the abnormal one in even thinking that there was anything odd about their marriage. They did not know the peculiar seamlessness of his character, in which no vulnerable chinks were to be seen, and which manifested not the smallest hint that he found his inability to offer love anything but normal.

Nor did they know that house which – though he insisted that Lucy was the complete mistress of it – was so singularly his own that she felt no more able to make free with it than with their honeymoon hotel. So quiet, so fearfully quiet a house! She felt the same guilt for thinking so as she felt towards Radford, for just as he gave her everything but love, so the house offered every convenience except homeliness.

So quiet! At night it was most noticeable, for she did not sleep well. Here there was no clanking night-soil cart as there had been at Alma Street; but neither was there that barely audible sound – more of an atmospheric pervasion than an aural sensation – of neighbouring people about her, like the gentle settlings of pigeons in a loft; only the great emptiness of night, scarcely stirred even in a high wind by the trees around the house, which merely whispered like well-trained servants. Nor did the house make those companionable creakings with which older dwellings seem to compose themselves for sleep. It was too new, too solid, too blankly well-kept for that. It knew its place.

The house was large, but not inordinately so: that would have smacked of ostentation. Its rooms were too small to be grand, but too capacious to be cosy. The windows, and the trees and shrubs outside them, were disposed so as to afford no prospect of the wider world to the sitter within; the Lessington Road might have been a mile away. Only in one of the spare bedrooms, by standing on a chair and fixing your eyes to the largest of the coloured window-panes, could you gain a chromatically distorted glimpse of carts and vans and bicycles, and life busily going on without you. What with this, and the heavy curtains all so pelmeted and tied and festooned with cords and fringes and pompons that they scarcely admitted more light when they were open than when they were closed, the rooms were rather dark; and as autumn drew on it was necessary to light the gas in the afternoon, the ponderous gasoliers that depended centrally from the ceilings making a decidedly dismal effect. Not that it was dust or decrepitude that they revealed: quite the opposite.

Radford detested dirt, and to him the slightest untidiness was dirt. Two maids were permanently occupied, so it appeared, in sweeping and cleaning, dusting and polishing. Lucy was always coming upon them. Whenever she opened a door, it seemed to her, she happened upon a black-clad figure with a brush and dustpan. She did not like them to go away because she was there, as was the custom, for they would only have to finish up later, and that meant a longer day for them; but nor did they welcome her efforts at conversation. It was not done, they were not used to it, and they were awkward and embarrassed. And so Lucy usually ended up beating a retreat, and trying to find a place that was not in the process of being scoured from top to bottom.

It might have been easier if she had been able to take some active part in the household. But it had been functioning without her for so long with such clockwork regularity that there was nothing for her to do. Radford handled all such things as servants' wages and tradesmen's bills; in his study he had careful accounts written out in calfskin notebooks, which would only have come to confusion if she had tried to interfere. Laundry was seen to by the maids, her clothes disappearing and then reappearing washed and pressed and laid out for her use, the whole operation occurring with a curious stealth, as if clothes were faintly shameful things. The cook planned the meals, insofar as they needed planning, for they simply rotated through an unvarying cycle that seemed to have been in place since Edward Stokes' day. Sunday was roast and Yorkshire pudding; Monday, hashed mutton or beef stew; Tuesday, steak-and-kidney pudding; Wednesday, saddle of lamb; Thursday, pork with apple sauce; Friday, chops; Saturday, porterhouse steak. The smells of these dinners wafting up from the kitchen became for Lucy the smells of their respective days, and sometimes they were her only means of identification, so monotonously uniform was her life.

Once, indeed, she suggested a change to the cook. There was gammon instead of chops when Radford sat down to dinner on Friday. His eyebrows went up, but he said nothing and ate his meal as usual. He was a slow, precise eater, cutting his food into small pieces and applying sauces with great nicety, as if he were conducting a chancy chemical experiment. Only from Miss Threadgold did the innovation draw a comment.

211

'I don't know why,' she said, 'there's just something about the flavour of gammon I've never taken to. Oh, don't misunderstand me! There's nothing wrong with the quality. It's just not a nice flavour to me, I don't care what anybody says.'

Radford still made no remark until after dinner, when he said to Lucy, 'I wonder why the butcher couldn't supply us with chops this week. He's always been very reliable.'

'Oh, it wasn't that,' Lucy said. 'It was my idea – I thought it would make a change.'

'Oh, I see . . . I'm sorry, my dear, I didn't realize you were fond of gammon.'

'Well – I'm not, specially . . . I just thought . . . Didn't you enjoy it?'

'The gammon? Yes – yes, it made a change, I suppose.'

She did not meddle with the menus again.

So quiet! Voices were never raised in that house. Radford and Georgina both spoke in muted tones: Miss Threadgold's steady purring drone, though more penetrating, was no louder. The very fires were so well-laid that they scarcely crackled, and the fall of the ashes in the grate startled the ear like a thunderbolt. The popping of the gas had a sup- pressed and apologetic sound, like the biliousness of an old gentleman. The doors were so well-oiled, and their catches fitted so smoothly, that you could enter the drawing-room as soundlessly as you might walk into an Arab tent. The loudest sound, indeed, was the ticking of those numerous clocks which Lucy had noticed on the day of her wedding; and that was such a stately, respectable and wholly predictable sound that it was more in the nature of a vessel to hold the silence and display its quality, as a glass reveals the purity of water. And they all struck too – the quarter, the half-hour, the three-quarters, the hour – cutting up and disposing of the time in orderly segments, just as Radford methodically cut up and disposed of the food on his plate.

Life in the Stokes household was entirely subject to time. The regularity of its routine did not change to accommodate Lucy's arrival: it merely swallowed her up. The day had as distinct a shape as an hourglass. Every morning Radford rose early. They shared a room with twin beds. Radford was as soft-footed as a cat, but Lucy always woke too. The long ritual of bathing, shaving and dressing followed: Radford always came to the breakfast-table immaculate. Over break-fast he read his letters. Occasionally he would take some into his study, and work there until half-past eight; more usually he set out for the factory at eight o'clock, kissing Lucy and his sister on the cheek before the maid brought his hat and, as the weather grew chill, his overcoat. In a coach-house at the back of the house there was a gig and an old pony that had belonged to Radford's father, but they were seldom brought out: Radford preferred to walk to the works, buying a newspaper on the way and occasionally some cigarettes, which he smoked as an occasional treat like cigars, always taking himself off to the conservatory to do so.

With Radford gone, the day was an empty tract with a few immovable landmarks. At half-past twelve a light lunch was served to Lucy, Georgina and Miss Threadgold. At half-past one, if the weather was fine enough, the ladies would go for a walk, usually down into the town where they could buy such small pieces of shopping as were not delivered to the house by tradesmen's vans; otherwise they would stroll round the garden. At half-past three there was tea, and at six o'clock Radford came home.

Before going up to change for dinner he would talk with the ladies about the day's events; and when he came downstairs again, washed and groomed and in a new, crisp-starched collar, he would take Lucy's arm and they would go into the conservatory to look over the plants that were under Georgina's care and to have a little talk by themselves. As far as Lucy could tell, this evening ritual was the only modification he had made to his bachelor habits.

After dinner he would usually spend some time with them in the drawing-room, but often he had work to do in the study; and perhaps once a week Mr Hallam, the works manager – a jug-eared man with thin hair plastered lankly either side of a central parting and a lugubrious expression, so that whatever the weather he always looked as if he had just come in out of the rain – would call at the house and be closeted in the study with Radford for an hour, the maid going in to them on the half-hour bearing a tray with a decanter of sherry, two small glasses, and a plate of of almond biscuits.

Lucy usually went to bed at half-past ten, and Radford would follow shortly after. Again there would be thorough ablutions before he came to bed. Sometimes he had a book, but he was not a great reader, and more usually he would turn over the pages of a shoe-trade paper before saying goodnight and going to sleep.

213

Thus the weekdays. On Sundays Radford slept late – until a quarter to nine – and exchanged his usual rather dapper waistcoats and neckties for sober charcoal-grey. This day was like a shapeless tent held aloft by two firm poles; the morning and evening visits to church. Chapel-bred as she was, Lucy made no demur about attending church both times; her faith was in any case moribund. Somewhere between these two poles were Sunday lunch and high tea. Radford rather plumed himself on not being particular about precisely when these were served, though the variation was never more than half an hour. 'I don't feel one should be fussy about these things on a Sunday,' he said. 'I think it's rather nice to let up a little, and take things as they come.'

And throughout all this, weekdays and Sundays, the clocks slowly ticked away; and Lucy listened to them, and tried not to listen, and in trying not to listen found herself harkening to them all the more intently, until they seemed to boom in her ears, and their tickings shaped themselves into compulsive rhythms that would all of a sudden shift like horses' hooves going from trot to canter and canter to gallop. They would alter their accents with strange syncopations, and turn themselves inside out, and then suggest odd guttural syllables repeated over and over, as if almost on the point of breaking into words; until it was the voices of the clocks that seemed to her the articulate element of the room, and the voices of her human companions the background noise, unmeaning and mechanical.

So insistent was the habit of routine that Lucy found herself submitting to it even in the few spheres of independent action left to her. One such was her weekly visit to her family in Alma Street. There was no special reason for it to be weekly, but the influence of that clockwork house prevailed, even to the extent that she went at the same time on the same day – Tuesday morning. This regularity in itself seemed to please Radford, so that a reference to it became part of his own routine. 'It's your day to see your family, isn't it, dear? Do give them my best regards,' he would say over breakfast on Tuesdays; and, when he came home in the evening, 'Ah, it was your day to see your family, wasn't it, dear? I hope they're all well.' He was so gratified that she even overheard him once saying to Mr Hallam: 'Yes, Tuesday – Tuesday should be all right, if they can deliver early. I'll remember Tuesday; that's the day my wife goes to visit her family.'

The Middleton household had at first threatened to collapse into the chaotic abyss left by Lucy's departure. Fortunately she was able to fill that gap with money. If Mrs Middleton was still too feather-minded to prepare a dinner for the boys, at least Lucy was able to ensure that the larder was full of things from which they could help themselves. For Radford gave her an ample allowance and, as she was not vain in the matter of clothes, she hardly knew what to do with it – except help her family, as had been her overriding aim when marrying him. Thanks to the money she conveyed to them, there was a great deal more comfort in the house in Alma Street than she had ever known when she lived there. Indeed, was it wholly unnatural in her to feel more relaxed in her old home than her new, and to conclude her visits with reluctance, putting off the moment when she would have to leave its rackety vitality and return to the world of ticking clocks? Certainly the memory of how often she had longed to escape from this house was mockingly present to her, and suggested ironic capacities on the part of Fate that her old optimism would scarcely have believed; indeed, it was only her continued refusal to completely abandon the hopeful view of experience that prevented her from forming the harshest conclusions. She had yet to fully apprehend, for example, that the surest way to get what you want is to cease wanting it.

The improved circumstances of her family were, at any rate, a matter for satisfaction; and Joanna seemed to be stepping forward from her gentle unobtrusiveness and quietly beginning to take charge. Dicky was now in rude health, as he demonstrated by wildly vaulting over the banisters. 'What a pleasure it is to see young 'uns in spirits!' Mrs Middleton beamed, as a muffled crash indicated that Dicky had come into passing contact with the aspidistra in the hall. 'I don't know what I'd do without 'em, Lucy. I may be a widder, but I'm a mother too, and that meks all the difference.' Mrs Middleton, in fact, touched upon the subject of motherhood often when Lucy visited, with many significant nods and smiles, and silences that Lucy felt herself unequal to filling.

Often she would protract her stay so as to step over and say hello to Mr Birdsall when he came home for his dinner, though she did not linger long. A certain element of protector and protégée had always been present in their relation, which Mr Birdsall now seemed to feel inappropriate, treating her with an awkward respect she did not look for. Even Nancy

Smallbones, who always made a pounce when she saw Lucy go by, seemed to modify her malice, restricting it to bland assertions that it was nice to see she didn't think herself too good for them, as if her status as a married woman gave her a certain diplomatic immunity.

A married woman: that was what she was above all, it appeared; not Lucy any more. And she wanted to cry out to them, *But I am still Lucy! I am still the same person!* For what was so disorientating about this disjunction of identity was the fact that she knew it to be a sham. She was an imposter, and about her old haunts she was as uneasily conscious of this as if she were actively engaged in a deception. While everyone supposed her to be in a normal marriage, she alone had to carry the knowledge of the truth suppressed within her.

But worse than that, she began to wonder whether she did know the truth. After all, Radford behaved as if there was nothing wrong; Radford never betrayed the slightest hint of awareness that their marriage was a farce – and, as she still regarded Radford as the keeper of the keys of sanity, she began to doubt herself. Was the emperor wearing clothes after all? It was as if the whole world except Lucy was maintaining that the grass was blue and the sky green – and in such a situation was it not natural that she should begin to suspect that it was she whose sight must be at fault?

So it was a strange hallucinatory life that she led. As far as the world was concerned, she was Radford's wife. As far as Radford was concerned, she was his wife. And as far as Lucy was concerned . . . well, just who *was* she?

One thing was certain. She was not the girl who had walked the woods with Matt Doughty in a trance of passion. That Lucy was dead and buried, and on no account must be resurrected. Whoever she might be now, that identity must never be allowed to assert itself in those silent varnished rooms.

And so she outwardly conformed to the image that people entertained of her; Mrs Radford Stokes, the manufacturer's wife, a girl some ten years his junior who had made a fortunate marriage. She played the part well, and gave no sign of the gnawing at her heart; for she had always been one of those ardently feeling people who look calm and cannot help it. Her large measure of beauty had much to do with this: it is plainness that gives most away, the thin lip and pale, lashless eye that are most vulnerably expressive. And Lucy, well-fed and well-dressed at last, was as handsome as she had promised to be. The richness and dark bloom of her looks, over which she had no control, did the work of making her appear contented far more effectively than forced effusions and determined cheerfulness could have.

And whom, after all, was she to confide in? Her mother? Even leaving aside the extent to which Mrs Middleton was financially beholden to Radford, which complicated things, hers was not a brain that anyone would find it worth their while to pick, even a daughter whose loving heart chose to disregard many of her incapacities. Joanna? She was younger than Lucy, and curiously unworldly. Connie, just about to be married herself, and prone to fiery blushes at the merest mention of the unmentionable? Unthinkable. No, there was nothing for it but to keep her own counsel, and hope to hear one day in the voices of the clocks some answer to her predicament.

There was one person who, inasmuch as they were swiftly becoming close friends, might have been a confidante to Lucy; but that person was debarred from such a role, not only by her extremely shrinking temperament, but also by her relationship to Radford. This was Georgina Stokes.

The terrible quiet of that house in which Lucy wandered like a forgotten visitor might have been unbearable indeed but for Georgina. Georgina broke its dismal spell with two things – friendship, and music, the one acting upon and fostering the other.

Georgina, of course, had shown her nothing but kindness right from the beginning of Radford's courtship. But when Lucy came to the house as a bride it was at first strained and difficult. Georgina, for one thing, was quite as much a creature of habit as her brother, and Lucy was continually conscious of encroaching upon her new sister-in-law's settled and extremely sheltered existence. With the blow to her self-esteem administered by the loveless honeymoon still fresh upon her, she could not rid herself of a feeling that she was in the way here, an intruder. Moreover, her friendships had been formed in the cobbled street and the closing-shop, with all the directness and plain speaking that such an environment encouraged; and while she liked Georgina, she could see no way of getting past all that soft-tongued correctness and civility that surrounded her sister-in-law like a cage of gauze.

In turn, Georgina seemed to regard Lucy with a certain awe. For though twenty-eight years old, she was as naïve as a schoolgirl: in this house, Lucy perceived, she had been bred up like a plant kept in a small pot; tended, cosseted, brought to a delicate bloom, but for all that, stunted. And in this paralysis of maidenhood, she saw in Lucy authority – the authority of a married woman. And most impressive of all, it was to *Radford* that she was married; Radford, who, as Lucy could tell from the start, was adored by his sister with something close to hero-worship.

It was sadly tempting to laugh at this misapprehension on the part of Georgina. If only she knew! But Lucy never laughed at Georgina, though many a less kind-hearted girl would have found some relief from her own trouble in doing so. Georgina had those eccentricities of solitude which, permissible in the elderly, are for some reason derided in the young. She was a great potterer in the conservatory, referring to favourite plants by name and even inventing personalities for them. She had odd little superstitions which, in her enclosed little world, she supposed to have universal currency: 'You didn't touch the newel-post for luck,' she would say on seeing Lucy descend the stairs, and then colouring dreadfully add, 'Oh! I'm sorry – it's just something I do, I – silly of me.' She was quite proficient at drawing, and had done some good sketches of Radford, but what she most enjoyed was filling sheets of paper with whimsical depictions of mice in bonnets and squirrels in Norfolk jackets and gnomes peeping round toadstools.

'I know it's not real,' she said, 'but I so wish it was sometimes. I wish I could get into the picture with them, or go down to the woods and see all the little creatures running around like that . . .' And she blushed again, as if conscious that what for her had long been a private amusement must appear silly to someone outside her closed circle.

Lucy, however, was not the girl to decry any exercise of the imagination. If she had learnt anything, it was that life was a subtle balancing act between reality and illusion, a teetering between ice and fire. But she feared that Georgina did not credit her with any such tolerance, and must think her very worldly-wise; and she could hardly convince her otherwise as long as their relation did not go beyond a desperate mutual obligingness.

It was music that broke this down. Georgina was a very capable musician, and more than that she loved it fiercely. She practised the piano a couple of hours daily, and often in the evening she played for them. Radford, while proud of his sister's accomplishment, seemed to regard the music as no more than a pleasant aspect of his leisure, like cigarettes or a good fire. Lucy, on the other hand, was transported. This was something different. This was something that stood outside time and circumstance, perfect and inviolate, regardless of whether the hearer was rich or poor, blissfully happy or inconsolable. Yet it did not have the cold self-sufficiency of a statue or a painting: it spoke. That she could not as yet understand all its language was of no moment: each new hearing was an adventure in understanding. Here was something that took her away from her personal unhappiness, not through cheap oblivion, but through engaging both her mind and emotions. It was a revelation.

Still she felt she could say nothing of this to Georgina; she was untutored, and probably she was completely misunderstanding what moved her so much. But at last she hesitatingly asked her sister-in-law about the piece of music she had heard in the hotel at Shipden, the melody of which had remained with her ever since. At Georgina's prompting she huskily hummed a few bars, and was rewarded with recognition.

'Radford was right. It is Schubert,' Georgina said, hurrying to the piano. 'This – is that it?'

'That's the one,' Lucy said, as Georgina picked out the melody. 'Oh, you know it! I was sure you would.'

'It's the "Ständchen". That's a serenade. It's a song originally, but there are all sorts of arrangements of it. Yes, I love it too, I haven't played it for ages . . . Oh, Lucy, I could have played it for you if I'd known!'

'Well, I – you see, I didn't know what it was called, or anything like that . . . The names of the pieces always seem so difficult,' Lucy confessed. 'I love it when you play, but I'm afraid I'm so ignorant—'

'Oh, don't worry about that! The names and things don't matter. I didn't know a fugue from a polonaise when I first fell in love with music – it didn't stop me enjoying it.'

'Will you – will you play it through for me?'

She sat and listened to the piece with an unnamable mingling of emotions; and when it was over her voice was not quite steady as she said, 'When did you first start learning the piano?'

'Oh, when I was quite a little child. Later I had lessons with the funniest old man – he was Dutch and he would say things like "Play more stronger if you please, it is Beethoven not embroidery!", and he had such a big tangly white beard, I used to imagine little mice living in it and him never knowing . . .' Georgina checked herself in a laugh, looking abashed, and went on earnestly, 'But I'm only the merest amateur, you know, Lucy. I know that's what ladies always say, it's what one is *meant* to say, but in my case it's quite true. Radford took me to a recital given by a concert pianist in Northampton last year, and when I came home – well, I couldn't touch the piano for weeks, I felt quite in despair.'

'That's how your playing makes me feel!' Lucy said. 'I so wish I could have learnt – but I suppose it's too late now.'

'Oh, my dear, it's never too late! Now if you wished to learn, I . . .' Georgina coloured again. 'Well, I was going to say I'd be happy to teach you, but that seems very presumptuous – the idea that I could—'

'Oh, I'd love it if you would,' Lucy said. It was time, she felt impulsively, to be direct. 'And you could teach me lots of things, Georgina . . . I mean, often I'm awkward here, and not sure of things, and I feel if only there was someone kind I could ask . . .'

She felt she had said that wrongly, for surely if there was anyone she should have been able to ask, it was her husband. But Georgina seemed too pleased to notice. 'Why, Lucy – if there's anything I can do to help you, I shall be more than glad; but really I'm sure you don't need any guidance from me . . .'

'No, Georgina,' Lucy said, 'don't speak that way: I want us to be honest together. I do feel out of place sometimes – you must have seen it. I'm only twenty, and I haven't been used to this sort of life, and it's no good pretending I have. So don't think of me as Radford's wife – I mean, yes that's what I am,' she added hastily, 'but don't just think of me like that. Because I want us to be friends, without that.'

'Oh, and we will be!' said Georgina, getting up and giving Lucy her hand as trustfully as a child. 'I always felt that we would, but . . . Well, I must confess I don't tend to think of you as twenty. Because you've done so much more than me, and you've got such assurance—'

'Me?' Lucy could not have been more astonished if she had been told she was an heiress.

'Oh, yes.' Georgina nodded solemnly. 'I do envy you that. Because – well, as we're being honest with each other – I feel a perfect goose in company. I always have. Oh, I make a show, because one has to; but really mixing with people has always been – always been torture to me.' It was said in her quiet, self-deprecating way, but Lucy saw that the pain in her eyes was very real. This, Lucy realized, was a genuinely defenceless soul. Other girls might have turned such a nature to account, and made themselves tyrants of timidity, demanding always to have their weakness taken into consideration; but Georgina lacked such calculation. The realization deepened Lucy's liking for her.

'And of course, there's Radford, you see,' Georgina went on. 'He's so good at mixing, and makes his way in the world so confidently. I feel I must be rather a disappointment to him in that regard, always lurking in the corners. So I try and make the effort for his sake – but I colour up so dreadfully, and end up saying such foolish little things . . .' Again Lucy could see how much pain, as well as relief, this confession gave her sister-in-law. She sympathized: she too knew what it was like to stand in the shadow of Radford's formidable correctness, to feel oneself messy, ill-defined, unsatisfactory beside that smooth, homogeneous personality; though Georgina, in her adulation of her brother, would not put it in those terms. 'That was why I was so glad about him marrying you,' Georgina went on. 'I'd always thought he ought to marry, though I was afraid he wouldn't find anyone to suit; he's very exacting, and rightly so. It's so much better for him to have someone to share his life whom he can be proud of, someone who – well, who isn't a silly goose, and can be the mistress of his house in a way I can't . . . That's a selfish reason for being glad about your marriage, isn't it? I didn't mean it to sound like that. I'm glad in every way.'

At least someone is, said a harsh whisper in Lucy's mind before she could squash it. 'Well,' she said, 'thank you; but I'm sure Radford is proud of you, Georgina. He—'

'So this is where everybody is!'

Miss Threadgold, lazy smile in place, had noiselessly entered and was seated beside Lucy almost before she was aware of it: she was curiously swift for someone who gave the impression of never having hurried in her life.

'Lucy's going to learn the piano, Dinah,' Georgina said. 'I'm going to try and be her teacher – if you can imagine that!'

221

'I'm sure you could teach anybody,' Miss Threadgold said. 'But music's one of those things you're born with, if you ask me. It's either in your blood or it's not. Look at those composers – they all started when they were practically *babes* in *arms*, didn't they? No, I'm sorry, I don't think music's a thing you can learn, I don't care what anybody says.'

'Well, I'm going to try, anyway,' Lucy said.

'Oh, don't misunderstand me! I'm not saying people can't learn to play the piano. I'm not saying that. Even I know better than that. But I think it's an instinct, isn't it? Like the one who was playing when he was so small his feet didn't touch the pedals . . . Oh, Dinah – ' she tapped her own wrist – 'honestly, your memory, it's a scandal, it really is! You'll know the one I mean, Georgina.'

'That was Mozart, I think,' Georgina said.

'Poor little mite. Really, it's not natural, is it? His little feet dangling.' Miss Threadgold gave her languid laugh, which seemed to originate somewhere between her throat and her nose, and caused no modification to the expression on her face – not even parting her teeth, which remained fixed together in the eternal, inexcitable smile.

That smile, indeed, could be considered to be Miss Threadgold's face in repose, and only its absence proclaimed an active emotion. It was a smile of contentment, the contentment of a cat in a warm window-seat: except that the contentment of a cat is infectious, and Miss Threadgold's effect on Lucy was quite of an opposite kind.

Dinah Threadgold reminded Lucy, rather, of a bird – a hen or pigeon of a fancy kind; soft, bosomy, clucking, hard-eyed. Though in her blonde voluptuousness she was of a very different physical type from Radford and Georgina, she was in fact a distant relation of theirs. She had lived in fairly reduced circumstances at Oundle, a little genteel public-school town down the valley, until old Edward Stokes' death; when, with Radford taking over the reins of the business and accordingly much away from home, she had been invited to live at the house in Lessington Road as Georgina's companion.

Miss Threadgold and Georgina were so very different that Lucy wondered at first how it was they got on so well, until she began to perceive things about her sister-in-law that her own intimate knowledge of Radford helped her to see. Georgina, so trim and daintily made, had the sort of physical gaucheness more commonly seen in great hoydenish girls who are all big feet and elbows. It was hard for Lucy – to whom the flesh, even in her poverty, had always been the agent of pleasure – to conceive of someone being afraid of their own body; but once she understood it, she understood much about Georgina's dependence on her companion. Dinah Threadgold, serenely drawling, absently stroking her own round arms with their light peach-bloom of fair hairs, reclining voluminously in a chair or walking with lazy robustness around the garden, was a reassuringly material presence, a screen of corporeal confidence interposed between Georgina and the world. Just as Miss Threadgold sometimes spoke for Georgina when shyness silenced her in company, so she acted as a sort of physical proxy.

Illness, for example, seemed to terrify and embarrass Georgina. A cold afflicted her with a dual discomfort, for it was as if her flesh were betraying her. Dinah Threadgold, on the other hand, had had everything short of bubonic plague and, as she said, didn't care who knew it. 'Oh! I had the impetigo terribly when I was a girl,' she would say. 'I looked such a fright my mother could hardly bear to come near me, and the doctor said he'd never seen a worse case. Oh yes, it was that bad, I don't mind saying it, I never have, that's just the sort of person I am, I'm sorry. The doctor tried all sorts of things, but in the end it cleared up on its own, and I wasn't one jot the worse for it. I believe in letting nature take its course, always have, and it doesn't seem to do me any harm. It was the same when I had the tonsilitis, and the trouble with my kidneys. I just went on as normal, even though I looked like death. I think it does more harm than good interfering with these things, that's my opinion, I don't care what anybody says.'

Certainly Miss Threadgold appeared to enjoy admirable health. Her appetite was large and steady: as with a cow, to picture her was to picture her eating. Placidly she munched, sipped and chewed, scarcely interrupting her smile. 'Oh! I can eat anything, I can. I've always had wonderful digestion, I don't know why, it's just one of those things.' All of this, Lucy saw, was peculiarly comforting to Georgina; for just as Miss Threadgold was, as she said, 'made that way', she assured Georgina that her nervous constitution was inherent. 'I can take any amount of cold, I can,' she said, 'always could. That's the way I am. But you're susceptible to it,

Georgina. It's in the breed. That's why I say you shouldn't go out today, when you're so liable to chills. I'm sorry, that's what I think. When I care about somebody, I just speak out, I don't care what anybody thinks of me.' And so Georgina, naturally enough, was glad to have her weakness thus excused, and did not go out. Any impulse towards independent action on her part was continually being discouraged by Miss Threadgold's solicitude – a solicitude that, looked at from another angle, was sheer manipulation.

That was how Lucy saw it. Was this unfair? Certainly Georgina seemed greatly to depend on Dinah Threadgold, who made herself conspicuously indispensable whilst disclaiming any credit for it. 'Oh, don't thank me, my dear!' she would say. 'You misunderstood me entirely if you think I need thanking. I can't help myself. I'll do anything for people I care about, I always have, I don't even think about it. There's no virtue in it. It's just me – just the way I am, I'm sorry.' But it was no less an exercise of power, Lucy thought, for being disguised as disinterested concern. The protective arm was also the arm of possession. The more Georgina lurked in the benevolent shadow of Miss Threadgold, the less she would dare to venture out into the light; and Lucy felt that Miss Threadgold knew it.

Unfair, perhaps, because she had to admit that she could not think objectively about Dinah Threadgold. Lucy hated the woman. She was sure the sentiment was mutual, though in a court of law she could not have pointed to any firm evidence of the fact. For, vastly opinionated as Miss Threadgold was, she somehow contrived to make nothing seem personal. Even her likes and dislikes were, she suggested, beyond her control. All was to be referred to natural laws.

'Well, I don't see why they should be prone to illness any more than anyone else,' Miss Threadgold said, alluding to a newspaper report on mortality amongst coal-miners. 'Really, we're all flesh and blood, aren't we?'

'But they're more likely to be ill, working in conditions like those,' Lucy said.

'Oh no, it'd be the other way round, surely! They get toughened and hardened, working like that. It makes them strong – it's only natural. Do you see what I mean? It toughens them. Oh, no, I can't agree with you there, Lucy, I'm sorry, I don't care what anybody says, it's just natural.'

That she never, in fact, agreed with anything Lucy said

was made less obvious by this habit of reading her own opinions off tablets of stone; and also by a sort of bland refusal to recognize Lucy's individuality at all. Often when the three women were together, Miss Threadgold would talk volubly to Georgina of things and people that Lucy could know nothing of, things and people that prefigured her coming here. But while she did not explain, she did not exclude either: she smilingly acknowledged Lucy's presence just as she would that of a dog or a baby.

In the same way, when Lucy haltingly expressed feelings, views or experiences of her own, she found them taken away from her by Miss Threadgold, set before the tribunal of Nature, and dismissed. Discussing once the childhood fear of the dark and ghosts, Lucy mentioned that she had found going outside an effective cure for the creeps: once outside the house, the possibility of the supernatural diminished.

'Oh, but there are all sorts of reports of hauntings in the open air, you know,' Miss Threadgold said. 'I'm sure it's quite natural for people to associate them with houses, but really they're no safer from them outside.'

'Yes, I see that,' Lucy said. 'But it just feels different—'

'Oh, I don't dispute that. I'm only saying what's common knowledge. People have seen strange things in gardens, you know – and on roads, and in churchyards, all sorts of places. Oh no, it stands to reason, they must be everywhere!'

But I don't care about other people, Lucy wanted to scream, *or what's natural or what stands to reason – it's what I feel!*

She did not, however, often as she longed to. She held her tongue out of consideration for Georgina, who seemed to regard them both as tremendously impressive people, and wanted them to like each other. When a mild clash did finally occur, Georgina looked as desperately unhappy as a child caught between quarrelling parents.

The occasion was trivial. The jobbing gardener had been taking cuttings and seedlings from the conservatory for his own use. Miss Threadgold said this was tantamount to stealing: Georgina didn't know what to think. Lucy merely said he could have as many as he liked, but it would be better if he asked first.

'But the point is, you see,' Miss Threadgold said, 'that's how it starts. You've only got to read the newspapers. Criminals always start out with petty crime. And if no one punishes them for it, they go on to do worse – that's only human nature.'

'I don't think our old gardener's likely to go housebreaking,' Lucy said.

'Oh no! I'm not saying that. Don't misunderstand me. That's not my point at all. But you know the saying – give them an inch and they'll take a mile. If they get away with betraying your trust once, they'll do it again, it stands to reason. I'm sorry, but it does, I don't care what anybody says. After all, those are Georgina's plants, and she's fond of them. If it was somebody else I perhaps wouldn't mind so much, but it's Georgina, you see. I can't bear to see somebody I care about being imposed on. I never have. I'm sorry, that's just the way I am.'

Lucy felt something like the snap of elastic within her. 'Yes, well,' she said shortly, using a gambit she had never ventured on before. 'I'm the mistress of the house, and I've dealt with it.'

Miss Threadgold became, if anything, more smiling, placid and obtuse. The only change was in her eyes, which dissociated themselves from the smiling mouth even more than usual. 'Oh! I don't dispute that,' she said. 'Even I know that. Don't misunderstand me. Of course you're the mistress of the house, dear, anyone would agree to that. I'm just looking out for Georgina's interests, that's all. It doesn't matter to me, not me personally. I'm just thinking of Georgina. I can't help putting her interests first. It's silly of me no doubt, but I always have, I'm sorry. It's just the way I am.'

About to say something more, Lucy stopped and let it pass. For one thing, her own sense of the imposture of her marriage made her chary of proclaiming her rights as mistress of the house. For another, Georgina already looked wretched, and Lucy did not want her sister-in-law to feel she was a bone of contention. Which she inevitably was, to some degree – and to a greater degree as time went on. For Miss Threadgold had come here as a companion to Georgina in her solitude, and it must be plain to the woman – who was no fool though she talked like one – that Georgina stood in less and less need of a companion as her friendship with Lucy ripened.

There was another reason why Lucy strove to contain her hostility to Dinah Threadgold. She feared, looking at herself, that it might merely be hatred searching for an object. Or hatred for Radford . . .? But that was just it. There was nothing to hate; no foothold for resentment in the sheer glassy surface of his nature. His life might be a claustrophobic exercise in joyless primness, but had he ever fostered any illusion that it would be otherwise? No, Miss Threadgold offered an easier handle for her bitterness, perhaps too easy. How could she hate Radford, when he continued to furnish her family with the security they had always lacked?

It was shortly before Christmas that Radford came to her with a proposal for finding Joanna a new situation, and one far above the glorified drudgery she undertook for the milliners.

'My dear, I was talking to Mr Aubrey Parmenter today,' Radford said as they made their nightly arm-in-arm sally into the conservatory. 'You know Parmenter's, of Nen Street, of course.'

'I used to work there,' Lucy said.

'Of course. Yes.' Radford did not like her to refer to her origins so flatly, and expressed disapproval in his usual manner, with a fleetingly pained look like a man experiencing a pang of indigestion. 'Well, Aubrey Parmenter is an old associate of mine, and was talking to me today of his sister, Mrs Silvie. She is a widowed lady of means, somewhat strong-minded, elderly, and not in perfect health. Mr Parmenter has long been urging her to come and live with him, for he has ample room, but she insists on maintaining a separate establishment – a house in a rather retired situation, out on the Cleatham Road, which she never leaves. However, she has been persuaded that she should have a companion-help to live with her, preferably a young woman of a quiet, gentle disposition, if one can be found to suit. "No vulgar giggling misses" were her words, I believe.' Radford doled out a smile. 'So at once I thought of your sister Joanna, and thought I would consult with you on the possibility of her taking the situation. Joanna has a very taking and pleasant manner, and I believe she would be eminently suitable. The situation would involve residing at Mrs Silvie's house, but of course she would have free time to visit her family; and there would be a generous allowance, the place is not really to be regarded as a job – more a matter of companionship, as with our own Miss Threadgold. What do you feel, my dear?'

'I know Joanna hasn't been happy at the milliners' for some time,' Lucy said. 'And this sounds much nicer . . . It was very kind of you to think of her.'

'Well, of course, we must see what she thinks of the idea, and whether she and Mrs Silvie take to each other. But I think my recommendation will count for something.'

'You've done so much for my family . . .' Her sense of gratitude was very real and, as so often, left her in a state of self-doubting perplexity. 'I don't know what to say . . .'

'Not at all, my dear,' Radford said; but he seemed gratified, and patting her hand he went on. 'I was thinking it would be nice to have the Parmenters here for dinner some time soon. We haven't done much entertaining, and I think the time is ripe.'

She supposed that to mean that she was up to it now, that she was fitting the mould of Radford Stokes' wife pretty well. Certainly she had learnt and adapted over the past half-year, but she could not contemplate playing hostess to shoe-baron society without a certain trepidation. However, this was one of the things she had vowed to undertake when she married Radford, and she was still determined to do her best, even if one affectionate gesture would have made her embrace her role with a thousand times more eagerness.

'Let's see – as well as the Parmenters, we could ask the Browns . . .'

'What about Mr Hallam?' Lucy said, for she liked the works manager with his pleasantly gloomy face and spaniel ears.

'I don't think so, my dear,' Radford said crisply. 'Now as for the Parmenters, they have a daughter in her teens, I believe. I don't know whether she's of an age to dine out yet. There's a son, Harry, but he's with the army in South Africa, and no prospect of him coming home yet, it seems. We must ask Georgina if there's someone she'd like to invite . . .'

'Yes, of course,' Lucy heard herself saying. A dimness had briefly swarmed in on her at the mention of the war in South Africa. Was Matt Doughty part of that far-away abstraction which, since the hysterical celebrations for Mafeking earlier in the year, had become a dull fixture in people's minds? She was assailed by an image of an empty veldt strewn with bleached bones, which was somehow entangled with the image of the crypt at Cleatham. But it was not just the horror of the image that made her thrust it away. It was the memories that it might lead on to, memories she had forsworn.

Mrs Silvie, as Radford had said, was the sister of Mr Aubrey

Parmenter, one of Cottesbridge's leading boot-manufacturers. She had married a prosperous leather-dealer who had died early, and had lived on as a solitary widow in a large house screened from the road by pines, half a mile out of Cottesbridge. It was a house of that stupefying ugliness and inconvenience which wealth seems to delight in, with numerous pointed scalloped roofs like those of a railway-station, and ironwork balconies and canopies all over its face, as if the house were of a savage disposition, and had to be muzzled.

Lucy knew this because she accompanied Joanna on her first visit to Mrs Silvie, on a December day of dank fog which, lurking thickly about the trees before the house, gave them the look of pillars in a ghostly hall, and made the invisible patterings of pine-cones falling upon the leaf-mould sound like the movements of furtive creatures.

'Now remember, Joanna,' Lucy said, 'if you don't fancy it, you can always say no. You haven't got to do anything you don't want to.'

'Oh I know, Lucy, but it is an opportunity, isn't it?' said Joanna, in whose small, fair-skinned face there was a subdued animation like the light through a butterfly's wing. The change in circumstances, the relief from pinch and trouble brought about by Lucy's marriage, seemed to have benefited her more than all the other Middletons; she had developed a new brightness and assurance, though her presence was still an unemphatic one. 'And the Misses Herring are getting so stingy in their old age, I just can't stay loyal to them for ever. And as for home . . . Well, it's not as if Mother will be on her own, and things are so much better there, now we're not short all the time.'

Lucy smiled. She guessed that Joanna had also found being the manager of that chaotic household a strain, and had jumped at the chance of an escape.

Mrs Silvie turned out to be a little eager, black-clad woman with a flat nose, black button-eyes, and a row of frizzy grey curls that proclaimed themselves so obviously a wig that they might as well have dropped upon her unwitting head from a height. Her first words on their being shown into the cluttered parlour were, 'Why, look at you! You are quite a sparkling pair!' Turning to look in the mirror that hung above the mantelpiece, Lucy saw at once what she meant. The fog had settled all over her in translucent drops, so that it hung in delicate beads upon her eyelashes, and formed a bright tiara on her hair; Joanna was in like case, so that they appeared like two jewelled and sequined creatures, rarefied and strange.

The incident set a happy tone for the meeting: Mrs Silvie seemed to take to them at once. She was not haughty and distant – quite the reverse. It seemed that in her seclusion she saw new people so seldom that she could not help touching them to see if they were real. She seemed especially taken with Joanna, and holding her by the elbows shunted her over to the window to look at her in the light. 'Why, haven't you got fine skin? What do you use on it, dear?'

'I don't use anything on it,' smiled Joanna. 'Just soap and water.'

'*Do* you?' fizzed Mrs Silvie, necklaces swinging and clattering across her bombazine bosom as she studied Joanna's face from all angles. 'Aren't you lucky? I know people who'd give a king's ransom for skin like that, and try all sorts of concoctions: buttermilk, mallow-root, pear-juice . . . Oh yes!' she affirmed, 'they do, you know! They'll try anything!' She transferred her attention to Lucy. 'And so you're Radford Stokes' wife – what a splendid figure you have! I'm afraid I haven't been to see him since he married, but I don't go out, you see. I don't. I get trembly, and I get shooting pains. You must tell him to come and see me. I hope he doesn't work himself as hard as ever?'

'About as hard, I think,' Lucy said.

'Then he shouldn't. He should attend to you, handsome creature that you are. Tell him I said so. Now you can't be local-born, I can tell that.'

'Yes – I'm from Cottesbridge.'

'*Are* you?' Each new piece of information, it seemed, was of equal fascination to Mrs Silvie. 'But then, I don't know Cottesbridge now. I never go down there now. Oh no, I don't.' Her little dried-up curls shook and rattled like winter oak-leaves. 'No, not I. I have got quite out of touch since my Harry went away to fight those beastly Boers. I call him my Harry, because he used to come and see me so often, and he's a favourite of mine. I mean Harry Parmenter, my nephew. My brother Aubrey's son – doesn't take after him a bit. Now tell me, my dear,' she said, seizing Joanna's arm, and speaking with a tremendous seriousness that made an amusing contrast with her look of an animated doll, 'now be quite frank with me – what is your opinion of this business in South Africa? Are you, what do they call it, pro-Boer?'

She gazed into Joanna's face, as if excitedly expecting invaluable wisdom.

'Well . . . I don't want anyone to get themselves killed,' Joanna said in her mild way.

'*Don't* you? Neither do I! Of course England must be right, she always is, but really I don't see the value of this dreadful dusty land. It's not like India. I told Harry so, before he went, but he didn't listen. You haven't met Harry Parmenter? I don't suppose you would – he left last year. He writes me though. Oh yes, he does. Come here.'

Mrs Silvie bustled them to a table, covered with a velvet cloth, which was even more densely crowded with knick-knacks than the rest of the room. It was set out as a sort of shrine, with numerous framed photographs, letters tied up with ribbon, and various other mementoes.

'This is Harry – that's his latest photograph, taken just before he went abroad,' Mrs Silvie said, thrusting the picture within inches of Lucy's face. 'He's rather plain. But we're not a family with a great deal in the way of looks, I'm afraid, as you are, my dears. I must say I feel like a little garden-weed between you two great sunflowers, how lovely and *tall* you both are! Well, that's Harry anyhow – a dear boy, and I only wish he'd never gone into the army, but he has rather impetuous ideas. He's a lieutenant with the North-amptonshires.'

The jolt this gave Lucy had to be disguised in an earnest scrutiny of the square, honest and hopeful face looking out of the photograph. 'The Northamptonshires?' she found herself repeating.

'Yes, my dear, and he's been out in that awful place practically since it began. Oh, do you know someone in the North-amptonshires? But of course I dare say you do, so many joined the colours. Well, he promised me that he wouldn't stay for ever in the army, but come home and settle down, and marry. Everybody should marry, even ugly people, because there are always other ugly people for them – well, you only have to look at our family. It's the best life there is. I only had twelve years of it before Mr Silvie died, but they were terribly happy years. He was a good man. Sometimes he drank more than was good for him, but he never chased after other women, as so many men do, I'm afraid. One can always tell if they do, because they have different smells about them when they get into bed and things of that kind.' Solitude and security had developed in Mrs Silvie a peculiar candour, so that she no longer seemed to acknowledge a dividing line between what was casual and admissible in conversation and what was entirely personal and frank. 'But I don't need to tell you about marriage, dear,' she went on, making a sandwich of Lucy's hand between her own. '*You* know it's the best of all possible worlds. I shall enlist you as an ally when Harry comes home, to persuade him to settle down. Because we are going to be seeing something of each other, aren't we, when you come to visit your sister? Yes, my dear – ' she seized Joanna's hand, making the same sandwich – 'I think you'll do for me. I think we'll get along. Yes, I do, you know. You'll probably want to see all over the house and so on, and so you shall, but I won't come upstairs with you. I don't tackle the stairs more than I need, because of the trembliness in my legs, and sometimes I get a feeling all along my left arm. My doctor says it's called angina something, which is a rather pretty name for something so unpleasant, isn't it?'

So it was settled: the practical aspects, including a tour of Joanna's future home, being quickly got over in Mrs Silvie's eagerness. It was agreed that Joanna should begin her new life after Christmas; and as the old lady seemed very far from the querulous invalid Lucy had expected, and life as her companion-help a far from burdensome employment compared with skivvying for the Misses Herring, Lucy was able to contemplate the outcome of the project with satisfaction, and reflect that all her family were now as well situated as she could ever have hoped.

It was the more necessary to keep this satisfaction before her, because of the disquiet aroused by the mention of the Northamptonshire Regiment. As they were returning down the Cleatham road, Joanna said with something more than her usual tentativeness: 'Lucy, didn't Matt Doughty join the Northamptonshires?'

'Yes,' Lucy said, with a forced smile, 'so I heard.'

Joanna said nothing more; she was no doubt interpreting Lucy's constraint as merely the slight embarrassment of a happily married woman being reminded of a former love. She could not know that great exertions of will were going on within her sister, with the aim of crushing the memory of what love was like, as a starving woman would struggle to drive from her mind the image of the food she craved.

IV

Mr and Mrs Radford Stokes entertained their guests for dinner a week before Christmas.

The season was marked in that household by the stiffest, neatest, most cropped and docked little Christmas tree that never dared to shed its needles upon the floor, and which seemed deliberately to hold out its candles at a perilous angle, as if wishing to be incinerated and put out of its misery; by a holly wreath on the front door, so very wreathy that it seemed to commemorate a death rather than a birth; and by a few sprigs of mistletoe, placed in such awkward and inaccessible corners that the very idea of kissing beneath them was a dismal impossibility.

For the dinner, however, a certain sedate glitter was put forth. The leaves of the large rosewood dining-table being pulled out, and the lucency of the silverware competing with the table's invariable high polish, the whole effect, in the light of festive candles instead of gas, was of a mildly coruscating affluence. Even the hothouse flowers that formed the centre-piece had a tamed and manicured look, as if they had never had anything to do with such elemental things as earth and water, and one might have expected the people who were to come in and seat themselves at those immaculately laid-out places to be at a similar remove from nature, and to be all sealed and varnished like toy soldiers.

Radford had been in to check this dining-room a score of times, and had made a similarly thorough investigation of the drawing-room, where the tendency of the great fire to produce little rebellious smuts had caused him inexpressible anguish; he had had the maid in several times to sweep round the hearth, and only decorum seemed to inhibit him from squeezing up the chimney and inspecting it for soot with an eyeglass. Lucy left him to it at last, to go and dress. Certain sardonic reflections on what immutable law of nature made

233

it absolutely necessary for her to have bare shoulders in order to eat cooling mutton in company, and why her introduction to complete strangers could only be achieved if she had the tops of her breasts showing, a lot of bits and pieces in her hair, and if she were seated in front of a bowl of clear soup that nobody in their right mind could actually want to eat: these she banished as disloyal. Not even her thoughts must be her own tonight. For she had formed a conception of this occasion as a test for herself: a test to see if she could *be* for a whole evening the person she was meant to be; to see if she could, in the language of segregation, pass for white. Poor Lucy's feeling of dissociation was so complete that her only means of negotiating her present existence was to completely separate the old, 'real' self – the Lucy whose flesh she had always inhabited – from the Mrs Radford Stokes that other people believed her to be.

Her duties as hostess she had gone over in the last few weeks with the thoroughness of a child learning the multiplication tables, and when the guests arrived she was prompt to go forward and greet them. Was there a certain defiance of Radford in this, a determined demonstration to him that she was keeping her side of the bargain, and that he could not point to any dereliction of duty on her part as an excuse for his coldness? Perhaps: but her relation with him was still too complicated by self-doubt, gratitude, and incomprehension for her to be aware of it.

The guests were not a varied set; they were all, in the valley parlance, in leather. There was Mr Aubrey Parmenter, owner of Cottesbridge's largest shoe concern, and fortunately unaware that his hostess had once worked in one of his factories, with his wife and daughter. There was Mr John Arthur Brown, who owned tanneries and warehouses, with his wife and his bachelor cousin, who was his agent in Northampton. There was an aged walking mountain of fat called Mr Leek, who was a retired leather-factor, and was supposed to know everything about the trade worth knowing. And there was a shadowy young man who was introduced by the bachelor cousin as Mr Miles Mellish, and who was apparently heir to so much leather-made money since his father's death that he did not really need to concern himself with leather at all.

This, then, was Lucy's entrée into the *haute-bourgeoisie* of the shoemaking towns. Who were these people? They were pretty much what they made themselves out to be: industrialists in a trade that had not long been an industry, who had usually started out from fairly small beginnings. The grand gestures that their counterparts in the North were capable of were not generally for them; a certain modesty of scale still clung about them; though there were big men amongst them, men like Moses Philip Manfield who would go on to knighthoods and renown. That use of two forenames was one of their idiosyncrasies, combining as it did a certain down-to-earth plainness with a boastful assurance, rather like the hideous redbrick Kremlins they built for themselves on the outskirts of the towns. They were Liberal in politics, if not in the wages they paid; in religion they were often Methodist, though it was doubtful whether theirs was a Methodism that Wesley would have recognized, and their reaction to the passionate open-air prayerfests that had founded their faith would have been a fastidious horror and an urgent summons to the police. They were intensely respectable, and also stupid – probably not more stupid than the men and women who worked in their factories; but it was a stupidity that always seemed to demand expression, and had no consciousness of itself.

Towards Lucy they were entirely polite. She was the woman Radford Stokes had chosen for his wife, and it was plain that they thought well of Radford Stokes, and did not believe him likely to make a bad investment. All the same, there was a sort of smothered vigilance about them; they took sidelong looks at her in the way a shoplifter takes goods from the shelves. Only the shadowy young man named Mellish kept that glint of speculation out of his glance. Though very well-dressed, he seemed to regard everyone present with equal awe, and a remark addressed his way produced in him the alarmed eyes and seat-shiftings of a schoolboy called upon to answer a tough question in arithmetic.

Talk soon turned to the South African war, and Lucy, her hostess mode coinciding with her natural sympathy, said, 'I believe you have a son with the army, Mr Parmenter? He's well, I hope?'

'Yes, thank you, Mrs Stokes, Harry was in fine form last time we heard from him. The trouble is that letters take an infernal time getting here from the Cape, and so one never knows what may have happened in the meantime,' said Mr Parmenter. He was a bulky man in his fifties, with short arms, a growling voice, a nose like a damson, and luxuriant dundreary whiskers that gave him the look of a benevolent old lion. 'I don't mind telling you that the army was never my choice for the boy. Leave that to the fellows who've got a tradition of it in their families – the Sandhurst type, you know. But there was no holding him. Once get him safe back in England, and I think we can persuade him to think again. I get the impression from his letters that he hasn't found the military life quite the glorious thing he expected from reading about it in books.' Mr Parmenter grunted amusement, and round the table there was a good solid middle-class chuckle at the mention of books. 'Well, I know his aunt will move heaven and earth to keep him here – my sister, Mrs Silvie, whom you've met of course. I must say she spoke very highly of your sister, Mrs Stokes, and can hardly wait to have her there. I'm sure it will work out very well. Mind, she won't find it a restful berth, I'm afraid. I don't mind telling you my sister would try the patience of a saint sometimes.'

'Joanna's a very patient person,' Lucy said. 'It's something I've always envied her.'

'Wish I had it myself!' said Mr Parmenter. 'But I've never had any more patience than a boiling kettle.'

'They do say it's a virtue,' offered Mr Mellish, the shadowy young man, speaking for the first time in a sort of desperate squeak, and immediately stopping his mouth with such a great forkful of greens that he quite choked himself.

'Will your sister take to the seclusion of Mrs Silvie's life, Mrs Stokes?' said Mrs Parmenter, a long-nosed simperer in brown marocain, whom to look at was to wish to slap. 'I'm afraid it wouldn't do for giddy girls, and there are so many of those nowadays.'

'I don't think that will trouble Joanna,' Lucy said. 'She's very far from a dull girl, but she's quite devout in her own way.'

She noticed that Radford was covertly observing her with a sort of pleased surprise at the facility with which she was handling her role. Certainly, now that the worst initial moments were over, she felt confident, though how much of that was due to the iced champagne of which she had already had two glasses she did not know.

'But this war – isn't it as good as over?' inquired Miss Threadgold. 'These people surely can't hold out against the British Empire. I'm sorry, but I don't see how they can.'

'The Yankees did, you know! Boston Tea Party – all that,' said the mountainous Mr Leek, who spoke only in an occasional dogmatic explosion, in the rare intervals when his mouth was not full.

'Oh, but they were British then,' said Mrs Parmenter. 'Before they became Americans, I mean.'

'Perhaps we should simply make the Boers British citizens, and then we won't feel so bad about them beating us.'

It was Mr Brown's bachelor cousin who had spoken, and a short silence followed his remark. Beating us! What sort of talk was this? The tone of the remark jarred too, though it was not entirely surprising; for while Mr John Arthur Brown was simply an upright, close-shaven specimen of the valley businessman, his bachelor cousin, name of Clayton Brown, had something uncomfortable about him. There was something irregular and not quite steady about that lean, angular face with its smoke-blue tolerant eyes, and about the way he slid his remarks into the conversation like a man sliding his stake on to a gaming-table.

'All very well to joke, Clayton,' grumbled Mr Brown, 'but what's this never-ending business costing us? That's what I want to know.'

The mention of cost, and hence money, brought an animation to the dining-table, like the rattle of a bucket in a chicken-coop. Mr Leek let off a few firecrackers of opinion about taxes: Radford discoursed learnedly about public finances. Mrs Parmenter, who throughout her whole life had only been put to so much exertion as was required to conceive and drop two children, opined that people nowadays seemed to be afraid of hard work. Meanwhile Lucy noticed young Mr Mellish nerving himself to speak to Georgina sitting beside him, a process that necessitated several deep breaths through the mouth, as if he were about to dive for pearls.

'Miss Stokes, do you—' A terrible and erroneous idea that he had a morsel of food on his lip visibly took possession of him, and he extinguished himself in his napkin for some moments before going on, 'do you suppose we shall have snow? Before Christmas, I mean,' he added hurriedly, and then to himself, 'It was before Christmas I meant.'

'Oh, I do hope so,' Georgina said. 'Snow at Christmas is so very seasonal, isn't it?'

'It is. It is,' said Mr Mellish, in his relief letting out so much of his pent-up breath that he nearly blew the candles out. His eye fell on the table decorations. 'Like holly,' he said; and then, through an irresistible association of ideas, 'And ivy.'

'Yes,' Georgina said, 'that's a carol, isn't it? A very pretty one – one of my favourites.'

'I'm sure it is,' Mr Mellish said agreeably. 'At least – I mean it's one of mine too. I meant it's one of my favourites too,' he explained to himself.

'Really, though, Mr Mellish, there's nothing particularly seasonal about ivy when you come to think of it,' said Miss Threadgold, at Georgina's elbow. 'We have ivy all the year round – not just at Christmas. Don't we? Oh, don't misunderstand me, I've nothing against ivy! But I don't see that there's anything festive about it. I never have, I'm sorry.'

Mr Mellish appearing quite crushed, Lucy put in, 'I suppose that's why we have it at Christmas – because it's an evergreen. It stands for life, even in the middle of winter.'

'Oh! I don't dispute that. Even I can see that. But I just don't see anything very Christmassy about it, I'm sorry. That's just me. That's just the way I am,' Miss Threadgold said, with her most droning complacency.

'Where will you be spending Christmas, Mr Mellish?' Lucy asked him. It was one of the duties of the hostess to bring all the guests out of their shells; and besides, she liked him better than any of the others. He was a pink-complexioned young man, with limbs as slender as those of a scarecrow, brown eyes, troubled eyebrows shaped like cabriole table-legs, vulnerable ears thin in the light were as transparent as a cat's, and lustrous black hair elegantly and expensively cut, but with a wave in it that caused it to jut up at the crown like the feather on a hat. His smile was of great sweetness when it came, though it tended to flit insecurely across his face rather like those smiles of a baby which all but a parent attribute to colic. Mr Mellish gave a grave consideration to Lucy's question before replying, 'Well, Mrs Stokes – at my mother's, I presume. At Northampton.' This simple information seemed to depress his spirits so much that Lucy was rather at a loss, until Mr Clayton Brown said, 'Miles' mother is rather a formidable person, Mrs Stokes. The Mellish fortune may have devolved chiefly upon Miles, but the Mellish strength of character seems chiefly to have devolved upon his mother. She takes her religion rather strong, doesn't she, Miles?'

'Rather,' said Mr Mellish, who seemed grateful for the intervention. 'Oh, a fearfully good woman, though, Mrs Stokes – Miss Stokes,' he added, including Georgina in his address by making a sort of sideways hop in his chair. 'I shall never come up to her, I'm afraid.'

'She tyrannizes you, Miles' said Clayton Brown, in his lazily composed way. 'You shouldn't allow it.'

'Oh, forgive me, I'm sorry, perhaps I'm quite wrong in this, but isn't duty to one's parents one of those things we seem to be losing nowadays?' said Miss Threadgold. 'That's one of the reasons society's in such a poor state, if you ask me. The general decline of respect as a principle. I'm sorry, but it is.'

'Respect has to be earned, surely,' Lucy said, forgetting herself for a moment.

'Oh! I don't deny that. Even I can see that. But I'm talking about decent families, of course,' Miss Threadgold said, turning her smile on Lucy. 'In other spheres of life, no doubt, there are parents who set a very bad example to their children, with all manner of vices. Luckily I've no experience of those sort of people, none whatever, and hope I never shall.'

'Unfortunately, you will have to meet them in heaven, Miss Threadgold,' said Mr Clayton Brown. 'I understand that is one place where they will have the prior claim. But who knows, perhaps there's a sort of ante-room to the afterlife, where they are washed and house-trained, so that nobody shall feel uncomfortable.'

'Oh dear! You quite misunderstand me if you think I'm shocked by that sort of joking at the expense of religion. To me it's just like *water* off a *duck's back*. I'm not saying there aren't others who might be offended – people who mean a great deal to me,' said Miss Threadgold, inclining towards Georgina with a look of martyred loyalty.

'Miss Stokes knows quite well what I mean, and knows I mean no harm, without the benefit of an interpreter,' calmly said Clayton Brown, whom Lucy was beginning to find agreeable, on the principle of my enemy's enemy.

'Do you know, Miss Stokes,' said Mr Mellish, who seemed completely to have missed all this in strenuously gathering himself to speak again, 'I can't think of any time of the year I like better than Christmas.'

Georgina, after a few moments' waiting to see if this was

all, said, 'It's a very cheerful time, isn't it? I remember I used to count the days to Christmas when I was a little girl.'

'Oh, so did I,' said Mr Mellish; then, with grave consideration, 'Not that I was a little girl, you know. I was a little boy.'

'Oh! Dinah, now don't you laugh,' Miss Threadgold said, *sotto voce*, giving herself one of her little slaps on the arm.

'Of course, spring is a very nice time of the year too,' said Miles Mellish. 'And summer, naturally. And autumn can be very nice too . . .' Seeing with alarm that he was coming round to Christmas again, Mr Mellish made a diversionary dive into the potato-dish and, cramming a steaming hot potato into his mouth, exerted himself greatly in pretending that it was not burning him in the least.

'Speaking of setting a bad example,' said Mr Parmenter, 'it appears that Walter David Ives' young scapegrace of a son has seen the error of his ways at last. You know, of course, that the young whelp got himself mixed up with that Wedderburn woman. Not the first, as we all know, but she usually tends to favour the older fellows, who aren't likely to harm anybody but themselves by the association. Well, Walter David Ives runs the biggest trade in leather in Kettenham, and that son of his stands to inherit. I suppose that's what the boy was counting on, and reckoned that his behaviour in the meantime didn't signify. Not so, it turns out. Walter David Ives had him up on the carpet and told him in no uncertain terms that the whole business would go to his sister's husband and he wouldn't get a penny unless he changed his ways. Pretty firm in the old man I call it: hope I should do the same with Harry if, God forbid, he ever got himself in such a situation. You can be sure the young sprig broke off that association pretty quickly: knew which side his bread was buttered!'

'I don't see how he could have done otherwise,' said Mr John Arthur Brown. 'The thing had gone on quite long enough. Luckily he's young, and can put it all behind him now.'

'It really would be shocking to see a young man permanently ruin his chances for such a sordid adventure as that,' minced Mrs Parmenter.

'But where does it leave Alice Wedderburn?' said Lucy.

The sound of her own voice startled her. She realized that it was she who had spoken, not the decorous hostess. She saw Radford's eyes flick over to her.

'Looking for someone else to dig her claws into, I presume, Mrs Stokes,' said Mr Parmenter.

'It would just about serve her right if she found all the men had come to their senses, if you ask me,' purred Miss Threadgold.

Though she knew it was dangerously out of place here, Lucy could not suppress a memory of the railway footbridge, and a pale veiled face turned to hers in despair. 'Well, no matter what you – what one thinks of her,' she said, trying to keep her voice conversational in tone, 'she's still been left in the lurch, in a way.'

'I'm afraid I don't follow, Mrs Stokes,' said Mr Parmenter.

'Mrs Stokes is making the very pertinent point that this woman, through no fault of her own, has been left without the means of support,' said Clayton Brown, idly examining his champagne. 'And that is an injustice.'

Mrs Parmenter put up a hand to her face, to mark her abhorrence of the turn the conversation was taking.

'No fault of her own!' said Mr John Arthur Brown, who seemed glad to be able to challenge his cousin as he could not his hostess. 'No, really, Clayton, I know you have this odd way of looking at things, and I know you like to provoke, but upon my word I don't know how you can make out that that Wedderburn woman's an innocent. Everyone knows the way she's lived for years, and only the presence of ladies prevents me from putting a name to it.'

'Better in the old days! Would have put her in the House of Correction! Had her beating hemp!' said Mr Leek, gobbling between each exclamation.

'And really, as to where it leaves her, as far as I'm concerned she can go back to the Hole where she came from,' said Miss Threadgold.

'But that's got nothing to do with it,' Lucy said. 'She can't help where she comes from, and . . . and besides, there wouldn't be women like Alice Wedderburn if there weren't these rich lecherous men looking out for mistresses. She's not likely to learn any better in the Hole, but they should certainly know better. They've had every chance of learning how to behave.'

Something had changed around the table, an intensification of constraint: Lucy saw that it was because she had talked about mistresses. It was all right, apparently, to talk about the subject with a lot of prurient innuendo, but not to say it out plainly. Only Miles Mellish, who was occupied in furtively trying to take a piece of ice from the wine-pail to cool his mouth, and kept losing his grip so that it slid around the tablecloth like a sliver of soap, seemed unaffected; and Clayton Brown, who looked amused. Across the table, Radford's eyes were like dull gemstones.

Mr Parmenter chose to be kindly condescending. 'You have a woman's natural clemency, Mrs Stokes, and it does you credit,' he said. 'But after all, as we're being blunt, it has to be said that that Wedderburn woman sells herself. She sells herself.'

'Well, isn't marriage the same?' cried Lucy. 'When you think about it . . . The woman gives herself to the man, and in return he gives her a home and supports her and everything. All that's different is they've gone through a ceremony.'

She knew at once that she had overstepped terrible bounds, but she simply could not stop herself speaking. The memory of the footbridge was too strong; and besides, she believed intensely what she said, though she had hardly framed the belief at a conscious level. It was a measure of how completely the impulsive emotion had overtaken her that she did not realize the relevance of her statement to her own marriage for several burning moments.

'A ceremony, my dear,' said Mrs Parmenter, clearly deciding that the time had come to my-dear Lucy into her place, 'that is sanctified by God.'

There was no arguing with God, and all the table seemed to think so; except for Clayton Brown, who remarked, 'So was slavery supposed to be, once upon a time.'

Dinah Threadgold chose this moment for a conspicuous display of social tact, as if to emphasize Lucy's lack of it. 'Oh! I must say I get tired of hearing that Wedderburn woman discussed. I'm sorry, but I do. It's almost as bad as when people talk about the Prince of Wales. Though on that subject, I must say it does seem that he has grown stouter than ever . . .'

Mrs Parmenter took her cue eagerly, and the subject of Alice Wedderburn, and Lucy's views on it, were left behind. Lucy felt for some time unequal to joining in the conversation, and when she at last did, it was in the conventional mode of the hostess again; but the consciousness of her lapse stayed bitterly with her. If only they had chosen something else on which to exercise their wagging tongues! But it was done now, and after all, why should she care a bean for what they thought of her?

Easier said than done. Only complete self-confidence and

complete self-loathing are indifferent to opinion: Lucy was far from the former, but had not sunk to the latter. She had wanted to prove herself; she had wanted above all to prove herself to Radford. Perhaps in that very desire there was a premonition that, if she did not win his good opinion soon, she would equally soon cease to care for it.

Genteel Cottesbridge did not keep late hours: the guests had left well before midnight. The adjournment to the drawing-room had been less of a trial, for they could split off into groups, and there was Georgina's piano-playing to cover any awkwardness; and Lucy was much occupied with Miles Mellish, who darted to a seat beside her as if in a game of fearfully earnest musical-chairs. From there he watched Georgina with a sort of crushed attentiveness, whilst simultaneously trying to answer Lucy's remarks, smooth down his hair, and balance his coffee-cup on his knee.

So the company departed, and left the house to the ticking of the clocks, which, as if indignant at being drowned out for so long, seemed to advertise their presence more loudly than ever. Lucy was glad to hurry up to bed while Radford was still making an inspection of the littered reception-rooms; he had not addressed a word to her since dinner.

It was cold outside, with freezing fog; but a good fire had been laid in their bedroom, and Lucy was kneeling beside it in her nightdress, letting its warmth lull her and still the busy fretting of her mind, when Radford came up.

'There's a glass and a plate broken,' he commented as he undressed. 'Jane's normally very careful, but she will get flustered when there's company.'

No one could have looked less flustered than Radford, who removed and folded his clothes with his usual deliberation. Only someone granted access to his private world like Lucy – and sometimes she suspected that he resented that access – could tell that he was not pleased; definitely not pleased. It was something about the upward tilt of his head, as if he were balancing something on the crown.

And yet he would not say it. To give expression to a grievance was to forfeit a little of the advantage, and lay himself open to counter-grievances; and she knew that his unearthly patience could sit out any mental siege, and force her to make the first move. The blame for any quarrel could then be laid at her door: she started it. Such grim games are played out by countless couples, and often their stalemate is broken only by death; but to one of Lucy's open, undevious temperament they were a torture. She was prepared to be the loser, if only to break the deadlock.

'Do you think everyone enjoyed themselves tonight?' she said.

'Yes, tolerably well, I dare say,' Radford said after a slight pause.

Lucy stirred the coals to make them blaze. 'I couldn't help saying that about Alice Wedderburn,' she said, trying to keep her voice light. 'I know she's not perfect, but – well, people seem terribly hard on her.'

'You made your opinion abundantly clear, my dear,' Radford said.

There was no mistaking the frost in his tone. She turned to look at him. 'So did everybody else,' she said.

Radford set his gold pocket-watch carefully on its stand. 'There are ways,' he said, 'of expressing an opinion.'

'What ways?'

Radford deposited his cuff-links in their little box – one, two. 'Since you ask, my dear,' he said, 'there are acceptable ways, and unacceptable ways. Yours was the latter. If you really intend . . .'

'Yes?'

He regarded her with hard composure. 'If you really intend meeting these people on an equality, you should not *gush* in that way. There is nothing so ill-bred. You should be in command of your feelings, not the other way around. I mean this as a general rule – leaving aside for the moment the substance of the views you expressed, which is so distasteful that I can only think you thought it up deliberately to shock and embarrass.'

'Well, you're wrong then,' she said. 'I'm sorry if anyone was shocked and embarrassed, but all I said was—'

'I know quite well what you said,' Radford said whitely. 'It's quite enough that my wife chooses to defend a common whore in public, let alone that she tries to repeat it to me in private.'

She was herself obscurely shocked at that word *whore* coming from Radford's lips; but it also seemed to encapsulate for her the same hypocrisy that had irked her at the dinner-table, and she was angry again. 'I don't suppose there was one man at that table who hadn't been with a whore at some time in his life,' she said sharply. 'That's what's so sickening . . . Except Mr Mellish. And you,' she added, beginning to tremble with a confusion of emotions she could hardly begin to disentangle.

Radford, after a rigid, smothered glare at her, broke his paralysis and went over to the bed. 'That,' he said, getting into bed, 'is precisely the sort of thing I mean. I really don't know what to think, my dear. I can advise you on your behaviour, but I can't help what's in your mind.'

They can't put their fingers inside your head . . . As soon as the memory of Matt's words came to her she pushed it away.

'I suppose,' Radford said, 'I should at least be grateful that you exempt me from your disgusting speculations.'

'That's why I liked you,' she said. 'Because you seemed different from other men in that way. Gentler. Not so swaggering.'

He made no answer: he seemed surprised by this sudden turn in the acrimonious exchange, and so indeed was she – the words had simply come. But once they had come, she felt hopeful of a change in the atmosphere, the oppression of which was dreadful to her; and out of the confusion of her feeling she traced an instinct which told her that now might be the time for the completest reconciling – a new beginning, indeed.

She remained gazing into the fire for a few minutes; and then, trusting to this instinct, she stood up and slipped the nightdress over her head. She crept over to his bed. Radford's eyes were open but his head was slightly turned from her. She did not lift the sheet but got up on the counterpane, naked, and began to caress him. When he turned his head his eyes took in her nakedness with a single appalled glance, as if it were a knife pointed at his heart.

'What in God's name are you doing?' he said.

'Oh, Radford,' she said, 'just hold me. Won't you just hold me . . .?'

He had shifted away from her. 'What the – just what the hell do you think you are doing?' he said, his voice going up, and pushed her hand sharply away.

Even now she could not believe that the instinct had led her wrong. 'This is what couples do when they make up after a quarrel,' she said huskily. 'This is what they do. Radford, it isn't dirty or wrong, it's normal . . .'

'I think you must be mad,' he said, sliding to the edge

245

of the bed and sitting there running his hand through his disarranged hair. His eyes were averted from her. 'I really think you must be mad.'

'Perhaps I am.' She knelt up on the bed. She had stripped herself, abased herself to no avail: a bitter shame was in wait for her, but anger came first. 'Won't you even look at me, Radford? Am I that repulsive to you?' With a half-distracted, half-parodic gesture she lifted up her heavy hair from her shoulders, throwing her body forward. 'Am I repulsive?'

Radford threw her the tiniest glance. 'Well, you certainly appear so, in that posture, my dear,' he said, barely opening his lips.

She let her hair fall: she looked at the counterpane. All was ashes, and she saw the extent of her defeat. She had given him the excuse he wanted now: the advantage was his.

After a moment she got up and put on her nightdress and stood looking down into the fire.

'There's one thing I don't understand,' she said at last, turning.

Radford, back in bed, gave her a frown, as if to someone who persists in talking over a trivial subject when it has been exhausted.

'I don't understand,' she said, 'why you ever wanted a wife at all. Why did you marry me, if you don't want a wife?'

And she saw then that she had stung him. All unwittingly, she had somehow pierced his armour, and she felt he would never forgive her for it. He could not disguise the twitching of his lips as he turned away from her in the bed and said, 'God knows. God alone knows.'

The room was intolerable to her. She managed to contain her sobs until she was out of it. She made her way blindly along the landing and at last slumped down upon the darkened stairs, hugging herself and letting her tears have their way.

She tried to be quiet, but the sound of her weeping must have reached the quick ears of Georgina. She came out of her room in her dressing-gown and timidly stole to Lucy's side.

'Oh, Lucy, dear – what's the matter?'

Lucy could only shake her head. 'Nothing,' she said, trying to recover herself; but the feel of the kind little hand on her shoulder only brought the tears bursting out afresh, and she was helpless.

'Oh, don't!' Georgina whispered desperately, sitting beside

her, and repeatedly patting her hand with a nervous fluttering motion. 'Oh, Lucy, dear, don't! Whatever it is, don't think about it! Think of nice things! Oh, dear, think of nice things!'

V

The beginning of 1901 saw two deaths. One was momentous, and scarcely believable: the old Queen died at Osborne. Victoria gone! Her great age did not lessen the surprise felt, and the sense of dislocation; she had seemed almost as much of a fixture of existence as the seasons. The other death was private and unnoticed, but was just as momentous to Lucy. It was the death of her respect for Radford.

It is all too easy to love where we feel no respect; but true respect must involve at least a degree of liking; so Lucy found. The scene on the night of the dinner-party had completed the alienation between her and Radford. Once the fire of emotion had cooled, she found on contemplating her husband that all trace of friendly feeling towards him had been burned off, and with it the respect for his character that had persisted through his primness, his coldness, his withheld affection. To her mind's eye he wore something of the jaded, shabby aspect of the food-smelling dining-room in the light of the morning after the party. The aspect that she must wear to his mind's eye she could only guess at: it was with mingled trouble and relief that she realized she no longer very much cared.

And so began a new year, a new reign and a new century; and though this was also the beginning of a new and dark era in Lucy's experience, to an observer – even one who knew her pretty well – there was no change, only continuity. She and Radford Stokes were married, and would presumably remain so for the rest of their lives.

And there was continuity. The relentless propensity of life to go grinding colourlessly on, just when it seems to the agonized nerves that it must surely make some dramatic pause, some arresting tableau to mark a crisis of human feeling, could not have been more convincingly demonstrated than in Radford's clockwork house. Radford continued in his regular habits of work and leisure; Lucy continued in her regular habits as the lady of the household. There was not even any sign of slow change or progression, except in one small, but to Lucy, crucial regard. She was haltingly, painfully but rewardingly learning the rudiments of music from Georgina, and its effect on her grew steadily. It was indeed redemption.

In the course of her studies she learned too about the lives of the composers whose works she well-meaningly maimed upon the piano; and in the tribulations of these long-dead men with their strange foreign names she found much reflection that fused directly with her own experience. The deafness of Beethoven, which at first seemed to her no more than a terrible mischance as she picked her way through *Für Elise*, became more significant as she recognized her own unhappiness and its ironic conditions. She saw now that great musicians were not made deaf by accident; or if it was an accident, it was of a different sort from the street accident or the scald from an upset kettle. She had long since ceased to believe in a benevolent power behind the workings of the universe, but nor could she quite believe that there was an empty neutrality instead. A person who walked past a dying man in the street might feasibly claim that he was merely being neutral: death was still the result. The sort of neutrality that consisted in visiting a composer with chronic deafness, or implanting incipient disease in infants, or implanting in human hearts desires that the conditions of life would not admit of, was surely indistinguishable from active malice. There was a blight laid across human endeavour: the question was, perceiving this malice, whether to continue out of defiance, or give in.

It was a smirking malice, that she knew. For the irony of her own situation was that externally everything seemed all right. Her family was secure. Joanna had settled in well with Mrs Silvie. In her own unassuming way she had even begun to alter her employer's habits, somehow persuading her to go out of the house occasionally, herself pushing the old lady's bath-chair when she was not up to walking. Sometimes Lucy would meet them on her own walks, and could see what a comfortable rapport was growing between her sister and the little lady with the wig roosting on her head like a fancy bantam.

'You handsome creatures,' Mrs Silvie would cry as they went along together. 'I feel just like a thorn between two roses! Mrs Stokes, I'll bet you dance beautifully with your lovely tall figure. Does Radford take you dancing? No? Well, I dare say he wants to keep you to himself, and I don't blame him. My Harry has always been fond of dancing, but he doesn't dance well – looks just like a big friendly dog standing on its hind legs. He does! If we could get this horrible war settled and have him home you could see for yourself.'

Radford take her dancing! That was funny – but there was not even a wry laugh left in her. There was ghastly humour in this discordance between appearance and reality, but it was only for ironic fate to appreciate. All she could do was play her part in the comedy: the comedy of a couple who preserved a perfect outward harmony whilst privately living in a state of profoundest separation: with not a spontaneous or confidential word to say to one another, with not the slightest meeting of sympathies or interests, and with a complete physical estrangement that seemed to Lucy to proceed on her husband's part from a simple loathing of her.

Even had there been some all-seeing spirit at hand to tell her that most marriages are more or less unhappy, it would have been cold comfort; for Lucy's sense of her self-worth was already so wounded that it would have been the killing blow to have learnt that her wretchedness was not even important – that it was only a single water-drop in a field of dew. It might even have dangerously intensified the blackest moods that came upon her, when Lucy felt that consciousness was a burden; when, staring into the loveless dark, it occurred to her that the chief obstacle to self-murder was indolence, and that if human beings came equipped with, say, a combination lock upon their hip, which at a turn guaranteed instant death, the earth would be populated only by the lower animals.

But these worst moments were, thankfully, fitful in their occurrence; and meanwhile there were great oceans of time to cross, with no landfall in sight. In fact as the winter, dragging its feet, slowly approached its appointment with the executioner spring, Lucy found herself living in two sorts of time. Memory of the past, which for so long she had held at bay, finally broke down her defences, swarmed in, and laid claim to her. She found herself compulsively remembering her time with Matt Doughty.

She had been right, of course, to suppress such thoughts, for the sake of her peace of mind. It is a fair bet that if something in life makes us very happy, it will at some time make us miserable in due proportion. Once remembrance was given free rein, there was no end to it: suddenly everything reminded her of her time with Matt, to the extent that it seemed her past self must have been a creature of supernaturally intense observation and receptivity. How else could the mere sight of a tea-tray bring to mind in such astonishing detail the tray of sandwiches that she and Matt had once shared on the narrow bed in his dingy lodgings? Yet that was doubly distressing, for she recalled too how uncomfortable that occasion had been – hardly a red-letter day. She even remembered longing to get out of that room which now she dwelt on with such fondness. Yet how could she have known then; how could she have foreseen that a day would come when the slightest unregarded details of this time would stand forth as heartbreaking emblems?

Whether Radford was equally unhappy she could not tell, given his increasingly inaccessible reserve; but somehow she doubted it. Had he given any hint to that effect, they could have begun some dialogue that might have led to frank mutual admission: 'Very well, we are unhappy – let us separate.' But even leaving aside the fact that mutual admissions were far outside the scope of their frozen relation, it was impossible. Radford Stokes, involved in the messy, unrespectable business of separation! Radford Stokes, with a failed marriage! Never. And besides, while her past was entirely lost to her, Radford in many ways continued to live in his. The presence of a wife was for much of the time no more than a mildly incommoding addition to his old way of life. If he had ever contemplated altering his habits in regard to, for example, entertaining and socializing, then he had certainly not done so – the party before Christmas had had no sequel.

No sequel, that is, except in occasional calls by two of the gentlemen then present – Mr Clayton Brown and Mr Miles Mellish. It was plain in the first instance that Mr Mellish had longed to call but lacked the courage, and Clayton Brown, whom the young man looked up to as the fount of worldly wisdom, had good-naturedly agreed to accompany him. But Mr Mellish was defeated by sheer weight of numbers on that occasion, and it was left to Clayton Brown and Lucy to keep up the conversation.

Not that this was entirely unwelcome to her, for Clayton

Brown had, after all, been her ally in the controversy over Alice Wedderburn, and she remembered that with gratitude. Moreover, that element of scepticism in him was refreshing to her in her discontent. Without ever being anything more than negligently well-dressed, dryly humorous, and idly observant from under his heavy, smoky eyelids, he conveyed the impression that he found Radford's upholstered, antimacassared, regulated and thoroughly conventional world rather ridiculous.

'D'you know this fellow hardly knows what to do with himself, Mrs Stokes?' Clayton Brown said, clapping the silent Miles on the shoulder. 'Money fairly coming out of his ears, and he wanders about complaining how time weighs heavy on his hands. Now if I had his fortune, instead of being tied to our wretched warehouse, wouldn't I know what to do with it? But it's always the way. What's that bit in Thackeray – "Which of us is happy in this world? Which of us has his desire? or, having it, is satisfied?" Pompous old humbug, mind you.'

'What would you do with a fortune, then, Mr Brown?' Lucy said.

'What would I do with it? Ask me rather what I *wouldn't* do with it. Live – live to the utmost.'

'That's rather vague.'

Clayton Brown smiled. 'So it is. I think you're in the process of trapping me into an admission that I *wouldn't* know what to do with it.'

'Not really,' said Lucy. 'I suppose I'm just wondering whether we can ever know what we really want. Except by getting it . . .'

'And then finding we don't want it,' Clayton supplied. He gave her a look of sharp curiosity before leaning back and going on in his normal tone. 'Ah, well, you may be right, but it's an experiment I'd willingly try. Miles, what do you say to making your fortune over to me, so that I can prove Mrs Stokes wrong?'

But Miles Mellish, rather overshadowed in Clayton Brown's urbane company, could only offer a nervous laugh in reply. However, once the initial breach had been made, Mr Mellish took courage, and began to call at the house on his own.

He did this with tremendous circumspection, seeming indeed to regard his coming at all as an impertinence, and perching on the very edge of his chair as if prepared at a moment's notice to be ordered out of the room. 'I hope I don't disturb you,' he would say, pulling his gloves all out of shape, and then trying to hide them. 'I hope I don't intrude.' And when Lucy offered him tea, he was as grateful and doubtful as if she had offered to prepare him a four-course banquet with her own hands, and do his laundry into the bargain. 'If you're sure it's not too much trouble,' he would say. 'If you're absolutely sure I'm not putting you out.'

Then there was the tea itself to be got through. Mr Mellish could not simply drink his tea and talk of other things: he felt that the presence of the tea required, as it were, a tribute.

'Tea's awfully nice, isn't it?' said he, vigorously rubbing both his knees. 'I like tea extremely. I can't think of anything I like better than tea.' He left off rubbing his knees, seeming to feel the friction rather scorchingly, and cast about him. '. . . Except coffee.'

'Oh! I find coffee bad for the digestion,' said Miss Threadgold. 'I always have, I'm sorry. I'm sure it's not good for the constitution generally. In fact I said so to a doctor I met once, and he said to me, "Miss Threadgold, if only everyone had your common sense – it *does* injure the health, and I've tried to tell people so for thirty years".'

'I'm sure you're right,' Mr Mellish said humbly. 'As a matter of fact My Mother—' he seemed always to refer to his mother, like the deity, in awful capitals – 'never takes anything stronger than barley-water, and says that if everybody followed her example there would be no railway accidents. I – I don't quite follow her reasoning, I must confess, but I'm sure she's right.'

Mr Mellish, in fact, was quite as sure that everyone else was right as Dinah Threadgold was sure that only she was right. So modest was he that Miss Threadgold could not provoke him into dispute, much as she tried. Her most complacent stupidities received his assent. Upon her asserting that Mellish was a Scots name, he timidly mentioned that all his family were English, that they had records of their ancestry in family Bibles going back to the seventeenth century, and all were English, and that he had been given to understand by His Mother, who was rather interested in such things, that the name was Anglo-Saxon in origin; but, he added, he was sure Miss Threadgold was right.

As it happened this, though Mr Mellish was unlikely to

realize it, was not at all a bad way of dealing with Miss Threadgold. And she needed dealing with, inasmuch as she was the dragon guarding the treasure-hoard – Georgina. Georgina was the person he came to see. So much was glaringly obvious to Lucy, to Miss Threadgold, and, though she was too shy to allude to it, to Georgina; but Mr Mellish went to such lengths to disguise it, and took such pains to be attentive to the two other ladies, that he ended up talking to Georgina least of all. He would be in the midst of some polite inquiry concerning her music or her drawing when a sudden consciousness would seize him, and he would make Lucy jump by springing round in his chair and saying, 'Mrs Stokes, I do beg your pardon, did you speak?'

'No, no,' said Lucy, 'do go on.'

'Oh! I beg your pardon. It must have been the fire crackling that I heard. It was the fire I heard,' he added to himself in an undertone. But in a moment he was twirling round again. 'Not that I mean to suggest, of course, that your voice is – that your voice in any way resembles—'

'You wouldn't say that if you'd heard me sing,' Lucy smiled. 'Do please go on.' And he would go on, at last, picking up his thread with all the ease of a man in thick mittens picking up a needle.

But despite all this it was clear that he liked Georgina, and that Georgina, though too flustered and blushing to say so, liked him. Lucy could see why. He was personable, honest, and gentle as a lamb: he never had an unkind word to say about anyone. The qualities that he lacked were precisely those which, taken to an extra degree, made for unpleasantness – self-confidence, shrewdness, and sophistication all being but embryonic forms of conceit, cunning and calculation.

It was an attachment that, with its potential for releasing Georgina from her imprisonment of backward shyness and dependence, Lucy was eager to foster, just as Miss Threadgold was eager to discourage it. She had already lost some of her power over that innocent young life to Lucy, and did not intend losing any more. So between Lucy and this woman she hated a new battle was joined every time the maid announced Mr Mellish and that familiar schoolboy crest of hair made its tentative appearance round the door with its invariable phrase: 'I hope I don't intrude?'

Unfortunately Lucy feared it was going to be a long haul,

given the extreme diffidence of both parties. Trying to push them together was like trying to bend butter. Mr Mellish clearly thought, for example, that to increase the frequency of his calls would be a highly presumptuous statement of intent, though it was noticeable that he did begin to frequent Lessington Road a lot. He had a gig, and almost every day he could be seen going up and down the road in it, never glancing at the Stokes house, but remaining very upright and abstracted as if it were the most natural thing in the world to traverse and re-traverse that quiet street six times a day like a moving-target at a shooting-gallery. His equanimity was quite a remarkable thing to see, for the pony was rather skittish, and often varied the exercise by breaking into an alarming gallop, so that all the evidence of Mr Mellish's passing was a whirl of dust, a flying hat and a feeble cry of 'Whoa!'

Under more usual circumstances, of course, Lucy would have discussed the matter with her husband. She would have sat up in some tender sleepy moment of the night and twiddled his hair and said, 'Do you know, love, I think Mr Mellish and Georgina have a taking for each other. What do you think of that?' And her husband would have said, 'Good Lord, I had no idea. How can you tell?' And she would have said, 'It's not easy, I know, they're so shy. I wonder how we can help them?' And they would have talked of it in low, intimate voices until they fell asleep in each other's arms.

Thus the fantasy. In reality Radford would not even have endured her touching his hair. As for what he would think of Georgina being courted, even with the caution of Miles Mellish, Lucy was deeply dubious. He was so used to having Georgina around, part of his hermetic, inviolable routine, just as much as his slippers and twice-daily bath. Moreover, his fondness for her seemed to have much to do with her status as the eternal sister – 'my sister,' as he usually and possessively referred to her, rather than by her name: the ideal sexless relationship. It was not difficult to see that this had contributed to making Georgina so childlike and naïve; not difficult to see, either, that the idea of Georgina having an admirer would not appeal to him.

No, there was no question of confiding in Radford, not that there had been for some time. The gulf was too wide, and she did not intend again trying to close it by any such humiliation as had concluded the night of the dinner-party.

They were a loveless couple and that was that.

And yet – even as her feeling towards Radford hardened from plaintive bewilderment to indifference to dislike – she could not help wishing to make some demonstration to him. Some demonstration that would show him that she was not as utterly repulsive as he found her. (Though was she? She had begun to wonder, and that was a motive too.) And perhaps some demonstration that would wake him, make him jealous, jolt him into valuing her? She was not sure about that, not sure whether she even wanted him to care any more: all was confusion, a confusion of revenge, boredom, longing to be loved, and self-disgust; but this confusion had enough of impetus to make her begin flirting with Clayton Brown.

She met him by chance one cold late afternoon in March. She had been on her weekly visit to her family in Alma Street, but disinclination to go home yet had made her turn her steps south out of the town, down to where the flood-meadows began, and take a look at the river. It was that sunset hour when the leafless trees lose in colour what they gain in definition, the pale silver birch and the dark moss-green oak alike appearing as silhouettes of purest black, their limbs thrown out against the sky in arresting and enigmatic gestures as if on the verge, at that bewitched moment, of communication. Returning to the town in this atmosphere, Lucy felt the final sinking of the sun below the horizon as a palpable withdrawal of warmth, like the shutting of a stove door. The darkness that now closed in upon her was of a teeming quality, almost as if it were a dense swarm of living particles, and she was glad when it was parted by lights approaching behind her, the beams making a commonplace stretch of country road out of what had been mysterious and oppressive.

The lights were the side-lamps of a smart little trap, the driver of which turned his head as she stepped aside to let it pass, and then pulled on the reins.

'Mrs Stokes, hello,' said Clayton Brown. 'Do you accept lifts from strange gentlemen?'

'It depends how strange they are,' said she.

He laughed. 'Jump up. It's a chilly evening.'

She was cold and tired, and glad of a lift; her motives seemed to need no further examination than that. She got up beside him in the trap, and they rattled off.

'Are you – going to visit your cousin?' she said after a

256

while, nervously. She had not realized how very close to him she would be in the small seat of the trap, and he seemed serenely disinclined to break the silence.

'Usual business visit,' he said. 'I bring the accounts, John shakes his head over them. I say we're doing pretty well, he says he can't see it lasting. Is Radford as pessimistic?'

'I wouldn't know,' Lucy said before she could stop herself.

'Doesn't talk business at home, eh? Lucky you,' Clayton said, casually, but missing nothing. 'Well, they always give me a good dinner anyway. I fancy John's wife thinks I never eat properly at home, being a bachelor. I don't like to tell her that I keep a very good table, even though I've no one to share it with. Married people always tend to look on single people as rather sad and helpless, don't they?'

'Perhaps that's to hide their envy of them,' said Lucy.

Clayton laughed softly. 'D'you know, it's wonderful to hear a bit of good downright cynicism, Mrs Stokes. I thought I was the only one to understand the meaning of the word in this dreadfully earnest part of the world.'

'Oh, no,' she said, 'you're not the only one.' But she was shocked, even now, to find that that was how she had begun to feel.

They were descending into Cottesbridge, and a glow-worm appeared to crawl across the steep townscape before them as the gas-lamps were lit.

'Ever get over to Northampton?' Clayton Brown said, tightening the reins as the pony clattered across the bridge and into the High Street.

'No, not often.' Never, she might have said, for she never went anywhere.

'You must come over some time. You and Radford.' The pause between the two sentences was barely discernible. 'As I say, I can give you a good dinner. It's not often an old bachelor gets a chance to entertain. Your sister-in-law too, of course. Though that means that crooning hag Dinah as well.' As Lucy was silent he went on cheerfully, 'Sorry, have I spoken out of turn? I rather thought you disliked her as much as I do.'

Lucy looked at him, and gave a small smile. 'Not dislike,' she said. 'Hate.'

'Thought so,' said Clayton, amused. 'Can't say I'm surprised. I fancy she always had it in mind to get her claws into Radford some day. Before you came along.'

'What?'

'That was my impression. Not that I think she had any chance, but it makes you think, eh? Lucky escape for Radford . . . in fact he's a lucky fellow all round, if you ask me.'

She did not wholly take in that last remark, for surprise had been succeeded by a wave of bitter, mirthless laughter. So Dinah Threadgold envied her her marriage to Radford! 'My God,' she said, shaking her head. 'My God.'

He let her have her laugh out; then said, with an air of tactful diversion, 'Do you see much of young Miles?'

'Oh yes, we do,' Lucy said, already feeling that she had revealed too much, and glad of the change of subject. 'At least – I think he comes to see Georgina.'

'He's a good fellow, even if he's never going to set the Nene on fire, let alone the Thames. It's quite true what he says about that mother of his, by the way. Fearful old Gorgon. That sort of miserable respectability that finds its chief pleasure prophesying hellfire for anyone who steps out of line.'

'Do you believe in hellfire, Mr Brown?'

He showed his teeth. 'Even if I did, I wouldn't let it alter my behaviour here on earth.' They had come to the corner of Lessington Road, and he pulled the pony up. 'Shall I set you down here, Mrs Stokes? We wouldn't want people to talk.'

She got down. 'Thank you for the ride.'

He shrugged slightly, regarding her. 'Do *you* believe in hellfire, Mrs Stokes?'

'In the afterlife – or here and now?'

He took out a cigar, laughing. 'Well,' he said, 'remember what I said – about coming over to Northampton some time.'

'Yes. I shall have to ask Radford.'

'Do.' He put a match to the cigar: the sudden upward illumination gave his lean face the look for a fleeting moment of a skull. Then he flicked the reins and, bidding her good-night, drew away.

And that was how, almost without conscious will, and with resentful confusion in her heart, she began flirting with Clayton Brown. Flirting was the only term for it, though in all truth that light word scarcely fitted the grim and joyless mood in which it was undertaken. She was out to make some sort of point, but she was far from being clear in her own mind as to what exactly the point was.

But it was easy to do, because of Clayton Brown. His combination of indolence and shrewdness needed no explanation from her, no declaration of intent. He offered nothing and demanded nothing. He seemed content to wait.

The same unspoken understanding determined their manner of meeting. Lucy's day for visiting her family coinciding with Clayton's day for visiting his cousin, she simply repeated the walk out of the town down to the river-meadows: he came along in the trap and picked her up.

Sometimes they merely drove around for a while; sometimes they stopped at pubs in the country and sat talking in smoky snuggeries. She would have a drink, not because she had any great taste for it, but because it helped to obscure the consciousness of what she was doing – and besides, it did not seem to matter if she became a toper as well. It was unlikely that Radford would get close enough to her to smell it on her breath when she got home.

Thus they went on, through the spring and into the early summer. The lightening of the evenings meant, of course, that they were more than ever likely to be observed, especially in such a gossip-infested community, whose first commandment was Be Censorious of Thy Neighbour. But Lucy hardly knew whether this was what she wanted or what she feared. Some mutinous voice, however, protested that this was not enough; that if report of her meeting Clayton Brown in this way got back to Radford, he would somehow assimilate the news in his nervelessly patient way, and go on as before, merely dropping his frosty temperature a couple of degrees. He would defeat her by fastidiously refusing to see such scanty evidence as anything more than a gauche girlish rebellion – simply confirming, indeed, what already seemed to be his mildly contemptuous opinion of her. She knew his capacity for outfacing her, the way he could make her feel like a child excitedly communicating something to an adult only to be wearily told that they knew all about it. No, something more was needed.

And so she despised herself for a coward when one evening, as Clayton was dropping her off at the edge of town, he said, 'You and Radford still haven't come to dinner with me in Northampton.'

'No . . . He doesn't dine out much.'

Clayton looked her full in the face. 'Come alone, then,' he said. 'Any time.'

'. . . I couldn't do that.' Coward, coward!

'You could,' he said, 'if you wanted to.'

She stared at the yellow spokes of the gig-wheels, and they seemed to glare upon her eyes like the rays of a merciless sun. What was Clayton seeing? Was he seeing a pathetic discontented wife, frittering away her time on an intrigue she would never dare to complete?

'It isn't easy,' she said. 'I've got to think . . .'

'Of course.' He took out his pocket-book and handed her his card. 'My address is on there,' he said. 'Write me when you can come.'

She took the card: it felt as heavy in her hand as an ingot.

'All right,' she said.

'I'll look forward to it.'

She was still standing with the card clutched in her hand when the gig rattled away.

Very well, she told herself, you've got the address. That doesn't mean you have to do anything with it. You don't have to write the letter. You don't have to do anything . . .

But if she did do nothing, would she not despise herself even more than she did already?

Her mind circled and circled round the same question, coming no nearer to an answer; and so when Radford said after dinner that evening, 'My dear, what do you say to a trip to Northampton?' she stared at him as if crediting him with an amazing feat of clairvoyance.

'Wh – when?'

'I was thinking of Saturday. My tailor's there, and I want to get measured for a new suit. Clothes have such a short life with all the factory dust. It would be an opportunity for you to do some shopping; one can buy much better quality there than here in Cottesbridge.' He looked at her quizzically. 'Is Saturday not convenient for you?'

'Oh . . . no, no, not at all.' She recovered herself. For a moment she had thought he was going to say Clayton Brown had invited them to dinner or something, and she knew she could not possibly bear to be in company with both Radford and Clayton together, not now. But it was no more than a shopping-trip. That, however, was surprising enough, for they never went anywhere. Was it a gesture of reconciliation?

'Of course, I can go alone, if you don't fancy the idea,' Radford said.

'No – no, I'd like to go,' she said. 'Thank you.'

'We could take the ten-fifteen,' he said in a satisfied voice. 'Have some lunch in Northampton, and come back on the three o'clock. How would that suit?'

'Very well.' The timetable, naturally, was already decided to the last detail; but she mustn't think of it in those terms. There was after all another chance, perhaps, for them to get back at least on a cordial footing with each other. Perhaps, she thought, they would be better when they were out of this forbidding house; she chose to ignore the unpromising precedent of the honeymoon.

Before Radford came to bed that night, she looked at Clayton Brown's card and then hid it in the drawer of her dressing-table, as if by that means she might forget its existence.

VI

The Northampton that Lucy and Radford visited that Saturday had been remade by the shoe in the last half-century, the industry turning it into a thriving, thrumming place that just missed being a city. Lineaments of the medieval town could be seen in the great central square and around the ancient Horsemarket, like family traits in a face, but it was in the warehouses and factories and the many leather-drays that the town proclaimed its current identity, not to mention the fashionable new suburbs of Duston and Kingsthorpe, where the shoe-barons had raised their immodest mansions, and where armies of maids shook dusters from Gothic windows of every shape and size, and pushed coach-built perambulators about the leafy streets.

Saturday was a capricious June day, sunlight suddenly spilling from the clouds on to the square with as physical an effect as the unrolling of great bolts of shining fabric, and as suddenly disappearing again, leaving the morning idly spitting rain like a vagrant piece of March. Radford, who had been watching the weather since rising as if they were planning a crucial military campaign, had made sure they brought umbrellas. Two: not for them the trifling and delightful pleasure of sharing an umbrella.

Their first call was at Radford's tailors: an intensely respectable establishment which scarcely deigned to advertise itself as a shop at all. There was no window display, no bell on the door, and as far as Lucy could see in the genteel dimness no counter or cash-desk or change-carrier. All was directed to maintaining the polite fiction that this was merely a private dwelling in which the residents, if they knew you very well, would make you up a suit of clothes out of the goodness of their hearts. And indeed when the tall bald man in pince-nez greeted Radford, and was introduced to Mrs Stokes and asked after their health and asked after mutual acquaintances and discussed the weather and the news, Lucy was half convinced they were simply going to say goodbye and walk out again, as if the introduction of commerce into such an encounter would have been the height of bad manners.

At length, however, Radford and the tailor touched on the subject of a new suit, as if it had just occurred to them; and Radford's tailor just happening to have some samples of material on his shelves, they decided they might as well look over them. Lucy meanwhile was given a chair, and from time to time was respectfully consulted: 'What do you think, my dear? What do you feel about the grey? I think the grey.' At last it was decided, money never being mentioned once; and the only discordant note was struck just as they were leaving, when to the horror of their host a harassed and underfed little man in shirt-sleeves poked his head into the shop from a room at the back, and humbly asked whether he might have his half-day.

Their next call was at a china-shop. A tea-set was wanted – a second-best tea-set, for the use of the servants in the kitchen; but Radford was no less fastidiously critical for that. Box after box was brought out.

'This is pretty,' Lucy said. 'What about this? And reasonable too.'

'Pretty,' Radford said, taking the cup from her, 'but not a good bargain, I think. See this handle? Not firm at all. Feel that. There's the faintest suggestion of give – see? In a year or so that cup will drop away from the handle. And probably scald the maid when it does.'

'Oh, I didn't notice that.'

'No, no, they won't catch us with a false bargain like that. Penny wise and pound foolish, as they say.' Radford had a habit, when pleased with himself, of tucking his thumb and forefinger into his waistcoat pocket and tapping the other three rhythmically: he did this now, whilst showing Lucy the cup again. 'There's a classic example of how buying the cheapest doesn't work out cheapest in the end. My father taught me that very early on. No economy worse than false economy.'

He was still dwelling on this theme when they had lunch in a tea-shop overlooking the square; and at last, in a moment of ungovernable irritation Lucy said, 'Radford, you really don't have to tell me about economy, I spent the first twenty years of my life scrimping and scraping to make ends meet.'

He looked quietly pained, as he always did when she 'lost her temper'. To Radford a sigh of annoyance or an impatient word was loss of temper. 'Yes, my dear, I know,' he said. 'I'm aware of that. That's why I was speaking to you of it, because I know you understand. There's no need to get cross.'

'I'm not getting cross – I'm simply saying . . .' She broke off, with a sort of terror of realization, as if for a moment she had stepped outside herself and seen the two of them at this tea-table. Was this the best they could do with life? Was this what thousands of years of human history, of struggle and tragedy and achievement, had come to? Bickering over trivialities – less than trivialities, over nothing – in a tea-shop? The terror of the moment was very real: it included, in a vivid flash, the image of those jumbled bones in Cleatham church crypt; and it made Lucy suddenly reach out and seize Radford's hand and say desperately, 'Oh, Radford, don't let's quarrel – ever – not if we can really help it. It's terrible that people should quarrel and make things worse in this sorry world . . .'

Radford raised his eyebrows, and looked uncomfortable at her holding his hand in public. 'Whatever you say, my dear,' he said, deftly drawing his hand away. 'I've certainly no intention of quarrelling. I never do as far as I'm aware.' He returned his attention to his raspberries and cream; and Lucy saw that she had followed up her 'loss of temper' with something just as bad: one of her 'outbursts'. An 'outburst' was any remark carrying more than a nominal emotional charge. Public ones were the worst. She held her peace.

When they went outside, the canopy of cloud had parted spectacularly again. The released sunlight was so strong that the patches of wet on the square were evaporating with the swiftness of breath from glass. Crossing the square, they paused to let a brewer's dray go rumbling by; as they waited, a little old lady in a bonnet and cape approached to ask them the way to Sheep Street.

There was probably nothing Radford liked better than giving directions, good detailed careful directions from which you couldn't possibly go wrong. The delight on his face was plain to Lucy, even though it manifested itself only as an extra punctiliousness. While he was about it, her ear caught over the rumble of iron wheels a sound of lilting music. Surprised, she followed the sound, and came upon a group of people, mostly children, gathered round a curious figure in the corner of the square.

It was a very old man, dressed in the fashion of half a century earlier, with gaiters and a kerchief and a brass-buttoned coat, and playing a violin. His hat was placed on the ground before him, and contained a few coppers. He had a white beard and wild straggling gypsy hair, and his open, colourless eyes proclaimed him completely blind. About his face there was an expression that Lucy found at once haunting and moving; for while it was superficially ugly, with its pursed mouth drawn up in deep furrows and grizzled brows contortedly meeting, there was a beauty in it too – the beauty of complete, rapt absorption. She did not know where he was within his own mind; but she was as certain as she was of her own name that he was not standing in Northampton market square on a showery June Saturday. He was held by the enchantment of his own music; pursuing some private path that the flow of sound laid like a silvery carpet before him.

Why the vision of this strange, heedless figure should touch her own heart so pointedly she could not say, unless it was a matter of self-recognition; but she was as irresistibly drawn as the little dirty-faced children who, gazing upward at the musician with round eyes, gathered close to her as chicks will gather round a mother hen, timidly touching her skirts and from time to time glancing at her face, as if to see whether she shared their fascination.

Of that there was no doubt; and she did not know how long she stood there listening to the fiddler's music. He made no pause between the tunes he played, but launched straight into a new one at each conclusion, so that the music formed an unbroken stream. Lucy was hardly even aware that rain had begun to fall heavily: the fiddler was sheltered by a porch, and the children, poorly dressed and street-soiled, were not of the sort to shrink at a wetting. It was only when Radford tapped her on the arm that she came out of her trance.

'What on earth are you doing?' Radford said. His glance, with typical economy, took in the fiddler, the children, and her dripping wet hair, with a tremendous weight of disdain for each.

'Oh! Radford . . .' She blinked at her husband through the rain, realizing at last how soaked she was. 'Such lovely music – just listen a moment—'

'Just look at you.' There was a pinched look about his nostrils. 'My good God, just look at you. Could you not at least put up your umbrella? Standing here in the street with a lot of ragamuffins . . . Come away, for God's sake.'

She had seldom heard him speak so sharply to her, but the effect of this on her was muted by the remains of her trance-like state; and it was in any case futile to argue. But she still hung back a moment as Radford urged her away, in order to throw some silver into the fiddler's hat. The old man did not acknowledge the clink of the money with so much as a twitch or a pause in his playing; she realized that she would have been disappointed if he had.

'How much did you put in there?' Radford said.

'Oh – I don't know, four or five shillings,' Lucy said, putting up her umbrella.

Radford sniffed. 'Perhaps I should take to begging, if it's that lucrative.'

She said nothing: there was nothing to say. The gulf between them had never, perhaps, been more wide; and she felt, like the blind fiddler, curiously distanced from her surroundings, and scarcely as if she were walking beside her wedded husband at all.

Lucy had underclothes to buy: Radford left her alone to do that, as such things embarrassed him. They arranged to meet under the portico of All Saints' when she was finished. Lucy felt the customary relaxing of tension when he was gone, like the unclenching of a clenched fist. She was tempted to go back and listen to the blind fiddler, but Radford would probably see her, or notice the extra time that had elapsed; so she got through the necessary business as quickly as possible. There was, after all, nothing to linger here for: their day out had left them as thoroughly estranged as they had ever been in the hushed rooms of the house in Lessington Road.

She was returning with her packages down the Drapery towards All Saints', through increasing rain, when she noticed a woman leaving from the side door of a dressmaker's and crossing the street diagonally before her. The woman was wearing a light cloak, and something about the brisk hurried movement of her figure within its folds, rather than the woman's face, fired in Lucy a leaping recognition. Without knowing why, she found herself running across to intercept the woman, splashing heedlessly through puddles and wetting her skirts.

266

The woman turned a startled and almost frightened face when Lucy drew close to her, and she seemed momentarily to shrink within the cloak which, Lucy now realized, was the very same that she had seen on the railway footbridge, ages ago in another life.

'Miss Wedderburn,' Lucy said – and then stopped, not knowing what more to say.

Alice Wedderburn, always pale, was paler, and the fine bones of her face were more prominent. An odd random thought flitted through Lucy's mind as they regarded each other: it's the eyes. It's the eyes that attract them. Against the whiteness of her complexion they were as green as new leaves.

'Do you – do you remember me?' Lucy said. 'Lucy Middleton.' The name came so naturally to her that it was several moments before she recollected and said, 'Well – I'm Lucy Stokes now. I got married.'

'I remember you,' said Alice Wedderburn. She continued to gaze at Lucy, not exactly with hostility, but with a sort of cool absence of trust. The rain was now coming down so hard that it seethed upon the pavement, and trickled in streams down Alice's face, which in its waxen whiteness seemed to resist the water like the petals of a lily; and instinctively Lucy drew close to her and held her umbrella over the two of them.

The change in Alice Wedderburn's expression as she did this was remarkable to see. The mistrust was lost in pure astonishment, which in turn produced that odd shrinking. The friendly action that Lucy had not even thought about seemed to affect Alice as much as if she had come up to her and struck her in the street. But in a moment she was mistrustful again, and in her old brittle tone said, 'Well, what brings you to Northampton, Mrs Lucy Stokes?'

'Oh, just shopping!' Lucy said, indicating the parcels under her arm, her eyes at the same moment straying to the bundle that Alice Wedderburn carried. It was plain to her, both from that and from Alice's demeanour as she left the shop's side door, that it was seamstress-work; but Alice, as if challenging her to doubt her assertion, said, 'Me too. I just took something in to be altered.'

She didn't look well, Lucy thought: the skin around her eyes was almost blue. Was she all alone? She recalled the gloating gossip about her at the dinner before Christmas. But despite that experience on the footbridge that bound them together, she could think of no way of asking after her welfare that did not seem mere prying; and all Alice's aloof defensiveness was in place again now. 'Have you – have you got far to go?' Lucy said.

Alice presented a brisk impatient smile. 'To go where?'

'Well – home.'

The smile was still on Alice's face, but Alice was not connected to it. 'Home? No, I . . . I . .' She rescued herself by becoming suddenly patronizing. 'My dear, why *do* you ask?'

'Well, because it's raining dreadfully hard,' Lucy said. 'Won't you take my umbrella? I'll be all right, my husband has one. Please – ' as Alice shrank again – 'please take it – just to please me.'

She thrust the umbrella into Alice Wedderburn's hand; and then, to forestall her refusal, quickly said goodbye and hurried across to All Saints'.

Radford was waiting for her under the portico. He gave her a look which left no doubt that he had seen what she had done; but he made no comment. Not, indeed, until they were on the train back home when, bleakly regarding the rainy countryside through the window, he said, 'I really believe you do it on purpose.'

She had thought she might get away without a reproof; but of course, Radford never forgot things. 'Do what on purpose?' she said.

Radford shifted in his seat, mouth set, eyes still averted from her. 'One would have supposed that making a show of yourself with beggars and street-urchins would have been enough even for one of your eccentric tendencies,' he said. 'But apparently not. Whether you reckoned that I would not recognize that woman I don't know. It was an unlikely supposition if so. Everyone knows her, by sight at least. My wife, it appears, knows her much better than that. I hardly know which is more repellent – that my wife knew that Wedderburn creature in the past, or that she sees nothing amiss in acknowledging her even now. More than acknowledging her.' He laughed stonily. 'Giving her her umbrella, if you please. You see, this is what I find so remarkable, my dear. Your sheer novel inventiveness in finding ways to embarrass and humiliate me. It's certainly a unique talent, if not an outstandingly useful one—'

'Why do you hate Alice Wedderburn so much?' Lucy said, cutting him off. She spoke calmly, but she could still be hurt when Radford chose to be scathing, and she was hurt now. 'You, Dinah, Mr Parmenter, all of them. What has she ever done that you people should hate her so?'

'Oh, my dear, you're the one who's so thick with her. I would have thought you well aware of that woman's manner of living. If not, I suggest you watch the cats on the roofs one night, that will give you an idea—'

'Oh, for God's sake.' All at once she hated him: hated his prim soft voice, hated his pursed lips, hated his lifted chin, hated all the deadly respectability he stood for; and her tongue was loosened as never before. 'What would you know about it, Radford? These shocking habits of Alice Wedderburn's. What on earth would you of all people know about that? Your narrow mind I can put up with. But don't talk about things you know nothing about. You just make yourself ridiculous.'

The relief that came of saying it was of a sick, unhappy kind; but it could not be unsaid. Nor did she know whether she would wish to unsay it. They were already living a lie; there was no point in compounding it. Radford looked at her for the first time, blinking, then looked away again. 'I really don't wish to discuss this subject any further,' he said.

She stopped herself saying that he had brought it up; she just wanted to have done with it. 'Very well,' she said; and they proceeded in silence the short distance to Cottesbridge. A denizen of another civilization, watching them then, might have marvelled that they remained in the same railway carriage together, and when they arrived at the station got out together, walked together, and went into the same house together – instead of, as pure reason would suggest, instantly severing all connection between them, and putting an end to an unendurable proximity. But while the bemused Atlantean might have understood that they were bound together by legal and financial conditions, it would have been more difficult for him to discern the greater, finer web in which they were entangled: a web made up of habits of mind. In spite of strong evidence to the contrary, accumulated from the very beginning of mankind, they were still governed by the Noah's Ark principle – that two by two is the best basis of human relations. Both Lucy's passionate unconventionality, and Radford's passionless conventionality, had been unconsciously formed by it.

Here, at least, they might have found common ground;

but nowhere else. The trip to Northampton had driven them further apart. Yet life was still to be got through. Normal faces had to be presented to Georgina and Miss Threadgold; and to that end, once she had shed her wet things, Lucy slipped for a few moments into the little-used front parlour to compose herself, and to think of some cheerful replies she could make to their inquiries.

It was from the window of this room that she saw a youth of about eighteen standing irresolutely about the drive, looking up at the house, and at last walking up towards the front door. Again, however, he seemed to hesitate, as if unsure whether this was the right house; so Lucy went to the front door herself and opened it.

'Can I help you?' she said.

The youth, who was dressed with mean threadbare respectability and had hair the colour of dull gold, still hung back from the threshold, staring at her. 'I'm looking for Mr Stokes,' he said at last.

'Well, he's—'

'What is it, my dear?' Radford's voice came like a cool draught at the back of her neck. A frown came and went on his brow as he saw the youth standing there.

'Can I see you, Mr Stokes?' the youth said, with more confidence.

'Not now.' Radford almost shouldered Lucy aside as he moved forward to close the door. 'Come to the office on Monday.'

The door was closed, and Radford turned to Lucy with a look that was as near to savage as his reserve would allow. 'The reason we keep servants,' he said, 'is so that they may answer the door, my dear, and not you.'

She ignored this. 'Who was that?'

'Someone looking for a job,' Radford said shortly, 'if you must know.' He turned away. 'I must say it seems rather late in the day for you to be taking an interest in my business, my dear.'

She watched him walk down the hall. The violence of her feelings was such that she felt she might scream. But she did not scream. She counted ten ticks of the hall clock and then followed him into the drawing-room, where she politely answered Georgina's inquiries and said yes, she had had a lovely time. As soon as she was able she went upstairs, and took out Clayton Brown's card from her dressing-table. She sat and looked at it for several minutes. Then she got out pen and paper and wrote him a note:

Yes, I will come to your house. Say next Wednesday. I'll come to Northampton by the noon train. Write me if this is no good. L.

Clayton Brown's answer came back by return of post. *I'll be delighted to see you Wednesday,* he wrote in his big careless hand. *I'll meet you at the station. Yours in anticipation, C. B.* And at the bottom: *P. S. Champagne?*

As soon as she had read the note, Lucy crammed it into the drawer with the card, as if it burnt her.

Acid politeness characterized her relations with Radford during the intervening time. A further shutter seemed to have come down over his personality, rendering him so inaccessible that he could scarcely be said to be there at all except as a physical body; but several times she found him looking at her when he thought she would not notice. There was a balefulness about these glances, but it was impossible to read him any more clearly than that. All she knew was that his presence produced such constraint that the very air of the house seemed heavy and viscous to move through, as if they were living at the bottom of the sea.

She had promised some time ago to go over and visit Connie Pollard, now Connie Lightfoot, who was pregnant and wanted to talk all about it; and that was her excuse for Wednesday. The day, anticipated with a mixture of defiance and dread, came as all such days come – both too quickly and too slowly. As she left the house and walked to the station she felt a curious envy for all the people she saw on the way who were not she, and for whom this day, which to her mind's eye wore a livid glaring yellow colour unlike all other days, was of so little moment that they would be unable even to remember what they were doing on it a week hence.

She did not have the carriage to herself: she was joined by an elderly matron who sucked liquorice comfits and talked to her about the price of things. As Lucy absently nodded and agreed, she experienced a dizzy sensation of unreality. Her companion plainly saw her as nothing more or less than a respectable married woman, off on a shopping trip; and yet here she was going to keep a tryst with a small-town rake, and surrender herself to him in protest at the mockery of her marriage . . . Was all appearance and reality, in fact, so fantastically discordant? Was the chattering matron really a spy in disguise, the trees in all their fresh dappled finery just stage-flats stuck about with green tinsel, the sheep dotted about the river-meadows mere dummies of wood and stuffing, the swifts wheeling and darting about the sky creatures of clockwork? She would not have been surprised, so unutterably alien did she feel.

But the liquorice woman got off at Wellingford, leaving Lucy alone for the rest of the journey; and once alone even the weird distortions that the physical world presented to her view faded, and simply left her face to face with the thought of what she was going to do. Face to face, indeed: for as the train chuntered briskly across the miles and Northampton drew near, the thought of what she was about to do became for Lucy a companion quite as real as the woman had been, and more insistent; she was trapped in the carriage with it, with nothing to do but stare into its leering face, and feel its hot breath upon hers.

As soon as the suburbs of Northampton came in sight she was on her feet and eager to be out: anything was preferable to being shut in here with this monstrous thought. The train seemed to take an age to draw into the station; but at last it was still, and she jumped out.

Clouds of steam were still swirling about the platform; and it was through them that she glimpsed, as through a rent in the curtain, the figure of Clayton Brown. He was right at the other end of the platform, leaning against an iron pillar with a cigar in his mouth, and scanning with his pale eyes the disembarking passengers.

She stopped dead. There was something about his posture, so relaxed yet coolly purposeful, that transfixed her with revulsion. Not so much revulsion at him – though she saw now that her attraction to him had only been a twisted version of that – but revulsion at herself. Adultery was adultery, of course, whether by romantic candlelight or grey daylight; but somehow all the trifling normalities of the scene, the whistling porter, the old lady fussing with her trunks, the little girl following her mother with hopscotch steps, the starling waddling after crumbs with the sunlight striking rainbows from its breast, all threw into relief the essential sordidness of what she was doing – doing with all the businesslike despatch of a visit to a dentist. She could not – she could not possibly go through with it!

Yet Clayton Brown was there, waiting; and once he spotted her she did not know what she would do. Cry off? But that would mean putting into words what she had not, thankfully, had to make explicit. And besides, what sort of pathetic coquette would he think her then?

But that didn't matter, she now knew: for he could hardly think worse of her than she thought of herself. All that mattered was to get away from him before he saw her. She turned and began to hurry down the platform in the opposite direction.

There was of course no easy escape: the platform presently gave way to a grimy wasteland of sidings and freight-boxes and coal-heaps, and she supposed she might be stopped on suspicion of trying to evade the ticket-collector. But no one observed her, and she managed at last, by crossing a siding-line and scrambling over a fence, to emerge in a side street, her skirts blackened with coal and her breath coming in sobs.

Wiping her face with her handkerchief, she tried to think what to do next. She couldn't go back to the station yet to get a train home, for there was no telling how long Clayton would wait for her, thinking that she had perhaps missed her train and would arrive on the next one. Then she thought of the market square, and the blind fiddler – she felt she could go and listen to him for hours: indeed, if there was anything that could lift her out of this wretchedness, it would be that music. But then it occurred to her how central and public the square was. Suppose Clayton should come by there in his trap, and spot her?

No: she must pass the time until it was safe to return to the station in some other way. The streets near at hand were narrow frugal places of grey brick and that familiar smell of leather-dust – similar indeed to the very place in which she had grown up. It was an unlikely haunt for Clayton Brown – unlikely too for her now, in her smart dress; but she felt safe here.

And so she spent the afternoon slowly and aimlessly wandering about a place that was entirely new to her yet hauntingly familiar; so that at every turn she fancied she might see Mr Birdsall standing smoking his pipe outside his house, or Lil Fry scrubbing her doorstep, or Nancy Smallbones twitching her curtains – or even, most strangely, her own self amongst the aproned closing-girls hurrying back to the factories after dinner.

It was a dreamlike experience, but chastening too. Some-how she had supposed that, despite her fine clothes, the people of these streets would recognize her as one of their own. But it was not so. Women paused in beating their carpets or interrupted their gossip to watch her go by, and their faces were grim and suspicious. Men lounging about gaslamps exchanged significant looks as she passed. It was a shock to realize that her old identity was so completely lost, even if she had no new one to speak of; and a shock to realize too what their estimate of her must be. For, thinking back to her own youth in such a community, she remembered that a lone, well-dressed young woman who came there was naturally assumed to be of one type only – the Alice Wedderburn type.

But then, was that estimate so far off, considering what she had come to Northampton to do? Lucy didn't know: she felt as if she could never make a confident moral judgement again in her life. All she knew was that all her defiance, her thirst for revenge, her rebellious urge had died when she had stepped off that train and found herself unable to go through with it. It was not inappropriate that she should half-expect to see herself in these streets: for the Lucy who had engaged in that pointless, self-despising flirtation with Clayton Brown these past months now appeared to her as another person entirely, whose motives were as murky as these dust-blown granite yards and alleyways.

What, then, would she have achieved had she gone through with it? Surely just a new depth of self-contempt. So she had attained at least that new level of knowledge from this disastrous day. Of course, she had laid herself open to possible exposure by Clayton Brown, if he should choose; yet, knowing him as she did, she doubted that he possessed the will or the energy to make capital out of their association. He would very likely laugh at her, but that was a price she was willing to pay.

At last she made her way back to the station. There was no sign of Clayton Brown. Her relief was mixed with guilt, for she had after all led him on, and stood him up – though she was under no illusions about the quality of his feeling for her, or about how he would have dealt with her once his own interest faded. She was seeing herself in all sorts of new lights today, and the self she now saw was not a nice one. It was all too easy to use one's own unhappiness as an excuse for behaving badly.

She boarded the Cottesbridge train, and for once the

thought of going back to Radford's house was not too intolerable, compared with what she had just gone through. Nature had not framed her for an adventuress. The sight of those backstreets had made her feel too that she ought to find some other outlet for her energies. She had money: now that the trade was declining after a boom caused by the South African war there would be many needy families in the valley. Even if she were personally unhappy, could she not work off her frustration in helping others, instead of dabbling in the squalid? It was an attractive idea: something good had come out of this horrible experience after all.

She arrived back at Cottesbridge in the late afternoon, called briefly to see Connie Lightfoot as a gesture to her conscience, and then hurried back to Lessington Road; and walked into a hurricane.

VII

It was nearly time for dinner, and she expected to find Radford dressing when she went upstairs to change. To her surprise there was no sign of him. She was just thinking how odd it was that he should vary his routine when the maid came and said he was in the study and wanted her to go and see him there.

This was excessively formal even for Radford, and was her first indication that something must be wrong. How wrong she did not guess, until she went into the study and found him seated at the desk with Clayton Brown's letter laid centrally on the blotter before him.

Lucy felt as if she had been slapped by an icy hand. She stared a moment at Radford, and it occurred to her, inconsequentially, that this was how his employees must feel when summoned to the factory office. Then she closed the door behind her and stepped forward.

She had no ready lies or explanations, not that she felt the want of them. She had already compromised herself enough with the Clayton Brown business, and only complete truth was tenable now.

Radford put a finger to his forehead and leaned his elbow on the desk. 'This,' he said, and swallowed. 'This – thing . . . there must be an innocent explanation for it. There simply must be. But I have been sitting here for half an hour racking my brains and I cannot for the life of me think—'

'There isn't,' said Lucy. 'There isn't, Radford. It's from Clayton Brown and I was supposed to – to go and meet him today . . .'

Radford put his hand over his mouth as if he was going to be sick.

'But Radford, listen to me – it isn't all you think. Yes – yes, I've been meeting him, but – nothing's happened. It's over, Radford, it wasn't anything. I mean, I did go to

276

Northampton today, but I came back, I didn't meet him because I saw that—'

'Well, of course it's *over*,' Radford said harshly, 'of course it's over, Lucy, you hardly need to say that, there is no question of its being anything but over now I've found out.' He picked up the letter between finger and thumb. 'That does not alter the fact that this – this *filth* would presumably have gone on and on if this letter had not been brought to me—'

'Brought to you?' Lucy said. 'What do you mean? You mean you didn't find it? Who did then?'

'Well, I don't see as that's of any account, but if you must know it was Miss Threadgold. She—'

'Right.' She was half-way to the door; for the moment everything else was driven out by fury and hatred. She was going to wring that woman's plump neck with her bare hands—

'Lucy!'

Radford had barked out the word: it was the shock of hearing him raise his voice that made her stop. 'That woman,' she said incoherently, 'she – this is a matter between you and me, Radford, no one else. She has no right to go prying through my things . . .'

'Miss Threadgold was acting, as she has always done, out of a concern for the honour of the family, and in particular that of Georgina.'

Lucy snorted. 'And she said so, no doubt.'

'I am not going to discuss Miss Threadgold, except to say she could hardly have done otherwise than bring this matter to my attention, however the information was gained. Because it is not merely between you and me, as you put it. Any – disgrace attaching to our marriage is sure to reflect upon Georgina. That is why Miss Threadgold acted, and I thank her for it.' He put his head in his hands. 'God knows poor Georgina has little enough to thank me for – bringing someone like you into a home that had always been absolutely pure and contented. It sickens me to think that she has been exposed to the – the filthy corruption of your company—'

'Well, Radford, so have you,' she snapped back, 'but it doesn't seem to have affected you very much, does it?'

It was a reflex, no more – none but a saint can endure insulting words without throwing a few back; but Radford blenched.

'Radford, listen to me,' she said. 'There's no point in us screaming at each other. I'll tell you it all, and then—'

'How long?' he said, cutting her off.

'I've been meeting him for a few months.' She came close to the desk, looking into his face – it was confusedly meant as earnest of her sincerity, but she saw how her physical presence seemed to make him recoil. 'He would give me a lift home in his trap. We would talk and ride around. No more. Nothing more.'

Radford's lip curled: it was an unpleasant sight, for despite his chill ways he was not a sneering type. 'So you say,' he said, 'but I have only your word for that.'

The pain of that mistrust went deeper than she could ever have guessed; and it was out of that pain that she said: 'True. But if that's not enough for you, you could always have me examined by a doctor. That would prove me innocent, Radford. That would prove it beyond a doubt.'

'You're filthy,' he said, his lips trembling. 'You're filthy.'

'No.' She shook her head slowly, putting her arms about herself in her distress. 'No, Radford. Clean. All pure. Untouched. That's just it . . .' Tears burnt her eyes. 'Don't you understand why I did it? Oh, don't you understand . . .?'

Radford looked away from her, his hand going up to his moustache. 'I don't – I don't feel that I am called upon to understand anything, Lucy. As far as I'm concerned, my wife has been – deceiving me and that is all there is to it.' He uttered a laugh. 'And to think I had that man here in my own house . . . However, I doubt he is greatly to be blamed. No doubt he had invitation enough. An open sore attracts flies . . .' He twitched at the sob she gave then, but went on levelly, 'And now I suppose everyone knows. This – involvement seems to have been carried out chiefly in public, and so I imagine it's common gossip.' He suddenly crumpled the letter and threw it across the room: in a man so self-controlled the action was as startling as a violent blow. 'I won't ask whether you were not inhibited by a sense of shame, because I know from your past behaviour that you never are . . . but could you not have considered the shame and humiliation that would attach to *me*? Could you not have considered *my* shame, Lucy?'

She struggled. It was on her lips to say that he had driven her to it; but she was no longer even sure of that, so persistent still was the sense of messy inadequacy that afflicted her when she tried to dispute with Radford. 'You – you don't have to feel that way,' she said helplessly. 'Nothing happened . . . I didn't know what I was doing. I just made a fool of myself. It's me that looks the fool, not you, Radford.'

'Oh! Oh, so I am supposed to simply disregard this whole business, am I? We're to carry on as normal, are we?'

She fixed him with a look through her dropping tears. 'But we're not normal, Radford,' said she. 'You know we're not.'

He went white to the lips. 'How dare you,' he breathed. 'How dare you suggest that I—' He left the sentence hanging in the air, and his face was curiously frozen for some seconds. 'There's no point in discussing it,' he said at last. 'The whole thing is so distasteful that I . . . I never thought I would be involved in something so utterly disgusting . . .' He would not look at her any more. He shook his head. 'I should never have married you.'

'No,' she said into the silence that followed, 'no, you shouldn't.'

He remained sitting at the desk, staring before him in apparent abstraction. It was as if she had already left the room; and so, wiping away her tears, she left it.

She did not come down to dinner: she could not face it. There was Dinah Threadgold, for one thing, though Lucy's anger at the woman had dissipated somewhat in the anguish of her exchange with Radford. There was Georgina too: she was highly susceptible to atmospheres, and would know at once that something was dreadfully wrong, even supposing Miss Threadgold had not told her all about it. But most of all she could not face Radford. Their being together at all now seemed an almost physical impossibility, as if night and day should coexist.

It was typical of Radford that he should go down to dinner that night, and dress for it too. While he was there she took the opportunity to move her things into a spare-room and make up a bed there. She sat in there numbly until she heard him come up much later; then she went to the door of their bedroom and looked in.

'I'm in the spare-room,' she said. 'I – thought it best.'

He nodded, removing and setting down his cuff-links with his usual care.

'I know this perhaps isn't the time,' she said, 'but we must – we really must talk about what we are going to do . . .'

'As I believe I said, there is nothing to talk about,' Radford said. 'The thing is done, and cannot be undone.'

'But if you'd just listen . . . I can't excuse it, but it isn't what you think—'

'Just go away from me, Lucy.' His back was turned to her, and his head was bowed. For the first time she pitied him, pitied him from the bottom of her heart: all the tangle of circumstance fell away, and he was simply a man suffering, and she would have given worlds to be able to put her arms round him and comfort him as such – if not as wife then as sister, as friend, as fellow-mortal, anything. He glanced over his shoulder at her. 'Go away,' he said. 'I can't bear you near me.'

She slipped away, and lay curled up into a ball, staring, for most of the night.

The day that followed was like nothing she had ever experienced. Mere consciousness was pain; and yet somehow this mental torment had to be accommodated with prosaic everyday existence. For Radford went off to work as usual, and once he was gone there was nothing for it but to come down and face the others. Georgina plainly knew there was something amiss, but Miss Threadgold had not, Lucy surmised, told her the story; for of course, her self-proclaimed role was the disinterested guardian, concerned only with protecting her beloved charge from the wickedness of the world and of Lucy in particular, and it would jeopardize that image if she tattled. But while Georgina merely looked troubled and unhappy, about Miss Threadgold there was a tremendously righteous air of having discharged a painful duty and expecting no thanks for it. She did not so much move about the house as float, her eyes half-closed as if in inward contemplation of her unspotted conscience. She was careful to avoid Lucy as much as possible – whether in order to escape her evil contagion, or because she feared that Lucy would kill her, it was impossible to tell. For the moment it did not seem to matter. As Radford had said, it was done and could not be undone.

But you wanted him to know, didn't you? asked a voice inside Lucy. Didn't you have some idea, at some point, of deliberately making him jealous, and making him love you?

Yet the acts and motives of her past self had become a tortuous enigma to her, and she could only reply to that questioning voice: I don't know! All she knew was that somehow she had brought the state of their marriage to such a pitch as made the former stalemate seem restful.

It was sufficient indication of that that Radford for the first time broke his inalienable routine. When he got home that evening he did not join them for dinner: he told the maid he had a lot of work to do and would take something in his study, and disappeared into it without another word. Dinner that night was the most dismal parody of that meal ever devised. Neither Lucy nor Georgina had any appetite, nor conversation; only Miss Threadgold went on eating and talking imperturbably, like one great incarnation of mouth.

After dinner Lucy could bear it no longer. She went to the study door and, fearing that if she knocked he would refuse her admittance, walked straight in.

He was working at the desk; and at her entrance he actually sprang upright from his chair, flinging the blotter across the papers on which he had been writing.

'What the hell do you think you're doing?' he demanded.

She was too wretched even to take notice of his face, which was furiously contorted in a way she had never seen it before. 'Radford,' she pleaded, 'this can't go on. We haven't got on well together, I know, and perhaps we never can, but this is just – just such hell, we must at least speak to each other—'

He pointed to the door, his other hand placed firmly on the blotter, his eyes averted. 'Get out,' he said. 'Just leave me alone.'

'What – what are you writing?'

She had certainly not stepped forward with any intention of snatching the papers from him – but that was plainly what he thought, and it was plain too, for a moment, that he would have struck her rather than let her do so. She shrank back, alarmed now at his expression. Then all at once he seemed by sheer will to summon up his old self-control: a shudder went through him, and he closed his eyes. 'Of course,' he said, 'we must talk about what we are going to do. But not now, Lucy.' His voice became precise again, and his hand mechanically went up to his moustache. 'Not now. Another time. Yes?'

After a moment she nodded, and quietly left him alone.

VIII

Lucy slept late the next morning, having had no sleep at all
the night before, and Radford had already gone to work when
she came down to breakfast. The day was insolently sunny,
and Georgina was in a hurry to get out to the garden and
potter with her beloved flowers; and Miss Threadgold, still
internally basking in the warmth of her own goodness, drifted
out with her. Lucy was so entirely at a loss that she was glad
to be rescued by the maid, who came to her with a timid
request about what she should do with regard to the
bedrooms.

'That spare-room will be mine in future, Jane,' she told
her; and she occupied herself for the morning in moving the
rest of her things into it and rearranging the room. The maid
was too well-trained to betray any interest or surprise, but
Lucy knew what she must be thinking. Perfect symbol of
separation, she thought as she regarded her new solitary
room! And yet even that was a sham, a distinction without a
difference. There was no reason why she should feel that this
development represented any change in their relation, when
since their marriage they had merely lain in the same room
as in a dormitory. But it did feel different to Lucy. Her
own chaotic upbringing had not hardened her to domestic
discord. That people in the same house should be at daggers-
drawn still struck sorely at her most fundamental sensibilities,
and that she should have helped create such a monster by
allowing herself to drift towards an adulterous liaison only
made the smart keener.

The window of the room overlooked the front garden and
drive. Lucy leant her forehead against the window-pane
and said aloud, 'You're a fool, Lucy. Oh, you're a fool,' while
her mind desolately confronted the fact that nothing she had
done in life had turned out anything but ill. In her over-
wrought state the friendly coolness of the glass against her

burning brow, in contrast to the general spirit of malicious opposition that seemed to animate the world around her, had an effect as of an unexpected gift; and in swift succession to this sensation she suddenly beheld, as if it had that moment materialized, a male blackbird perched upon the topmost twig of the cherry-tree that grew near to the window. He was singing in a jaunty, bubbling, whimsical way, as if he just liked to hear himself, and thought his elevated perch quite the best spot in creation. Lucy was close enough to him to see the liquid tremble in his throat and the dot of reflected light in his eye. The sight and the sound, so remote from her present trouble in every aspect, seemed for that very reason to offer relief from it; and she was just wondering whether she could quietly steal open the window, so as to hear the joyful song better, when the blackbird turned himself about, cocked his head downward, and flew away with a rapid chittering.

She was bitterly disappointed, but saw in a moment what had alarmed him: a man was walking up the drive towards the house, whom she recognized as Mr Hallam, the works manager. Supposing him to have come from the factory on some errand for Radford, she went down to meet him; and it was only as she stood facing him in the hall that it occurred to her that Mr Hallam, second only to Radford in the works hierarchy, was an unlikely person to be sent.

She still did not guess even from the expression on his face, for that was habitually gloomy. It was only when he took her gently by the elbow – for he was the most unassuming of men – and guided her into the front parlour, that she knew that something was wrong.

As he told her, some part of her mind detached itself and registered how odd it was that this news should be delivered in this room which was so seldom used. And indeed the fragmentation of her mind seemed to leave it useless and uncomprehending, so that she heard what he was saying without really understanding it. It was something about a fall. A fall from the high crane doors of the factory, four storeys up. A fall to the granite yard below. It had happened this morning. He had gone up there to inspect some glacé kid, and then someone had looked round at the crane doors to see him toppling over, and he had plunged down: it was all over in a flash. It was a terrible thing, and Lucy heard herself saying so, but still she could not quite grasp why Mr

Hallam had come to tell her about this dreadful accident. She didn't really know anyone at Stokes' factory, except for Radford of course. Radford. . . .

Mr Hallam hurried forward and put his hand under her arm. She must have been about to fall; that was why the room was pitching and swaying. He lowered her to a chair. The distance downwards to the seat seemed endless, like four storeys.

'There was absolutely nothing that could be done,' Mr Hallam was saying. 'Such a tragic thing to happen . . .'

She heard herself thanking Mr Hallam for coming to tell her; and another part of her mind seemed to detach itself, and noted that her gratitude was very real. For suppose it had been poor Georgina who had had to receive the news! And then Lucy began to break down as it came to her that, not only would she have to tell Georgina herself, but that in one way it would be easier for Georgina to bear. For Georgina, unlike herself, would be able to believe that it was an accident.

Part the Third

The Long Shadow

I

'Well, well, John, and how do you go on?' said Mr Aubrey Parmenter, who was dining with Mr John Arthur Brown, and who before the meal was warming his substantial seat at the first fire of a mild autumn. 'I haven't seen you since – when would it be? – poor old Radford Stokes' funeral. Dear, dear, never dreamed I'd see that. Man of half my age, near enough. Terrible business.'

'What a lesson for us all!' said Mrs Parmenter, omitting to explain precisely what the lesson consisted of, but giving that windy sigh which is taken to indicate unimpeachable piety.

'Well, I consider myself as tough as the next man,' said Mr John Arthur Brown, 'but I don't mind telling you it fairly knocked me up. Couldn't put my mind to anything for days. Radford was a different sort of man from old Edward Stokes, and perhaps none of us knew him quite as well, but still he was a fine man of business, a thoroughly decent fellow. I tell you, to think of him being lost like that – well, it fairly beat me down.'

'I had the foreman check our crane doors for safety straight away,' said Mr Parmenter. 'But of course, there's only so much you can do in that way. It only takes one moment of carelessness, absent-mindedness even . . .'

'Well, of course, if that's how one is to take what happened,' said John Arthur Brown. 'And I'm not saying it wasn't that way. I don't suppose anyone will ever know for certain. But there seems to be a pretty strong undercurrent of opinion that—'

'Fellow jumped!' put in perspiring old Mr Leek, who was present as always when there were comestibles to be had. 'Plain as a pikestaff! Took his own life! Known a score of similar cases!'

'You think he was a suicide, eh?' Mr Parmenter said, stroking his luxuriant whiskers. 'I must admit you're not the first person who's said it. It's crossed my mind more than once.'

'Radford Stokes was the least careless man I ever knew,' said Mr Brown, who was one of those men who appear mildly hot-tempered when they are only serious. 'His father introduced him to that factory when he was still at school. You're not going to tell me he was the sort who didn't know what he was doing when he was around the crane doors. It just isn't like him.'

Mrs Parmenter stirred. 'But suicide – oh, dear, at least I mean . . .' She searched around for a word less shocking to her particular brand of idiocy, but could not find one. 'I mean, what you suggest he did – that is a sin, surely?'

'I dare say it is, Mrs Parmenter,' said Mr Brown. 'That's not my province. But people don't commit it just on the spur of the moment. They get driven to it. Driven to it. And that's where the subject of sin comes in, if you ask me.'

'Oh, you mean these rumours about young Mrs Stokes,' Mr Parmenter said. 'Yes, she doesn't come out of it well, I'm afraid. I think that's a pretty general feeling. But look here, John, I hope you won't mind me saying this, but a lot of the rumours had to do with your Clayton, you know. Now what does he have to say about it?'

'Oh! I don't know. He didn't have much to say before he moved to London. And I'm not saying he didn't get himself mixed up with Mrs Stokes – I've really no idea. But you know Clayton. He's never made any bones about the sort of fellow he is: never claimed he's a saint. It's in his nature – he is a man, after all. And if a pretty married woman starts throwing herself at anyone who looks her way . . .'

'She was a flighty type, I'm afraid,' said Mrs Brown, a younger, robuster version of Mrs Parmenter, who was pregnant on a professional basis. 'Poor Radford! It was common knowledge that he'd married a flighty piece.'

'Well, I remember when we dined there last Christmas,' said Mr Parmenter. '. . . Dear me, there's a sad thought, none of us guessing what was coming to Radford! I say, I remember when we dined there: now young Mrs Stokes tried her best, I think, and was very agreeable on the whole . . . but she did go and make rather a show of herself in the end, banging on about that Wedderburn woman, and trying to make out she was practically pure as the driven snow, if you please.'

'There you are,' said John Arthur Brown, 'my point exactly.

288

It's highly revealing that she should choose to defend that Wedderburn woman, if you ask me.'

'Birds of a feather flock together!' exploded Mr Leek, moistly. 'Takes a trollop to know a trollop!'

'Whatever's happened to that Wedderburn woman, by the way?' said Mr Parmenter. 'Don't seem to hear of her nowadays.'

'Dropped out of sight, it seems,' said Mrs Brown. 'But it was bound to happen. Men won't go on paying for that sort of soiled goods for ever.'

'Well, it's no more than she deserves,' said Mrs Parmenter. 'But at least . . . Well, I never thought I would hear myself putting in a good word for Alice Wedderburn, but at least she never made any pretence of being anything but a single woman, entrapping single men: at least she never defiled the marriage bed like young Mrs Stokes.' Mrs Parmenter then blushed at having mentioned the marriage bed, for all the world as if she had not lifted her nightdress in it every Saturday for the last thirty years.

'And such a thoroughly respectable man as Radford, to end up married to someone like that,' said Mr Brown. 'That's the pity of it. Of course, I don't suppose she showed her true colours to him at first. But it's pretty clear that he cottoned on to what she was really like. I thought he didn't seem his usual self just before the end.'

'Mrs Stokes has—' came a piping voice from the large armchair by the fire, and then stopped in a cough. The voice had its origin in Mr Miles Mellish, who had been sitting there all this time feeling the heat on his legs excessively, surreptitiously rubbing his shins, and too shy to ask Mr Parmenter to move so that he could get out. Having cleared his throat and got his voice back to a normal pitch, Mr Mellish began again. 'Mrs Stokes has always been awfully nice to me. She has always made me most uncommonly welcome – and – and she gives me tea, you know. Uncommonly nice tea.' He stopped, stroking down his errant crest of hair, his eyebrows thoughtfully twisted. 'Sometimes three cups,' he said.

'Oh, hush, Miles,' said Mrs Parmenter absently, as if he were a noisy parrot. 'Well, there is one consolation. At least we won't be called upon to meet her any more. She will hardly go about much on her account as a widow; and I don't suppose there are any respectable people in the valley who would extend an invitation to her now.'

'What *is* she doing, anyhow?' said Mr Brown. 'Is she ever seen about? And what about the factory?'

'Well, my sister's seen her once or twice, I believe,' said Mr Parmenter. 'Because, as you know, Mrs Stokes' young sister Joanna is employed as her companion, and so Mrs Stokes goes over to visit now and then. There's one blessing, anyhow . . . Miss Joanna doesn't resemble her sister in the least . . . a very quiet, decent, modest girl.'

'It's rather hard on poor Mrs Silvie, having to receive the woman in her house,' said Mrs Brown.

'We-ell, you know my sister,' said Mr Parmenter, 'she rather lives in her own little world – all wrapped up in our Harry, mostly, and what he's doing and when he's coming home from the war and so forth. If you were to try and tell her what Mrs Stokes is like, she probably wouldn't really listen, but just go on talking about Harry, bless her.'

'I don't think Mrs Stokes is "like" anything.' It was the voice of Miles Mellish, speaking much more firmly this time, and escaping from the chair by the fire at last by climbing over the arm as if it were a stile. 'I don't think she is like anything but a frightfully nice woman who has always been very nice to me. And if it's all the same to you I'd rather not stay and hear her talked about in this fashion. I'm very sorry, Mr Brown. Perhaps you could give my portion of dinner to – well, to somebody who hasn't got any, you know.'

'Miles, don't be an ass . . .' began Mr Brown; but Miles Mellish, having faced about and made an apologetic bow to all present, was already out of the door, a dignified exit hardly impaired at all by his getting his coat-pocket caught on the door-handle, and momentarily springing back like a catapult.

'Not to worry, not to worry, John,' said Mr Parmenter when Mr Mellish had gone, making a tolerant hushing motion. 'You mustn't mind young Miles. I understand he's got a taking for Miss Georgina Stokes, and so he sees these things differently.'

'Georgina Stokes, eh?' said Mrs Brown. 'Well, that's hardly a connection to gratify Miles' mother, given what we know about Radford's widow; but then I suppose Georgina isn't a blood relation of the hussy, so perhaps it will be all right. Certainly it will be the very best thing for Georgina to be taken out of that house, and away from that shameless creature's influence.'

290

'Well, what is the situation in that house, Aubrey? Does your sister hear anything? I suppose Mrs Stokes inherits?' Mr Brown asked.

'As far as I can gather,' said Mr Parmenter, 'Radford's will – oh, yes, drawn up some time ago, typically thorough – makes ample provision for both Mrs Stokes and Georgina. But the bulk of the property, the house and the works, go of course to his widow. Cecil Hallam is an excellent manager, and Radford's lawyers are very capable; and he had that factory running so smoothly that it won't come to any harm for now, with Hallam in charge. But of course it won't be the same without the guiding hand of the master.'

'I don't suppose she means to take it in hand herself?' said Mr Brown.

'Oho, that would be a turn-up. But I don't think it likely,' said Mr Parmenter. 'The sensible thing for her to do would be to sell up: I've no doubt that's what the lawyers will suggest. It would make a tidy acquisition, for someone with the means to take it on.'

'Stokes' works, eh?' Mr Brown said. 'Not a bad little concern at all.' Over the faces of both the gentlemen there stole something veiled, filmy, and gloatingly cautious at this turn in the conversation. 'Yes, someone ought to take it on – out of respect for Radford's memory, I mean.'

'Oh, yes, precisely. Terrible to see all his work go to waste . . .'

The incense thus lit at the altar of Mammon made the air of the drawing-room quite thick and soporific; and it was with the sudden fluffing motion of a dozing hen that Mrs Parmenter said, 'Well! All this is very shocking; and I can only hope that that Mrs Stokes is suffering in her conscience. But I very much doubt it. That sort never do, do they?'

II

Lucy's ostracism by local society was tempered by two things: firstly, she did not want to see anyone anyway; and secondly, their strictures only echoed what she thought of herself. For some time after Radford's death, she accepted their estimate of her as nothing less than the truth.

They were wrong, however, if they thought she did not grieve. The mourning she wore would have had to have been the most Stygian shade of black before it could have begun to reflect what was going on within her. Whatever she had felt or been unable to feel for Radford, whatever divisions, misunderstandings – hatreds, even – that had existed between them, whatever their relationship had been or not been, the one bursting fact that filled her mind and threatened to split it asunder was that, if she had not married Radford Stokes, he would have been alive today.

Fact it inescapably was, to her, though the official pronouncement was death by misadventure. She could not believe for a single moment that Radford's plunge from the crane doors had been anything but deliberate; and nothing but his marital situation, she was convinced, could have prompted that act. Even had Mr Hallam come to her with a sheaf of papers proving that Radford had been thousands of pounds in debt, had embezzled thousands more, and was within days of being publicly called to account, her self-accusation would not have diminished in the least.

Mr Hallam, of course, did not come with anything of the kind. Radford Stokes' business was on the firmest of footings, as Mr Hallam demonstrated when he came weekly to the house with the accounts. This was a later development. For the first few months, everything was left to Radford's solicitors, and the grief of the house was not trespassed upon; but as time went on, the conscientious Mr Hallam called regularly to consult with her on matters to do with the factory.

Lucy was practical, and her mind, though dazed with grief, was sharp enough; but virtually everything that Mr Hallam set before her and laboriously explained on those evenings in the study was simply Greek to her. All she could do was give her assent to his suggestions about everyday matters; the buying of stock, the repair of machinery, the paying of wages, the pursuance of contracts; and if anything more problematic came up – a labour dispute, an army order that would entail liaison with government officials – she would simply have to ask Mr Hallam to take charge and do as he thought best.

Cecil Hallam could, of course, have been swindling her prodigiously, though the solicitors kept a close eye on things: but Lucy simply knew that he would not. He was one of those melancholy, kind, unassuming men who are entirely trustworthy, and are destined never to reach the heights because of it. Just about the only independent action that Lucy took, or wished to take, was to insist on Mr Hallam's salary being raised. For the rest, she simply struggled as best she could with the largely incomprehensible; though the diversion was, at least, not entirely unwelcome, in that it forced her to think of other things besides that terrible plunge, and a surreal, ghastly image of herself standing behind Radford as he dropped.

Still, it was clear even to her wounded mind that this was no way for Stokes' works to be run. The jobs of numerous people who did not have her comfort and security depended upon that factory functioning at its very best, especially with the present downturn of the trade; and that it could not do in this betwixt-and-between fashion. The most sensible course in the long run, as the solicitors had hinted to her, would be to sell up: a buyer could surely be found among the big manufacturers of the valley.

Of course it would have been very nice and romantic and gratifying if Lucy had decided to prove the likes of Mr John Arthur Brown and Mr Aubrey Parmenter wrong, and run the works herself – if she had swept into the factory office, set about mastering the mysteries of the trade, and gradually earned the respect of her male coevals as a sterling business-woman. Such things, however, do not happen. She had wit enough to know that she would have bankrupted the place in six months, as would anyone, male or female, attempting to do the same with no experience. Fortunately she felt not

293

the slightest inclination to transform herself into one of those entrepreneurial Boadiceas so beloved of romancers. Perhaps as a result of having been herself at the sharp end of the trade, operating a sewing-machine in an airless workshop, she saw no glamour in it, only a dismal tedium. And that particular factory now held such an abhorrence of association for her that she could not even have borne to go near it.

She would have to do something, of course, factory or no factory: she was a young woman with a life ahead of her. But it was not easy to see it that way. She could not see a time when she would be able to do anything but what she did for months after Radford's death – lurk in lonely, self-punishing agony in the house of clocks, the house that seemed less than ever her own now that it was her own completely. Her one activity, if such it could be called, was to serve as prop and stay for Georgina, who was at first so prostrated by the news that a breakdown seemed imminent. Feeling that she was responsible for depriving Georgina of her beloved brother, Lucy found a double anguish in the way her sister-in-law clung to her, depended on her, and lavished on her all the timorous affection that had lost its primary object. Something even of the idea that she was not a fit person for this innocent girl to cleave to, and that she would surely corrupt her, took root in Lucy. Miss Threadgold clearly seemed to think so, though a certain hesitancy characterized her now. For one thing, she must know her own position in the household was in some doubt; for another, the death of Radford, all unexpectedly, caused the decisive weakening of her power over Georgina. The comfortable, opinionated sturdiness on which her charge had been accustomed to rely in the more trivial trials of everyday life, was the very last thing to be of help to a grief such as Georgina's now; and in Miss Threadgold's voluptuous amble about the silent house could be seen the lineaments of a woman who was learning to tread carefully.

So Lucy, torn between a conviction that she was unworthy to help Georgina, and a natural pity for the girl whom she loved dearly, did what she could to help her recover. The process was swifter, or at least smoother, than she had anticipated: she had reckoned without Georgina's religious faith, which was quiet, firm, and most importantly – and what is so rarely the case – actually did her some good; at least when she was left to reflect on it alone, and was not troubled by the officious visits of the vicar of the parish, who, besides having the standard-issue clerical face of frightful pop eyes, horse's teeth and beetroot complexion, brought with him such a doleful line in sanctimonious bromides that Georgina was invariably set back several days. With Lucy, who did not bother to hide her unbelief, he was loftily impatient, demonstrating to her – not for the first time – that the very people who are most insistent that their faith be respected will not respect an honest lack of it.

But Georgina, for all her timidity, had her own sort of strength. 'I'm not sad for Radford any more,' she one day announced to Lucy, with a face the shining vulnerability of which made Lucy want to weep. 'I've been thinking of all the things he'll miss, and the happinesses he can never enjoy; but you see, that's wrong, because where he is all those things don't matter any more. They're like the toys you had when you were a child: you look at them affectionately, but you've moved on to other things.' There might have been an element of determined wishfulness in this, but the important thing was that Georgina had decided to face down her grief in her own way, and Lucy admired her for it. She even partly envied her for her faith: only partly, for any acceptance of that afterlife in which Georgina believed meant that one day Lucy would have to meet Radford again, and look him in the face.

But except for Georgina, Lucy shunned even such human company as cared to be associated with her. Mrs Silvie, as Mr Parmenter had said, lived to some extent in a world of her own, and did not realize the extent of the opprobrium attaching to Lucy's name; but all the same, Lucy restricted her visits to her and Joanna to a bare minimum. Her own family in Alma Street were similarly untouched by the cloud of disapproval that hung over her in shoe-baron society, but all the same Lucy did not see much of them. Her mother's blundering, good-natured sympathy was in itself a source of pain, for the simple reason that Lucy did not feel she deserved it; she felt rather as she had as a child when, feigning illness to escape school, she had been fussed over by her mother and had her perfectly cool brow tenderly stroked. Punishment was more bearable than pity, and her self-imposed solitude was her way of administering it.

Despair does not require the rent garments and wild cries of an Elektra: it can coexist with the small business of everyday life – as Lucy all too piercingly perceived from thinking of Radford's death, and his behaviour before it. And despair was not too strong a word for Lucy's state of mind, even though it had to be accommodated in a house of gaslight, tradesmen's bills, parlour-maids and laundry, instead of the blood-haunted palace of Agamemnon. It was a despair dry, deep, settled, and unreachable by any of the conventional forms of comfort. The continued presence of pleasant things in a world in which something terrible has happened is only an objective phenomenon, and meaningless to a mind over which a filter of despair has been placed. The admonition 'cheer up' may be backed up by eminently reasonable references to the persistence of sunshine and flowers; but if the rays of the sun appear to the eye as jabbing spikes, and the scent of flowers to the nose as the stench of death, then where is cheer to be found?

In such a frame of mind the passage of time was scarcely observable. Radford's house, as she still continued to think of it, was in any case a place well insulated against the signs of the changing seasons; and with her emotional life suspended in an aspic of guilt and regret, with none of the flux of thought and feeling that gives a sense of personal chronology, Lucy felt herself to be marooned both in space and time. She might have been some fairy-tale character agelessly imprisoned in a castle – the castle of her own anguish; and she would not have been surprised to have seen an enchanted forest of thorns growing up around the neat villa-eaves of the house in Lessington Road.

Such, indeed, would have made little difference to her situation, for no one came there. Secluded she might be, but she was well aware of her ostracism – malice having in common with bad news the quality of travelling fast. She knew that the worthies who had attended Radford's funeral would as soon have thought of acknowledging Alice Wedderburn as acknowledging the widow of Lessington Road.

No one came there – except one. Mr Miles Mellish, with typical delicacy, had immediately ceased his equestrian haunting of Lessington Road on Radford's death and, after a prompt call to pay his respects, tactfully retired from the scene for some months. At length, however, as the long year drew to its close, Mr Mellish began to make his presence known once more. Too retiring at first to intrude physically over the threshold – for Mr Mellish modestly assumed as a general principle that he was unwelcome wherever he went,

296

unlike most young men who start from the opposite assumption – he began to send proxies of himself, as it were, in the shape of little baskets of delicacies, hothouse flowers, albums of sheet-music, books, and other gifts, miscellaneous indeed, but alike in two regards: they were all fearfully expensive, and they were all chosen so that all three ladies of the household could enjoy them. The handwritten note that accompanied them was likewise unvarying: *Mr Miles Mellish presents his compliments to Mrs Stokes, Miss Stokes, and Miss Threadgold, and hopes they will do him the honour of accepting this small token of his esteem.* It was written in a fine, free-flowing hand, which gave no hint of the agonies its composition had cost Mr Mellish, who had hesitated for two days over the order of the three names, and had even wildly considered writing them crossways as on a theatre poster. He had hastily recalled the first version, which hoped they would *do him the honour of accepting this small trifle*, Mr Mellish being suddenly struck with a misgiving that the note implied the enclosure of a confection of cream and sherry, and had run all the way down the street to stop the messenger boy, who called him some very disobliging names when he caught up with him.

The gifts became a regular occurrence, but it was not until the new year of 1902, over six months after Radford's death, that Miles Mellish plucked up courage to call in person; and then the mere sight of the three women seemed to affect him with such poignancy that he could only sit biting his lip and going red in the face. Lucy's thanks for his latest gift only seemed to throw him into worse confusion.

'The game pie? Oh, I beg you, don't mention it. Really, it was nothing. Absolutely nothing. Mere rubbish – not fit to eat, really. At least – I don't mean there was anything wrong with it, you know, or that I would send you anything not fit for . . . It isn't worth mentioning, that's what I mean . . . It wasn't worth mentioning, that's what I meant,' he explained to himself in an undertone; and after biting his lip some more, and doing terrible things to his gloves, he hastily took his leave.

It was one of the pleasant points about Mr Mellish's character, however, that he did not let his social diffidence get the better of him, gloomily declare the battle lost, and retreat: he simply tried and tried again. And though he still prefaced his every entrance with an anxious, 'I hope I don't intrude?', as the new year grew older it must have been plain even to his modesty that he did not intrude at all, but was very welcome. Certainly Lucy was always very glad to see him: to her soul, frozen in its own dark winter, his visits were like those gleams of sunshine that, breaking across a January day, seem brighter and purer than the continuous rays of summer. And more importantly, it was plain to her that Georgina, as her recovery from her bereavement proceeded, liked Mr Mellish quite as much as she ever had, if not more: indeed it seemed to Lucy that Mr Mellish's gentle attentions were crucial to the completion of that recovery, and that knowing herself admired and loved was not only healing Georgina but making her something of a new person, stronger and more confident.

In a world in which the cruel, the afflicting and the tragically defeating seemed to be dispensed by the hand of Providence with a liberality hardly reconcilable with its reputation for kindness, this was a fine thing. In fact, it was so fine and worthwhile a thing that Lucy, who felt her own influence on the world had so far been almost exclusively malign, was determined that here at least she would do some good – break the bonds of self-pity and introspection that immobilized her, and help the couple in every way she could.

Which would have been simply a matter of, figuratively, taking the twain by the scruffs of their necks and pushing them together – but for one thing. Miles Mellish was not made universally welcome. There was the blonde, bland, sleepily watchful obstacle of Miss Threadgold, who used her every artful stupidity to discourage and undermine him. The more Miles' friendship with Georgina ripened, the more Dinah Threadgold stood upon her ground as Georgina's oldest and most faithful confidante, with the continual implication that only she genuinely had the girl's interest at heart. And Miles Mellish was quite unequal to her: he was too incurably polite to ignore her as she deserved. Lucy knew that she was going to have to confront Dinah Threadgold if she was to be a friend to the potential couple. Indeed, she had seen the shadows of a confrontation for some time, but in her mood of sterile hopelessness had felt it hardly worth the trouble. But that was merely thinking of herself: she must think of Georgina and Miles.

Then one day Mr Mellish's call, which normally brought Georgina hurrying from whatever she was doing, did not elicit the usual response. She was upstairs, and did not come down; Miss Threadgold said she had a headache. Mr Mellish was so determined to show that he didn't merely come to see Georgina that he stayed rather longer than usual, though his conversation was somewhat fragmented by his jumping expectantly out of his seat and facing the door at every slightest noise within the house. When he had at last gone, Lucy went up to Georgina's room, where the girl sitting on the bed presented to her a face of such transparent misery and confusion that Lucy knew at once this was no headache.

'Miles was asking after you,' Lucy said, sitting down beside her. 'He was very disappointed not to have seen you.'

Georgina burst into tears. Oddly enough, in tears all traces of the awkward naïveté that made her often seem like a very young girl disappeared: a woman approaching thirty was there instead, acknowledging herself, with a curious dignity, to be at the mercy of emotions no less painful for being the universal human burden.

'You and Miles,' Lucy said, 'you surely haven't – fallen out in any way?'

Georgina shook her head. 'But I don't think I ought to see him any more, Lucy. Not the way it . . . well, the way it appears.'

Lucy frowned. 'How does it appear?' As Georgina did not answer, Lucy went on, 'It doesn't appear anything except very nice to me. Miles likes you a great deal and you like him the same way, I think. Don't you? There's no need to be shy, Georgina, not with me . . . So what could possibly be wrong with that?'

'Well, Dinah said – she said that I perhaps couldn't see what was happening, and so she would have to tell me for my own good . . . She said that I mustn't make myself seem cheap, that I would get myself a reputation for leading men on, and . . . Oh, she meant it for my own good!' Georgina added hurriedly as she saw Lucy's expression. 'She said I probably didn't realize the impression I was making, and she was just trying to protect me . . . Oh, but, Lucy, I never dreamed that that was what it must look like, it just never occurred to me . . .'

Lucy's grip on Georgina's hand tightened. She felt as if she had just seen some well-loved picture daubed with obscene graffiti.

'She said it was all too easy to get a reputation that way,' Georgina said, wiping her eyes.

'Hm. And she gave examples, I suppose?'

Georgina stared, looking young and helpless again. 'Oh – oh, Lucy, I'm sure she didn't mean—'

'I know very well what she meant,' Lucy said. 'Never mind, my dear. It'll be all right.' Oh, Dinah, you fool, she thought. You fool. You've gone and done it now. Were you counting on me being so guilt-ridden and ground down and spiritless that I would just let you get away with it? Did you think I was broken for ever? Well, perhaps I might have been. But now you've done the very thing to shake me out of it. You fool!

She stood up: such a towering anger was upon her that she felt as if she rose up ten feet. Certainly that was how Georgina seemed to see her, for she said in alarm, 'Oh, Lucy, what are you going to do? I know you and Dinah don't get on, but she meant well . . . I don't want there to be any trouble—'

'There isn't going to be any trouble,' Lucy said. She spoke sharply, but the sharpness was not meant for Georgina: it was simply the first rumble of the coming storm. She patted her sister-in-law's hand, and went in search of Dinah Threadgold.

She was in the conservatory, admiring Georgina's plants. Was this meant to be a tableau showing her in benevolent communion with the innocent and untainted spirit of Georgina, over which she stood in loyal and selfless vigilance?

'You surely can't have thought it wouldn't get back to me,' Lucy said without preamble. 'What you said to Georgina. So I can only suppose you thought I wouldn't do anything about it.'

Miss Threadgold looked at her, all amiable surprise. 'Oh, I'm sorry! You'll really have to explain a bit more clearly, dear. I can't follow that sort of insinuating mysterious way of talking, I never have. Plain speaking and plain dealing, that's always been my motto, I can't help it, it's just the way I am.'

Lucy's palms were damp: she made herself unclench her fists, realizing that she had never been so close to hitting someone. 'All right then,' she said, 'speaking plainly, you're a nasty meddling bitch, and this time you've gone just too far. You've made Georgina feel terrible about her attachment to Miles, and you did it because you can't bear to lose your power over her. That's the most vicious trick that even you've played, and believe me, I've seen through every single one.'

'Oh dear! Pardon me if I don't join in this sort of cursing-match, I never have been able to, I don't know why, perhaps it's just the way I was brought up.' Miss Threadgold's expression was as serene as ever, but for the first time her speech had quickened and lost its usual drone. 'All I can say is that I put Georgina's interests before everything, I always have, I don't care if people think I'm foolish for it, it's just the way I am. Call me old-fashioned if you like, but I don't believe girls should be taught to play up to the men. I dare say that makes me rather out of place here, but it doesn't matter, it's not me I care about, it's Georgina. And when I see her coming under a bad influence, I speak my mind. I'm sorry, I always do where Georgina's welfare's concerned . . .'

Miss Threadgold tailed off, for Lucy had turned away from her and stepped into the passage. 'Jane,' she called to the maid who was just going into the kitchen, 'when you're free, will you have Miss Threadgold's trunks brought down, and help her with her packing.'

Lucy turned back to Miss Threadgold, whose smile was visibly decayed. 'Oh, pardon me! This sort of joking is, I'm sure, appreciated in certain circles, but I've never had any taste for it, I'm sorry—'

'No joke,' Lucy said. 'You're leaving. Today.'

Probably Dinah Threadgold's mouth had been fixed like that for so long that the smile could never quite leave it, but it was as near gone as it ever would be. 'I think we should ask Georgina about that,' she said.

'No.' Lucy was quite in control of herself now. There was something cold, clear and final about her which she hardly recognized as coming from her own conscious will. 'This is my house. You've got no place here. Not any more. You're leaving.'

Even Miss Threadgold's obtuseness could not dismiss this. 'And where am I to go? Really, I can hardly believe my ears – I've become accustomed to much in your behaviour, thinking you didn't know any better, but really this is . . . Where am I to go?'

'Back to where you came from. Who was it you lived with in Oundle, some great-aunt? Go and inflict yourself on her, poor woman. And don't try and have any communication with us. Is that plain enough for you?'

'*You* ought to go back where you came from,' Miss Threadgold hissed. 'Radford should never have taken you out of it. He should have left you in the gutter where you belong – and if only he had, he'd be here today!'

Lucy felt that one strike home; but to her own surprise, and as an indication of her growing strength, the wound was not mortal. 'And you'd have been at his side, I suppose, Dinah?' she said. 'Well, it's too late. He's not here: I am; this is my house.' She turned away. 'I'll have your things taken down to the station in the trap.'

And victory was hers. Miss Threadgold left that afternoon, after delivering to Georgina a long martyred speech, full of righteous refusals to dwell on her wrongs or to blame anyone except those who knew full well their blame and would have to answer for it one day, and of earnest assurances that if ever Georgina needed her she would fly to her side, which Lucy did not even bother to listen to. She could not help but feel satisfaction at her triumph; but inwardly she was perturbed at the chief weapon she had used. 'This is my house!' Well, she supposed it was; but in the calm after her anger she reflected on how little it seemed so. For the whole house was terribly redolent of Radford: all his possessions were there, all his domestic arrangements were still in place, the whole mechanism was geared to that fastidious presence that was now eternally absent. And it struck her that if she was to continue to live here – live in any sense other than mere vegetable existence – she must begin to make some more changes.

One other realization was presented to her in perfect clarity. She had made herself another enemy – one who had formerly been sequestered in this enchanted house where nobody came, and whose malice had been accordingly circumscribed, but who was now at large, and who would lose no opportunity of further blackening Lucy's name. Given Miss Threadgold's part in the events that had preceded Radford's death, there was no doubting the account she would give of the circumstances of that death, and who was to blame. But then that was pretty well what Lucy believed too, even if her self-hatred was less intense than it had been, and she was already so far beyond the pale that it seemed of no moment what people thought of her.

Georgina was, inevitably, distressed by the manner of Miss Threadgold's leaving: so tender-hearted a person could hardly be indifferent to the breaking of so long an association. But even her humility could not pretend, on reflection, that

Miss Threadgold's hints about her and Miles were anything but unjust. Self-doubt and dependence had long distorted Georgina's feelings, and without them she would probably have realized some time ago that she disliked Dinah Threadgold very much – not an uncommon emotional conundrum, and one that has sustained many marriages.

'You know why I did it, don't you, Georgina?' Lucy said that evening. She knew she had done the right thing: she just wanted to be sure that none of Miss Threadgold's poison was still in Georgina's bloodstream. 'It was because of what she was trying to do with you and Miles. What she said was rubbish and she knew it. Nobody could look at you and Miles with anything but sheer pleasure and happiness that here are two very nice people getting to know each other. She was simply trying her spiteful best to keep you apart. And that's why I told her to go.' As Georgina still looked a little tearful and doubtful, Lucy went on, 'I mean, I may be wrong; but what gives you the greatest happiness in life? What is it you look forward to when you wake up in the morning? When things are all grey and dark, as they too often are, I'm afraid, what is it that stands out in the distance, like a green hill where everything will be better, if you can only get to it . . .? Isn't it that person you love, and who loves you?'

Georgina gazed at her for several moments. 'Oh! Lucy,' she said, 'you make me sad.'

'Do I?' Lucy smiled. 'I don't mean to.'

'No – I mean, it's true what you say, and that is how I feel about Miles, though he is a funny fellow sometimes . . . But I'm sad for you because you must have felt that, Lucy. I know you must have, because you put it so well – and now it's gone . . .!'

Lucy's emotion on hearing this was too poignantly complex for her to trust herself to speak: all she could do was pat Georgina's hand.

'Do you think he was – put out today, when I didn't come down?'

'No,' Lucy said. 'No, not at all. And nothing's going to come between you and Miles, Georgina, I'm going to see to it. There aren't so many chances of happiness in this world that we can afford to let any pass by.'

'I always felt that she was hostile to him, but I suppose I tended to trust her judgement instead of mine. Perhaps that was a sort of hiding – not wanting to take responsibility . . . It will be strange without her.'

'It will,' Lucy said. 'As if it isn't strange enough . . .' Thinking of her resolution earlier, she said, 'Georgina, you've felt it too, haven't you? That everything's all set out just as if – if Radford was still here?'

Georgina nodded. 'Do you think we should change things?'

'I don't know . . . I couldn't bear to at first. It seems terrible – as if that person never even existed.'

'Oh, no,' Georgina said firmly. 'It wouldn't be like that – not even if every last trace of Radford was wiped off the earth. Because he'd still be alive in my memory, and my heart. And yours too, Lucy.'

Again Lucy could not speak.

'So if we put away his things, it's only because he has no need of them any more – not because we're deciding to forget,' said Georgina. 'We know we'll never do that.'

And so, together, Lucy and Georgina tackled all the personal effects that had lain untouched since Radford's death, from the study to his bedroom, where everything down to his cuff-links still stood as if awaiting his return. As they worked, packing some things away for storage and others to be passed on to charity, the conviction grew on both of them that this was the right thing to do, and they managed to keep their spirits briskly up. It was all the more surprising therefore for Lucy to find herself breaking down as she folded away one of the dove-grey waistcoats of which Radford had been so fond, and helplessly sobbing out, 'I wish he had been happier – oh, I wish he had been happier!' And it was Georgina's turn to comfort her then, telling her that he had been happy, of course he had been happy: kindly meant, and the one thing above all others that Lucy could not believe.

III

It was in May, almost a year after Radford's death, that Lucy made one of her still rare visits to Mrs Silvie and Joanna, and found the old lady buzzing about the house as if she had never had wobbly legs in her life.

'And how are you, my dear? You still look a little peaky – but see here, you must touch my hand, because I'm so full of happiness that it will probably go straight from me into you, like one of those electrical rods,' Mrs Silvie said, seizing Lucy and tugging her over to the little shrine-like table of photographs and letters. 'There – take a good look at that funny face, my dear,' she said, thrusting at her one of the pictures of her nephew, 'because you will be seeing the original very soon. Perhaps I shouldn't count my chickens like that, some people would say that's just inviting bad luck, but I'm not superstitious. Are you superstitious, dear?'

Lucy said no.

'*Aren't* you? Good! It isn't Christian, after all. I wear green all the time, and some people wouldn't be seen in it for love or money. Oh, no, they wouldn't, you know! But anyhow, you know what this is all about, my dear. They're signing a treaty and settling this dreadful war at last. And my Harry will be coming home! Of course he isn't my Harry, he's Aubrey's Harry, but he knows I shall simply demand to see him as soon as he comes. I will, you know!'

'That's wonderful news, Mrs Silvie,' Lucy said. 'Will he definitely be leaving the army?'

'Oh, without a doubt! He's going to resign his commission or something. I gather he's pretty well disillusioned with the whole business after his time in South Africa, and between you and me he says some rather naughty things about the generals and the government and so on. Well! I could have told him it was a mistake right from the start, but that doesn't matter now. The main thing is he's coming home. Such travails as he has suffered! Wounded – getting separated from his platoon and lying for hours under the dreadful sun, and in danger of getting eaten by lions and Zulus.' Mrs Silvie turned to Joanna. 'Was it Zulus, my dear?'

'I don't remember him saying anything about Zulus, Mrs Silvie,' Joanna said gently.

'No? Perhaps I mean zebras. Well, I dare say there were some of both around the place, anyhow. And such diseases! I won't even mention some of them – Joanna had to look them up in the dictionary for me and then we were quite put off our lunch. Harry writes that I must prepare myself for his being terribly yellow in the face. Not that he ever had much beauty to spoil, bless him, quite a Parmenter in that regard – not like you, my dear – I don't know which of you two creatures has the nicer skin, it's like choosing between silk and satin!' said Mrs Silvie, grabbing a hand each from Lucy and Joanna and pressing them to her cheeks. 'And I know what you're thinking – I do! You're thinking I shall tire myself out and get those wobbly feelings . . . But I can't help it – when I'm happy, I feel as if I'm just going to go off bang!'

Such happiness was inevitably infectious, even to a nature in which the capacity for it had been so blighted as Lucy's, and she walked back to Lessington Road in lightened mood. Part of her reason for making the visit today had been the knowledge that Miles Mellish would be calling at home: in the months since Miss Threadgold's departure she had employed all sorts of strategems in order to give Miles and Georgina a chance to be alone. Accordingly she made her usual slow and noisy entrance into the house, so as to give Georgina time to go and sit at the piano and turn over some music, and Miles to go and lean his elbow against the mantelpiece in a supremely conscious attitude and examine the vase thereon as if he had never seen anything like it. This time, however, she had only just taken off her gloves when Georgina came running out to the hall and flung her arms round her.

They were engaged. What Everests of diffidence Miles had had to conquer to make his proposal Lucy could guess; how he had gone about scaling them she never knew; but somehow it had been done, and here was Georgina blushing and asking her if it was all right, for all the world as if she were an awesome parent instead of close on ten years her junior; and here was Miles Mellish bashfully coming forward from the mantelpiece whither he had withdrawn from force of habit, the crown of his hair more recalcitrant than ever, and his ears seeming positively to glow like twin side-lamps. Having kissed Georgina and congratulated her, Lucy did the same to Miles, which occasioned in him so much confusion that he was compelled to go back to the mantelpiece and examine the vase all over again; and for some time he could make no contribution to the conversation beyond an emphatic throat-clearing like the tearing up of a cardboard box.

'As if you needed to ask me,' Lucy said, 'when it's the very thing I've been hoping for all this time!'

'Well,' Georgina said, 'of course I would have had to have asked Radford . . . and besides, you helped to bring us together, and have been such a friend to us – isn't that so, Miles?'

'Harrumph!' answered Miles.

'Well, it's the best news I've heard since – for ages,' said Lucy. 'And as we're going to be sort-of relations, Mr Mellish, I can call you Miles now – if you don't mind.'

Miles tore at his cardboard box, very energetically.

'So, is it official? Are you going to announce it? What about a notice in the newspaper?'

'Perhaps not just yet,' said Georgina. 'As I said, I had to be sure of your approval – and of course, there's Miles' mother to consider.'

Miles, after a last bout of ripping and tearing, came away from the mantelpiece and said, 'You see, Mrs Stokes—'

'Lucy.'

'Harrumph – Lucy – of course . . .' Miles seemed about to make a dash back to the mantelpiece, but thought better of it and went on, 'You see, though I am in possession of my own fortune, My Mother retains a good deal of – of influence. Oh, quite rightly – she's such an admirable woman, I shall never be worthy of her; but she is a little exacting, and will of course expect to be fully consulted over the matter of my marrying. Not that I have any doubt as to her approving my choice – that is, I mean the one who has so wonderfully and – and amazingly chosen me. No one could disapprove of that; not even My Mother . . .' Here Miles looked a little depressed. 'But the fact is, she will need to be approached carefully, at the right time. She's staying with friends at Huntingdon at the moment, but when she returns I must really address myself to – to facing her.' (Miles more downcast than ever.) 'Not that I mean to suggest that she's anything but a thoroughly splendid woman. But she does like to be consulted – about everything.'

Lucy was in some doubt as to the capacity of Georgina's nerve to stand up to the fearsome Mrs Mellish; but a glance at her sister-in-law's face showed that in her happiness she was prepared for anything. Lucy was about to suggest that Miles invite his mother to visit here – it was one consequence of her outcast state that she had lost all social fear, and didn't give a hang for strong-minded matrons – when it occurred to her that that very outcast state meant it was best if Georgina distanced herself from her as much as possible, at least until she was married and the approval or disapproval of Mrs Mellish was beside the point. It was a sad reflection; but she forced herself to betray nothing of this, and simply repeated her congratulations, and added that if there was any help they needed she must be the first person they asked.

Discreetly she left them alone again; and in her room allowed the melancholy that had been lurking under her wholly genuine happiness for them to well up. It was an entirely selfish melancholy, as she recognized; it had to do with the prospect, which now could not be far distant, of being quite alone here. Her family were in the process of settling into a larger house, not too far from the old neighbourhood but much healthier and roomier, which she had rented for them; but even had this arrangement not been made, she knew that this lonely echoing pile was hardly the place for her little brothers to be brought up in.

Was it part of her punishment that she should be forever alone? That she could even ask this question showed that she was groping back to life, for hitherto solitude had been not only desirable but the only thing that was bearable. But as for the alternatives to solitude, one was out of the question. How little the gossips of Cottesbridge society knew of her, if they supposed her to be carnality personified! The pairing urge was extinct in her; and if perpetual solitude was to be her punishment, she could only be grateful that she was not under a worse sentence, and that she would never again have to enter the portals of that grim prison known as love.

IV

Georgina and Miles' engagement had been a fixture for some
weeks, though yet to be intimated to the fearsome Mrs
Mellish, when Lucy going into the front parlour one morning
to retrieve some sewing glimpsed from the window a figure
lurking about the trees that lined the drive.

Recognition did not come for a moment, until a glint of
sun upon the figure's fair hair put her in mind of the youth
who had been hanging about in just such a way on the day
she and Radford had returned from Northampton, and who
had apparently been looking for a job. The youth was now
leaning against the bole of a tree, and looking up at the house
with a speculative air, as if debating whether to approach.
The mixture of lounging and furtiveness in his manner gave
Lucy no very easy feeling; so she decided to be as secret as
he and, leaving the house by the side door, made her way
towards him round the back of the trees, which being low
and in full new foliage effectively screened her until she was
directly behind him.

'Were you looking for someone?' she said, stepping forward. The youth started, his lips still pursed in the act of
whistling; but after a moment he regarded her very coolly,
and said, 'You're Radford Stokes' wife, aren't you?'

'Widow.'

'Yes, that's what I meant.' The youth's lips resumed their
whistling shape, though no sound issued from them; and he
examined Lucy in a very frank and critical manner which yet
had something covert about it.

'What do you want here?' Lucy said.

'I've got something to tell you.' He checked himself, head
on one side. 'Something to ask you, I mean.' His speech had
that worst of all accents, the genteel imposed upon the native
with no intermedium of education, and resembled his dress
in that regard.

'Go on then.'

He smiled defensively, showing those white strong teeth that against the fairness of eighteen-year-old skin can look more heartless than the most wolfish maw. 'It's not very private here.'

She studied him for a few seconds. Georgina was not in, having gone out driving with Miles, and already Lucy was glad of it without knowing why: something simply told her it was best if no one else knew of this. 'Come into the house,' she told him.

In the back parlour the youth slouched aimlessly around with his long limbs, ignoring her invitation to sit down. He did not say his name and she did not ask it. There was something both primly affected and insolently brash about him that put her on edge, and he seemed to know it.

'I've come to ask you a favour,' he said, looking sidelong at her. He had very attractive blue eyes, and he seemed to know that too.

'Is it about a job?'

'A job, no thank you. I've got myself a position, thank you very much,' he said loftily. 'Not that it pays very much . . . What did your husband say about me?'

'He never said anything about you,' Lucy said, coolly enough, but with a feeling of constriction at her chest.

'No? I dare say he wouldn't. I knew him pretty well, as it happens. Probably better than you.'

'I doubt that very much. Now will you—'

'Did you know he made advances to me?' He observed the effect of that, with the intent, interested look of a boy setting a match to a beetle.

'I don't believe you.'

'He even wrote me letters. He would have done a lot more if he hadn't been frightened. And if I'd let him, of course,' he added with a very moral look.

'I don't believe you,' Lucy said again, mechanically; and she did not know whether he could tell how completely she lied when she said that. For belief was too strong a word for the utter penetrating conviction that entered her: the whole of her married life with Radford turned itself inside out in her mind, and in the space of moments was transformed from a harrowing enigma into a tragedy no less cruel but now completely intelligible in every detail. The flicker of revulsion that went through her as she saw and understood

310

was merely the reflex of a cultural conditioning that in her own lonely trials she had almost sloughed off, and was succeeded by a bright pure flame of pity. If only he could have told her . . . The thought was not even finished: how could he have told her that, of all things? How could he have confessed his shame to she whom – as she now perceived – he had hoped might cure him of it? The thought of Radford being driven to such expedients as approaching this youth gave her, it was true, another shudder; but that in turn was followed by an acute realization of the despair that must have driven him.

Another reversal occurred within Lucy as the youth stood looking curiously down at her. She became her late husband's defender unto death.

'You can get locked up for that sort of thing,' the youth said brightly. 'Remember that Oscar Wilde one? It was all over the papers.'

'I remember,' she said. 'And that young lord got off scot free, didn't he? He was lucky.'

The youth tossed back his hair petulantly, and then smiled. 'I don't suppose you and him had much of a married life, did you?'

Lucy smiled back. 'Oh, you'd be surprised. You had a lucky escape, really. You wouldn't have been able to stand up.'

The youth coloured: like most conscious Adonises, he was at heart a prude. 'Your husband made improper advances to me,' he said. 'And I don't see why I should keep quiet about that. Do you?'

'My husband's beyond your reach now. He can't be hurt by anything you say about him.'

'No. But the people he's left behind him can.'

She was about to say, truthfully, that it didn't matter a damn to her what people said, when her eye fell on one of Georgina's books on the work-table, and a terrible thought smote her. Could this youth's revelations endanger Georgina's marriage, and her hard-won chance of happiness? Miles was a good fellow, but would he be able to stand up to that powerful mother of his if such a scandal tainted Georgina's name, and set Mrs Mellish against the marriage?

It was a small chance, but Lucy had sufficient experience of life by now to know that if there is any possibility of things going awry, they will. Nor could she say what effect such a revelation might have upon Georgina's sheltered and sensitive

311

nature. She could not risk it: she could not allow the youth to tell his tale – which, she knew, would find plenty of receptive ears. The happiness of two people who were very dear to her was at stake.

'When you say "keeping quiet about it", you're talking about money, I suppose,' she said, regarding the youth with such open, settled distaste that he could not meet her eyes.

'Well, like I say, I don't earn much,' he said.

'Neither do a lot of people, but they don't resort to blackmail,' she said, then made herself stop. There was no point in antagonizing him. 'So. If I give you money, you keep quiet about your . . . association with my late husband. Is that correct?'

The youth look gratified, but also looked as if he wished to linger it out a little more. 'Well, I suppose that's a possibility. I mean, by rights I should report the matter to the police—'

'And what are they going to do about it? Imprison a dead man? Don't come that priggish stuff with me. You didn't go to the police because you'd got nothing to gain by it – you're not interested in anything but lining your own pockets. And I'm not so sure that the police would think you an innocent victim, either, to look at you.'

'Now listen here—'

'No, you listen. Don't expect me to admire your virtue and pay you off as well. It's going to be one or the other. Now which is it to be?'

The youth was sullen, but attempted a smirk too. 'I didn't think you'd want it known. I should have come before, but as it happened I wasn't in such need of the money. What Radford gave me lasted and—'

'What Radford gave you?'

'Yes.' The youth gave her a supercilious look. 'I suppose you didn't know about that either. Well, he did. I *was* going to go to the police last year, you know, and I told him so; and he gave me money to stop me. I wouldn't have taken it, but as it happened I did need it rather badly at the time . . .'

Lucy did not listen to his whining self-justification, which served as proof that nobody believes themselves to be entirely without ethics: she was thinking back to last year and the time before Radford's death. 'When was this? That time last summer when I saw you in the drive, and opened the door to you? Just before . . .?'

The youth nodded, pouting. 'Radford got very worked up. I suppose he was thinking I might go to the police anyway

– but I couldn't help that, I couldn't help it if he didn't trust me . . .'

Just before Radford's death . . . Lucy felt as if an earthquake were moving beneath her feet. The entire set of suppositions on which she had based her mental and emotional world this past year was thrown into doubt. Her view of her husband's death had been wholly solipsistic: from the moment she had conceived of it as a deliberate act she had drawn a direct line connecting that fatal plunge and herself. No other known circumstance had come into the picture – and such too had been the judgement of her accusers in the plush drawing-rooms of Cottesbridge. And now came the news that, when Radford had made that ascent to the crane doors, his mind was shadowed by the threat of exposure as an unspeakable indulger in unnatural practices. With anguished pity, Lucy envisaged those last days of her husband's in the light of her new knowledge. If he had thought of his estranged wife at all, it was probably only as a supplementary aspect of his shame and failure.

In the sheer shock of this revelation she uttered a quiet moan; and the youth, misinterpreting it, said righteously, 'Well, look here, Mrs Stokes, I didn't come here to upset you. Not at all. I'd rather get the unpleasant business over as quickly as possible . . .'

Lucy came to herself, and threw him a sharp glance. 'Would you? Then let's do it. What do you want to do with this money you're hoping for?'

'Get to London,' the youth said airily. 'I've got no real prospects here. It's a one-eyed hole. I'm wasted here.'

'Yes,' she said grimly. 'I think you are.' She went over to the bureau and took out pen and paper. 'I will give you – let's see, a banker's draft's no good, I suppose you'll want cash. I'll get it through Mr Hallam . . . I will give you enough to see you settled in London, and set up in . . . What is it you want to do?'

'Be an artist,' said the youth, in the tone of those who suppose that for an artist's life the chief requirements are an aversion to work and a bohemian temperament, talent being an optional increment.

'All right then. Enough to set you up and support you until you're . . . established. How does that sound?'

'Well, of course I can't tell how much more I may need in time—'

'Oh, no.' Lucy faced him, and fixed his eyes with her own.

'I am going to give you a good deal of money. And with that money you are going to go to London and have your heart's desire. And that is going to be the end of it. You are not going to have any more communication with this house or anyone in it. I wasn't born to this, you know. I was brought up in Alma Street, near the gasworks, and I worked in a factory till I was nineteen. My father used to use the strap on us sometimes, and I've seen more fights than you've had hot dinners. So you see I don't mind playing rough. Do you see?'

It was he who at last turned away his eyes: he did not call her bluff. He was worthless, but he was not stupid; he had got what he came for.

The business was soon concluded, it being agreed that the youth would collect the money from the back door on the Friday following; and it was only when he was gone that Lucy gave way to the tremulousness that she had taken care to hide from her visitor. She sat shakily down and hid her face in her hands, and waited for her turbulent feelings to settle down so that she could tell what they were.

Pity: pity for Radford, there was no mistaking that. It remained with her as strongly as before. But quite apart from that, a new and dramatic realization was appearing before her. She had been presented with a chance to clear her own name. If she had simply shrugged and let the youth tell his tale to the world, then everyone would have seen Radford's death in the light in which she was now seeing it: the blame that hung about her would have been swept away. She might even have been pitied herself, as the wife of a man so unspeakably perverted.

But of course this was not a new realization. It had been subconsciously present all the time she was buying the youth off. And, thank God, it had not tempted her for a single second. Yes, she could have cleared her name by letting him blab, at the expense of endangering Georgina's happiness. Yes, she could have cleared her name, at the expense of Radford's memory. She could have delivered him over to the gossips instead of herself, to be fingered and mauled and traduced and insulted; and how they would have enjoyed it, especially as he could no longer answer back, as she could if she chose!

She could not deny that the yoke of blame still irked and pained her, and that it would be wonderful to be rid of it.

But not at such a price. She would continue to shoulder it, and keep the truth suppressed. Let Radford rest easy in his untimely grave: he must have had little enough mental rest, she knew now, when he was alive. Let Georgina and Miles start their married life free of any blighting shadow. Let people still think of her as the scandalous widow of Lessington Road, who had driven her husband to take his own life. The decision had been taken almost without conscious volition: the heart with which Cottesbridge did not credit Lucy had stirred from its paralysis and led her – it might be towards redemption, it might be towards further ignominy; all she knew was that she would follow it in the future, unhesitatingly.

And so no one knew of the youth's disclosure. No one knew of it when Lucy paid and packed him off; and no one knew of it when, some months later on a bright autumn morning, Georgina Stokes and Miles Mellish were married at Cottesbridge church – the approval of the groom's formidable mother having been at last won, after a long and gruelling inspection of her prospective daughter-in-law which, Georgina confided to Lucy, she would not have gone through again for the world. And no one knew of it when Lucy waved goodbye to the couple, who were to live at Miles' home in Northampton after the honeymoon. No one knew of it, just as they did not know how wretched at heart she was at parting with them, for she was gaily dressed, and laughed and threw rice and kissed them affectionately; and Cottesbridge society, observing, said she was as shameless as ever.

Fortunately the terrible emptiness of the house that she had feared once Georgina was gone was mitigated, for a while at any rate, by negotiations for the sale of the factory, which brought both solicitors and buyers there frequently in the following weeks. The decision to sell had been taken some months earlier, and there had been no shortage of interest. Mr Aubrey Parmenter and Mr John Arthur Brown had been prominent among the prospective buyers; but in the end they had got cold feet, the current depression in the trade consequent on the end of the Boer war bringing out all their native caution. Stokes' factory went at last to a newcomer from Norwich, which had its own specialized boot industry.

Norwich was certainly the previous home of this Mr Bressart

and his family, but rumour pointed to foreign extraction. German, some said: others went so far as to suggest Jewish origin. But whatever the truth, the Bressarts in the flesh turned out to be no more nor less than prosperous, pious, satisfied; stiff-necked and thoroughly English people. The only un-English thing about them was their conspicuous good looks, which Lucy had ample opportunity to observe, as much of the business of the sale was done sociably at her house, her unclean reputation presumably having yet to reach them. Mr and Mrs Bressart were fine, dark, stern-looking people in their forties, from whom had come a stronger distillation of beauty in the person of their daughter, who was about Lucy's age. Her name was Helena – Lucy envied her that; and in her at least there was a faint, decorous touch of the unconventional. She dressed rather in the aesthetic style, with much flowing lace at her sleeves, and her black hair in short curls on top of her head, and she had a remarkable nonchalant self-confidence: she moved about the world as if it were a place in which she belonged as completely and comfortably as a fish in a pool, whereas Lucy had long had a sense that her own existence was an awkward and disabling mistake that must somehow be accommodated. She noted too, if not with envy then with wistfulness, how great a separation there was between them in spite of their identical years; Helena Bressart having her life all before her, and presenting a mere *tabula rasa* of personality, in contrast to that of Lucy on which experience had already written much in a crabbed hand.

However, the sale being concluded, Lucy would never want for money; and that same experience having taught her that money, alas, is the most important thing in the world – a fact disregarded only by those who have a sufficiency of it – she immediately resolved that she would not succumb to such a convenient amnesia about its power, and applied herself to doing things with it. As winter drew on and the shoe-trade slackened after a long boom, there was much distress among the working people of the Nene Valley, and Lucy looked for ways to relieve it. In neighbouring Kettenham, where things were very bad, private benefactors had set up a soup-kitchen; but she knew from her own impoverished youth that want must be keen indeed before it would submit to be relieved in such degrading publicity. Her own alternative was achieved by meeting Jane the housemaid's aunt, a staunch Methodist who, although not very poor, continued to live in the Hole, where she attempted to light a candle against the darkness with Bible-classes and sewing-circles. Lucy visited this devoted woman, Mrs Blades, in her little frugal house at the end of one of the worst streets in the Hole, and thereby got to know at first hand the families who were in worst distress. Remembering the gifts with which Miles Mellish had penetrated the shell of their bereavement, Lucy began to work upon a similar plan, placing a regular order with her butcher and baker for large quantities of filling and nourishing provisions, and having them sent individually to the households that were in need. Though she insisted on anonymity, it soon became known that it was Mrs Stokes who was behind this most practical assistance; and though there were one or two proud refusals, in the main her activities in that intractable place came to be gladly accepted, the more readily perhaps because the knowledge that she was of humble origin herself took away any suggestion of condescending patronage.

She was much occupied with this work, and so managed to keep at bay the glooms that the empty house might have inspired in her; for except for a piano-teacher who came once a week to continue the tuition begun by Georgina, she was completely alone there, and her circle of acquaintance was intensely limited. Georgina and Miles, settling into their new home in Northampton, were near enough for fairly frequent reciprocal visits, but otherwise her social life was restricted to her family; and she had not been to Mrs Silvie's lately, knowing only that the old lady's beloved nephew Harry was now at last home from the war, and presumably being pressed to her necklace-encrusted bosom – a private scenario on which she did not wish to intrude.

Thus she went on into the winter, feeling her life to be, if not exactly fulfilled, at least justified, and touched by no extremes of sorrow or joy; until one dank, raw day in early December, when she called at Jane's aunt's in the Hole to discuss with her the distribution of sacks of coal in the district. They talked the matter over for some time in the stalwart old woman's tiny parlour hung with crewel-work texts; and when at last it was time for Lucy to go, Mrs Blades said she would walk a little way with her.

'Well, well, and the season of the birth of the Prince of Peace coming round again!' said Mrs Blades who, though

317

she talked like a Sunday-school book, was good-hearted. 'There'll not be much peace or good cheer for a lot of folk in these parts, I'm afraid. If it's not want, it's broken heads and broken vows. Every year I hope it'll be better, and that His spirit will enter here, and every year I'm disappointed. And yet I still have hopes, my dear – I always have hopes.'

As they passed down the grim street, which was in all conscience as effective a destroyer of hopes as was ever devised, they came to a house of more than commonly dingy appearance, and divided up into several dwellings, outside which stood a man with the familiar patched elbows and harried expression of the rent-collector. He was shouting up at one of the upper windows, where movement could be discerned behind a ragged curtain.

'It en't a bit of good you hiding there, and glining at me behint them drapes, my beauty! I see you there, burn you! You git yourself out of there by three o'clock, else I'll be back with somebody to break down the door! You can't say you en't had notice!'

'Dear me,' said Mrs Blades, 'there's someone who just won't be helped, try as I might. And she's in desperate need of it too – sick, and with a little child, and no money. God have mercy on her soul! And yet I can understand it, in a curious way. She's proud: some might say she's got little enough to be proud about, but it's pride just the same. You'll have heard her name, no doubt, Mrs Stokes. Alice Wedderburn, the one who got herself talked about so much, not so long ago.'

'Good God . . .! Alice Wedderburn – here?'

'The very same,' said Mrs Blades, shaking her head, and interpreting Lucy's reaction as the usual one of ladies on hearing that name. 'She was born in the Hole, you know, and she left it to – well, to do as we all know she did; and now she's got nothing, and she's come back here to die. Yes, she's consumptive, poor creature – a true daughter of the Hole in that, I'm afraid! And she can't be long for this world, though some might say she'd be better off in the next, if God is merciful to her . . .'

Mrs Blades' homily faded in Lucy's ears as she hurried across to the house, pushed open its peeling front door, and ran up the worm-eaten stairs. The door that faced the front was, as she expected, closed, and when she knocked there was only a faint scuffling within.

'Alice,' she said, tapping again, and placing her lips close to the door, 'it's Lucy. It's Lucy Stokes. You know me, Alice. Please let me in.'

The ensuing silence was broken by the muffled crying of a child: not the reflexive vocalizing of a small infant, but the quite different weeping of a child in whom consciousness is sufficiently developed for it to perceive that the world into which it has been forcibly summoned is an unwelcoming place, which it might have declined to visit had it been granted a choice in the matter. The crying continued in spite of audible hushings; and at last Lucy was rewarded by the sound of a key in the door, which opened a fraction.

'What do you want?' said a sharp voice, which also unmistakably had tears in it.

The room was too dim for Lucy to see much of the speaker. 'Won't you let me in, Alice?' said she. 'Just for a moment. It's so long since I saw you. I heard that you're not well, and—'

All at once the door was flung open with a sort of flouncing defiance which was so characteristic of Alice Wedderburn that Lucy hardly needed the sight of the green eyes that flashed at her as she entered. Those striking eyes, indeed, were almost all that remained of the Alice Wedderburn who had once stepped haughtily down from carriages in silk and jewels. Lucy had lived most of her life in communities where tuberculosis was common, and a glance was enough to tell her that Alice was in the advanced stage of the disease. Poverty, which showed itself in its most abject form in every detail of this dismal room and of Alice's dress, had undoubtedly done its part in wasting her figure, but it was something more specific and terribly final that had given her face that sunken, taut, and curiously visionary look.

'Well? What is it? They're sending Lucy Stokes in as a bailiff now, is that it?' said Alice. There was a little saucepan of something over the meagre fire, and she turned away as she spoke to stir it and, Lucy perceived, to hide her face.

'I just thought I'd call and see how you were, and . . .' Lucy stopped. Such euphemistic talk was nonsense in a situation as desperate as this plainly was. 'I want to help you,' she said.

Alice's back was still turned to her. 'Why?' she said.

Before Lucy could answer, her eye fell on the frowsy bed, and on the little girl of two or three who was sitting upon it. Her face was still marked with tears which must have been

319

called forth by Lucy's knocking, the child supposing that it was the irascible rent-collector; but now she was regarding this less intimidating visitor with a shy interest.

'Hello,' Lucy said. 'What's your name?'

'Sophie,' came the reply after a moment, in the soft whisper of a child who is used to having to keep quiet.

Alice Wedderburn had turned now, and was staring at Lucy with an intense challenge that the pallor and emaciation of her face made almost unbearable. 'I – I never knew,' Lucy said helplessly.

'Well, you don't know everything about me,' Alice rapped out. 'And after all, why should you know, Lucy Stokes? Who are you to me anyway?'

'I'd like to be your friend,' Lucy said, 'if you'll let me.' She already felt with utter conviction that she was not going to allow this situation to continue, no matter what Alice said. It seemed to her that this meeting was the inevitable destination of a journey begun on the night she had first met Alice on the footbridge. She inclined her head towards the child and said, 'The father . . .?'

The corner of Alice's mouth twitched. 'What do you think? Oh, yes, he knows, vaguely. But don't even say it, Lucy. Don't even think it.' She reached up to feel some grey washing that hung on a string over the chimney-piece. 'Let them rot,' she said with sudden energy. 'Let them all rot and burn in hell. I hope they do – I really and truly hope and pray that they do . . .' Her voice had begun to break in tears, causing the child's widening eyes to threaten the same; but then she was attacked by a fit of coughing – not the delicate consumptive's cough of the stage Traviata, but a horrible, retching, deafening hack that left her doubled up and clutching blindly at the mantelshelf.

The attack triggered in earnest the tears of the watching Sophie, who wailed desolately; and it spurred Lucy into action too. She went quickly to the bed and gathered up the child on to her hip, and with her other arm she hugged the sick woman to her breast.

'Don't cry any more, Sophie,' she said, 'nor you, Alice. I think we were meant to meet somehow . . . We're going away from here, and you're coming home with me.'

V

Lucy could only hope that Radford's shade was not aware of the infamous intruder that she had brought into his prim and proper house; though given what she now knew of him, she saw that very prim-and-properness in a different light, and as something that had a good deal of desperate camouflage about it. But certainly the censorious view of her taken by local society received the most powerful of reinforcements by her taking in Alice Wedderburn and her illegitimate child. The news went like a tremor (not a disagreeable one) through the drawing-rooms of the valley. Actually taking that Wedderburn woman and her by-blow into her house . . . and not caring who knew it! In a respectable neighbourhood like Lessington Road! Two of a kind! It just confirmed what they had said about that Mrs Stokes all along – that was all there was to say. Though considering that was all there was to say, they managed to say a lot more, and at great length.

They were right, at least, in that Lucy did not care a damn what anyone thought. That did not mean, however, that her new responsibility was lightly or easily taken up. She had brought Alice and her daughter home with her that very day, and established them comfortably in the big house, and meant, as she told them, that they should stay there permanently, entirely supported and cared for by her: such had been her instant and final decision on seeing them in that squalid room, and she would not change it. So far so good. But of course she had embarked upon a very serious undertaking.

The whole house, for one thing, had necessarily to orientate itself towards the needs of a small child and a sick woman. The maids already had quite enough work: so one of Lucy's first actions was to engage a nurse to help with looking after Alice, and a girl – poor, kindly and eager for a job – to help with Sophie and with all the extra laundry.

Three rooms upstairs were given over to the guests, as Lucy insisted they be called: a bedroom for Alice, a bedroom for Sophie, and a room that she had converted into a little private sitting-room for them. This part of the house Alice was to consider as her own place, and neither Lucy nor the servants were to think of it as anything less.

And then there was the fact that, as Lucy had seen at once, Alice Wedderburn was dying. Dr Munro, Radford's old physician, whom she called in to attend the sick woman, confirmed it.

'You think of nursing her here, Mrs Stokes?' he said.

'Yes. Is it . . . practical?'

'Oh yes! She'll do as well here as anywhere else. That's what I'm trying to tell you, Mrs Stokes. I can't say how long it'll be . . . but she isn't going to get better. If you're going to keep her here, you must be prepared for her to die here.'

Lucy nodded. 'I'm prepared for that.'

So she was; though the harsh prospect was made infinitely worse by the fact of little Sophie, who, though she had had a grim enough time of it in her short life, could hardly be expected to be resigned to her mother's mortality. In the meantime, however, there was the immediate concern of making the patient as comfortable as possible, and that was complicated by Alice Wedderburn's temperament.

Alice did not have the proverbial heart of gold. It was no doubt unlikely that she should have, given that the circumstances of her life had led her to place a higher value upon other and more useful organs, and there was besides the inevitable fractiousness of illness; but the fact remained that she was not an easy person to care for in either sense of the phrase. When Lucy brought her to Lessington Road she had no possessions beyond a couple of frocks, the last faded and outmoded remnants of the days of her glory; but the new clothes with which Lucy replaced these did not meet her demanding standards, and neither did the dressing-table that Lucy furnished for her use, or the mirror, or the meals that were brought up to her, or the illustrated papers that were ordered for her amusement.

'Look how my hair comes out,' she said, dragging the brush through it and scowling at her reflection. 'Isn't it enough that I'm ill – do I have to go bald as well? It's so quiet here. I don't know how you stand it. Couldn't you go and play the piano, and leave the door open so I can hear? No – don't bother – you only know that dreary whiskery stuff. Don't you know any of the new lively things? Can't you play "Ta-ra-ra-boom-de-ay"? Can't you play the cake-walk? I suppose you wouldn't. It's all so miserably respectable here. Whatever made you marry that Stokes one, anyway?'

'Why does anyone marry?' said Lucy, by way of answer.

'God knows. God only knows.' Alice's eyes met Lucy's in the mirror, haughtily. 'Mind you, I could have, you know. If I'd wanted. I had offers. I had offers that most women would have jumped at. But I chose not to. I like my freedom.' She gave a snort of laughter. 'Catch me getting tied down like you did!'

'Well, we all make mistakes,' Lucy said vaguely.

'What do you mean by that?' Alice turned on her. 'What are you trying to say? Come on – come out and say it plain, if it's me you're hinting about—'

'Hush, hush,' Lucy said, 'you'll make yourself ill again. I didn't mean anything.'

'Well, I am ill, aren't I?' Alice said, looking down at her paper-white hands. 'It's not as if I can get any worse . . . I don't know why you put up with me, Lucy. Why do you?'

Lucy shrugged and smiled. 'Whatever I say I shall be in the wrong, so I shan't answer that.'

'It's not as if we were ever friends,' pouted Alice. 'Not real friends. It's not as if we ever knew each other well, is it?'

'Isn't it?' Lucy said. '. . . Anyway, I couldn't leave you in that awful place.'

'Oh! I would have managed somehow. I was born in the Hole, remember. I'm no stranger to that life . . . No, thank God you took me out!' she said with one of her little contrary reversals. 'I don't mean for my sake. I mean for Sophie's. It doesn't matter about me.' She looked at Lucy with a naked candour that revealed the truth beneath the triteness of her next words: 'She's all I've got.'

For Alice loved her daughter with a fierce and possessive love. She was given to dramatic statements, but Lucy knew she was burningly sincere when she said, after a particularly bad night of coughing blood, 'You know, I would have put an end to all this long ago if I were alone, Lucy. If life's a burden to you, I think you should throw it off, always have. Throw it back in God's face. It's not that much of a gift, after all, though we're supposed to be forever on our knees thanking him for it . . . But there's Sophie, you see. I carried on living because of Sophie.'

The little girl's impact on the household, indeed, was in

strong contrast to that of her mother. She was as good-tempered as Alice was difficult. Much of this could be attributed to the change in her circumstances: for the first time she was warm, well-fed, well-clothed, and had ample space to play in, and that scared, preternaturally mature look born of having to hide and skulk and be quiet at the creditor's knock quickly left her. But besides that she had a naturally affectionate and happy disposition, and soon endeared herself to everyone: a development that produced in Alice both pride and jealousy. There was something almost tigerishly fond in Alice's look as she combed the child's soft brown hair and held her at arm's length to be inspected, and then at last relinquished her to Lucy for her walk in the garden.

'She calls you Auntie Lucy,' Alice said one day, when Sophie had been helping to trim the Christmas tree downstairs.

'I know . . . Do you mind?'

'I don't know . . .' Alice regarded her suspiciously, then made an impatient gesture. 'How can I mind? She owes you more than she owes me.'

'Nonsense,' Lucy said. 'And what's this talk of owing? Love isn't about owing.'

'Love.' Alice was scornful. 'Of course, she hasn't any real aunties. No relatives. At least . . .'

'Her father?'

'He doesn't count . . . I do know who the father is, Lucy. If that's what you're thinking. I only had them one at a time, for your information.'

Lucy said nothing: she had learnt to ignore these accusations. They came her way simply because she was there.

'God! If he tried to take her from me – my God, if he was to try—'

'Might he do that?'

Alice calmed down, and smiled crookedly. 'No. Not he. He gave me money to get rid of it, you know. They're fine ones, men, aren't they? They hate us very much, my dear. And do you know when they hate us most? When they're lying on top of us.' She studied Lucy's reaction. 'Did you have a happy marriage?'

Lucy looked unseeing at the sewing in her lap. 'No,' she said.

'I didn't think so. Not that there's any such thing, anyway. If you didn't feel like killing each other for most of the day, then you didn't do too badly . . . When was the Bible written down? Thousands and thousands of years ago?'

'Yes, most of it, I think.'

'There you are, you see. It's all full of lovings and marryings and so-and-so cleaving to so-and-so – just the same as now. All those thousands of years of it, and it still doesn't work! When are people going to see what a fraud it all is?'

'Perhaps they always have,' said Lucy.

These conversations took place in Alice's sitting-room; for though at first she came downstairs, and moved restlessly about the house, it was not long before that was too much for her strength; and by the time the new year came in she was confined to her bed. Even there, however, her store of nervous energy would not let her be still. She demanded constant diversion, and if nothing else availed, then Lucy would simply sit with her and talk – or listen, for Alice did most of the talking, flitting from one subject to the next, now self-justifying, now defiant, now airily pretentious, now painfully honest; but often bad-tempered. But even the cantankerousness was, Lucy saw, a displacement of something else: it was the last, frustrated expression of that animal vitality that the men had found so fascinating in Alice Wedderburn – a fascination of which she was alternately dismissive and proud.

'I haven't kept anything of what they gave me, you know. Except, I suppose, Sophie, but that was something they never meant to give. They always looked so pathetically pleased with themselves when they handed over some wretched brooch or necklace or some such, as if they'd made it with their own hands, instead of simply having the money to walk into a shop and buy it. Not that they always did even that for themselves. One said to me, "Oh, my man always does such things for me." That'll give you an idea, my dear. Mind you, the things that came my way weren't rubbish. There wasn't much of my jewellery that came from Cottesbridge, you know. Bond Street more often, sometimes Paris . . . All gone now.'

She spoke only vaguely of her downward path from these glamorous heights. Perhaps its very inevitability made detailing superfluous; but more than that, in her tetchy pride she seemed to prefer giving the impression that the final, dismal course her life had taken had been a matter of choice rather than compulsion. 'They were such weaklings, really,' she said.

'I'd had enough of them.' This was not mere perversity, Lucy perceived: admiration and attention had been Alice's life, and to admit that she had simply been thrown over would have been a blow quite as killing as the disease that was consuming her.

'I could have settled down, like you, you know,' she said. 'But that wasn't for me, I decided. Like being buried before my time. I'd always gone my own way, and I wasn't going to change for anyone. So you needn't look sorry for me, my dear. I've never done anything I haven't wanted to. And I've lived ten times as much as you. Ten times.'

For she hated to be an object of pity, even as she fretfully sought it; and her relationship with Lucy, already ambiguous, was further complicated by her dependence on a woman who, whatever the talk about her, was settled and respectable, and who, though she did not want to be the lady-bountiful, must appear so to Alice's peculiar bundle of nerves, hypersensitivity and resentment. It was plain that, though she spoke with genuine contempt of the men in her life, Alice did not like women very much.

'You needn't think you're any better than me, you know,' she said. 'Just because you went into a church and signed your name in a book. It still comes to the same thing.'

'I know,' Lucy said. She remembered using precisely that argument at Radford's dinner-party – how long ago it seemed! – when she had been defending Alice Wedderburn in her absence. But it was no good saying this to Alice: she would not take kindly to the thought of herself as a person who needed defending.

Most of the time, indeed, Lucy was able to bear in mind both Alice's illness and her understandable bitterness. But one morning her tongue got the better of her. Alice had had a bad night. With her breakfast tray on the bed, she impatiently called for her hand-mirror and, after peevishly examining her thinning hair for some moments, she threw the mirror down. Then, with a sudden scowling movement, she swept the breakfast-things on to the floor. Tea and butter and jam covered the rug, and were all over Lucy's skirts.

'That was a mean, spiteful thing to do!' cried Lucy. 'Look at the mess you've made.'

'Well, you've got maids – *you* won't have to clean it up. Let them do it, that's what they're paid for.'

'They have quite enough to do, without you making more

326

work. And I shouldn't be surprised if this skirt's ruined—'

'Oh, don't fuss! You've got money enough! You could buy all the skirts you want. And besides, you're lucky you can wear a skirt! I shall never wear a skirt again – but nobody cares, nobody cares!' Sophie appearing in the doorway that moment, Alice stretched out her arms to the child and said, 'Come here, Sophie, and give Mummy a kiss – because Auntie Lucy's been horrid to her, and she's made her upset all her nice breakfast, telling her off and saying she doesn't want us here any more!'

Lucy left them alone and withdrew, mentally counting to ten several times. When the child had been taken away for her bath by the little nursemaid, Lucy returned and, fixing Alice with a level look, said, 'It isn't true that nobody cares, Alice. A lot of people are taking a lot of trouble over you, and they don't expect any thanks for it – just the normal consideration that anyone, sick or well, would show. And if you've got anything to say to me, say it to my face, don't use the child in that way. It isn't fair on anyone.'

Alice merely looked mutinous and refused to speak; but later that day, Sophie approached her in the garden, solemn with responsibility, and said in her ear, 'Mummy says she's sorry.' Lucy could not help smiling: though that evening Alice gave no sign that anything at all out of the ordinary had taken place between them.

Georgina and Miles came to visit. Georgina at least was rather shocked at the thought of Alice Wedderburn in her old home (Miles, in his modesty, did not presume to judge anyone); but she was too loyal to Lucy, and had too much in its genuine form of that oft-counterfeited article, Christian charity, to say so directly. But while Miles was accompanying Sophie down the garden, and looking very earnestly attentive as she told him the names of plants, Georgina put her hand on Lucy's arm and said in an agonized whisper: 'This poor woman . . . is she going to get better?'

'No,' Lucy said. 'No, she isn't going to get better, I'm afraid.'

Georgina looked through the french windows at Miles and the child, and her eyes moistened. 'Oh, Lucy . . .!'

'I know. This might seem a terrible thing to say, but I think that for Sophie's sake it can't come too soon. I suspect Alice is beginning to think so too. Because – do you see? – the older Sophie is when it happens, the worse it will be.

She'll understand more, and be less able to adapt.'

'Oh, Lucy . . .' said Georgina again. 'I don't know how you bear it, seeing it going on every day . . . It must be heart-breaking.'

'Yes . . .' It was, of course; but Lucy wanted words to say that life was a continuous process of heartbreaking, and that certain circumstances, joyful or sad, merely retarded or accelerated the process. But this was hardly an insight to be offered to Georgina in her newly-wed happiness, and so she merely said, 'You get used to it; and it's best not to show what you feel, for both their sakes.'

It was, indeed, an experience gruelling to the nerves and emotions that Lucy had let herself in for; but then she had known that from the moment she had taken her two charges out of that squalid room in the Hole. Death had touched her twice, in the persons of her father and her husband, and she did not doubt her capacity to cope with it. As time went on, too, a grimly mocking acceptance seemed to surface in Alice, and flash out between the stormy clouds of her moods.

'I'm not afraid of it, Lucy,' Alice said quietly one day; and threw her a wry smile. 'Do you know why? Because you're coming with me. Oh! Don't worry, dear – I don't mean I'm going to lay you out with a pistol when my time comes or anything like that. But you see what I mean, don't you? I'm just catching an earlier train, if you like. Nobody's staying behind. You're all going to come after me, sooner or later.' She pointed a bony finger towards the window, and the tree-lined street beyond. 'Each and every one of you – you're all coming with me, you know!'

But the ungraspable thorn at the heart of this situation, as both Lucy and Alice were aware, was little Sophie. Alice's love for her seemed to wax brighter as her strength faded: it seemed to light her wasted frame from within like the glow through a parchment lamp. And as Lucy and the little girl became closer friends, Lucy participating in the child's intensely lived life as her bedridden mother increasingly could not, a curious and complex look began to be seen on Alice's face as she regarded the two of them: wistful, proud, jealous, but also somehow appreciative.

So, Lucy was much occupied with her two charges; and with her work with Mrs Blades continuing, she had little time for visiting. She had had a couple of notes from Mrs Silvie, full of exclamation marks, inviting her to come over and meet the returned hero, Harry Parmenter, who was often at her house. She had replied that she would come very soon; but the new year of 1903 found her promise still unkept. So, one February morning of frost and sun, when the lawn – its shaded places still ice-blue and bristly while its exposed portions were dewy-green – looked as if it were sown with two different species of plant entirely, Lucy's sister Joanna called at Lessington Road, charged with persuading Lucy in person.

'Oh, dear! I'm afraid I've been very rude,' Lucy said as she gave Joanna some tea in the back parlour where it was warmest. 'It's just that I've been so busy . . . Is Mrs Silvie very annoyed with me?'

'Oh, nothing like that,' Joanna said. 'She just wants everyone to meet Harry. He says he feels rather like an exhibit at the fair. And the poor fellow has to share himself out between Mrs Silvie and his parents, who have the first claim really, though Mrs Silvie won't admit it.' Joanna had blossomed: she looked a lovely young woman, her fairness having lost its watercolour delicacy and her voice its slightly other-wordly note, though it was still soft.

'And what's he like? It'd be a pity if he was a horrible brute, after all this.'

'Oh no,' said Joanna smiling, 'he's not! I wondered if he might be rather stiff-necked and pleased with himself, the Parmenters being so rich and respectable, and him being an officer in the army. But he's very kindly and down-to-earth – a bit like a big friendly dog, as Mrs Silvie said.'

'Well, I'm glad he's home safe, and out of the army. What will he do with himself now, do you know?'

'He's starting up as a leather-factor. Helped by his father, of course. And . . .' Joanna licked her lips, and regarded her sister gravely. 'I ought to tell you, Lucy. In case you do come to see Mrs Silvie, when he's there with Harry, because he does come over often . . . They're great friends . . .'

'Who?' said Lucy; and had a feeling as if a spectral hand had reached out from some great distance and touched her on the shoulder.

Joanna licked her lips again. 'Matt Doughty. He's back in Cottesbridge. He was with Harry Parmenter in the Northamptonshires, in South Africa; and they came back together. As I say, they're great friends. Harry says Matt saved his life one time in the war, though Matt says it wasn't anything like that. But Mr Parmenter certainly sees it that way, and he's got the two of them started in this little leather business, as partners. Matt's quite the hero to the family . . . He was quite surprised to see me at Mrs Silvie's; and he asked after you.'

'Did he . . .?' Lucy was in that dumbstruck state of feeling in which straightforward physical objects become baffling to manipulate, and she did not know how long she would have gone on stiffly gripping the cup and saucer at a canted angle if Joanna had not taken it from her.

'Well, I thought I should tell you – he's often there with Harry, and it might have been awkward if you'd bumped into him out of the blue.'

'Yes . . .' The sense of the dead past rising up was so strong it seemed almost to blind her. She blinked at her surroundings, at her dress, as if she could not imagine how she came here. Then the blind mist lifted, and she was Lucy Stokes, the widow of Lessington Road again, and the past that had stood before her so bright and solid that she had only to reach out and touch it faded into something worn, ambiguous, and lost. She made an effort to say something, though she knew that whatever she said would be impossibly strained and artificial. 'Is he – is he all right?'

'He was wounded – he walks with a stick now. That's why he was invalided out of the army. But he seems very contented with life, and glad to be home.'

'Isn't it funny how things turn out?' Lucy said with a suddenness and brittleness so unnatural in her that Joanna looked quite troubled; then she smiled. 'I'm glad he's safe and well,' she said. 'Thank you for telling me, Jo.'

And that was the end of it; or would have been, but for the uncomfortable fact that Lucy could not go on ignoring Mrs Silvie's invitations to come and call. She tried, indeed, to put off the reckoning, even if she could not shrug off the stunned, stupefied feeling that the simple news of Matt's return to Cottesbridge occasioned in her; but shortly after Joanna's visit there came another note from Mrs Silvie, which seemed to leave her no avenues of escape.

My dear Mrs Stokes,

You think I'm going to scold you – but I'm not! Quite the contrary! It has occurred to me why you have been so shy of calling at a house where you are so very welcome. It has to do with this poor fallen creature you are sheltering! I don't just mean the demands upon your time that she must make, but the fact that she was rather scandalous and disapproved of, so I hear, though I am rather out of touch – and so you think I would not like to see you because of that! My dear, it's like your discretion – just like your sister too, the most tactful creature! But you needn't worry on my account! I applaud you! Do we not all know the beautiful story of the Magdalen, in the most beautiful of Books? That you may be enabling this unfortunate woman, by giving her the ease and space to reflect upon her misspent life at its end, to repent of her sins and contemplate her coming meeting with the Almighty, seems to me the most admirable act! And so now you know my feelings, and have no excuse for not giving me the pleasure of your company! And Harry, of course – no, you are not going to avoid meeting him, you know! He fully agrees with me on that subject, by the way. And is very anxious to meet you. Now, he always visits me on Fridays – other times too, but Fridays I can absolutely vouch for – and so if you don't come this Friday, I shall positively hate you! No I won't – how could anybody hate you, you lovely creature, with your sweet soft eyes? I swear when you and Joanna are both by me I feel as if I'm being looked at by some magical beings of classical antiquity – I fancy I mean dryads, or is it centaurs? Or were they the ones that were half-horse? Such an uncomfortable combination, one can't help feeling. Well, I have said my piece! And I shall expect you on Friday, you know – I shall!

With fond regards
Agnes Silvie

How could she not go now, without snubbing the old lady? She had, of course, no qualms about meeting Harry Parmenter: it was the possibility that Matt might be with him that caused her to tremble and perspire when she thought of the coming, inescapable visit.

Yet, she told herself, there was no reason for such trepidation. Three years had passed since she had last seen him – three whole years had loaded upon her their burdens of experience, and had surely done no less for him. In that time the raw clay of her selfhood had been through such shapings, such firings and shatterings, such complete transformation that only in the vaguest sense could she be said to be the same woman who had parted with him in Mr Birdsall's little parlour. If they did meet, it would be almost as much a meeting of strangers as her introduction to Harry Parmenter, the only effective difference being that they knew each other by sight. And did even that count for anything? She had no way of knowing how much she had changed physically, our own appearance being of all sights in the world the most inscrutable; but she certainly did not associate the face she now saw in the mirror with her self of three years ago. As for Matt, he had been at war in the heat and disease of Africa, and she knew already that he had not come through unaltered. Lame! She could not deny the mournful start that that news had given her, remembering Matt's litheness of limb; and she was pierced too with a memory of Matt stepping out of the ironstone brook with his bare legs seeming to welter in gore. But if there had been premonition in that moment, it had been misleading: when she had urged him always to be careful, she had been envisioning a future in which he was all to her, always, and bloodshed the only thing that might come between them. Instead the prophecy seemed to have come true only when they meant nothing to each other, and her reaction to it could only be the uninvolved and generalized sympathy that anyone would feel for a man wounded in war.

No – she did feel more than that, of course; but how much more she could not tell. During the worst frustration and estrangement of her marriage to Radford she had thought of her time with Matt with aching nostalgia, but that too was a stage in her life left behind. Indeed the nostalgia, she had known even then, was no more than a means of escape and a shunning of reality. And if she had reached any point of conclusion by now, it was that reality was not to be shunned. Reality was a thug who could not be avoided by crossing the street: he simply came after you more insistently brutal than ever. The memory of Matt had once acted as a palliative drug, but it had no such function now. She was not sure whether, as a piece of mental furniture, it was an asset or an encumbrance; and his actual presence was likely to be no less ambivalent in its effect upon her.

But he was back in Cottesbridge, and it was reasonably likely that she would come across him at some time; thus the one thing she felt with conviction was that it was best to get it over with. And so she hardly knew what to think when, having nerved herself to go to Mrs Silvie's on Friday, she found neither of the young men there.

'I can't think what's become of Harry!' complained Mrs Silvie, hovering at the window and trying to see past the jungle of macramé-clad potted plants. 'He always comes on Friday mornings – always! I shall be so bitterly disappointed if you don't meet him at last, Mrs Stokes! Whatever can have happened?'

'Well, they have their business to run now, you know, Mrs Silvie,' Joanna gently admonished her.

'Oh, pooh to their business,' Mrs Silvie said, darting back from the window and sitting down by Lucy with a sulky flop. 'If it isn't beastly Boers, it's beastly leather. Men can be dreadful creatures, can't they, Mrs Stokes? They can be so thoughtless. And they look so ghastly with their clothes off. I remember, when I married Mr Silvie, thinking that those statues in the galleries were very misleading. Unless those ancient Greeks were made differently. They did eat a lot of olives. However, I soon got used to it. Well, my dear, it's a pleasure to see *you* at any rate – you haven't quite deserted me like my horrid nephew. And how does your patient go on? About as bad as ever? The poor creature . . . I hope she is preparing her soul. Oh! I knew there was something. I have some tracts for you to give her – they'll help turn her thoughts in the right direction. Is she chapel? Mind you, they are not at all High. Joanna, dear, where did I put those tracts . . .?'

Lucy had to suppress a wry smile at the thought of Alice Wedderburn's likely reaction on being presented with devotional literature; but as it happened the tracts were never forthcoming, for at that moment there were voices in the hall, and the maid came in to say that Mr Parmenter and Mr Doughty were here.

Mrs Silvie bounced out of her seat like a firecracker. 'Harry, you brute, I am going to scold you quite severely!' she cried to the young man who appeared in the doorway of the sitting-room – doing no such thing, however, but instead embracing him so vigorously that the dusty curls seemed in some peril of being knocked clean off her head.

'Sorry we're late, aunt,' said the young man, 'only we've got something for you, and we had to go and buy a basket

333

to put it in. It's on the hall table, shall I – Oh!' – catching sight of Lucy – 'I do beg your pardon, how d'you do?'

'Well, well, come in both of you,' fizzed Mrs Silvie, 'and let me introduce you to Mrs Stokes. This – ' she hauled the young man over – 'is my nephew Harry, about whom you've heard so much that you're quite sick of him already.'

Lucy shook the large frank hand of Harry Parmenter, whose broad square frame almost eclipsed the slighter figure who had followed in his wake.

'And this is Matthew Doughty. I believe Joanna said you'd met – but anyhow, here they are!'

She was not obliged to shake hands with him, but still some sort of greeting had to be made. She heard her own voice saying 'Hello', though she was not in the least conscious of having spoken; and in the same dreamlike way she heard Matt's voice say 'Mrs Stokes', though she did not quite connect the voice with the man who had come into the room leaning on a stick; and then, thank heaven, she did not have to do any more, for Mrs Silvie took charge, buzzing around them with a great torrent of excited words. Thank heaven indeed, for in spite of all her brisk self-chidings about getting it over with, Lucy found herself quite stricken and helpless – the result, she ruefully saw, of ignoring the rule that any given dreaded experience will always be at least three times as bad as you expect it to be.

There was a diversion, anyhow, in the shape of Harry's gift, which turned out to be a black and white kitten, and which, as it explored the room getting to know everyone, was for some time the centre of attention.

'I know you said you wouldn't have another one after old Tab died,' said Harry, 'but this little one needed a home, and so I thought of you straight away.'

'Oh, he's a treasure!' said Mrs Silvie, as the kitten made a climbing-frame of her many necklaces. 'You knew I was hankering for one, you cunning boy! I shall call him Harry.'

'Well – I think it's a female.'

'Oh, you can never tell at this age. Joanna, dear, ring for some milk – oh, and tea for us. Mrs Stokes, would you like to hold him?'

Lucy was glad, indeed, of the excuse to turn her attention to the kitten, and be spared the necessity of looking at the visitors. Harry Parmenter was just as his photographs suggested: a big, kind-looking young man, with stiff brown hair swept back from a high forehead, a square jaw, and a gentle mouth; his voice was simultaneously deep and boyish. That Lucy was seized with shyness of him, when his manner was all unaffected openness, was entirely due to the fact that he was the friend of Matt Doughty; a close and firm friend, as was revealed by the way he unfussily put his hand beneath Matt's arm to help him into a seat.

For Matt, it was clear at once, was very lame. His right leg was quite stiff from the knee down, and the boot on his right foot, though carefully made by a Cottesbridge 'craft' to disguise its nature, was plainly, to Lucy's experienced eye, a special boot – a cripple's boot, in other words. She could not have foreseen how strongly this sight affected her: the image of Matt's well-shaped bare legs as he laughingly bathed them in the brook recurred to her with the force of a slap across the cheek.

It might have been unbearable if Matt had not changed in other ways; but he had, to such a degree that ten rather than three years might have elapsed since their last meeting. The hair that used to grow thickly from a double crown was not only shorter but seemed to have lost its old unruly spring, and there were even one or two strands of grey at his temples. Like Harry's, his skin had been burnt and dried by the sun; but Harry was clearly of a brown colouring to begin with, whereas the loss of Matt's old fairness of complexion was stark. Where he had been slender he was now somewhat gaunt, no doubt because of the trauma of his wound; but the effect of this was to bring out that slight severity that had always lurked in the shape of his brows, and to inhibit the old mobility of his mouth. He still appeared a man of attractive looks: though it might have been better if she had, Lucy did not think, 'Dear me, he's rather ugly', on seeing him. But the inescapable fact was that he was not the man she had known, and it startled and dismayed her without her being able to pinpoint why. As for his reaction upon seeing her . . . she could not tell. He had formerly been a man whose changing emotions were as externally visible as cloud-shadow upon a field, but that too seemed to have gone: one thing and one thing only she could tell from his now hard and uncommunicative face, and that was that he found her greatly changed too.

'Now, Harry, you must think of Mrs Stokes as a friend immediately, and not a stranger,' said Mrs Silvie, 'for the poor dear was forced to hear so much about you when you were away – not that she's heard half your adventures, and you must tell them to her, because they are quite thrilling.'

'Oh, I'm sure Mrs Stokes wouldn't stay a friend very long if I was to bore her with all that,' said Harry. He smiled, but Lucy sensed that he liked talking about his experiences in the war a good deal less than his enthusiastic aunt supposed.

'Now, Matthew, are you comfortable there? I'm afraid my chairs are so low and squishy. We'll bring your little table over when the tea comes,' said Mrs Silvie. 'Isn't it a treat to entertain these two returning heroes, Mrs Stokes?'

'It's a pity we couldn't all have returned,' said Harry, amiably enough, but plainly uncomfortable under his aunt's adulation.

'Now, Harry, don't talk that way,' Mrs Silvie said. 'You're here, and Matthew too, and that's the main thing. I've never had the slightest interest in leather – which is very naughty of me I know because that's where all our money comes from – but I'm glad of it now, if your little factor's business is going to keep you here.'

'Don't worry, aunt,' Harry said, 'I'll go no more a-roving, that's for sure. Mrs Stokes – there's another from the same litter in need of a home, if you'd like one.'

Lucy looked up from the kitten, which was doing soft-mouthed battle with her hand. 'It would be nice to have one,' she said, 'I'm sure Sophie would love it.'

'Ah, your daughter?' Harry said.

'Now, Harry, don't be more of a noodle than usual . . . I told you, about the unfortunate woman that Mrs Stokes is nursing, and her child,' Mrs Silvie said, giving his knee a slap.

'Oh! Good heavens, I am sorry.' Harry coloured. 'What a blundering fellow I am – quite the stupidest . . . How is the lady?'

Lucy liked Harry Parmenter already, and liked him better for the way he did not even think twice about using the word lady for Alice. 'She's very ill,' she said, 'but comfortable, I think.' Was Matt looking at her? She could not even turn her head: the awkwardness of the situation paralysed her. Yet the crowning paradox was that everything was apparently normal. That she and Matt had once passionately loved was a fact known not only to them but to a lesser extent to Joanna; yet not a ripple of that past turbulence disturbed the calm surface of the gathering in Mrs Silvie's sitting-room.

The tea came: Joanna poured out. During an interval in which attention was focused on the kitten lapping its milk and getting its paw in the saucer, Lucy noticed from the corner of her eye that Matt was having difficulty reaching the little table to put down his teacup: the stiff leg, which in a high chair would be reasonably manoeuvrable, left him helpless in Mrs Silvie's sunken armchair. Remembering Matt's old impatient self, she suspected he would not make a good invalid, even a partial one, though of course he might have changed in that too. She got up and moved the table closer.

'Thank you,' he said, looking up at her. '. . . Bit of a nuisance.'

'Yes,' she said. 'I mean, it must be for you.'

'Well, you get used to it, you know . . . There were a lot of fellows worse off.'

'Oh yes, I should think so,' she said. His accent had softened, presumably through association with the Parmenters, as had hers through her marriage to Radford; the crooning Northamptonshire gutturals opened out, the consonants less blurred. She took in for the first time his clothes, which were formal and well-cut and sat well on him, and she remembered how he used to hate what he called 'getting dolled up in a chapel-suit'.

'Oh, you'll soon be skipping about like a two-year-old, Matthew,' said Mrs Silvie, overhearing their exchange. 'You're walking much more easily than when you first came here, you know.'

'Well, I'm certainly getting about better, ma'am,' Matt said. 'But the doctors tell me this is about the best I can hope for. I shall never do Cossack dancing, that's for sure.'

'Seems hardly fair, does it?' said Harry, his brows puckered. 'Me coming through without a scratch.'

'Oh, that's not true, you know, Harry!' said Mrs Silvie. 'What about your dreadful shoulder wound, that nearly put an end to you?'

'All healed up in no time.'

'Well, that's your Parmenter constitution. All the men of the family have had the constitution of an ox – and the brains too, some would say . . . But I'm only teasing! There's the most dramatic story about Harry's wound, Mrs Stokes,' Mrs Silvie said, turning excitedly to Lucy, 'and how Matthew saved his life.'

337

Matt looked extremely embarrassed, and Harry uncomfortable too at a repetition of a story that had obviously been told many times, but he said with quiet emphasis, 'It's true.'

'Harry and Matthew were separated from the rest of the men after a skirmish, and quite lost in this dreadful sort of scrubby desert, with no water and the sun beating down and dangers on all sides,' Mrs Silvie explained, with a wealth of illustrative gestures that made her necklaces fairly rattle, 'and poor Harry was horribly wounded—'

'Simple flesh wound,' Harry said, with a deprecating grimace at Lucy.

'Well, but you were losing absolute buckets of blood, my dear, now that you can't deny, and it made you so weak you could hardly stand. Now you can see, Mrs Stokes, that our Harry is not exactly a sylph, or do I mean a nymph? Well anyhow, he is a stocky chap – big-boned like all the Parmenter men – whereas Matthew is built like a bird in comparison. But Matthew got him back to camp, Mrs Stokes – all through miles and miles of bushes—'

'Bush, aunt,' said Harry, laughing.

'Well, some ghastly wild place anyway . . . teeming with Boer snipers ready to pick them off, the devils!'

'Jolly brave men,' Harry put in, 'tremendous fighters.'

'Hush, Harry. Yes, Matthew got him back to safety, even though Harry lost so much blood that he quite passed out, and Matthew had to hoist him on his back and actually carry him most of the way. Can you imagine carrying that great bulk of a fellow through miles of brush or whatever it's called? Isn't it the most heroic affair? And that's how Matthew saved Harry's life. I think he should have had a medal.'

'So did we all,' said Harry, with some bitterness. 'Unfortunately the commanding officer was a fool. Not that he was any exception to the general rule in that respect . . . Sorry you've had to put up with all this talk of me, Mrs Stokes, you must be jolly fed up with it. I'm sure your sister is, for she's had to suffer it for ages,' he said with a hesitant smile at Joanna, who in his presence seemed to be even quieter and more self-effacing than usual: Lucy wondered if they did not get on. 'But at least Matt's getting the tribute he deserves.'

Throughout Mrs Silvie's account, Matt had been drinking his tea rather determinedly and plainly wishing it over; and

338

now he looked relieved that the kitten had come to investigate him and provide a diversion. 'Perhaps, Mrs Silvie, you could call it Harriet if it does turn out to be a girl,' he said, stooping awkwardly to pick the kitten up. Lucy, on whom Mrs Silvie's narrative, embroidered though it was, had made a deep effect, observed Matt's hands running through the kitten's fur – his beautiful hands, at least, were unchanged – and thought, randomly, how odd it was that her own hands had been touching that same fur just a few moments ago. Not odd, though. Not odd or significant or poignant or ironic or any of those things; for with every moment that passed in that overfurnished room it became plainer to Lucy's consciousness that she and Matt Doughty, whatever they had once been, were now nothing to each other. She had expected discomfort and awkwardness of this meeting, if not to such a painful degree, but she had not anticipated so forceful a demonstration of the power of time and circumstance to reshape human lives until nothing was left of what they had once been.

'No,' Mrs Silvie said, 'if it's a girl, do you know what I shall call it – if Mrs Stokes will allow me? Lucy. I've always thought that quite the prettiest of all names. Whatever were my sainted parents thinking of when they named me Agnes? It always makes people think of that horrid little prig in *David Copperfield*, who never does anything but float around looking angelic. Don't you think Lucy is a pretty name, Matthew?'

'It's a very pretty name, indeed, ma'am,' said Matt.

'I say, aunt, what d'you think? We've an order from Bressart's, to supply them with box-calf. Isn't that a feather in our caps?' said Harry. 'You'd know the Bressarts, of course, Mrs Stokes?' He blushed at having, even so indirectly, alluded to the matter of her widowhood.

'Yes, I saw a good deal of them when they were buying my late husband's factory,' said Lucy, who was past any such embarrassment. 'I hope they're prospering.'

'As far as anyone is at the moment,' said Harry. 'We certainly didn't pick the best of times to start up on our own account. This Bressart order's a godsend.'

'Things will pick up,' Matt said. 'It's only a temporary lull. Nobody's going to stop wearing shoes. The more confident people are in the trade, the healthier it will be. No good spreading gloom and despondency.'

That too, then, had not changed – that determined

hopefulness; though there was a dogmatic note in it that was new. Or had that always been implicit in Matt's view of life as a thing to be attacked and overthrown?

It didn't matter: there was no point in her tracing out these vague shapes of perception. He had changed, and she had changed, and there was no more to be said. After the tea, and some more general chat about the state of the trade, Lucy took her leave, Harry promising to send over the kitten for Sophie. She shook hands with him and said it had been a great pleasure to meet him at last – this was true as well as conventional – and Matt very punctiliously stood up, using his stick with a practised movement to bid her goodbye. With assurances to Mrs Silvie that she would not leave it so long till her next visit, Lucy left the house and walked home.

'Well – we can never again be as we were,' was the thought that at length presented itself, distinctly and calmly, to Lucy's mind as she came into Lessington Road.

'And I'm glad of it,' was the succeeding thought, as she entered her own home.

The visit to Mrs Silvie's had, after all, achieved more than just getting an unpleasant experience over and done with. It had removed from Lucy, with a relative minimum of pain, one last illusion – an illusion, indeed, that she had hardly recognized as such; like some memento she was not even aware she possessed, found wrapped in tissue in a forgotten drawer, and revealing itself to have been hardly worth the keeping.

VI

After their call upon Mrs Silvie, Harry Parmenter and Matt Doughty repaired to the warehouse down by the river which was the locus of their fledgling leather-factor's business. Mr Aubrey Parmenter had made the premises over to them jointly, complete with stock – various lengths of second- and third-grade leather that he had been storing there and hardly known what to do with – and had cautioned them not to expect a gold-mine out of it: it was a start, no more. There was of course a certain element of testing their mettle in this, but no one was more delighted than Mr Parmenter when they began to make a success of it. Harry, as the son of Cottesbridge's largest manufacturer, had the contacts, but Matt knew leather; and he had moreover a good deal of drive and energy. They now employed half a dozen people, and Matt already had his eye on a larger warehouse that stood empty further along the river. After unpacking and inspecting a load of leather that had come in by dray during their absence, Matt left Harry at work in the little pine-panelled office and went to look again at the empty building – an excuse to be on his own for a bit.

His leg was hurting him a little, but he had trained himself to ignore it and keep moving, for it got stiffer the less he used it, and he did not intend being restricted in what he wanted to do by his own body. He could always put the soreness in perspective by recalling what the pain had been like when he had lain in the makeshift field hospital at Bloemfontein with his knee shot to pieces; he could always put his disablement in perspective by remembering the men who had died like flies around him, sometimes a dozen a day being carried off by typhoid. He knew that he was very lucky not to have lost the leg, or indeed his life: he had seen men die from the infection of far more minor wounds than his own. The stiffness, the aching, and the cobbled-together knee that still

341

looked like a snarl of fleshy knitting, and had made his right leg shorter than his left (by a tiny amount, indeed, but just let the able-bodied try it, and see if they could walk straight) were altogether a fair price to pay considering the grim alternatives he had seen in South Africa.

Those sights he had seen still haunted his dreams intermittently, but the worst of the horrors had faded now, and he hoped that a kind forgetting would presently supervene. Anger, at least, had quite left him – in contrast to Harry, who had gone out to South Africa a bright-eyed son of Kipling and had come back with his honest soul baffled and scarified by his experience of British administrative muddle, arrogance and incompetence. Harry's outrage was the greater because he was of the officer class himself, if at a junior level, and it all came as a revelation to him; whereas Matt had never expected anything better. Matt had already been an embittered man when he joined up: what he had seen had disgusted but not surprised him, and by the time he left the Cape – his wound had come in a skirmish in the last months of the war, some time after his rescue of Harry that was such a talking point – it was as if much of the bitterness, so long the dominating element of his emotional constitution, had been worked out of him. There seemed no point in getting into a righteous lather over the injustice of life, which was so universal that fighting it was like trying to push back the wind with your hands: the wisest course was to accommodate yourself to it. Here was a signal difference between him and Harry Parmenter. The bond of loyalty and affection between them was strong and true, but Matt found he could not share in his friend's tortured indignation over the war which Harry had joined as a crusade and found a bloodbath, and which he was now always trying to express in his decent, bewildered way. Matt could understand Harry's disillusion, but it was something he himself had passed through a long time ago – not in the butchery of the veldt, but in his disgraced departure from the valley of his birth. That, he considered, had been the turning point of his life; and it was with sympathy but a little impatience that he saw Harry struggling to maintain an idealism that he himself had outgrown and abandoned even before he had landed at the Cape. Though he was the same age as Harry – twenty-six – he often felt that he was the elder partner in the friendship.

It was, he supposed, an unusual friendship: the disparity

of their backgrounds had been echoed in the army, where Harry had been a lieutenant and Matt a ranker in the same battalion, though he had just been made a lance-corporal at the time of the dramatic episode that had brought them together. However, that same army that had perpetuated these class distinctions, also unwittingly confounded them once it was in the field, where everyone's blood was seen to be the same colour – except that of the generals, which stayed firmly in their bodies. To the fact of Matt having saved Harry's life – an event of which Matt had only a dim and harrowing memory – was added their common place of origin in the Nene Valley and Harry's own genial democracy of manner, which were quite enough to put them on the best of terms. All that was needed was that extra, subtle, intuitive element which makes two men know they are going to be friends – quite as wonderful in its way as the element which makes people fall in love – and that had soon established itself in their convalescence, Harry from his wound and Matt from the heat exhaustion sustained in that gruelling and now embarrassingly famous trek with Harry's unconscious form slung across his shoulders.

Embarrassing it certainly was to hear it continually alluded to, but Matt could not deny, and saw no reason to deny, the satisfaction that he had felt on returning to Cottesbridge a hero. After the miserable circumstances of his exit from the valley of his birth, Matt had certainly never contemplated returning there. It was Harry who had persuaded him – insisted rather – during the long wait at the Cape for the ship to return them to England. And Matt was glad he had done so. He had left Cottesbridge a petty thief: workless, hopeless, and bitter, and full of furious contempt for the smug and narrow-minded place that had frustrated his dreams and exiled him. Sweet, then, to return as the sworn friend of the son of the town's biggest manufacturer – to find, on their arrival at the station, that same manufacturer shaking his hand with tears in his eyes, and Mrs Parmenter embracing him, and both of them urging him to consider their house his home as long as he wished!

Even then, living almost as one of the family and fêted by them and their connections and acquaintances, he had wondered whether he might not find Cottesbridge intolerable, its painful and humiliating associations glaring at him from every brick and tile. That, indeed, would have quite undermined the sense of triumphant vindication he felt; but as it turned out, he found no impediment to holding his head up high. He had just enough sense of a continuity of self to give him a vengeful thrill in regarding the scenes of his downfall, but in the main he felt himself to be an entirely new and different person from the one who had left here three years ago. After all, was he not treated as such by the wealthy society that now received him as a hero?

It might have been better, perhaps, if there had been someone to remind him that he was the same person in spite of everything that had happened; even to remind him that the general approval in which he now basked, and the acceptance which the world now offered him, were the result of mere accident, and proved that the universe was an amphitheatre of the arbitrary rather than a court of appeal in which good intentions were taken into account. But there was no one: no one who knew him as he had been, and as he was – except one.

As he looked over the warehouse, Matt's thoughts turned to his own accommodation. He had left Cottesbridge for the army practically penniless, and the terms of his invalidity being hardly generous, he had come back with very little money. The gratitude of the Parmenters and their setting him up in business with Harry had changed all that; even so, he had initially chosen to take as little out of their profits as possible, just enough to keep him in modest lodgings. Not liking to be beholden to anyone, even in such a special case as this, he had been all the more determined to make a success of a venture to which he brought no capital, but only his leather-working skill and his energy. He wanted to justify and repay their faith in him; and now, indeed, he took the lead in the enterprise, devoting himself to it with a single-mindedness that Harry, who had never known poverty, could not match. It was partly at Harry's urging that he had begun lately to draw a salary more appropriate to the work he put into the business, and it was with this in mind that he now contemplated moving into more commodious quarters. There were one or two houses to let in the choicer parts of Cottesbridge – not on a par perhaps with the Parmenters' and the Browns' places, but sufficiently respectable to invite such people to, in time. He was not going to rush into anything: if he took a house he would want it fitted out properly before he invited anyone, and he had seen now at first hand the sort of things that would be required.

For valley society, which for all his ambition had once seemed as remote and unattainable as the furthest stars, had opened to him. The piquancy of the story of his rescue of Harry, and the friendship thus begun, had made of him something of a minor celebrity in the towns, and the friendship itself – though sincerely valued – had the added value of securing him access to the drawing-rooms of local society. And Matt would have rejected as idealistic fallalery any suggestion that these drawing-rooms were not in themselves particularly worth entering, or that the mere wealth and status of this society were not particularly good reasons for admiring and emulating it. He remembered well what it was like to be poor, and he saw nothing very noble in it. He remembered too the degrading circumstances of his exile, and he could not help but feel a glow of pride at his transformation from branded outcast to associate and equal of men who had once wielded such power over him. If he remembered too a time when other aspirations than the merely material had beguiled his dreams, and when the possession of a well-cut suit such as he now wore would have seemed to him a laughably trivial thing to feel satisfied about – well, that simply showed how naïve he had been then, and how much precious energy he had wasted, burning it away in clouds of romantic incense.

Well, the warehouse was in need of a few repairs, but it would double their storage space. He would have to talk Harry round. Though impetuous in many of his ideas – he had come home vowing to write a book about his experiences in South Africa, and never got beyond the first page – Harry could be over-cautious in matters of business. He didn't look ahead as Matt did. After all, suppose another war broke out, and army orders flooded in, and the factories of the valley were crying out for leather? Yes, they definitely needed more space.

Matt strolled on by the river, thinking of the warehouse, thinking of the house he would take, but really thinking of neither, or allowing them merely to hover about the margins of his mind. For of course, that was filled by the thought of his meeting with Lucy Stokes. Changed he might be, intensely cool and unblinking the gaze he now turned upon life certainly was, but he could not come face to face with his former sweetheart and contemplate the event with indifference.

That meeting, of course, had not been his first indication

that the woman he had loved was still in Cottesbridge – far from it. Very soon after his return he was aware of the widow of Radford Stokes as a frequent subject of gossip in the Parmenters' circle. It had taken him a little while to connect this semi-notorious figure with the girl he had known. That she had married was not in itself a surprise: he was not a vain man, had always regarded himself during their love affair as supremely lucky to have captured her heart, and did not suppose for a moment that she would take the veil once he was gone. That the marriage should be to someone like Radford Stokes, and such an obviously material arrangement as everyone proclaimed it, did surprise him. That she should have earned herself such an unhealthy reputation, one which involved the probable suicide of her husband, and one which she seemed concerned rather to confirm than refute by taking someone like Alice Wedderburn into her house – that deeply surprised him, and the surprise was not far from shock. The strength of his own reaction had indeed surprised him, for after all his experiences had led him to take a not very exalted view of human nature. Why then be astonished at what was only further supporting evidence for that view? The reason was, as he soon came to realize, that he had always tended to exempt Lucy from it. Even in the bitterness of their separation, which had lasted long into his soldiering career, and had indeed blazed in his mind as the central emblem of his failure, he had never taken the disappointed lover's easy way out – the sullen pretence that the lost partner was never worth loving anyhow. He had said harsh things to her on their parting, and thought harsher ones in the ensuing months; but even as the general anger and resentment that he had taken abroad with him had hardened into a protective shell, and he had come to terms with his disappointment by adopting it as a first principle, and never expecting much of his fellow-mortals; even then the remembered figure of Lucy had remained outside the rather pitiless light in which he now saw human experience.

But she had changed – of course she had changed. It was stupid of him, he realized, to have thought, 'She looks older', when he had seen her in Mrs Silvie's sitting-room. He had left her a nineteen-year-old girl, and now she was a young woman, married and widowed, well-off and experienced; and the experience had, by all accounts, not been of the choicest kind. It was absurd of him to have felt that peculiar jolt of dismay (which he was sure he had not shown, for he had schooled himself in hiding his feelings), as if he had seen the moon fall ruinously from the sky. After all, had he really supposed that Lucy alone was invulnerable to the harsh dealings of time and circumstance, which he had accepted as universal and inescapable, and to which he had accordingly adjusted his own philosophy?

Matt Doughty, at the time when he had been passionately and wholeheartedly in love with Lucy Middleton, had been a young man who tended to see the world in bold primary colours, and to be blind to the enigmatic greys and halftones of which so much of life is so frustratingly composed. If he had changed greatly in the matter of his ideas, he had not perhaps changed so greatly as he supposed insofar as he still could not take those ideas in half-measures, or in any form that was not absolutely cut and dried. And so he could not simply accept that his meeting with Lucy had perturbed and perplexed him in unexpected ways, and let it go at that. It had to be fitted in. And it did fit in, very neatly. It came as the culmination of a process which some might call disillusion and the death of idealism, others a pragmatic reconciling with reality. It showed him that his ideas were right. For if that bright, generous and impassioned soul could end up marrying for money and then driving her husband to suicide with her dubious behaviour, was romance not gone from the world for ever?

VII

Sophie was delighted with her kitten, which Harry Parmenter brought to the house in person. As his parents and their kind would, Lucy knew, as soon have thought of entering a brothel as crossing her threshold, let alone stay for some tea as he did, she was rather touched and pleased. She found much to like in the young man, who seemed to be slowly and hesitantly disentangling himself from the assumptions and prejudices of his class and learning that most detested of perversions, the art of thinking for himself. Slowly and hesitantly; for he was no quicksilver visionary blazing a trail of rebellion, but a steady, unspectacular fellow who still sometimes spoke in the accents of a friendly schoolboy, and who was, as he confessed to Lucy, 'No great shakes in the brain department.'

'I must say you're awfully good with children,' he said in reference to Sophie. 'She's a sweet little girl, but it can't always be easy for you, I should think.'

'Well, I have got plenty of help,' Lucy said. 'And I'm used to it in a way, because I've got four younger brothers.'

'Yes, of course, I remember your sister Joanna telling me. The youngest – Dicky, isn't it? – wasn't in good health at one time, I believe. I hope he's doing better now?'

'Much better, thank you,' Lucy said. 'Mother has to practically tie him down now, he's so lively.' She was somewhat surprised that Joanna had talked to Harry of their family – her impression from her visit to Mrs Silvie's had been that they had very little to say to one another; but then perhaps Mrs Silvie had been orchestrating the conversation.

Alice Wedderburn's first reaction to the advent of the kitten was to mourn that it should be she who provided such treats for her daughter, but these plaints were growing less common as her illness worsened. By the time the spring weather came, unusually mild and gentle, Alice was very weak, and could do little but lie flat and feel the sunlight, which seemed to go right through her skin just as it went through the new leaves that flickered outside her window.

She talked less now, and sometimes she held Lucy's hand, a thing which her old defensiveness would never have allowed. When she did speak, it was usually of Sophie; but on one occasion she startled Lucy by suddenly mentioning that first meeting of theirs upon the railway footbridge, an event that she had never so much as alluded to.

'Why did you do it, Lucy?' she said. 'I've never really understood. What was I to you, after all?'

'Well . . . to tell you the truth, I suppose I was interested in you, the same as everyone was. You were such a talking-point for folk . . . But I used to feel a sort of sympathy for you – I know you don't like that idea, and I don't mean sorry for you – I just used to wonder what it would be like to be you. And so when I saw you on the footbridge I – I didn't stop to think, really.'

'Perhaps it would have been better if you hadn't come along that night,' Alice said, but absently, as if such remarks were now only habit. She stirred, restlessly exploring Lucy's fingers with her own, which felt as slight as chicken-bones, and then said, 'I ask because . . . I keep thinking you wouldn't have done it if you didn't mean it – mean that I should live . . . just as you wouldn't have taken me and Sophie out of the Hole and brought us here if you didn't mean to – to make everything all right. D'you see?'

Lucy squeezed her hand by way of answer.

'Because – because these aren't trivial things that you've done, Lucy. And – as we're talking of these serious things, or at least I am, my dear, holding up the conversation single-handed as usual – ' a smile like a wince crossed Alice's face – 'what I'm trying to say is: Sophie is going to be an orphan.'

'No, she isn't,' said Lucy.

'Oh, Lucy . . .' Alice frowned and tapped her hand petulantly. 'Don't fob me off with that fake optimism. There's no point. You know as well as I do that I am going to die quite soon and there's no use pretending otherwise—'

'I'm not,' said Lucy. 'All I'm saying is that Sophie isn't going to be an orphan.'

This was not a spontaneous reply made with the intention of soothing the fretful patient. Lucy had thought long and seriously about the question of what was to become of

349

Sophie, forcing herself to put aside the immediate response of her heart and be as hard-headed as any lawyer in tackling the implications. There might be legal impediments, though as a well-set up young widow with a large house, she thought that unlikely. She even made herself consider what the position would be if she married again, though she was certain that was not going to happen. What if the entirely hypothetical Mr X didn't take to Sophie? Then she wouldn't marry him in the first place. What if he tried to edge Sophie out, as it were, once they were married? He couldn't do that effectively: nowadays, she knew, a woman's property remained her own when she married, so she would always have independent means wherewith to protect the child. She even made herself address the question: would you feel the same if Sophie wasn't such a pleasant and likeable child? – as, indeed, she might not be in time: there was no telling how the loss of her mother might affect her. Yet none of these questions diverted her from her first conclusion – that she would adopt Sophie as her own. But that conclusion was itself entirely hypothetical, for the consideration that governed all others was, of course, what Alice wanted.

Alice regarded Lucy for a long time; then said, with a little burst of her old fractiousness: 'So, you've quite made up your mind to take her from me!'

'I'm going to do whatever you want me to do,' Lucy said. 'It all depends on what you want. All I'm saying is, you've only to say the word, and Sophie will always have a home here with me.'

'Properly – formally?'

'Yes. If it's possible to do it – and I don't see why it would not be – I will adopt Sophie and bring her up.' She stopped herself saying, 'As my own': this was bitter enough for the sick woman without that.

Alice gave a long writhe in the bed, and let go of Lucy's hand. 'I don't want you to have her!' she cried. 'It isn't fair!' And then, feverishly seizing Lucy's hand again, 'But I don't want anyone to have her – that's what I mean – but if I must, I do want it to be you, Lucy . . . There, that's the first nice thing I've ever said to you, isn't it? Well, you're lucky – I don't say many nice things!'

Lucy laughed. 'I'm flattered.'

'Well, you should be,' Alice said, changing in a moment, and fixing her with a baleful look. 'Because Sophie's very precious. She's part of me, and I'm trusting you with her. And I want her to turn out right . . . This is where you expect me to say, "I don't want her turning out like me"; but that's just what I'm not going to say. I do want her to turn out like me, d'you hear, I want her to be the perfect image of me: Alice Wedderburn's daughter! And I want her always to keep my name . . . and . . . and . . .'

A fit of coughing paralysed her for some minutes. Lucy held her until it was over; and when it was, Alice lay back exhausted and regarded her with eyes from which the rancour had disappeared.

'You – you're sure, Lucy?' she said.

'I'm sure.'

Alice managed an impish smile. 'Oh, my dear!' she said. 'What have you done? They talk about you now – what *will* they say if you adopt Alice Wedderburn's illegitimate daughter? You really have done it now, haven't you?'

VIII

It was late summer. Georgina and Miles had been away for some time, paying visits to Miles' relations around Anglia, and they were paying their first call at Lucy's house since its temporary resident had left it on her final journey, some four months ago.

Miles had brought a picture-book for Sophie, and the two of them were going through it in the garden-seat just beyond the french windows, an occasional fragment of their talk drifting through to the parlour where Georgina and Lucy were sitting.

'The poor, poor woman,' Georgina said. 'I suppose . . . I suppose at least she's out of her pain now . . .'

She looked at Lucy with a sort of hopeless appeal. Lucy knew what she wanted to hear, and wished she could say it: that Alice had had an easy death. Alas, it would not have been the truth. In one of Georgina's books Lucy had read a harrowing account of the death of the poet Keats from the same malady, and that seemed comparable with what Alice had suffered at the end. No doubt, as the clergyman at the funeral had suggested, there was some holy plan behind all this, but Lucy couldn't see it, and she didn't much care to have it explicated to her. As far as she was concerned, an eternity of bliss could not make up for one single minute of what Alice had gone through in those last days.

However, these were not thoughts to be expressed to Georgina who, though she was not one of those religious people who are forever tilting at unbelief but are very quick to yelp if it gives them so much as a smack in return, would still have been hurt by what was in Lucy's mind; so she merely said, 'Yes, she's out of her pain now. She was thankful, I think, that it was over – as we all are.'

'. . . Sophie?' said Georgina in a small voice.

'She's very brave,' Lucy said. 'It was bad at first, of course.'

The initial desolation of the child at the loss of her mother had, indeed, been such as to make Lucy want to hurl curses at the heavens. She had been able to take much upon herself – the care and support of the woman and her child, the nursing through to death, the responsibility for the orphaned girl – none of these burdens had bowed her down, and they had established such a pattern that her automatic response to Sophie's bewildered grief had been to wish to take it on herself. And this, of course, was one thing she could not do. She could not shield Sophie from this: she must stand helplessly by and watch the full weight of premature woe descend upon the little girl's head. However, as the beautiful doctrines of the faith in which she had been raised would no doubt assert, the child was full of sin anyway, and deserved it.

'But thank God she's got you!' Georgina said. 'How terrible if there had been no one . . . There isn't any sign of the father, I suppose?'

Lucy shook her head. 'There was never likely to be. Sophie's birth certificate is one of those "father unknown" ones . . . But at least that's made it easier for me. Well – not easy: the adoption was much more of a long and complicated business than I thought it would be. But Radford's solicitors were very helpful, and Dr Munro too, who said she should stay here with me.'

'What's that?' Sophie was inquiring of Miles, pointing to a picture in the book.

'That's a pumpkin,' answered Miles.

'What's a pumpkin?'

'It's – er – well, it's rather like a great big apple. Well, not like an apple really, because it grows on the ground, I think, and not on trees . . .'

'She likes you and Miles very much,' Lucy said. 'It takes her out of herself to see other people. I don't want her to think I'm the only person in the world.' Sophie had, not unnaturally, clung fiercely to Lucy in the aftermath of her mother's death, and had been unable to sleep alone for some time, fearing perhaps that she too would be taken away from her in the night. Curiously, the one other person who had been able to calm the child in those first weeks had been Lucy's mother, who had often come over then, and in whose vague croonings and half-forgotten bits of songs there seemed to be something primevally soothing.

'We must try and come over more often,' Georgina said.

'I must say it's nice to be home again – I didn't think we'd be away so long. You'd never believe how many Mellishes there are scattered around the country.'

'What's that?' came Sophie's voice.

'Well, it seems to be a sort of goblin. Or is it a gnome?' said Miles, who was applying himself to the picture-book as if he were undergoing a searching examination which he was afraid he was going to fail. 'No, I rather think gnomes have beards, so it must be a goblin . . .'

'But there's only one Miles,' said Lucy, smiling.

'Oh yes! He's an original, bless him . . . But Lucy, you wrote me that you might be going away.'

'I think so. Now that Sophie's over the worst of it, and starting to smile and take an interest in things again, I thought of taking her for a long holiday by the seaside. She's been a bit peaky, and I think fresh air and new things to see will do her good.'

'I think it will do you good too, my dear. After all, you've both had your share of heartache here, haven't you?'

'Yes,' said Lucy after a moment, 'I suppose we have.'

Shipden was her first thought, for the spot was attractive; but it was untenable now because of its associations. They went instead to Great Yarmouth, where Lucy found a small-ish private hotel that lacked the intimidating grandeur of the well-remembered Metropole, and from which it was only a short walk down to the sands.

She was growing used now to her maternal role, and indeed Alice's last feverish injunction – 'You will love her, won't you, Lucy? You will give her all the love I can't?' – had been unnecessary. Sophie was a pleasure; and Lucy's own subconscious renunciation of a life for herself made her a fitting protector for a three-year-old child who was understandably prone to feelings of insecurity.

She could not help ruefully noticing, however, that wherever the two of them went, the mere fact of her wedding ring elicited from everyone a consideration that must always have been denied to Alice when she had her child with her. Sympathetic smiles, doors held open, cheerful remarks about what a bonny little girl she was . . . How acceptable they were, as a genteel young widow and her child! It was so tempting to proclaim the truth: that the child was the bastard of what they would no doubt call a whore, and her widowhood was the remains of a loveless marriage to a man who had secretly preferred men. And yet none of this had set any visible Cain-like marks upon them: did that not say everything that needed to be said about the hypocrisy that surrounded her? That people should be so sentimental about children and so prudish about sex struck Lucy as revealing a curious blindness to cause and effect. Her own untouched state did not debar her from perceiving that a great deal of high-flown nonsense was thought and talked about the sexual act, and always would be until it was viewed neither as very shameful nor as very interesting, but merely, like eating, as one of the inevitable and unreflecting parts of life.

'Dear, dear, I'm afraid she'll miss a father terribly!' the chambermaid well-meaningly remarked. Lucy, remembering her own father, was not so sure about that; but the presence of the sea having already set her thinking about her own marriage, she wondered whether some desperate smothered desire to be a father had been present among Radford's motives for marrying her. He might have made quite a good father, she thought, in spite of his frigid reserve – so much of that, after all, had had its tangled roots in his guilt and shame. How sad it all was! But she kept her thoughts to herself, as she was well used to doing by now, and shared in Sophie's delighted fascination with the sea, the sand, the starfish, the pop-weed, the seagulls, and all those natural minutiae which are wonderfully new to every child, and which, it occurred to Lucy, are not unlike the perfect shining fruit displayed on the top of the market stall – the real stock underneath, as the eager purchasers discover when they get home, being rotten and misshapen.

The effect of the holiday on Sophie was, however, as Lucy had hoped: she was restored to abounding health, and greatly improved in spirits and in confidence. Lucy noticed with a sensation between pain and pleasure that the child sometimes, when absorbed, would absent-mindedly call her Mummy instead of Auntie; and she could only hope that Alice would have understood.

Autumn was at hand when at length Lucy and her charge left the North Sea breezes and pellucid light of the Anglian coast for the inland valley of their home. Two letters were awaiting her on her return. One was a welcome-home note from Georgina and Miles; the other was from Mrs Silvie, and was so startling that Sophie, seeing her expression, said with alarm, 'What's matter? What's matter, Auntie?'

Lucy mustered a smile. 'Nothing, sweetheart. You know all those shells you got in Yarmouth: why don't you go and show them to Jane?'

When she was alone she slowly re-read the letter, which was penned with something more than Mrs Silvie's habitual excitement, and concluded with an urgent summons to her house. The news concerned, not unusually, Harry Parmenter: it also concerned, more unusually, her sister Joanna.

'Still waters,' Lucy found herself saying aloud, as she immediately got ready to go out. 'Still waters, that's what they say'; and she reproached herself for her obtuseness, and for not thinking it strange that Harry and Joanna, two of the most easy-going people she knew, had not seemed at ease with each other. She should have remembered that mutual awkwardness was a characteristic not only of enemies but of lovers, and such Mrs Silvie's letter indignantly proclaimed Harry and Joanna to be. How long it had been going on Mrs Silvie did not say, but it was long enough for Joanna to be pregnant.

IX

'In my own house,' Mrs Silvie said again. 'That's what hurts me more than anything, Joanna. That you and he should have . . . met, and carried on, in my own house. When you came here, I never thought – I never for a moment dreamed . . . I can't go on.'

She could, however, go on, and did; and had plainly been doing so for some time, for Joanna was pale and red-eyed, and regarded Lucy like a prisoner awaiting execution.

'Mrs Stokes, is it kind in your sister to abuse my trust in this way? I speak only of kindness for the moment. I quite put aside for the moment the indecency, the shocking indecency of the whole business—'

'Oh, nonsense, Mrs Silvie,' said Lucy. 'We all came into the world in the same way. There's no point in getting worked up about that.'

'Well, really, Mrs Stokes!' Mrs Silvie's mouth was as round as her eyes, and the dusty curls vibrated. 'I hardly expected you to condone this dreadful deception!'

'I don't,' Lucy said. 'Not the deception part of it, anyway, if that's what it is. Now what is the truth of it, Joanna?'

Joanna, looking rather surprised at her sister's briskness, faltered out: 'Well – of course Harry and I first met here, and . . . and then we started meeting on my days off, and so one thing led to another, and . . . oh, Mrs Silvie, there was never any intention to deceive you, really, it was just one of those things that happened . . . and I love Harry, I love him so very much—'

'Boh!' The explosive exclamation that Mrs Silvie gave at this point seemed likely to lift the wig right off her head. She beetled fretfully around the room, her swinging black skirts making havoc among the bric-à-brac.

'I suppose there's no doubt?' Lucy said to Joanna.

Joanna shook her head, miserably.

357

'And you've told Harry?'

'Just this week.'

'And what did he have to say?'

'Oh! He came straight to me, and started to make a clean breast of it, as he put it,' fumed Mrs Silvie. 'Clean, indeed! As if anything could be clean in this frightful business. I feel quite defiled . . . Well, I wouldn't listen to him any more. I ordered him straight out of my house and I told him I won't have him here again. I would have immediately done the same with your sister, Mrs Stokes – I would! – but I thought I had better consult with you first. And of course Harry has gone and made the same clean breast to his parents, and is almost as unwelcome there, I believe.' She sank into a chair and fanned herself with a newspaper. 'My Harry! My Harry, with so much before him: surviving those dreadful Boers, and wounds, and diseases . . . only to go and ruin himself in this way! Oh, Joanna, how could you, how could you?'

'Well, Mrs Silvie,' Lucy said, 'it takes two, you know.'

Mrs Silvie turned pink. 'Mrs Stokes! How can you suggest – my Harry – my Harry has always been the most upright young man!'

A salty riposte occurred to Lucy at that, but she suppressed it. 'All I'm saying is that, however we look at it, Harry and Joanna – well, neither of them did anything they didn't want to do,' she said. 'Is that so, Joanna?'

Joanna nodded.

'Nonsense! My Harry would never have been caught in this way – yes, caught! – if he hadn't been led astray, and tempted and inveigled and I don't know what else . . . I brought you here to be a companion-help to me,' Mrs Silvie burst out at a now tearful Joanna, 'not a – a Delilah, taking your scissors to my poor Samson!'

'Very well.' Lucy stood up, and extended her hand to Joanna. 'I think we've heard all we need to. Come on, Jo. You're coming home with me, now. We can send for your things later. You don't want her here, I understand, Mrs Silvie?'

Mrs Silvie looked somewhat startled, as if she still had several rounds of outrage to discharge, and did not expect to cease fire so soon; but after an open-mouthed moment she waved them sweepingly away, crying, 'Yes! Yes, take her away! Take her out of my sight! I don't want to see her ever again! She's spoilt everything – she has!'

Joanna allowed Lucy to lead her by the hand out of the house; but once among the dismal pines along the drive she stopped and burst into tears afresh.

'Oh Lucy! It's so horrible, leaving the house in this way! I'm very fond of Mrs Silvie – we both are – and I never meant it to end like this!'

Lucy regarded her sister with a rueful sigh. She was not the one to say, 'You should have thought of that before'; looking before they leapt was not, she realized, a characteristic of the Middletons; even Joanna, who had seemed so quiet and sensible. Her own history underlined the point more than sufficiently. 'Never mind, Jo,' she said. 'Come home with me, and we'll sort something out. I don't suppose you've told Mother?'

'No . . . Do you think I should?'

'Well, she'll have to know sooner or later. Oh, we'll cross that bridge when we come to it . . .' She hesitated before giving vent to a question that had been nagging her. 'Jo . . . When Mrs Silvie said that about "in her own house", she didn't actually mean . . .?'

'Oh, no,' said Joanna hastily. 'Good heavens, no.'

'No . . . not with all those photographs staring at you,' Lucy smiled. 'Oh don't cry any more, Jo! We'll sort it out, somehow.'

X

Matt returned to his new home after calling on the Bressarts. It was a Saturday, and he had recently allowed himself time off work on Saturdays, their first year's trading accounts showing that they were doing remarkably well despite the slump. He knew that he and Harry's status as returned war heroes had much to do with the willingness of local manufacturers to do business with them. Another fortunate circumstance, in a curious way, was the slump itself, for several of the valley's older leather-dealers had gone swiftly to the wall, having become slack and complacent during the long boom years and being unable to adjust to the new conditions; and Parmenter & Doughty were able to step into the breach. Luck, then, had played its part in his prosperity, but he had put in a great deal of work too, and he felt that he deserved a little more leeway for leisure at last.

The house that he had taken, just a few weeks ago, was a square-bayed villa in a quiet, tree-lined street off Nene Road; not very large, but well fitted out. He had rented it part-furnished, but the elderly owners who had gone off to cultivate their liver-spots at Eastbourne had clearly been of very old-fashioned tastes, and Matt was having all their superannuated movables shifted into storage, and was refurbishing the house more in line with what he had seen in the grander houses of the valley. As a result he was rather squatting than living there just yet, a single room upstairs being set aside for his use while the rest of the house was worked on by the decorators and furnishers. In this room he now changed out of his best clothes and, with a slice of cold pie in his hand, wandered about the dust-sheeted rooms examining the progress of his new home.

Of course, some of the big houses of the district had that same old-fashioned look, if not quite so gloomily: the Parmenters' place, for example, was somewhat stuffy in its respectability. Much more to Matt's taste was the Bressarts' house, which he had visited again that morning. Respectable it certainly was, but it had elegance too: the elegance of people who knew what could be done with money. Or one of them did, at least – Helena, the daughter: it was her influence that he traced in the Bressarts' light and airy rooms with their oriental touches.

Sometimes he felt that he and the Bressarts were fated to meet. They were both, after all, partial outsiders here: the Bressarts as newcomers, geographically speaking, to the close-knit shoe-baron elect of the valley; Matt as a man who, though native-born, had only just joined that elect and was still surprised to find himself part of it. His surprise, however, was daily receding before the growth of his assurance – some might have said that his humility was going the same way – and what contributed most to that assurance was his association with the Bressarts. This had begun, of course, as a matter of business; but his new identity (he felt it to be no less) gave him the entrée not just to the manufacturers' offices but to their drawing-rooms as well. Once he had the confidence to go about independently of Harry, there was no doubt about which drawing-room he most often chose to enter.

Certainly the value of the Bressarts' business account played its part in this, but he could not deny that something else drew him, something that appealed to heart rather than head; though he might have recalled a time when he would not have thus separated the two. Helena Bressart fascinated him. Some of the fascination lay in the fact that not so long ago she would have been far above his reach, he admitted that; but he could not tell, and did not wish to speculate on, what role the pedestal played in his mental image of her: whether he wished her to be on it, or stepping down from it. But the effect of her beauty upon him was straightforward enough, even if he could not quite disentangle it from the background of peacock feathers and blue china which set it off so well, or indeed from the general pleasure of experiencing the exquisite best of everything after his grinding early years and the grimness of war. She certainly appeared to his eyes as a high-water mark of human quality: there was no blemish about her. His lame leg could be considered a badge of honour, but even so he was never more conscious of it than when beside Helena Bressart's classical grace.

But it was not just her looks. He could not get over her assurance, her unruffled self-confidence – something he himself had been at pains to cultivate. The world to her was a very simple and accommodating place, something like a well-pruned apple tree to which one hardly needed to reach up to gather the fruit. So much of his young life had been spent in an exhausting battle with the world that Matt could not help but be impressed, and wish to be a party to the secret.

Given that very assurance, however, it was difficult to know where he stood with her. There were several young misses of Cottesbridge society who found him an interestingly romantic figure, and at suppers and at-homes he found himself being plied with excited questions about his experiences, which he would have preferred to forget. If this did not tend to turn his head, it was because he was quite as fastidiously exacting, in a different way, as when he had been a poor boot-finisher in love with Lucy Middleton and refusing to bow to the chapel-suit conventions of courtship. Helena Bressart, though always very conversable, was quite different from these naïve gigglers who would make of him a parlour Heathcliff. He supposed the term he wanted was well-bred. Not for her that constant anxious agreement: a look of unperturbed scepticism would appear in her dark-lashed eyes if he said anything flashy or meretricious. That too, he supposed, showed supreme self-confidence. She knew what she thought about everything. Again an instructive contrast, when he had spent so much of his life progressing through a series of beliefs and finding each one betray him or otherwise prove unsatisfactory for negotiating the world.

And was much of what she thought, in fact, conventional? If it was, it only occurred to him as such when it touched upon something in which his own private knowledge and feelings were involved; as today, when she had spoken of Lucy Stokes.

'Of course, we didn't really know her history when we came here, and Father bought up the factory,' Helena had said. 'We saw quite a lot of her then. She seemed a very agreeable woman – a little outspoken, but I like that. There was really nothing to suggest the sort of woman she was. I suppose it's impossible to tell, isn't it? Her giving a home to that Wedderburn woman could I suppose be interpreted as a sort of philanthropy, though she might have considered the homes that creature broke in her time. But this business of bringing up the woman's child as if it were her own seems to me extremely curious. After all, she has the means: she could have provided for it in some other way, and spared herself a lot more disapproval.'

'I . . . suppose Mrs Stokes doesn't care what people think of her,' Matt had said.

Helena smiled, raising one charcoal-black eyebrow and looking beautifully dubious. 'Doesn't she? I wonder if anybody truly, genuinely doesn't care what people think of them. Isn't unconventionality merely another pose? When someone claims not to care what impression they give people, I'm always suspicious. It's like these eccentrics who dress like frights and say it's because they don't care what they look like. If they really don't care, why go to all that trouble – why not just dress normally?'

'I don't know,' Matt said hesitantly. 'I don't entirely understand Mrs Stokes, but I wouldn't say it was a pose.' Some instinctive impulse made him want to defend Lucy; and yet he had been deeply disconcerted by this new development in her scandalous career: the adoption of Alice Wedderburn's illegitimate child. He could no longer begin to guess what was going on in her mind. And yet there had been a time when he had understood her, and she him, with an electric sympathy that went beyond words: it was perplexing to find that so completely lost. Had Lucy changed that much? But then, that was all in the dead past, part of his old identity, and he wanted Helena Bressart to have nothing to do with that discarded husk of self. Helena was the present; Helena was – dare he think it? – the future.

'Oh, Matthew, you've made me feel terribly cynical now,' Helena laughed. 'But then men are always more charitable than women – to other women at least.'

'Well, I don't know. I don't suppose anyone will ever understand her.' He laughed too, but soon changed the subject, for he found he did not like talking about Lucy, even though that was all just a memory, dead and gone.

He did not much like thinking about her either, but he found he was doing so as he cast a critical eye over his new home. Strange that they should both have ascended, and by such different routes; strange that her way should involve, in effect, selling herself . . . But no, he had given over being disappointed about that. Besides, it was unlikely that their paths would cross much now, so good luck to her . . .

'Hullo! Anybody home?'

The front door was open, and Harry had stepped into the hall. Matt went down to him. The stairs were not steep and he could manage them without too much lurching effort.

'Sorry to barge in. Thought I'd come and see how Castle Doughty's coming along,' Harry said.

'Say sorry for not coming sooner,' Matt said, patting his shoulder.

'Yes, I . . . have been a bit of a stranger just lately, haven't I? Neglecting work too. Sorry, Matt. Had a lot on my mind.'

Matt made no comment, for it had been quite plain to him for the last week or so that something was amiss with Harry. Their friendship was such that confidences did not have to be laboriously invited: they would come in their own good time.

Harry drifted from room to room, looking at everything and seeing nothing, mechanically replying to Matt's remarks. He did look worn and troubled, Matt thought: his face bore scarcely more colour than the sheeted shapes and fresh white-wash amongst which he moved. Matt was concerned, but not overly so, for he had known his friend get conscience-stricken over the slightest thing.

And then Harry, leaning against a stepladder with his head on his crossed forearms like a man about to be scourged, poured it all out.

Matt could hardly believe what he was hearing; and astonishment was swiftly succeeded by a deep dismay. What fools people could be! Everything the two of them had worked for since their return hither more than a year ago seemed set at hazard by this supreme piece of folly: all the sturdy, practical foundations they had laid for a new and productive life seemed undermined. For a moment, indeed, anger possessed him. Hadn't they seen enough of mess and muddle, of effort wasted and lives blighted, in South Africa? Hadn't Harry learned, as Matt had, to rein in the destructive passions, and to look at life with a cool and unromantic eye?

But as part of that same process, Matt had learned to control his impatient temper, and he held his peace; and he could not help but be moved when his friend at last turned to him a face puckered in that frown of concentration which men believe disguises the fact that they are wretched enough for tears.

'So this is why there's been no visits to your aunt just lately,' Matt said.

Harry swallowed and nodded.

'And your parents . . .?'

'They haven't quite thrown me out, let's put it that way,' Harry said. 'Or disinherited me, yet. But it's been pretty good hell at home, as I'm sure you can guess. And what Joanna's been going through at my aunt's I daren't think.'

Matt winced. Joanna Middleton! It seemed he wasn't to be finished with that family after all. The girl had always seemed so quiet, refined almost; but then, as Helena had said, you could never tell. But the whole thing was so very unsuitable, so shabbily disreputable: no wonder the Parmenters were beside themselves.

'I don't know what to do, Matt,' Harry said. 'I just don't know what to do – can't think straight at all. Feels as if my mind's turning . . .'

'Come upstairs,' Matt said. 'I've got a bottle of whisky in my trunk somewhere, and we can have a drink on it, at least.' His own mind, after the initial shock, was quite sharp again, and it was working swiftly – as he saw it would have to if this thing was to be settled, for Harry seemed at the end of his tether.

'I never meant – we never meant anything like this to happen,' Harry said, as he sat on the edge of Matt's bed and accepted the glass Matt offered him. 'It was just one of those things that ran away with us . . .'

'When did you last see her?'

'Oh, more than a week ago now. My parents have forbidden me to go near her. I've written, but all I got was a note from Aunt Silvie saying that Joanna had gone to stay with her sister.'

It occurred to Matt – quite separately from his own feelings about this unfortunate matter – that a man who had not so long ago been a courageous officer at war should hardly allow himself to be 'forbidden' like that. Yet he reminded himself that there was a strong streak of conventional dutifulness in Harry, which tended to take over at moments of crisis. And he knew that Mr Aubrey Parmenter could be a highly domineering father.

'Well, at least you know she's all right for the time being,' Matt said. 'With her sister, I mean. They were always quite close – er, so I've heard. However, that doesn't mean there's any time to lose.'

Harry, who had drained his whisky at a gulp, looked bewildered. 'In what way?'

'Well, look here, my old friend. I don't imagine you confided this to me just for the hell of it. I mean, what you want is my advice, for what it's worth . . . isn't that so? So, I'll give it to you. Face your parents, tell 'em you're sorry – sorry for letting them down and so forth; you'll have to swallow some pride, but that can't be helped; and say that what's done can't be undone, but you're going to try and sort it out in the quickest and most efficient manner you can.'

Harry shook his head. 'I'm sorry, Matt . . . I'm the most thick-headed fellow, and I still don't follow you.'

'Harry, you've money, haven't you?' Matt said patiently. 'Of course you have. Then use it. Find somewhere out of the way where Joanna can go until the baby's born. And then when it is . . . Well, it will depend on what she wants to do with it, but the wisest course, as I'm sure you can get her to see, is to have it adopted, or provided for in some such way. Then she can have some sort of normal life afterwards – that is if we act now, keep the whole thing absolutely quiet, and plan it like a – well, like a military campaign.'

Harry stared into his empty glass. 'Can – can it be done?'

'By poor people, no. That's where they get caught. But money can do it. Money can do anything, Harry. And if we can't raise enough between us, I'm willing to bet your father will be only too happy to chip in, once you impress on him that this is the best possible solution to the problem, d'you see?' Matt was talking rapidly, in his old impetuous way, and pacing up and down with scarcely a thought for the complaining of his leg. 'In fact it's the *only* solution that I can see. The only one that makes sense. After all, Harry, think of what you want from life. Think of our leather business, and the way it's just starting to take off. Think of how young you are. D'you want a thing like this to drag you down for the rest of your life?'

Harry gave his friend a sad smile. 'You sound very worldly, Matt.'

'Well, I should hope so,' Matt said with a slightly annoyed laugh. 'What else should I be – heavenly? We don't live in the clouds, Harry, we live in this world, and there's plenty of good living to be had from it, if we go about it the right way, and don't let ourselves get all tangled up in the first snare that we come upon.'

'I know there's truth in what you say,' Harry said after a moment, rubbing a hand distractedly through his stiff brush of hair. 'And yet I can't help wondering . . . Well, suppose you'd thought like that when we were alone in the bush together that day? Wouldn't it have made sense, as you put it, to have left me there instead of dragging me back to safety? Didn't you let yourself get all snared and entangled by doing that?'

Matt shook his head. 'It's not the same,' he said; but for some moments was perplexed as to how to go on. 'Look, Harry, you're not thinking straight at the moment.'

Harry sighed. 'No,' he said. 'No, I'm not.'

'Well, we've got to be brisk about this. And if you can't manage it, then I'll have to be brisk for you. Now, why don't you let me talk to Joanna about what I've proposed?'

'That should be me.' Harry's frown was emphatic.

'Well, all right, perhaps I can talk to her sister, and raise the subject of what we're going to do about Joanna with her. What do you say? I can be your go-between.' Awkwardly Matt levered himself down on to the bed beside Harry and gripped his arm. 'Now cheer up, do, my old friend! It'll all be settled as neat as you please. I know you're feeling all confused in your mind now, but you'll be glad one day.'

'Not just in my mind,' Harry said. 'My heart too . . . But I don't know. You've always made the right decisions so far, Matt – with the business. If you're sure—'

'I'll go over there this very evening.'

XI

Lucy was at the bottom of the garden with Sophie, looking at the pond, which was a source of unfailing interest to the child. The river backing on to the end of the garden, their pond was visited by all manner of aquatic life, some of which Lucy found it hard to put a name to in response to Sophie's questionings; and this prompted the ironic realization that, though she had been such a passionate lover of the country in her younger days, and had believed herself to be naturally at home there as she was not in Cottesbridge, she had really known very little about it.

It was appropriate that, in the midst of these reflections, the sharer in those lost and deceptive rural idylls should come to call: the maid came up the garden to tell her that Mr Matthew Doughty was here. Still, Lucy was startled and flustered for a moment, a moment in which her old social fear seemed to resurface and tremulously suggest that she say she was not at home. But then, if society had lost its terrors and become a matter of indifference to her, why should she hesitate to face Matt Doughty, whom she had known when he was as poor as she?

Of course she knew why: it was because of that very shared past that she could not be easy in his presence. It was no use her pretending that her feelings were untroubled by meeting him; that would be lying to herself, and she had come to great grief in her life by lying to herself. A sudden understanding resolved her indecision. Matt was Harry Parmenter's friend, and so this must surely be something to do with Joanna. The latter was presently in the spare bedroom Lucy had given her, where she spent much of her time. She often read the Bible there, though not with a look of ineffable comfort, rather with the look of someone consulting a manual which turns out to contain none of the answers that might reasonably be expected of it.

'We must go in now, dear,' Lucy said to Sophie. 'The light's fading, look. We'll come and see the pond again tomorrow.'

'And the river?' Sophie said hopefully.

'We must see. Not if it's too high.' The bank was not very safe when the river was up: it was an unsatisfactoriness on the part of Nature that had always annoyed Radford.

Matt was waiting in the parlour that overlooked the garden. Lucy could see him indistinctly as they approached up the path, and in that crepuscular light the dapper figure waiting near the fireplace might have been taken for Radford's ghost. Then they went in, and the figure turned, and at once could have been none other than Matt.

'Mrs Stokes – I'm very sorry to intrude on you,' he said.

'That's quite all right . . . Er, this is Sophie.'

'Hello, Sophie. Glad to meet you.'

Lucy was obscurely pleased to see that, though he was so very much the well-set-up young gent, there was no awkwardness in his manner with the child, just as there would not have been in the old Matt.

'Have you got a bad leg?' Sophie inquired sympathetically: Matt's lameness had been very noticeable when he came forward, perhaps because he was far from being at ease, and her mother's long illness had left Sophie with a tender interest in infirmity.

'I'm afraid so,' Matt said. 'But it's getting better.'

'Oh good,' Sophie said.

'All right, sweetheart,' Lucy said, bending for a kiss. 'Go and see Jane, and get washed and ready for your supper. I'll come and see you when you're ready.'

Sophie gave her that curious half-bashful, half-possessive kiss that children give in the presence of strangers, and soon Lucy and Matt found themselves alone for the first time in almost four years.

'Is it really getting better?' Lucy said quickly, to break the silence; and as Matt looked blank she added, 'Your wound.'

'Oh, that! It's not much more than a nuisance. I sometimes do without the stick now . . . Mrs Stokes, I'm afraid I haven't come about a very pleasant matter, and it may seem strange my coming at all. But I'm sure you'll understand once I explain it to you.'

'Very well.' She sat, inviting him to do the same; at the last moment she wondered whether she should put her hand under his arm to help him be seated as she had seen Harry do, but he managed it unaided.

'Your sister . . . She's – she's here, I believe?'

'She's here, yes. She's in her room, and won't hear anything we say. You've come on behalf of Harry, I suppose?'

'Sort of. You see, he confided in me, and we agreed that we should – well, put our heads together, and see if we can't sort this business out. Harry isn't really thinking straight at the moment, and I wouldn't imagine your sister is either, and so, well . . .'

She heard him out in silence – a part of her mind noticing the way he argued it out with himself, eyes intent on the floor and hands making quick gestures, just as he used to do when they walked together in the country; but her chief attention was to the matter of his argument, and against that she reacted violently. A few years ago she would have been unable to stop herself bursting out in protest; but she was older, and she waited until he was done.

'I don't see what all this has to do with Harry and Joanna,' she said at last.

Matt frowned, but said in the same measured, reasonable tone, 'Well, it's what I'm suggesting as a way of . . . negotiating this difficult question. Now if—'

'Negotiating!' said Lucy, unable to keep still any longer, and springing up. 'Really, you talk as if you were trying to sell me a few rolls of leather! These are human lives we're talking about. Three human lives. Joanna's child might be easy to ignore just at the moment, but time's going to change that whether we like it or not. Time's going to turn this "difficult question", as you call it, into a person just like Sophie. But not quite like Sophie . . . Not if I can help it.'

Matt seemed taken aback by her abruptness, and for a moment she was reminded of Radford's expression when she was having one of her 'outbursts'. But then he recovered himself and said in an altered tone, 'I'm sorry. Perhaps I've put it badly. But it needs someone to talk coolly about it, and I thought – I thought we were the ones to do it.'

Lucy forced herself to come and sit down again. 'What does Harry feel?' said she.

'He's sorry – sorry that it's come to this, and that he's behaved badly. He wants to make amends, and . . .'

He stopped, for Lucy was shaking her head. 'No,' she said. 'I mean what does he feel? The point is, Joanna is in love with Harry. She's told me about it, though it wasn't hard to see. She's told me about the way they met, and the way they went on meeting, secretly, and – well, it's plain that she loves him very much. I should have known that from the first moment, because I know Joanna's not the sort of girl to have put herself in this position lightly.' Matt's looking embarrassed, she thought: how absurd, when we two once kissed as if we could never tire of it, and spoke such words to one another as might have set the grass alight . . .! She wrenched her wandering thoughts back. 'So, from what I've heard and seen, this whole thing doesn't sound like something to be negotiated. It seems to me like a love affair. Now is it, as far as Harry's concerned? Because it doesn't sound to me as if his heart wasn't in it. I don't know him very well, but I don't see him as an insincere person somehow. Isn't that what we've got to establish first?'

Matt sighed, and looked ironical. 'Perhaps . . . But what then? You're surely not going to tell me that love conquers all?'

The personal and private note, the consciousness of their former relation, which till now they had successfully ignored, was all at once formidably present: they both knew it. 'No,' Lucy said. 'My God, no, I'd be the last person to say that. But I think it should be given a chance. In this case, I think it should be given a chance.'

'What chance has it got against such – such forces of disapproval? Why not take the easier way out?'

She shook her head. 'You wouldn't have talked like that once, Matt,' she said: it was the first time she had used his name, and the word was as conspicuous as a flash of light in the room.

'No? Well, I've been around and seen a few things since then,' he said. 'And I've learned that by beating your fists against the world you don't break anything down. You just break your own heart. The best thing is just to bend yourself to the conventions and—'

'Oh, conventions! Let them go to hell! I've seen so much misery brought about by people acting the way other people think they should, as if being different were some terrible sin . . . Why, I can remember you saying something like that yourself – something about the way folk will hate you for being different just as much as if you'd done them a bad turn.'

'Aye, and I was right, though I didn't know it at the time. That's why I advised Harry as I did. Better to be safe than sorry . . .'

'No, Matt, no. I can't take that cold, cautious way of thinking. Jo loves Harry and she's bearing his child and I believe Harry loves her too, if he'd only listen to his better nature; and I think we should be bringing them together, not pushing them apart. There isn't much to life, you know: it's a poor show really, considering the struggle we have being dragged into it; and what there is of it is too precious to waste. I remember you saying something like that too – don't you remember the bones at Cleatham? I believe it even more than I did then.' She stopped. She was about to say that these convictions had been strengthened by a sense that her own life had been a waste and a failure; but her feelings were already dangerously wrought up in a way she had never intended, and she quietly concluded, 'I don't want Joanna and Harry to miss their chances, that's all.'

Even that seemed tinglingly significant, in the circumstances; but Matt made no response for some time, and sat brooding, his eyes cast down.

'Those things I once said,' he got out at last, 'they were – they were a long time ago, Lucy.'

'I know. It was wrong of me to bring them up,' she said correctly.

'No – not wrong... I don't know, I still feel that this business could be sorted out—'

'So it can. If Harry loves Joanna, then they should be married as soon as possible, and be damned to the rest.'

It was an idiosyncrasy of Lucy's to look tall when she was most forthright; and she had never looked taller than now. Matt, in his sitting position and not able to rise with any ease, was very conscious of it.

'But there're Harry's parents,' he said. 'And Mrs Silvie. They won't like it. After all, Joanna is—'

'My sister?' Lucy said, smiling harshly. 'Well, they'll have to put up with it. They needn't have anything to do with me if they don't want. But it isn't that. Oh, yes, Joanna is rather unsuitable, and no doubt they'd got much better things in mind for Harry, but what they really can't bear the thought of is that their Harry has got a girl into trouble. Isn't it?'

'I can't say what they feel. But I'd imagine they don't want to see him – dragged down.'

'And that's how you feel, too, isn't it?'

This came out sounding hostile, though she had meant it merely as a question. His glance was unfriendly, but also

372

uneasy. 'He's my friend, and I just want what's best for him.'

'As long as it doesn't drag *you* down.'

He flushed. 'That isn't very fair,' he said: it was his turn to invoke the past. 'You never used to be unfair.'

'Oh, Matt, it doesn't matter what you and I say to each other. It doesn't matter what we were or what we are. It's just picking over dead bones, however you look at it. It's the living that we need to concern ourselves with: Harry and Joanna. And think how much worse it might have been for them. Harry's not poor – far from it. They could marry and live comfortably for the rest of their lives. If they were both poor then there really would be difficulties. But money makes it all right, like it does most things. Think of . . . think of how much worse it might have been.' What she had been about to say was, 'Think of how it would have been for us'; but she was trying to purge her persuasions of all personal references. But of course that was impossible, as his expression showed. Everything they said on the subject inevitably carried a personal implication, if they chose to see it.

Matt sighed again and got to his feet. 'We don't seem to be getting very far,' said he.

'That's because it isn't really up to us, is it?'

'What do you suggest, then?'

'We should bring Harry and Joanna together. Of course I must ask her if she wants to see him, though I don't think there's any doubt of that. And you must ask Harry the same . . . Unless you don't want any part of it?'

After a moment Matt's gauntness broke up in a wry, reluctant smile: the effect was like the instant erasure of four years. 'I'll bring him here, shall I?' he said.

'Whenever you like.'

'Of course, you know it's not a very good look-out for the game if the umpires don't agree.'

'Well . . . like I said – we don't really matter, do we?'

Matt was left with some disquieting thoughts after this interview. He had not expected to be outfaced so completely; he could not help marking with a certain dark amusement that she had even used one of the very same arguments as he, to the opposite conclusion: the argument that money made the whole thing easier to settle.

He was still not wholly convinced; but it was something else that disturbed him. Various ideas that had assumed the status of pillar-like certainties in his mind had wobbled momentarily, if not fallen. Ideas about himself: for it had pained him to have his practicality dismissed as calculation, his coolness as coldness, as she had seemed to suggest. And ideas about Lucy: he could not quite reconcile the woman he had seen with the notorious widow of Lessington Road who had become such a figure in the town's mythology; such a figure, indeed, that he had perhaps tended to take the town's censorious estimate of her on trust. Of course, he told himself, there must be something in it. But once his own rather indignant feelings about the encounter had subsided – for he felt he should have come out of it better – he could not help being impressed by the memory of that tall, strong-limbed woman who had risen up to challenge him and passionately state her case. She seemed, in fact, to have much in common with the generous, warm-natured girl he had once known. Such uncompromising individuality was not the sort of thing to which his heart any longer inclined, for he had changed, but he could still admire it, and feel that she had been rather misjudged.

That feeling was further reinforced by the evidence of her tenderness to the little girl she had adopted, which he had seen on his first visit, and which was demonstrated again when he went back to Lucy's house the next day with a nervous and self-chastising Harry. With a friendly lack of ceremony she greeted Harry and led him into the small parlour where Joanna was waiting; then she closed the door on them and suggested that Matt come out to the garden with her and Sophie. A croquet set was in place on the lawn, and Sophie, though the game as properly played was beyond her small limbs, was enjoying herself greatly in trying to get the balls through the hoops. Lucy, rejoining her, seemed to enjoy herself no less; and Matt, called upon to have a go, soon found himself laughing along too.

However, he could not forbear glancing back several times at the house, and wondering what was going on within. Lucy met his eyes on one of these occasions, and he said, 'D'you think we should go to them yet?'

'No,' said she. 'Leave them be for a while. Let them talk it out in their own time.'

As she stood there, her arms encircling Sophie from behind and helping her to hold the croquet mallet, Matt had a strange presentiment of her as the woman she would be, or should be, when she was thirty or so years older – the sort of sturdy, handsome, much-loved, strong-minded woman to whom people turn for advice. Would she be such?

Observing his eyes upon her, she seemed to take his expression as one of renewed doubt at their manner of proceeding with regard to the couple indoors. 'It'll be all right,' she said. 'How did Harry seem today? You did tell him what we – well, what I suggested?'

'Yes,' he said. 'I told him.'

'And how did he react?'

Matt hesitated. If he were to be truthful, he should say that Harry had seemed enormously relieved, relieved at being thus nudged towards the course which his better nature had always favoured. For that was the way it had been. 'Of course Mrs Stokes is right,' Harry had said, stamping about in the way he had when moved. 'Of course she is. And it's very good of her to be so decent. I'll come and see her and Joanna at once.' But Matt baulked at telling Lucy this, for no one likes to admit they were wrong. 'Well, he seemed glad that it was going to be settled, one way or another,' he said at last; but at once felt that these were weasel words, and added confusedly, 'For what it's worth, I do believe that his feelings for your sister are . . . well, that he does love her.'

Lucy was saved from replying by the troubled couple's coming forth from the house at that moment, and approaching them arm in arm.

'Mrs Stokes,' said Harry, who was looking very boyish and dishevelled. 'I haven't yet thanked you for letting me come here, and for all the trouble you've been put to . . . I mean, apologized for all your trouble rather, and for – well, for what you must think of me, quite rightly, and I can't make any excuses for myself—'

'Oh, never mind that!' said Lucy, smiling. 'Have you two sorted it out? That's what I want to know.'

Harry took a deep breath. 'We're going to be married. As soon as possible. Because we want to be.'

Lucy looked at Joanna's shining face. Some tears had clearly been shed there, but of the sort that preface relief and happiness; some perhaps by Harry too, though she thought none the worse of him for that. 'Well, congratulations!' Lucy said, and embraced them both. 'That's fine news!'

'Yes,' Matt said, 'congratulations.'

'What I said goes for you too, Matt,' Harry said. 'I'm sorry to have burdened you with all this, my dear fellow, especially when – well, when the answer was staring us in the face all the time! Of course I must tell my parents at once. Set the whole thing before them.'

'I should come with you to do that,' Joanna said.

'Well, it depends. Not if it means that we go cap in hand, as it were. That's not the way it should be. I'll tell them; and if we don't get their blessing, we'll do without it,' said Harry.

'And then there's Mrs Silvie,' Joanna said. 'I'm afraid she's not going to be easy to convince.'

Matt too was preoccupied with these objections; but Lucy said, 'Well, nothing worthwhile's ever easy! Don't let's stand around with long faces. Let's go into the house and have a glass of sherry or something – we should be celebrating. After all, Harry, you're going to be my first brother-in-law!'

Sophie was plucking at Lucy's skirts, asking to have the matter explained to her; and while the other two went on into the house, Matt hung back to speak to Lucy. He found himself undecided what to say, and settled for, 'So, it has turned out for the best after all.'

'Well, it won't be easy, as they know . . . But yes, I think it has turned out for the best,' she said. 'Things do, sometimes. But not for everybody.'

XII

Lucy and Joanna stayed up late talking that night. In Joanna, normally reserved, a great store of emotion had been opened up by the recent events, and Lucy let her talk it all out. She was happy now, and sanguine about the future: marriage to Harry, the baby; Joanna was adjusting her views to embrace it all. There was much resilience behind that eggshell complexion and trusting manner.

Lucy was happy too, and thankful, for from the very start she had been firmly convinced that this was the best course, and she had meant everything she had said to Matt during their meeting yesterday; though she had never meant to let her own feelings get so entangled with what she had said, and she still felt uneasy about it. She supposed she let herself get carried away simply because it was Matt sitting there, and with Matt she had once had no need of inhibition: it was too easy to forget that he was not the same man that she had known, and that the instinctive empathy was gone.

Well, it was decided now, and she was glad. She liked and trusted Harry. It had been agreed that Joanna would remain here, and be married from this house, just as soon as the banns were called or a licence procured: Harry in the meantime must try and bring round his disapproving family. Lucy had no illusions about how easy that would be; but then she had no illusions about this whole business. Matt had been very wrong if, as she suspected, he thought her a fanciful romantic trying to blind the eyes of reality with stardust. She believed, as she had told him, that Joanna and Harry's love must be given a chance. But she also knew that love by itself had not the strength to get two people through a single day of the most humdrum and undemanding nature. Indeed, she had strong misgivings about its place in human affairs altogether; and if she had come to any settled creed, it might have been expressed thus: that before we can love each other,

377

we must cease to believe in Love – love with a capital letter, love the magician, the all-conquering. The false god must be dethroned, and its worshippers reconciled to the sight of the unsatisfactory earth, not dazzled by stage lightning, or dazed by conjurer's sulphur.

Joanna yawned, saw the time, and was apologetic. 'I've been keeping you up, going on so. But we're so grateful to you – and Matt – for helping us. Somehow we just couldn't seem to see the wood for the trees . . .' She got up and drew aside the curtains. 'The rain's stopped, and there's a lovely bit of moon. This is just like when we used to share the old bedroom in Alma Street – d'you remember, Lucy? – and we used to stay awake talking, and looking at the moon between the chimney-pots . . . What ages ago that seems! Like another world.'

'That's what it was,' said Lucy.

XIII

It was a December afternoon, and Matt was working late in the office of the leather warehouse. It was a time of heavy dun mists that snuffed out the days even before their short course was run, and the gas had been lit in the office for several hours. Matt had put in a lot of extra work lately, with Harry much occupied with his marriage, which had taken place last month before only the necessary witnesses. He didn't mind the work: it was what he thrived on; but he still could not help wishing sometimes that Harry had never met Joanna Middleton. The couple seemed happy enough, he supposed, but he wasn't sure how long that would last, living in rented rooms as they were at the moment, and still not really reconciled with Harry's family. It was all a very messy business. Helena Bressart had been greatly surprised at it.

'Such a rushed marriage,' she had said to him the other day, and then with an impish look: 'I don't suppose I should ask you whether it's true what one hears – that there was, how shall I put it, a pressing reason for their marrying?'

'That's right,' Matt said with a smile. 'You shouldn't ask me.'

'You're a tormentor, you are, Matthew. I truly believe you were sent to torment me.' She narrowed her eyes at him. 'What did you think of it all?'

'I wished them all the happiness in the world.'

'No you didn't. Or at least, you didn't believe it if you did. I know you, you're like me: you keep your feet on the ground. Yes, we wish them all the best and so forth; but inside we think it all a very hole-in-the-corner affair, and not what would do for us at all.'

Matt's heart gave a double beat.

'Well, isn't that so?' she said. 'If either of us ever thought of marrying someone, we wouldn't want it like that, would we?'

'Oh, I see!' said he, laughing with an oppressed feeling at his chest. 'No, no, not at all.'

'Hmm. I don't know, you didn't look too sure there for a moment. Perhaps you're the head-in-the-clouds type after all: elopements with a ladder against the balcony and all that.'

'Good Lord – not with my leg. I'd probably end up falling into the cucumber-frames,' he said. She gave a peal of satisfying laughter; but he wondered whether he had come close to making a fool of himself there for a moment. It was still sometimes difficult to adapt to Helena's oblique way of talking, which baffled even as it fascinated him . . .

Matt frowned down at the papers on his desk. In fact it was not business that was now detaining him. He was making out a list of guests to be invited to a dinner at his house before Christmas, and it was costing him some pains. He had no doubts about the suitability of the house for receiving company, for he had spared no time or expense in fitting it out during the last few months; but now that he came to the summoning of that company, the very thing that all the effort had been directed towards, unexpected hesitations came upon him. He had written the names *Mr and Mrs Bressart and Miss Helena Bressart* at the top, for therein, after all, lay his aim of aims; but though they had been highly civil to him – and rather more than that, he fancied – still when it came to inviting them to a party at his own house, he was a little diffident. Of course, he was thoroughly respectable now, and quite a figure in the town in a way. But if they did accept, he must make doubly sure that everything went absolutely smoothly. The onus was on him as host. Those dark eyes of Helena's did not miss much.

The question of the other guests was not unproblematic. The Browns he was pretty sure of: he had got on good terms with them through Harry. As for Harry himself, he had discreetly signalled to Matt that he wouldn't at all mind being left out: Joanna was beginning to show, and they both preferred to live quietly for now. The Parmenters he was undecided about. Their disapprobation of their son's marriage was none of his business, and there was no real reason why they should not remain on good terms; but there was still an awkwardness, and he could not get rid of a feeling that they somehow looked on Harry's disgrace, as they saw it, as something to do with him. Or was he being over-sensitive?

He put a question-mark next to the Parmenters. The next name on his list had, by any reasonable criteria, no right to be there at all, though for some reason he had underlined it. It was Lucy Stokes.

She had been so shunned by local society, he knew, that she hardly ever went out; would she want to do so after all this time? He didn't know. He was sure she wouldn't relish coming on her own, but he had thought to get round that by inviting her sister-in-law, Georgina Mellish, and her husband. Yet if he was slightly nervous of entertaining the Bressarts and their kind, why on earth was he considering endangering the whole thing by including amongst the guests a woman whose name was mud to them? Was this not a terrible risk?

But he did want Lucy to be there: he found that he had underlined her name for a second time. He acquitted himself of a boastful wish to show her how he had got on, for the simple reason that he intuitively knew that Lucy would not be impressed. The old Lucy would not have been; and neither, he felt, would this new Lucy who was revealing to him more and more resemblances to the old. He was undoubtedly curious about her: that, he supposed, was a straightforward enough motive.

He got up to warm his hands over the little stove that stood in the corner of the office: cold and long sitting had made his leg stiff and aching, and he limped like an old man. Surely it couldn't be that he wanted to offer a challenge, to throw down some sort of gauntlet, to this wealthy society just as it was opening up to him? For that was how it might appear. And he was simply not in the business of making such defiant gestures any more; they got you nowhere. After all, look at Lucy herself, who no longer seemed to care what the world thought of her: look at the way she had ended up. Although he had to confess that she was not the abject creature he had been led to believe. Her unaffected tenderness to the little girl, and the way the child seemed to love her; the way she had taken charge of Harry and Joanna . . . In fact there was no doubt about it, she was a fine woman, and he could imagine many a man, younger than he and less realistic about the way the world wagged, falling in love with her.

He didn't know what to think; and that was precisely what he didn't like.

He went to the little grimy window and smeared a hole to look out. The dark afternoon had become evening, and the river was shrouded in freezing mist; the pollard willows looked as lifeless as a petrified forest. It was a bitter, dismal, spectral evening: just such an evening as that on which Scrooge had his reluctant encounter with Marley's ghost; and Scrooge, beholding that ghastly visitor entering his room without troubling to open the door, could not have been more surprised than Matt when, casually answering, 'Come in' to the knock upon his own office door, he turned to see Luther Benson.

'Matt – Matt, my old shopmate!'

Luther Benson it was, from the crop of foxy hair to the long skinny shanks, and it was Luther Benson's voice that thus familiarly accosted him; and yet how changed was this shambling scarecrow from the fly, cocky, limber fellow who had once led Matt a rubbery, shady dance around the valley! The buoyant step had become a hesitant shuffle; the gaily shabby clothes that had given him the look of a careless coster had given place to the dingiest of pop-shop cast-offs; the slender frame had become gaunt and stiff, the shoulders hunched with defeat; and the face, once so cunningly comical, was white and haggard, with no light in the eyes but a sunken gleam that seemed like the last dim reflection of a hope disappointed almost to extinction. And yet, as if trying to deny what Matt's startled gaze so plainly apprehended, Luther came forward to greet him with a feeble shadow of the old jauntiness, saying again, 'My old shopmate! My old shopmate . . . after all these years . . . it does my heart good!'

'How did you get in here?' Matt said.

'Your ware'us-man downstairs told me to come up, when I said I was a friend of yourn,' Luther said. 'Leastways, he did after a bit of persuasion . . . I don't reckon he quite believed me at fust; and really, who's to blame him, looking at me—' here there was a shaky approximation of the old elastic smile— 'and looking at you, compare and contrast as they used to say at school, not that I ever did, more's the pity. And just look at you!' Luther said with a gesture of admiration. 'So it's all true what I heard! Yes, I heard all about how Matt Doughty was one of the town's up-and-coming young businessmen, and quite the coming man, and all the rest of it – and I believed it! Why, I always knew you had it in you. Right from the fust day we met, I knew you had it in you. But upon my word, not that that means any-thing you'd say and I dare say you'd be right – well, upon my soul then, it still knocks me side'uds, to see you again, and set up so smart!'

'It's – it's been a long time,' said Matt, recovering now from his first shock, but still as deeply disturbed by this apparition as if his own double had walked through the door.

'Four year,' said Luther, who seemed to reconsider a half-born impulse to extend his hand, and instead put it awkwardly in his pocket. 'Four year, and you've hardly changed a bit. Excepting that spot o' rustiness in one of your pegs,' he said, nodding sympathetically as Matt crossed the room to his desk, 'and that's what you might call a trophy of honour. Oh, yes, I've heard about it all . . . and that didn't surprise me neither! When I heard, I just said "Don't surprise me: no more'n I expected from that masterpiece of a man, my old friend Matt Doughty." And so I thought I'd look you up, just as old friends and shopmates, like,' he concluded, with a strained and anxious look which his grin rather accentuated than concealed.

'Well, I'm glad to see you again, Luther,' Matt said, though this was very far from the truth. 'You'd best have a seat.'

'Thanks, shopmate . . . I can't pretend I en't a mite blown – them stairs of yourn – don't seem to have the wind I used to . . . I don't suppose, by any chance, you've got a drop of summat reviving in this here hive of industry . . .?'

'Hm? Oh no,' Matt said, 'I'm afraid not.' He frowned and tried to drag his mind back to the point; he had just been assailed by a mental vision of Helena Bressart walking into the office and finding this fellow here. Nonsense, of course, for she would never do such a thing; but it brought his unease into powerful focus. 'So . . . what have you . . . what have you been doing since we . . .'

'Since we last met,' Luther said. 'Without saying goodbye, as you're too polite to say, my old shopmate.'

'It wasn't the goodbyes I was bothered about at the time,' Matt said grimly.

'I know. I know.' Luther hung his head. 'What can I say, Matt? I left you in the lurch, all them years ago – no two ways about it. All I can say is, I would have got word to you that the game was up, if I'd had time. But as it was, there was only time to save me own skin. Don't think I haven't fretted over that, since then. Don't think—'

'Oh, it doesn't matter,' Matt said. He did not want to be reminded of that time; he wanted a veil drawn over it for ever. And that was why he did not like Luther sitting in this room. The Matt Doughty that Luther had known, and the Matthew Doughty that he now was, were effectively two different people, and he wanted them kept that way.

'I don't blame you if you still feel bitter over that,' Luther persisted. 'You got every right. But there's mebbe justice behint it all, any road. I mean, you've turned out all right – and you've deserved it, shopmate! – whereas old Luther Benson, he . . .' He gave Matt a wry, intimate look. 'He went to the dogs, didn't he?'

'I always thought you were the surviving sort.'

'So did I, shopmate. So did I. But in the end there was a couple of rather determined policemen who decided I'd survived for too long, and a judge who was of the same mind. So while you was serving their majesties under the flag, I was doing the same – leastways, detained at their majesties' pleasure, in Norwich gaol. Which en't,' he added with a catch in his voice which he tried to disguise as a laugh, 'which en't the sort of place I'd advise a man to go, Matt, not if he wants to keep his – his mind in one piece . . . But there!' He wiped an unsteady hand across his face. 'You don't want to sit here listening to my cautionary tale. It en't a tale you stand in any need of, shopmate, and I'm glad of it. You're set up nicely, and I'm out of jug now and breathing God's pure air, none the wuss for a bit of leather-dust in it, and everythink's turned out for the best, eh?'

'I suppose so,' Matt said. It should not really have surprised him that Luther had been in prison, and it would certainly account for his crushed and broken look; but still the atmosphere of the gaol-cell, pestilentially blowing into his new and respectable world, made him recoil still further. 'Where – where are you living now?'

'Oh, back with my old stepmother in the Hole! Not the choicest of berths, and she weren't best pleased to have me back, but then blood's thicker than water. Not that she's any blood of mine, but she had enough out of my old man, so that evens it out.'

Well, he has somewhere to live, thought Matt: that's something. He shifted a little under Luther's gaze, in which that forced gaiety was joined with an appeal almost childlike in its nakedness.

'Well, I'm sorry things haven't gone well for you, Luther,' he said. 'If there's . . .' He coughed. 'If there's anything I can do . . .'

'Do? No, shopmate. All I want to know is that you don't hold it against me; the way I ratted on you all them years ago. It's been playing on my mind—'

'No, please – it's forgotten,' said Matt quickly; for so it was, and he wanted it to stay that way. 'Look, Luther, it's been good to see you again, but I ought to be getting along home . . .'

'Of course, shopmate. You're a busy chap now, I understand that. But if I could just – well, mebbe you don't like me to bring those old times up . . .'

'Not at all,' Matt said, colouring slightly.

'No, no, I understand if you don't. But it's because of old times that I feel like I can ask you . . . Well, when I said there was nothing you could do . . . Matt, I'm down on my luck. I know I gin you that story many a time in the old days, and mebbe there was times when that was all it was – a story; but I'm past that now. What you see now, shopmate, that's all there is of old Luther.' He reached across the desk to clasp Matt's arm: Matt just stopped himself from withdrawing it. 'A chap don't step out of gaol all set up to tek on the world, I'm afraid. Mebbe that tells him he shouldn't have gone there in the fust place, I don't know; but one thing's for sure, it don't do much to keep him from going back there. And I don't want to, Matt. You can have as much spirit as you like, but in them places it – it don't last long. I got to have work.' He had given up the attempt to be his old jesting self now: his face was all appeal. 'That's why I come to you. You know there's no chance for a chap like me, 'ithout somebody gives him a helping hand. And – well, no pretending now, that's why I come to you. You with your own factoring business and all, I thought . . . I don't care what it is, sweeping the floors, anything . . .'

'Luther, I wish I could help you there, but we just don't have any work to give.'

Luther grimaced. 'I know what you're thinking of, and I can't blame you. You're thinking, if you couldn't trust me then, how could you now? And all I can say is—'

'No, no,' Matt said, 'don't say that.' In fact that thought had occurred to him, though he had quickly dismissed it. But it was indeed those 'old times' that were disturbing him – or rather, their unexpected eruption into the present. He simply wanted them consigned to their former oblivion; and that went for Luther too. 'I just can't help you in that way, Luther. But look . . .' There was a cash-box in the desk drawer, and he drew it out and took money from it. 'Let me – let me help you out this way. Tide you over. How would that be?' As he spoke he somehow felt as furtive and embarrassed as if it were he who was begging for help.

'Well, shopmate, I . . .' Luther gave a glum, beaten sort of smile. 'I'd rather have earnt it somehow . . . Mebbe you don't believe that, because it's the sort of thing I would have said in the old days, but I . . . Well, I can't say no to it. I need it bad, Matt.'

'Certainly,' said Matt, with forced briskness. 'Quite natural. Look, here's five pounds and, what is it, some odd shillings. No, no, please take it.' He found his hands a little unsteady as he pushed the money over.

'Well . . . thank you, shopmate. I don't like to tek it, but . . . thank you.' Luther put the money in his pockets, and then said with a sort of timid cheeriness, 'What about tekking a drop wi' me on it, for old times' sake? We could go down to the Clicker's Arms, mebbe, just for—'

'Oh no, thanks all the same, Luther,' Matt said hurriedly, 'that'd be very nice, but really I – I've got to get home.'

'Ah.' Luther hesitated, then followed Matt's lead and got to his feet. 'Mebbe some other time, eh?'

'Er, maybe. The thing is, I'm – I'm very busy, with the warehouse and all, so . . .'

'Course you are.' At last there was a spark of life in Luther's eyes. Was it the money? Or was it a glint of that old, knowing irony? 'Well, old shopmate, I won't tek up any more of your time. And I won't keep thanking you. Just say, God bless, and good luck. Not that you'll need it, I reckon.' Again his look seemed to have something of that old slyness as he stuck out his hand; this time Matt was prompt to take it. 'Goodbye, Matt. Mebbe I'll see you around.'

Matt mustered a smile. 'Goodbye, Luther.'

His visitor was gone at last. Matt sat heavily down and wiped his brow. Strange, strange experience! All manner of indefinable emotions had overcome him; but overriding them all had been the urgent necessity of getting rid of this man who had strayed into his new life, as hideously incongruous as a crow in an aviary.

It had been sobering, indeed, to see Luther so changed. But then that was just it: he was changed too. Luther must surely have seen that. Instead he had seemed to think that there was some link between them beyond that of an old, perished friendship. And there was none . . . Well, he had helped him out with money, and money was what mattered after all. All that stuff about wanting to earn it through work was probably just the old Luther talking. Though Matt had to admit he had seemed sincere.

Had he perhaps done the wrong thing, fobbing him off with some cash, and hustling him out? Should he have found some work for him – anything, as Luther had said? But no. Even as he thought of it, he recoiled again. To have Luther Benson always around, a permanent reminder of the unsatisfactory and compromised past, a continual drag on his efforts to rise in the world – it would be intolerable! No, his only regret was that he had not had more money on hand to give him, so that he could have been more effectively bought off. He wanted those old times laid to rest for ever, and it would have been cheap at the price.

The list of party guests was still on his desk, and Matt quickly covered it up, just as if the names thereon were their owners' faces, with watching eyes; though he could not have said which of those faces it was that he did not want to see him at that moment.

XIV

'What's that, Auntie?' said Sophie.

'It's an invitation to a party,' Lucy said. 'No, not that sort of party, I'm afraid. A grown-up party, not much fun at all. But we're going to have a proper party at Christmas, aren't we?' She had lately been occupied in helping to make friends for Sophie on their visits to the Gardens, feeling that she needed to associate with other children, and knowing that the parents of this genteel neighbourhood would never let their fledgling prigs near the dreadful contagion of Alice Wedderburn's child. 'A proper party, with games and everything.'

This prospect was plainly so new to Sophie's experience that she could only contemplate it in solemn silence for some minutes; but then, observing Lucy reading the embossed card again, she said, 'Aren't you going to your party, then?'

'Oh, I don't think so!'

'You could wear your best frock,' Sophie said after a moment, as if this were an argument she could not imagine anyone resisting.

'Yes, I could, couldn't I? We'll see,' Lucy said, putting the invitation away in the bureau. It was the umpteenth time she had done so; and similarly well-thumbed was a letter from Georgina, saying that she and Miles had received the same invitation, and how nice it would be if they could all go together. That was one reason in favour of accepting; but the reasons against were so numerous and compelling that she did not know why she was even continuing to consider it.

She went upstairs and made ready to go out. She had taken up her work in the Hole with Mrs Blades in earnest again, for it was going to be another hard winter for the poor of the town; and she often visited Joanna and Harry, to lend what help she could to the newly-married couple. Indeed she always seemed to be going restlessly hither and thither lately, almost with feverishness; for some reason the more she busied herself the less it seemed to satisfy her. Even as she pinned on her hat, the urge to be out and doing something was more fully formed in her mind than an actual destination.

After a moment she decided on visiting Joanna and Harry. Whilst happy enough in their marriage, they were always vulnerable to a feeling that it could not be such a good thing as it self-evidently was, simply because others did not treat it as such. Harry's parents, whilst grudgingly reconciled to what could not be undone, had not been near them; Mrs Silvie was still in a huff. They were isolated, a thing that Harry in particular, used to moving in a large circle of acquaintance, found perplexing, and it reassured them for people to call. Even, Lucy thought ruefully, the widow of Lessington Road; for her reputation was surely worse now; it was her sister, after all, who had ruined young Harry Parmenter . . . She could just hear the clacking tongues.

Which was another reason for her to refuse Matt's invitation. Not because it would mean having to mix with the gossipers, and resist the temptation to smack them in their smug faces; she didn't care about that. It was because it might spoil it for Matt to have her there. She could guess how eagerly he anticipated this occasion as the confirmation of his new status, and the presence of so dubious a quantity as Mrs Lucy Stokes could only imperil its success.

On the other hand, he *had* invited her; and he had also gone to the trouble of inviting her closest friends, Georgina and Miles, whom he hardly knew — Georgina said Miles had met him just once. Why *had* he done it?

She hurried out. Thinking about his motives troubled her, and set tingling nerve-ends that she had thought cauterized and deadened for ever more.

It would be better for everyone if she did not go, she decided, as she had decided twenty times in the past week. It would be better for her peace of mind, and better for his. He had probably sent the invitation out of a friendly obligingness, and would breathe a sigh of relief when he received her polite negative reply, which she really must write soon. As for this nagging curiosity that tempted her to go, and which she was always worrying at like a hole in a tooth, she must simply suppress it. Curiosity was not such a terrible thing in itself, but she was afraid there was more to it, and a visit to his house, a whole evening in his company, might see that fear confirmed. She had a feeling of not quite being able to trust herself, a feeling not unlike being in the grip of feverish illness; except that it was not the cottony grasp of her hands and the straightness of her step that she could not trust, but her heart.

She left the house, and walked down into the town; and the confused press of her emotions, which could not be stilled, seemed to demand some more congenial environment than the clattering streets which indifferently received her. She experienced, in fact, with some of the old sharp hunger of her days in Alma Street and the closing-shop, a longing for the country; and the return of this longing, for all her fine resolutions to do the sensible thing, was in itself an ominous development.

XV

All the invited guests were present at Matthew Doughty's evening party just before Christmas.

There were Mr and Mrs John Arthur Brown, who formed a sort of centrepiece of unimpeachable respectability for the occasion; the aged Mr Leek, who was growing so unthinkably fat with advancing years that to look at him was to suffer a sympathetic pang on behalf of the coffin-maker and grave-diggers who would presently have to deal with him; Mr and Mrs Bressart and their daughter Helena, like a triptych representing three forms of handsomeness – the severe, the mature, and the elegant; Georgina and Miles Mellish, who by marrying each other had somewhat overcome their mutual diffidence in company, but were still apt to throw each other mutely pleading signals when separated; and Lucy Stokes. And no one was more surprised to see her there than Lucy herself.

Everything was in order: nothing had been omitted. There was no sign, for example, that the glassware had only arrived that very morning, and that Matt, immaculate now in evening dress, had been running round tearing his hair out at a vision of his guests having to drink their wine out of custard-cups. There was perhaps an air of conspicuous newness about everything – a suggestion that the tablecloth was not merely newly laundered but newly unwrapped from the draper's brown-paper, that the drawing-room rug curled very slightly at the ends not from age and wear but because it had until recently been rolled up in a carpet-shop, and that the large and undeniable walnut sideboard, in such a boastful state of polish, had nothing in it but the cabinet-maker's tickets. However, this was a recommendation rather than otherwise to shoe-baron society, which liked things new, and whose attitude to the past might be summed up in Mr Leek's comment on his one visit to the British Museum: 'A lot of old dusty lumber and rubble such as you might dig up in Wellingford quarries! I wouldn't give you ten pounds for the lot!'

So, here was Matt, moving amongst his guests before dinner as nimbly as his lameness would allow, seeing that Mr Leek had a stool for his gouty foot, making sure that Mrs Bressart, who had a slight chill, had a seat near the fire, and taking care to circulate continually and to talk to everyone. He was circulating at such a rate, indeed, that he rather caught out Miles Mellish who, having acquitted himself well with, 'I do think this is most awfully agreeable of you to invite us, Mr Doughty, and I'm so glad to be here,' soon found his host bearing down on him again before he had thought of something else to say, and for want of new inspiration was constrained to repeat the whole formula word for word – a failure which left him telegraphing helpless contrition to his wife across the room for some minutes afterwards.

'Mrs Stokes, I'm so glad you could come.' Thus Matt to Lucy. Whether he was really glad she couldn't tell, but his smile was easy enough: the smile, alas, that she remembered so well. At least her presence had not caused anything more than surreptitiously raised eyebrows and a certain heaviness of articulation when people spoke to her, as if she were foreign or slightly deaf. She reflected again that money was the philosopher's stone: her reputation might be equivocal, but she was Radford Stokes' widow, and she had money, and she was well-dressed from the best shops; and it was those things that spoke with the louder voice.

'I like the house,' she said, with truth enough, though it did remind her rather of a hugely enlarged doll's house, and had she entered the kitchen she would have expected to see cardboard frying-pans with rashers of bacon painted on them. 'You must be very pleased with it.'

'Oh, thank you! Yes, it's coming along,' Matt said, and she saw his eyes flick restively round the room as if to reassure himself that everything was in place. 'And how's Sophie?'

There was, then, nothing half-hearted about his having her here: he didn't mind acknowledging Alice Wedderburn's child. She saw Mrs Brown's interested eyes slide round. 'She's very well, thank you. Very excited about Christmas. We're going to have a children's party on the twenty-seventh.'

'You must have a heart like a lion,' Matt said smiling. 'She's a charming little girl, though. Does you credit.'

This took her unawares: she could only thank him, stammering, before he was off again. Well, now there was time to try and relax a little, and talk undemandingly with Georgina, and feel the long-unaccustomed draughtiness of her evening-gown, and take in the furnishings of the drawing-room which were quite up-to-date and oriental, and ask herself again why she had come.

And receive again the inescapable reply: because she couldn't, God help her, keep away.

Time too to watch Matt moving amongst the guests, and to notice as perhaps only her eyes could what he took such scrupulous pains to conceal: that all his courteous attentiveness – and he was playing the host admirably – had a focus, and the focus was the elegantly seated, darkly glowing figure of Helena Bressart.

Ah! Much was clear, now, about Matt's aspirations; and from that same realization much became clear to Lucy about herself, and the confused feelings she had brought here crystallized into something all too recognizable.

She had indeed been wrong to come. But she was here now, and the evening must be got through.

The other guests, however, seemed not to regard the evening as something to be got through. It was a raw, bone-freezing night without, and here they were comfortably, even royally, entertained by a most obliging and interesting young man, with a good dinner in prospect; even the stately Mr and Mrs Bressart were unbending a little, and the beautiful Helena looked, as she always did, as if she were in exactly the right place at the right time. The company were in good spirits as the time for dinner arrived; and in the elaborate foolery of being paired off to be 'taken in' to dinner, Lucy found herself on the arm of Mr Bressart. Poor Georgina was consigned to Mr Leek, and found some difficulty in taking his arm, which could hardly extend more than an inch from his blubbery side; whilst Miles, paired to his alarm with Mrs John Arthur Brown, could not resist a terrible compulsion to quickly reach up and smooth his errant crown of hair and, unluckily choosing the arm with which he was linked to Mrs Brown, nearly dislocated that lady's shoulder.

Matt, Lucy noted with dull unsurprise, took in Helena.

Though she had grown pretty well into the social role which marriage to Radford had conferred on her, Lucy still found the rituals of social eating faintly ludicrous. The white dress-fronts of the men, so perfectly designed to make even the merest spot of gravy show up like a giant graffito; the obligation to present the same undemonstrative appreciation of both the dishes that turned your stomach and the ones that you wished to gobble in platefuls; the wooden-headed refusal of such occasions to recognize the sheer irreconcilability of eating and talking at the same time; the duty of the men to 'help' you to this or that, which made you feel like a child and hardly gave them time to eat their own meal – a duty which Miles, in his well-meaning way, fulfilled so conscientiously that Mrs Brown could hardly see over the mound on her plate; and the way that every eatable, whether hot soup or cold sorbet, was of a uniformly lukewarm temperature by the time it had made the journey from the kitchen to the sideboard, and thence all round the table.

Lucy could not help noticing that sideboard. The dining-room was large enough for the company, in the sense of *just* large enough; and that sideboard, so bulky and amply made, was rather commandingly present. She could tell from the way he kept glancing at it that Matt too had his doubts about that sideboard; or rather, half-doubts, which would not have amounted to anything had they not joined with half-doubts about the servant he had engaged to wait at table. She was a very smart and brisk young woman, but somewhat broad about the hips; and, though she adroitly negotiated the narrow passage between sideboard and chair-backs, Matt's glance could hardly have been more jittery if she had produced a shattering collision every time.

Lucy, remembering her own nervousness as a new hostess at Radford's party, at just this time of year, sympathized; but even that sympathy was oppressively unstraightforward, and could not be felt without catching on a snarl of other feelings. She watched Matt's dark head inclined to hear something Helena was saying, and the knowledge that came over her was like the grimly undeniable knowledge that a painful illness which one thinks long cured and over is returning. She blinked at her plate of salmon, and wished herself a thousand miles away. An emotion which she did not want, and which was unlikely to be anything but injurious to her well-being, had again been thrust upon her; an infection which, if inflicted by the hand of man rather than by supposedly beneficent Nature, would have been condemned as the cruellest invention of misplaced ingenuity, had taken hold after an incubation of she knew not how long, and she must submit to its ravages. It is seldom pleasant to have old saws proved to us, and the lesson that first love is after all the deepest was one that Lucy would willingly have dispensed with, especially as that scourging pedagogue Fate had chosen to administer it just when she and that love's object seemed more widely separated than ever before.

'You'll be glad to know, Mrs Stokes, that your late husband's factory is still a thriving concern,' said Mr Bressart at her side. As the purchaser of Radford's business, he had plainly hit upon this as a convenient common ground for conversation, and he did not trouble to shift it throughout the meal, simply talking to her about the shoe trade. She did not mind this, however: Mr Bressart liked the sound of his own voice, and only required her to agree with him, and in her present state of mind she felt unequal to doing much more.

'. . . I doubt we'll see another large-scale war in our time,' Mr John Arthur Brown was saying. 'Not between the civilized countries, at any rate. Their whole system of trade and finance is too interlocked for that: the whole thing would just come crashing down. But of course the Empire will always require a large military presence, and that's where the security of the boot trade lies, in the long term. Though the War Office will insist on buying cheap nowadays, penny-pinchers that they are.'

'No more wars?' said Helena. 'Well, we have a soldier amongst us, perhaps we should ask him about that.'

'Oh, I don't know,' Matt said. 'I'm no expert – I only felt like a cog in a great wheezy clanking old clock most of the time. But wars don't stop just because they don't make any sense, that I do know.'

It struck Lucy for the first time that there was nothing in Matt's house to remind him of his service as a soldier, no trophies or campaign mementoes. That was clearly a time that he wished entirely to forget, just like – just like another time.

'Well, peace and prosperity, that's my motto; peace and prosperity,' said Mr Brown. 'Not that there's a great deal of prosperity about at the moment, not in the trade at any rate.'

'Well, that's where I think what you said about the long term comes in,' Matt said. 'After all, if Harry and I had only taken present conditions into account, we would never have started up as factors at all. But things can only get better. As long as the trade makes sure that it – what's the word – diversifies. Look at Saunds. The whole town depends on army boots, and that's why half the men are out of work, and up in arms about it – and quite right too. But we're hopeful. After all, the shoe trade isn't going to die like the mail coach.'

'Nothing like leather! People will always need a pair of shoes!' burst out Mr Leek, uttering two phrases so often heard in the valley towns that they had taken on something of the aspect of religious liturgy, and an obedient murmur went round the table like a congregational response.

'True, true. You know, Matthew, I think that's just the sort of spirit this town needs,' said Mr Brown. 'We older fellows are inclined to get a bit down in the mouth at times, and it's quite a heartening thing to see, the way you and young Parmenter have set up for yourselves. You're thinking of moving into new premises, I hear?'

'In the new year, I hope. We're rather cramped for space where we are now.'

'Oh! I don't think so, you know,' put in Miles Mellish, and threw an admiring glance round the dining-room. 'I think it's really quite commodious here – though perhaps the sideboard is—'

'Miles, we're not talking about this house, we're talking about Mr Doughty's warehouse,' said Mr Brown impatiently.

'Sorry,' said Miles. 'Silly of me. Sorry. I thought you meant this house . . . I thought they meant this house,' he explained to himself, diving at his champagne-glass, and getting the bubbles up his nose.

'But talking of this house, Matthew,' Helena said smiling, and talking slowly as self-confident people do, in the assurance that they will be listened to, 'you've quite done wonders with it. The Johnsons were a very old and staid couple, I understand, and I rather expected to see ponderous mahogany and dusty petit-point everywhere. Who says men have no taste?'

'Well – thank you,' Matt said, meeting her liquid-dark eyes. 'I must admit I did rather overhaul the place. It'll do, for now.'

Is it really possible to be happy for someone when we are miserable? Would we not rather see a lover writhe in the ghastliest region of hell, than see that lover happy without us? However, Lucy tried: seeing Matt so proud, well-thought-of, and plainly hopeful of a successful issue to all his prospects, she tried to be happy for him, and wish him well; and there was heroism in her so very nearly succeeding. There was, thank goodness, no one here who could have the slightest suspicion of what she was feeling, or who could guess at what had once existed between the two who were now merely host and guest. That most difficult feat of cutting oneself adrift from the past had been achieved – by Matt if not by Lucy.

After dinner – which had been a great success, the maid and the sideboard having continued on good terms with each other right to the end – came the gravitation to the drawing-room, effected at last with difficulty by Mr Leek, who was in some danger of having to join the ladies with his carver chair clamped to his ample seat like the shell of an upright tortoise. Tea and coffee circulating, and the hour drawing later, Lucy could at least comfort herself that it would soon be over, even though her heart was torn by a contrary wish not to go at all, when she found herself for some time seated beside Matt and talking with him.

He looked relaxed at last, as if conscious that his hurdles were safely got over; and she could not help saying, 'It's been a lovely evening, Matt. It's always difficult – entertaining in a new home.'

This was private language, if coded; but after a moment he gave a relieved smile and said in a low voice, 'Well, I'm glad it went off well. I was afraid of – oh, I don't know, all sorts of things. What the kitchen looks like I daren't think. I only hired the cook and the maid last week. They don't get on, to be honest, and it's a wonder we haven't heard them throwing saucepans at each other.'

To no one else but me, she thought, could he talk like this; to no one else but me – and yet it's no good!

Presently, when Matt had rejoined the Bressarts, Georgina escaped from Mr Leek, who was telling her a funny story, the point of which was somewhat blunted by his continually falling asleep in the middle of it, and came and sat by Lucy.

'It's been very nice, hasn't it?' Georgina said. 'Though I wish Miles hadn't had so much champagne, I'm sure those odd faces he keeps pulling mean he's got the hiccoughs. Mr Doughty's quite the coming man, isn't he? You know, in years to come I shouldn't wonder if we don't see him one of the big men of the valley like Sir Moses Philip Manfield. Especially – ' she lowered her voice – 'especially if there should be an alliance, as it were, between him and the Bressarts. And I wouldn't be surprised if there were, you know.'

Before Lucy could counterfeit a reply she became aware of a commotion in the hall – the maid's voice, on an agitated note, mingled with a voice that she thought she recognized but could not place. She just saw Matt, seated beside Helena Bressart, turn his head with an expression of dawning horror, and then the attention of the whole room was seized by the drawing-room door being flung open and by the shabby figure who stood there, wildly gesticulating with his long thin arms and crying 'Matt! Matt Doughty, my old shopmate, I'm here, a bit late mebbe but I'm here!'

And Lucy remembered him. Luther Benson, though much changed from the way she remembered him: the raffishness gone seedy and a little pathetic. He did not look well either, but the blast of sour breath confirmed that it was drink that made him stagger a little as he came forward into the room, bowing ironically to the ring of astonished faces.

The maid, frantic, followed in his wake, still ineffectually plucking at his sleeve and saying in an anguished whisper to Matt, 'He wouldn't tek no, sir, he just barged straight in and I couldn't stop him, no matter what I—'

'Never you mind, gel, you done nowt wrong,' Luther said in the same loud, emphatically pitched voice, 'Mr Doughty's only having a gathering of his friends – ' he bowed swoopingly and blew a kiss to Mrs Bressart, who stared stonily at him – 'and so it's only right that old Luther Benson should be here, seeing as how he's Matt's oldest friend from way back, en't that right, shopmate?'

Matt had risen stiffly to his feet, and as he stood confronting this tattered Nemesis, Lucy was reminded of the way he had stood, in just that posture, regarding the bones in Cleatham crypt.

'Luther,' he said quietly, 'I didn't ask you to come here—'

'Hark at him!' Luther said with admiration, reeling round in a half-circle, and bestowing a wink on Mr John Arthur Brown. 'Hark at him! Apologizing! He's the soul of politeness, en't he? Course, you and I know it was just an oversight that I weren't invited, even though I knew him when most of the company here present, greetings all, wouldn't have spoke to him in the street. You and I know he's not the sort of chap to be ashamed of the people he once knew, and pretend they never existed, and sneak 'em a few bob and say there now my man, clear off and don't come near me again in case I catch summat nasty off you, don't we? Why, you know him as well as you know your own pa, don't you, miss?' Luther said catching Helena's eye. 'But mebbe you don't know him as well as old Luther Benson—'

'That's enough,' said Matt, who had gone white. 'You're drunk, Luther. I think you'd better leave—'

'Don't know him as well as old Luther Benson, oh no!' shouted Luther, dancing out of Matt's reach with something of his old sly suppleness, and circling round Mr Leek's chair. 'You don't know the times we had when we wukked together at Whiting's, all them years ago – such times we had, eh Matt? Until we was asked to leave, as you might say, on account of certain items of stock going missing, and always going missing when Matt was around, curiously enough! Old Josh Whiting don't git about much now, I hear, but I'm sure he'll remember that if you ask him. Ah, but it's wonderful what a few years wi' the colours and a new suit will do – even make a fellow think he's a different man altogether – oh, but not Matt, not old Matt Doughty, he don't pretend to be nowt but what he is. He'll have told you all about them days when he slunk out o' town one step ahead o' the policeman's arm—'

'Luther.'

Lucy rose, approached him, and placed her hand upon his arm. He stared a moment into her face, and for the first time his exaggeratedly sardonic expression faltered.

'I know you,' he said. 'Why – Lucy Middleton!' He began to make another expansive gesture. 'Burn me, quite a reunion—'

'Yes,' she said. 'It's been a long time. But this isn't the best place for it.' She could only try to limit the damage: Matt, paralysed, was beyond helping himself. Except for Matt and Lucy, no one in the room had said a single word: their silence was sufficiently eloquent. 'You've had a drop too much, Luther. The best thing for you is to go home.'

'Home! No, the party's just starting—'

'No, it isn't. It's late.' She spoke firmly, and did not relax her hold upon his arm. 'I'm going myself, now. Will you please come with me, and see me home? It's a dark night.'

Luther regarded her with fuddled perplexity; seizing her

advantage, she steered him to the door, talking casually, and presently had got him out in the hall before he knew he was there. Miles in his helplessly helpful fashion had followed, and she said quickly to him, 'Miles, can you get me my wrap? – the closet there, I think – thank you; and could you say my goodbyes for me?'

In the drawing-room, the maid was still stuttering out her apologies, and Matt was murmuring something soothing in reply: from the rest of the company came the same, frozen, audible silence. Luther showed some shakily mulish inclination to go back in there, but she had him now, and soon she was propelling him down the front path and out into the misty street.

They walked on in silence for a few moments; then Luther wrenched his arm away from her, and leaned heavily against a high garden wall so that the brickwork rasped against his hollow cheek.

'He asked for that, burn him,' he said in the same, mutinous tone; but he scrubbed his sleeve across his eyes, and Lucy saw by the light of the street gas-lamp that he was weeping.

'How?' she said.

He flung a red-eyed look at her over his shoulder, then turned his head again. 'Like I said. Like I said. Mebbe I am a bad 'un – mebbe he didn't want to be reminded of me; but when I went to see him it was like he . . . he didn't want to admit as he ever knew me. Like he just wanted me to fade away and . . . not exist any more. I didn't expect him to chuck his arms round my neck, not the way we parted all them years ago . . . but I thought to be treated like I was human at least, especially by Matt Doughty of all people, who never had any side. And I'm sick of being treated like I en't human, no matter what I done – it gits so you start to believe it yourself . . . And so when I heard about him having his posh do, and when I'd had a few drinks, I thought I'd . . .' He scrubbed at his face again and gasped, gulping down the cold air; then tried to smile. 'Well, missus, you certainly en't done yourself any good with that straight-laced lot in there, coming out wi' me like this.'

Lucy shrugged. That was the last thing she was concerned about.

'Whatever happened to you and Matt?' Luther said. 'I thought you and him—'

'No,' Lucy said, 'that was over a long time ago.'

'Well, I en't sorry. For what I just did, I mean. Or mebbe I am . . . I don't know!' he said confusedly. 'I . . . I shouldn't have had that last drink . . .'

'It's always that last one that causes the trouble, isn't it?' Lucy said, smiling ruefully. 'My father used to say he wished he could miss that one out, and go on to the next one. Come on, Luther. It's bitter cold, and you're not dressed for it. You'd be better off at home.'

XVI

'Yes! In trouble at Whiting's once for stealing, so it appears,' said Mr John Arthur Brown, who was paying a seasonal call on Mr Aubrey Parmenter. 'I seem to remember something of the sort, though I didn't make the connection with young Doughty. Of course, one knew he wasn't quite out of the top drawer, but even so . . . The whole episode was quite an eye-opener, I can tell you.'

'Well,' Mr Parmenter said with a portentous clearing of his throat, 'one can't entirely forget what he did for Harry in South Africa, of course. But I can't help wondering if Harry wouldn't have got into . . . well, the scrape he did get into with this young woman, which we've just had to make the best of . . . I say, I can't help wondering if he wouldn't have done it if he hadn't got mixed up with young Doughty. We were wrong to encourage the friendship, no doubt, but then Matt seemed a decent young fellow, if a little rough at the edges. However, these things will always come out, it appears; they always come out.'

'Poor Harry,' moaned Mrs Parmenter, 'he was dragged down, dragged down by inferior people; I shall maintain it to my dying day.' She still had a fit of the vapours whenever her daughter-in-law's condition was mentioned, which might have prompted an unsympathetic observer to ask her by what route her son Harry had come into the world.

'Well, I shall certainly advise Harry to dissolve that partner-ship as soon as may be,' said Mr Parmenter, 'though the boy has such wrong-headed romantic notions there's no knowing what his reaction will be.'

'You still see Harry, then, Mr Parmenter?' gently inquired Mrs Brown, who had a habit of lacing her sweetest remarks with a spice of malice.

'We are still not on the best of terms with the boy,' Mr Parmenter said, his florid face flushing a deeper colour. 'But of course he's our flesh and blood and, as I said, we're making the best of things . . . Have you seen young Doughty since this shocking exhibition, John?'

'Only in the street to say good morning to,' Mr Brown said. 'One can't cut the fellow dead, though it does make one look at him in quite a different light. I must say he's holding his head up pretty well.'

'Well, I certainly don't wish to see him again, after that night,' said Mrs Brown. 'I was never so humiliated and embarrassed in all my life. I was talking to Mrs Bressart the other day, and she left me in no doubt as to where they stand. Quite insulted and indignant she was, and you know she's not usually a woman to express herself strongly. Of course young Doughty had begun to make himself quite a fixture at the Bressarts' place, you know; it was business at first, but there was no pretence of business later on. Well, whatever he was hoping for from that quarter he'd better think again.'

'And so it was Mrs Stokes who took charge of this drunken fellow, I understand?' Mr Parmenter said.

'Oh well! What would you expect?' said Mrs Brown dismissively. 'I was going to say I didn't think well of Matthew Doughty for inviting her in the first place, but it's perhaps just as well he did, or there might never have been an end to it. But of course, my dear, I forgot –' smiling at Mrs Parmenter – 'you're in a way related to Mrs Stokes by marriage now, aren't you, so perhaps I shouldn't breathe a word against her.'

Mrs Parmenter could only moan again in reply: 'Dragged down! Dragged down!'

XVII

Occupied with preparations for Sophie's first Christmas without her mother, Lucy's mind was still wholly taken up with the events at Matt's house.

Even as she had propelled Luther Benson out of the house, she had known that the situation was past saving; and her heart went out to Matt at the thought of what he must be going through, especially with the memory of her own lapse at Radford's dinner-party. She knew well how unforgiving the close-knit local society could be. That the approval or disapproval of these hidebound and narrow-minded people no longer mattered a bean to her was beside the point: she knew Matt's ambition, and she knew that it did matter to him. And she was, besides, not able to be objective about Matt any more – if she ever had been.

Dwelling on an unforgiving world, however, also brought Luther Benson and his plight into her reflections. During their old association she had never much trusted him, and his action at Matt's party was not such as to commend him, unless one recognized that slighted unhappiness rather than malice lay behind it; but before they had parted that night after Matt's party, he had confided to her, briefly, the grim details of his recent life, and it did not take much percipience to see that his spell of hard labour in prison, physically enfeebling as it had been, had had a far more devastating effect upon his spirit. And what was there for him now? What beneficent influences did his life contain, that might help towards recovery and reparation?

Still thinking of these things, she went to see her old friend Mrs Blades in the Hole; and inquired of her whether she knew anything of Luther and his circumstances.

'Benson? Oh, yes, he's back in his old haunts now. Living with his stepmother again, I reckon,' Mrs Blades told her. 'Nobody was much surprised when he went away to gaol, and I'm afraid not many were glad to see him back. He played a few slippery tricks in his time. Mind you, he's been looking hard for work since he come out, there's no denying it. Much good it'll do him, I'm afraid, with his history. We're all God's children, of course, but there's some you can only look at and say, well, they're a lesson – a lesson, that's all.'

Lucy, however, having learned from Mrs Blades where Luther lived, went there directly to seek him out. The cottage was squalid even by the standards of the Hole, and looked like a ramshackle outbuilding of some larger place, rather than a complete human dwelling. In the alley leading to it, a half-wit boy was throwing stones at a cat upon a roof, and the overflowing gutter was as green and slimed as the surface of a pond. Luther's stepmother was just such an ill-natured, ill-favoured, and ill-affected old curmudgeon as he had always jestingly portrayed her: one of those creatures the world could easily dispense with, the very ones who always go on living in it for an unconscionable time. After much suspicious glaring, she admitted that Luther lived here, but he had gone out. On Lucy's establishing that he would not be long, she was grudgingly given permission to wait; and she sat on a broken wheelback chair whilst the old woman pottered about making the hollowest pretence of housework ever seen, interspersed with a great deal more glaring. No stranger to the bleakest aspect of poverty, Lucy was still appalled by the bareness and filth, and the element of grim optical illusion in everything that met her glance; the grey dishrags that turned out to be laundry, the scrap-iron that turned out to be cooking utensils, the dirty hole in the wall that turned out to be the fireplace. But she had not long to view these things before Luther came in.

He had been just about to say something to his stepmother when he saw Lucy, and to her utter surprise he stopped dead and did something she had never seen him do before; he blushed from his frayed collar to the roots of his carroty hair.

'Don't ask *me* what *she* wants,' grunted Luther's stepmother, who was one of those people who give a contemptuous emphasis to every personal pronoun. '*She* wouldn't tell *me*'; quite an untruth, as the old crone had not even asked.

'Hello, Luther,' Lucy said. 'I was wondering if I . . . if I could ask you a favour.'

'Me?' Luther stared a moment, then spread his hands in bemusement. 'No harm in asking, missus.' He threw a significant glance at his stepmother.

'Oh! I'm not wanted, en't I?' she croaked, a stupid question if ever there was one, and stamped into the next room to do unconvincing things with a broom with no bristles.

'Well, it isn't really a favour,' Lucy said when she had gone. 'It's more of a – business proposition.'

'Man alive, a business proposition, eh?' said Luther, who had recovered from his flush of embarrassment, but still seemed uneasy at having her here. 'Long while since I had one of them, missus. But I'll tell you now, I en't exactly overflowing wi' capital, if there's an outlay required.'

'No,' she said. 'But there is money in it . . . What I mean is, will you come and work at my house?'

He did not answer.

'I know this is . . . a bit sudden, and I don't expect you to say yes or no straight off . . . I need someone to work in the garden, and around the house. There's no male staff, you see, and there's a lot of heavy work needs doing, and repairing and decorating, and I've been meaning to get a good handyman in for some time . . .' There was a reasonable measure of truth in this, but still she felt it to be rather transparent, and wondered if he would refuse it as a put-up job born out of pity. 'I can pay you a decent wage, if not a craft's wage, and you could have your midday meal at the house, and . . .'

She faltered and stopped, for he had turned away from her. She thought for a moment this was a brusque dismissal; but then she saw him pass a hand across his face, and fetching a deep breath he turned to face her again.

'I like the sound of that business proposition, missus,' he said, with a faint echo of his old waggish tone; but his voice trembled too. 'I like the sound of it a lot, and – and if I was a praying man . . . When can I start?'

Luther came to the house that very day; and he was there on Christmas Day and Boxing Day too, though she protested that this wasn't necessary. But he was eager to show willing; and, as he said, cleaning out the garden pond was more of a holiday than spending the festive season with his stepmother.

There was plenty for him to do, as the jobbing gardener had left after Georgina's marriage. Looking about her, Lucy saw how badly she had let the place go through the blank time of her widowhood and then the nursing of Alice Wedderburn. She remembered Radford's fastidious pride in his home, and felt ashamed.

'The house really hasn't been touched since my husband died,' she said to Luther as he made a bonfire of garden rubbish. She regarded the peeling paintwork of the conservatory, the missing slates from the outhouse where the old spring-cart was kept. 'It's funny how you stop noticing . . . Have you got everything you'll need, Luther?'

'There's everything in that tool-shed bar a left-handed spanner,' Luther said. 'Only thing I need is strength anew to do it all, and that'll come.' He had made no further attempt to thank her since she had come to him in the Hole, or say what this chance meant to him; but now, his eyes on the leaping flames, he said hesitantly: 'Have you . . . seed anything of Matt Doughty since . . . since the other night, I wonder, missus?'

'No, I haven't,' she said lightly, as if her thoughts had not been full of him every waking moment. 'But then, I don't, as a rule, you know; and of course he's very busy.'

'There's some things that seem right before you do 'em, and right at the time of doing 'em, and even right just after you've done 'em,' Luther said musingly, 'and then blame me if they don't turn out to be wrong after all . . .! Mind them sparks don't land on you, my duck,' he said to Sophie, who had come out to join them, and was examining the bonfire.

'It goes right up high, don't it?' she said, throwing back her head to see the smoke spiralling heavenward.

'Right up high,' Luther said, 'and then meks clouds.'

'It never does,' said Sophie, looking at him sidelong.

'Course it does! Why, where do you think the clouds come from then? All the chimley-smoke going uppards, o' course. Fancy you not knowing that, my duck.'

Sophie looked shy, pleased, and dubious all at once; and Lucy knew that she would be asked for the truth of this before bedtime.

There was something about Luther that Sophie took to. Lucy could see that with his rubbery physique, comical mouth, and rapid, unserious way of talking, he lacked the stiffness and solidity that made adulthood so dully imposing to a young eye. He was more congenial to that exaggerated and highly coloured world in which a child moved. And Luther took to Sophie in return. Perhaps it was because he himself had had to be old in the ways of the world virtually from the cradle, and childhood represented something lost and untainted to him whose relations with adults had always been hobbled by a dog-eat-dog opportunism. Whatever the reason, he had a rapport with children, and Lucy did not know what she would have done without him on the day of Sophie's party after Christmas. Her invention and patience were exhausted long before the young guests' appetite for games; but the day being, though cold, bright and clear, she presently ushered them out on to the lawn, where Sophie called to Luther, engaged in lopping the old apple-trees, to come and play.

'Do – please!' Lucy said to him at his inquiring look; and the burden was lifted from her for the rest of the day, for Luther was the tireless orchestrator of a score of games, and the uncomplaining centre of a whirling turbulence of children; a sort of human maypole around which they at last danced themselves to the end of their energy.

'I don't know how you do it,' she said to him afterwards, when the young guests were gone. 'I'd started to feel like King Herod!'

'All right when they en't your own, and you know somebody else has got to git 'em to bed,' he said. 'Excepting one, of course, and she's no trouble I'll bet . . . It's funny, she's like you, en't she? Though she en't quite your own . . .'

'Is she?' Lucy had never thought of it; it surprised her.

'Don't tek that wrong, I mean, I know she is your own, in all the ways that matter—'

'No, no – it's all right.' She thought of Sophie, running and laughing today, and as she had first seen her cowering on the bed in a sordid rented room. 'I can't imagine being without her now; that I do know.'

The new year set in with sleet and slush followed by a hard and enduring frost: the high causeways of Cottesbridge were clogged with embankments of sullied ice, smoothed into grotesque contours by the freezing wind, and looking more like something that had been quarried and dumped there than an innocent consequence of winter weather. Outdoor work being suspended, Lucy turned her attention to the interior of the house, and resolved upon a comprehensive redecoration, room by room. Declaring off limits the room currently being decorated only increased Sophie's curiosity, and Luther said he liked having her around while he worked. As it happened she was not likely to get in the way, for the simple processes of painting and stripping and papering had for her a fascination that called for a grave, still watching, and that Lucy faintly remembered from her own childhood,

408

when grown-up activities that now seemed commonplace and even tedious had worn the aspect of magic arts.

It was fortunate that there was this to engage Sophie's attention, for she was still a year off school age, and having no brothers or sisters she required much entertainment. Her favourite resource, the garden and pond, was untenable in the bitter weather. It was not until February that there was a partial thaw, and some watery sunshine; Sophie pleaded one day to be allowed out, and Lucy relented. She was very busy with her monthly accounts, settling tradesmen's bills and the servants' wages, but Jane the housemaid undertook to go out with Sophie and keep an eye on her; and having made sure the child was well wrapped up, Lucy returned her attention to her housekeeping. At length she was finished, and she closed the desk, stretched, and decided to go and join Sophie. She had just stepped out of the french doors when Jane came tearing across the lawn to her in wild despair.

'Oh, Mrs Stokes, I can't find her ... That dog from number twenty got in through the vegetable patch again and I just went to shoo it away, and when I turned round she'd gone and I can't find her, I can't find her—'

Lucy was already half-way down the long garden: it was her body rather than her conscious mind that impelled her towards the pond. Dimly she heard Jane shouting to her as she hacked and splashed her way into the scummy half-frozen water, pushing at great lumps of ice with her hands.

'. . . I looked there, Mrs Stokes, I looked there first . . .'

Lucy was still disbelievingly sweeping the pond with her red-raw hands when she saw Luther, who had observed them from the window of the room where he was working, come running from the house at full pelt. There was a curious purposefulness about him and he ran straight past them without a look or a word, on to the very end of the garden.

He vaulted the fence there, and Lucy understood. She heard the icy splash of him going into the river and then she was dragging herself out of the pond and running after him.

By the time she had clambered over the fence, hampered by her sodden skirts, Luther was already climbing out on to the frozen river-bank. The little dripping bundle he held in his arms did not move. There was a sensation in Lucy's throat like a key turning in a lock; but before she could let out the cry she was cut off by a long wail issuing from

409

somewhere around the breast of Luther's shirt, the voice unmistakably Sophie's.

'She's all right,' Luther gasped. 'Must have slipped down the bank . . . no harm done.'

The child sobbed as if her heart would break: Lucy did likewise, rendering incoherent the scolding that was as natural an impulse of her relief as the embracing. At last practicality prevailed, and the drenched and shivering little girl was hurried inside. She seemed to have taken no hurt that a hot bath and dry clothes would not cure, but Dr Munro was summoned just in case, and in the meantime Luther had to be got out of his wet things, and some old clothes that had belonged to Radford's father found for him. Distractedly Lucy asked him whether he wanted to go home, but having thoroughly warmed himself before the kitchen fire he said he might just as well stay and carry on with his work.

Throughout all of this, Lucy's emotional state was too wrought up for her to do more than stammer out her gratitude to Luther; but once Dr Munro had been and confirmed that all was well, and Sophie, exhausted by it all, was asleep in bed, Lucy went to the room where Luther was occupied in whitewashing the walls.

'All right, is she?' he said, pausing half-way up the stepladder.

She nodded. 'She's been told – told not to go near the river,' she said.

'Well, in one ear and out the other. Probably wanted to see the ice, same as on the pond.'

His skinny hand was resting on top of the stepladder, and she reached up and squeezed it, clutching it tightly for some moments, until she had to brush a tear from her eye again.

'There, missus,' he said awkwardly. 'It's all right now. Forget it ever happened, I would.'

She smiled, but shook her head. 'I don't forget things,' she said.

XVIII

Well, Matt decided after coming away from the Bressarts'
house and being told once again that they were not at home;
that was the last time. A man could only dance attendance
so long and still keep his self-respect.

Walking blindly away down the street, he noticed that he
was still holding in his hand his card, which he had meant
to leave. He looked at it a moment, and then tore it up and
threw it to the wind.

But bravado rather than resignation was in this gesture:
his mood was black. The partial glimpses of himself as a self-
deluded creature – vainly pinning vague hopes on vaguer
futurities that he had been vouchsafed over the past few weeks
– were not enough to counteract his bitter disappointment at
what seemed the wreck of all he had achieved. Nor was there
the comfort there should have been in the reflection that
much, if not most, remained, and that he still had money
and reasonable prospects for the future. For though he prided
himself on being a practical man without illusions, he still
had the habit of thinking in terms of symbols – the very
hallmark of the idealist – and his intimacy with the Bressarts
had been the most potent symbol of his new-found success.

However, they – and she – no longer wanted to know him:
that much was plain; a reaction echoed in varying degrees
by most of the valley hierarchs whose drawing-rooms had
formerly been open to him. Numerous ideas were hammering
at the closed doors of his mind to be let in; realizations, some
fully formed, some shadowy yet, that a social approval that
could chop and change so swiftly was hardly worth seeking;
that to have tried to cut himself off from his past so completely was as foolhardy as it was doomed; that he had partly
brought this on himself; that pride came before a fall . . .
But he kept them out, and remained alone with his anger
and indignation.

411

Damn Luther! That the disastrous intervention of his former associate was an accident waiting to happen was one of the realizations he kept at bay; the emotion that still seared his heart after his humiliation made him see it as an arbitrary act of malevolence, whether by Luther himself or by Luther as fate's instrument.

One slip, then: one slip in life, and you were finished. It seemed hard, very hard. Of course, the unrelenting hardness of life was one of the articles of his new creed, its corollary being that you had to adapt yourself to it on the principle of 'When in Rome . . .' So it was rather inconsistent of him to protest at the hand fortune had suddenly dealt him. But poor Matt did protest, inwardly and wretchedly; which perhaps suggested that his creed, like others less private and more celebrated, was all sound and no sense, and not much use when it was put to the test.

Of course, what Luther had revealed was true. Matt had not sought for a single moment to deny it. He might in fact have brazened it out with judicious lies, but this had never occurred to him, and he would have rejected it out of hand if it had – another indication, perhaps, that his worldly creed was only the thinnest of coverings over his true nature. But he did firmly believe that it was unfair that he should continue to be punished for ever for that long-ago lapse. Were there no second chances in life?

Or had some other punishment been enacted that awful night? For it had more than once occurred to him, in the course of his long brooding over his fall from grace, that his fate had been sealed not when Luther had drunkenly crashed into his drawing-room, but some time earlier, when he had hustled his former friend out of his office with a hasty five pounds . . . Yet what in God's name was he supposed to have done? Thrown his arms around him and sworn they were blood-brothers? It was all a long time ago, they had changed . . . No: nothing could excuse what Luther had done, because nothing could repair it. There were just some people you couldn't help, he told himself, and Luther had proved that himself.

Matt went home to his plush house; but the place offered no consolations, in particular none of that sense of self that should be a home's first attribute, and it was his sense of self that was in need of restoration. The house seemed to have nothing to do with him; virtually all of it, he now saw, had been fitted out in obedience to quite other criteria than his own tastes; chosen for him rather than by him. It was, besides, haunted by memories of that awful night: he could see Luther circling that leather armchair with his demon's grin and his mocking, devastating words; he could see Helena's haughty, remote face as she left. Worst of all, he could see that that expression had always been there in essence, and only his vanity had prevented him from recognizing it. (Another of those shut-out realizations was that he would soon have found her quite as contemptible as she found him, but he would not let that one in either.)

Inwardly gnawing thus, he roamed about his own rooms, which all felt as if they should have been fenced off with gold ropes, and should have had string tied across the chair-seats to stop people sitting in them; and at last his restlessness drove him out of the house and he went to call on Harry and Joanna.

The hasty wedding having left them no time to find a permanent domicile, the couple had moved into this set of rooms in an old high-ceilinged townhouse off the High Street. They were spacious, but fearfully old-fashioned and inconvenient compared to Matt's house. They were also, he noted with perplexity, curiously comfortable, and he found lately when he visited the couple that he was reluctant to leave.

Of course, the friendliness of his hosts had much to do with that. Joanna always gave him a warm welcome: six months' pregnant now, her prettiness had matured, and several times Matt found himself looking at her with puzzled attention and then realizing that she reminded him of her sister. As for Harry, he was so warmly and faithfully what he had always been that Matt almost wished he was in a position to carry him through another few miles of scorching bush to convey his appreciation.

The staunchness of his friend and partner towards him in his trouble touched and perturbed Matt deeply, and that he could not think of it without a flicker of self-disgust alongside the glow of gratitude was perhaps because he remembered that in Harry's trouble he himself had not been so staunch and open-hearted, and had considered that trouble chiefly in regard to its effects upon himself. Wanting words to express this, he could only try to repay the friendship in kind, and hope that his visits in some way conveyed his contrition for having cast doubts on this match at first, and his pleasure at being proved wrong.

Harry's loyalty was all the more affecting in that he had

nothing to gain, and much to lose by it. Their factoring enterprise was one in which personal goodwill counted, and Matt had lost some of it now; it was not only social credit that was likely to be withdrawn as a consequence of that night. Sitting in Harry and Joanna's parlour that evening he thought of this, and thought too: 'What a mess we've both of us made, when everything seemed set so fair!' And yet Harry did not look unhappy with his lot . . . Am I unhappy? Matt asked himself, and was not only surprised but relieved by the emphatic 'Yes' his heart returned. For in the past year or two he had even come to believe that unhappiness was a sort of failure of the will, a weakness. He had not thought that the true weakness might lie in refusing to acknowledge it.

This evening he found himself asking Joanna, as he often did, how her sister was: he had not seen her since the awful night.

'Oh, yes! I knew there was something I had to tell you,' Joanna said. 'There was very nearly a dreadful accident with little Sophie. She wandered off and fell into the river at the bottom of the garden—'

'Good God,' said Matt, turning white. 'Is she all right . . .?'

'Yes – right as rain. Luckily this Luther Benson, who Lucy's got working for her, managed to get her out . . .' Joanna intercepted, too late, a warning glance from Harry.

'Took him on as a gardener and handyman,' Harry said quickly. 'Anyway, the little girl's perfectly all right, so that's a blessing. Well, old man, I hope you're staying for dinner?'

Matt blinked at him, groping out of a pit of dark thoughts. How could she? She had been there that night, she had seen what Luther had done to him. She had even, he thought, tried to save him. How could she? 'Dinner . . . er, no, that's very kind of you, Harry, thanks all the same, but I – really must be going . . .'

XIX

Lucy had just put Sophie to bed when she heard the knocking, and she came down the stairs to find a wind-blown and agitated Matt delivering his hat and coat to the maid in the hall.

'Lucy, how could you?' were his first words.

He spoke impetuously, in his old manner – was so much, in fact, the Matt she had known and loved as he stood there in the gaslit hall below her, turning up his face in urgent appeal, that it was like a blow to the heart.

'How could you?' he said again.

'Hello, Mrs Stokes, how are you? Very well thank you,' she said lightly, to cover her feelings; but she saw at once he was in that emotional state in which flippancy feels like sand thrown in the face, and she said in an altered tone, 'You mean about Luther, I suppose.'

'I just heard . . . I just heard, and I came straight away to find out if it was true.' He had walked swiftly all the way without his stick, and it was plain that his lame leg was hurting like the devil; the pain made his face white.

'You'd better sit down,' she said. 'Come on. There's a fire in the parlour.'

He followed her, trying to make nothing of his limp; but he did not sit down, leaning instead on a chair-back and frowning at his hands.

'Maybe it's no business of mine,' he said in a suddenly perplexed tone; but then, lifting his eyes to hers, he burst out, 'Oh but, Lucy, you were there that night! You know what he did! You saw it all. And then to go and give him work . . . take him under your wing as if . . . I just don't understand.'

'Luther needed work,' said she simply. 'He was down at the bottom with no way up. You know he's been in gaol?'

'Yes, he . . . he told me,' Matt said, lowering his eyes again.

415

'Well, he had no chance, unless someone gave him one. So that's what I did.'

He was blunt. 'D'you think he deserves one?'

'Oh, Matt, what do any of us deserve? Look, I don't condone what he did that night. But when a man's as low as he was ... I know it's no consolation, but I really believe he's sorry.'

'A bit late in the day for that,' Matt said, though with gloom rather than rancour.

'Why don't you sit down?' she said.

'Yes ... all right,' he said, but abstractedly, and he did not do so: she could tell he hardly knew whether he was sitting or standing. His face had that look, achingly familiar to her, of tortuously tracing out an idea; so he used to look in their old days in the country, the days of the haymaking, the bloody brook, and the house on the hill. 'I don't know ... I just can't forgive him for what he did. And to think of you giving him a job, just as if nothing had happened. It was as if something blew up in me and I had to come ... Is his work all right?'

'Yes. He's finished the dining-room, and he's starting on this room tomorrow.'

'That's another thing I can't understand. I mean, you know perfectly well what he's like. He didn't go to gaol for nothing. How can you be sure you can trust him in your house?'

'I don't know.' She hesitated. 'You might as well ask how you could be trusted when you came back to Cottesbridge.'

This was close to the bone, and she felt at once that she had cut too deep; but he did not flinch, though he was silent for several moments.

'Well,' he said, 'I'm not trusted any more.'

'No .... and I'm sorry about that. That isn't right either, and that's what I'm trying to say, that everybody deserves another chance ... I'm so sorry about what's happened, Matt. But I was sorry for Luther too. It's a sorry world, I'm afraid.'

'It is that,' he said bitterly. 'But I thought at least there was some ... some logic in it, some key to it ... some way of getting along in it without being floored at every turn!'

'Well, there isn't,' said she. 'That's exactly what there isn't. There isn't any justice in the world, and I don't just mean that some people are poor and others rich and all that. It's unjust in another way. It's like playing with a pack of cards

416

that isn't complete. We can be as cunning and skilful at it as we like, and work out all sorts of infallible systems of winning, but it's no good because there's a card missing. And so when we lose we wear our hearts out even more trying to make sense of it . . .'

'But there's got to be some fairness!' he protested.

'Well, there isn't: I've stopped looking for it. There isn't any, unless we make it ourselves, and even that isn't easy. It's just random. You had luck: Luther didn't.'

He seemed about to reject this, but pondered instead. 'What about you?' he said. 'Do you feel you had luck?'

'I don't know,' she said, unable to look at him. 'It depends when you're talking about . . . Anyhow,' she said hurriedly, 'Luther saved Sophie from drowning. If he hadn't been here . . .'

'Yes,' he said, 'I heard about that.' He sat on the arm of the chair; she saw a sad shadow of his old litheness in the action. 'I don't know what to make of it. This talk of luck . . . I worked damn hard to make a success of that factoring business: Harry'll tell you so. Since I came back to Cottesbridge, I've put everything into getting on and making something of myself. I thought I'd succeeded. I thought I'd earned some respect. And then along comes this ne'er-do-well and—'

'Are you talking about respect?' she said. 'Or just respectability?'

He flushed, and said hotly, 'Is respectability something to be despised, then?'

'You would have thought so, once.'

He made an impatient gesture. 'I thought the moon was made of green cheese once. I thought you could reach up and pick the stars like apples off a tree once. I thought you could disregard what the world thought and what it expected of you, once, and just go your own way. I thought love made the world go round, once.' He looked sharply at her. 'We both did, didn't we?'

'Well . . . we were wrong,' she said softly. 'Events have certainly shown that. But sometimes I think I'd rather be wrong than right, if right means believing instead in a lot of petty little conventions, and giving up your soul altogether—'

'As I have, you mean.'

She did not answer. Meanwhile the fire roared in the grate, casting a cosy glow over the room, and inviting them to ease;

417

but the twain still faced each other in impromptu positions; Matt propped against the chair, Lucy standing near the hearth, as if they had just met by accident and were on the point of parting; their arrested postures in themselves indicative that a large freight of feeling was present, and precariously balanced.

'Those old ... dreams of ours,' said Matt, his eyes fixed on the floor. 'If I betrayed them ... well, can you say you didn't do the same?' He gestured around at the comfortable room.

She shook her head. 'We both lost. We both let it beat us. We both took the thirty pieces of silver, Matt. All we can do is admit that.'

'I'm not sure as I do. Not in the way you mean. Silver's better than bronze, Lucy, better than grovelling for halfpennies. I don't see why I should be ... ashamed of what I've achieved, ashamed of the position I've got to.'

'No,' said she. 'No more than you should be ashamed of what you once were.'

'Why, who says I am?' he said, with a laugh, but his face showed that he was stung. 'I just don't want to be forever pulled back by it. What's past is past. It's finished with.'

'Yes,' she said, 'it's finished with.'

He stood, awkwardly; he seemed about to say something, or modify something he had said, but at last he shrugged and said, 'Well, I'm sorry to have burst in on you like this. When I heard, I didn't stop to think, I just ... just lost my head a bit. Bad habit of mine, I'm afraid.'

'Not a new one, though,' she said, faintly smiling.

'I haven't changed completely, then?' he said, his tone a little sardonic; but the exchange had been curiously exhausting for both of them, and the resentment only flickered between them in the lowered atmosphere.

'Only you can tell that,' she said.

She saw his limp as he said goodbye and left the house. She felt she should have pressed him to stay and rest a while longer at the same time as she felt the sheer impossibility of doing so, of spending any more time in close proximity to him without disastrous self-disclosure. For though she had spoken her mind – no other way of proceeding seeming worthwhile to her nowadays – she had certainly not spoken her heart.

XX

Matt set off down the Lessington Road, not particularly cognizant of his direction, which was in any case rendered doubtful by the fog. The thaw had been accompanied by the return of the murk and mist of December, and the slush at his feet mingling with the palpable grey-white air made the whole world seem to be in some intermediate, amorphous, half-crystalline state, and nature in the grip of a primeval metamorphosis. The very light of the street-lamps, feebly penetrating the haze, had the look of some rotten, submarine luminescence.

He stumped on blindly thus for some time, the pain in his leg fiercely present but impressing itself on his mind as no more than an aspect of the powerful anger burning within him. It was an anger that was for some time complete in itself, leaving no room for thought; and it was only gradually that he came to see that his animus was no longer chiefly against Luther.

Against Lucy, then? Perhaps: certainly he had not liked some of the things she had said. But it was his inability to answer them to his own satisfaction that irked him. This, of course, was the time when you were supposed to think of the perfect reply, the unanswerable last word that didn't occur to you at the time; but all his spinning brain was doing was throwing off a series of sarcastic rhetorical questions. So, he had become cold and conventional, had he? He had become enslaved to a lot of puffed-up narrow-minded false values that he would once have despised, had he? That was all his life came to, was it? That was all there was to say about his struggle and his triumph and his failure?

If it had been anyone else but Lucy, he felt sure he could have found a satisfactory answer. But every time he saw her he became less sure of himself, which was incidentally why he had lately resisted more than one wayward impulse to go and call on her. The trouble was she didn't really need to say anything in accusation or reproach: the mere fact of her was like a light that cast a long shadow behind him, a shadow that revealed much of his true shape. He could have rejected with a thousand cogent arguments any insinuation that he had allowed himself to become cold-hearted if it were not for that warmth that was hers, that warmth of heart which she seemed almost physically to emanate, and which silenced him more effectively than any words. How well he remembered that wonderful warmth of hers, from their time together all those years ago! So accustomed was he to thinking of that past time as lost beyond recall that it bewildered him, affronted him, set his whole world on end to see it flashing out from Lucy's soft eyes, and to hear its accents unchanged in Lucy's dark-toned voice; he could not have been more bewildered, in fact, if he had turned a corner in the fog and bumped into his old self in his finisher's apron and cap.

He did turn a corner, but came upon nothing but a denser concentration of fog; so dense, indeed, that every landmark was swallowed up in it. He stopped, and turned himself about. He was in a street, but he had not the faintest idea which one. He had been walking along so deep in thought that he had entirely lost his bearings; and the whiteness, which had about it a stealthy, just-visible motion like the movement of the minute hand on a clock, closed off every perspective.

'This is ridiculous,' he said aloud, and the sound had the quality of a voice spoken indoors rather than in the open air. 'I'm lost, quite lost, in my own home town!'

For a moment he was stricken by an almost childish distress, sharper than any fear he had felt in that long confusion of blood and boredom that had been his experience of war, and which seemed to long for a loving hand to materialize from the fog to lead him to safety. But after a few moments, looking upward, he perceived the faintest red glow through the mist, like a horizontal streak of watercolour laid on with the thinnest of brushes; and all at once knew it to be the light from the iron furnaces that rimmed the escarpment of the valley to the north. His mental map righted itself immediately, and he turned his footsteps in the direction that would lead him home.

'I know where I am now, at least,' he said, again aloud;

but the statement invoked another question – not where was
he, but who was he – and that he left unanswered.

XXI

Luther's work proceeded apace, and by March he had finished the redecoration of the ground-floor rooms and had made a start upstairs. Whilst the work itself had lost its novelty as a spectacle for Sophie, she and Luther had become yet firmer friends, and great was her pride at being daily entrusted with the carrying in of the tray of sandwiches and tea that was provided for him at midday.

'She'll be going to school soon, I should think?' Luther said to Lucy.

'Yes,' Lucy said. 'I wish it didn't have to come in a way . . . but it'll be better for her, mixing with a lot of children of her own age.'

'What name will she go under?'

'Sophie Wedderburn,' Lucy said, and paused. 'That's what Alice wanted . . . And yet I don't know what to do for the best. She might get teased as Alice Wedderburn's child. It's all very well to say she shouldn't be ashamed, but it's easier for a grown-up to shrug that sort of thing off.'

'I should send her as Sophie Stokes,' Luther said decisively. 'When she's older, and can stand up for herself, she can tek the name if she likes. Mud sticks,' he said with his crooked smile. 'I should know that.'

'Would you like to have children yourself, Luther?'

He considered. 'No question about the liking,' he said. 'But I shouldn't want to trust myself with 'em. They might turn out like me.'

'Oh, you shouldn't think like that. Mud can always be washed off, you know. It doesn't stick for ever.'

'Don't it? I'm not so sure.'

It was on a dark gusty day in March that she made one of her charitable visits – she disliked the term but had to accept it – to the Hole, where she noticed several groups of unknown men, in bowlers and shoemakers' aprons, hanging about the grimy streets.

'Men from Saunds,' Mrs Blades told her. 'They came over to Cottesbridge all in a body, to ask for work here; for there's hardly a pair on the books in Saunds, as you may know, ma'am, and the unemployment's something chronic. I'm afraid they'll have no luck, for things aren't so very much better here. Most of 'em will go back peaceable, I've no doubt; but the trouble is there's some who are getting treated at the pubs by folk as felt sorry for 'em, and I'm afraid it might not end so peaceable, for Saunds is a rough little town, as you know, ma'am. "All hair and teeth like a Saunds man", as they say round here. I just pray God they won't start a-fighting, there's trouble anew in the world 'ithout them making it wuss by tearing at each other like dogs in a pit.'

Lucy saw more of the Saunds men lounging about street-corners as she set out for home; but they seemed more defeated and apathetic than troublesome. It was mid-afternoon when she got back to Lessington Road and went upstairs to see how Luther was getting on.

The bedroom on which he had been working that morning was still swathed in dust-sheets, and his paints and brushes and trestles were all in place; but of Luther himself there was no sign. She went downstairs again, and found Sophie in the kitchen helping to shell peas.

'Benson, ma'am?' Jane said. 'Why, I thought he was upstairs still . . . I never heard him go out.'

'He's gone home, Auntie,' Sophie volunteered. 'He said he had a bad head.'

'Did he? When did he go?'

Sophie's face puckered with a child's vagueness about time. 'Well, I was upstairs . . . and I showed him the pretty things in that box, and then I came down for my milk, and then I saw him going out the door, and I said where're you going, and he said he had a bad head so he was going home.'

'What pretty things did you show him?'

'Them ones in that box, Auntie,' said Sophie: grown-ups could be very dense. 'Them ones I like. He said he liked them as well.'

Lucy returned upstairs, a horrible knowledge hovering at her shoulder. She knew the box Sophie meant: it was a jewel-box that still stood on the dressing-table in Radford's old room. A quantity of Stokes heirloom jewellery was contained within, unused: Georgina had taken a few pieces with her on her marriage, but she was not a woman for glittering ornament, and some residual guilt inhibited Lucy from wearing them. There were also some antique coins and medals that had been collected by Radford's father. Lucy had not put the box away because it had been a special pleasure of Sophie's, ever since she first came here, to open it and gravely examine all the pieces before carefully wrapping them in gauze again and putting them back in their compartments.

There the box was, on the dressing-table. Lucy had not prayed for years – if there were any Power to hear she did not consider it worthy of human supplication – but still she found herself breathing some sort of beseeching murmur as she drew the jewel-box to her and lifted the lid.

It was empty.

Disappointment was her first emotion, as she sat heavily down with the open box in her hands: bitter and crushing disappointment, which even overbore her anger at having been duped and taken advantage of. The disappointment was not confined to the individual case, though that was bad enough, for she had begun to like Luther as well as trust him; but her view of human nature, on which she had based all her recent conduct, had suffered a severe blow. That there was something disjointed and inimical in the universe as a whole she had come to accept, but she had hoped and believed that the human beings adrift in it were capable of being the exception to its harsh rule. It was difficult to resist some cynical conclusions, and some might have found relief in a smile of satire and an inward resolution to wash their hands for evermore of the whole mortal tribe; but she could not find even a sour pleasure in this classic manifestation of the old Adam, and was saddened beyond words.

'Oh, Luther, why?' she murmured. 'Why did you have to go and do it? There was no need . . . no need.'

She could not even bear to see the paraphernalia of Luther's recent and apparently so appreciated work, and she closed up the bedroom that he had been painting with all the apparatus just as it was, postponing its removal until such time as she was in better heart to face it. Where Luther had gone and what he meant to do she did not know, and was not much interested: presumably he meant to slip off with his booty in his old elusive way, thence to pop up somewhere else and delude someone else into thinking him a reformed character. The question of pursuit, and recourse to law, occurred to her, only to be dismissed. The jewellery meant nothing, and she had no retributive urge; besides, her feelings about Luther, though not of the friendliest just now, were still coloured by the fact that, if it were not for him, Sophie would very probably not be alive today. And so she decided to do nothing; nothing but, in the old phrase, put it down to experience, though it was an experience she would much rather not have had.

It told upon her spirits, nonetheless, and she was low for the rest of the day, to such a degree that Sophie, who lacked the superdeveloped ego of most children and tended to notice the woes of others, several times asked her what was the matter. She roused herself for the child's sake, and was able to present a semblance of cheer as she went through Sophie's favourite picture-book with her before bedtime; but once the child had gone to bed, gloom overcame her again, and she sat before the fire encompassed with dark thoughts, listening to the rising wind moaning down the chimney and feeling dreadfully alone. And so it was with an almost dizzying leap of the heart that she heard the maid say that Mr Doughty was here to see her.

She sprang up at his coming in; but neither of them could quite manage a coherent greeting.

'I'm sorry to keep barging in on you,' he said, 'only I felt I ought to see you and ... well, apologize for some of the things I said the other week. About Luther, and everything. I didn't express myself very well, perhaps, or perhaps I expressed myself too well ... Anyhow, I felt I ought to come and say sorry ...' He tailed off; for he was himself not entirely sure why he had come. He had simply been drawn back here almost against his will, and indeed had hovered about Lessington Road several times this week resolving to knock and then going away again.

Lucy knew none of this; she only knew that he was the person she most wanted to see in the world, whilst knowing too that her reasons for feeling so were untenable. But in her hurt and dejected state she was not equal to manning all the defensive battlements that she had erected to keep herself safe, and she said in a tone in which the tremulous emotion must have been plain, 'Well, you needn't be sorry, Matt. It looks as if you were right after all ... Oh! I don't know – I 'don't know what to think,' and grateful that here was some-one to whom she could unburden freely, she told him in brief what had happened.

The act of telling was itself therapeutic, and helped clear the mists of confusion that had closed round her in her solitude. It was a sad story, but she knew now that she did not regret her involvement with Luther, and knew she would do the same again; and finding her faith not entirely destroyed as she had first thought, she brightened.

There are few human pleasures quite as intense and irre-sistible as the pleasure of saying, 'I told you so'; but Matt struggled manfully against it, and was as tactful and sympath-etic as it was possible to be. But when he asked her whether she had gone to the police, and she replied that she had not and had no intention of doing so, he could not maintain his restraint.

'But he's stolen from you,' he said. 'He's stolen from you – and not just trifles either – after abusing your trust . . . You, the one person in the world he ought to show a bit of gratitude to!'

'Oh, I don't care about the jewellery,' Lucy said. 'Let him keep it, if he can square it with his conscience.'

'But . . . but it's bare-faced thieving. He shouldn't be allowed to get away with that. Surely you've got to tell the police. Surely you've got to have the law on him, the way he's treated you.'

'No,' she said. 'No, I'm not going to. Probably he does deserve it; but I'm not going to be the one who sends him back to prison. I feel very let down . . . but I'm not going to do that.'

She was in earnest, and Matt knew it; but while his mind acquiesced, his body told a different tale as he paced restlessly round the room, using his stick again, she noticed. At last he came to a halt and shook his head. 'Well,' he said, 'you know your own business best . . . but he's a lucky cuss, that's all I can say. You acted with the best of motives when you took him on, I know, but you shouldn't have done it, Lucy. You shouldn't have given him that second chance.'

'Why, is nobody ever to have a second chance?' she said. '*You* had a second chance, didn't you? Everything seemed ruined and finished for you when you left Cottesbridge all those years ago, but you came back, and you had a second chance.'

He regarded her reflectively as she spoke; and when she had done he said with a strange blind look: 'Well, I'm not sure as I've done any better with my second chance than Luther has with his ... Which makes me think there's only one chance in life, really. Win, or nothing.'

'No, no, no,' she said passionately, 'there has to be a second chance. There always has to be a second chance for people – and a third and a fourth ... Because we're frail, Matt. We're not made of iron, we haven't got lumps of stone for hearts. It might be better if we did, but we haven't. And it's no good trying to live life that way.'

'Is that what you really think of me?' he said wonderingly. 'Iron and stone ...?'

'Perhaps that's the impression you want to give,' she said, and then after a moment, 'but I know better.'

'Do you?' He seemed to consider this. 'I wish I did. I wish I was half as sure of things as you seem to be.'

It was her turn to be surprised. 'Me? I don't think I'm sure about anything in the whole world. I used to be, once.'

'So did I. But I lost it, somewhere.'

'Perhaps that's not such a bad thing.'

'I don't know ...' His glance took in the repapered parlour. 'This was his work, I suppose?'

She nodded unhappily; it had bad associations now, and she had been half considering whether to have it done again.

'My God!' he said with renewed vehemence, 'the sheer gall of it ... I still don't understand why you won't have him ... brought to some sort of account for what he's done.'

'What good would it do? And besides ... he saved Sophie from drowning that day. He saved her life.'

'True ... But I don't see what difference that makes in this case.'

'Well, it does make a difference,' she said; and as he frowned she repeated, 'It does make a difference, Matt. It just does.'

'I don't see it.'

'Well, I don't know how I can make you see it ... All I can say is the old Matt would have seen it.'

She felt she should not have said this, and indeed had hardly intended to, the pressure of the thought giving it verbalization against her will; even so she could not have expected his reaction.

'Damn it all, Lucy,' he said in a voice in which real misery

427

was apparent, 'I *am* the old Matt,' and in unconscious confirmation of his words he pushed back his fringe of dark hair with a gesture so familiar, so characteristic and so well-loved that it brought back to Lucy the days of their joy as vividly as if they were at that moment standing in the abandoned mill with thunder and rain without.

'Oh, Matt, are you truly the same? In every way?' was what she wanted gladly to cry; but an inner voice warned her that her heart in its vulnerability was likely to hear in such a remark just what it wanted to hear, and not what was intended. So she checked herself, saying instead, 'Of course you are . . . I'm sorry. I didn't mean to suggest—'

'What you suggested last time?' he said. 'That I've sold my birthright for a mess of pottage, or a new suit, or a set of calling-cards, or whatever fits? That I've lost my soul, and turned into a prig and a snob and everything I once detested?' He smiled, to show there was no bitterness in his words; and indeed his voice was gentle as he went on, 'Well, I certainly seem to be a man of extremes, if nothing else.'

'You put it very harshly,' she said. 'I certainly never meant to say anything as bad as that to you.'

'No, no,' he said, 'you said some very true things, Lucy. But I resisted them – and I still do resist them – because I didn't feel *here* that that's what I am.' He pointed to his breast. 'But then that's not a place to be trusted, is it? It plays you false . . . or at least it's played me false. I don't think it's ever played you false, Lucy.'

The tenderness in these last words threatened such a breach in her defences that again she had forcibly to remind herself that he always had an impetuosity of expression even when talking of neutral matters. 'Oh, you'd be surprised!' she said, with a light laugh.

He shook his head pensively. 'No, not you . . . And that's why I know I should be guided by your instinct in this business about Luther. And yet it makes me so wild to think of him sneaking out like that, and not even having to look you in the face with the knowledge of what he's done! I reckon he should have that much punishment, at least.'

She shrugged. 'What can we do?'

'Well . . . we could at least go and see if he's done a bunk yet. I imagine he's well away from Cottesbridge by now, but it's worth a try. What do you say?'

'Well . . . all right.' She had as little real hope as he of finding Luther, but it was true that her inaction had contributed to the oppressiveness of her mood, and perhaps she would sleep better tonight if she at least made some effort to resolve the situation.

So, after she had put on her hat and cape, they left the house together, their destination Luther Benson's dingy home in the Hole. A violent wind had sprung up, leaping out at them from round corners with a mad shriek, shaking the early blossom from the suburban trees, and dragging troubled swarms of cloud across the evening sky; and as the twain came to the narrower, closer streets leading to the Hole, the wind fairly hooted down the alleyways and yards, and in its sudden head-on gusts was as unpleasantly physical as a sheet flapped in the face. Hearing the regular tap of Matt's stick upon the cobbles, Lucy said to him, 'Is your leg very bad at the moment? I mean, needing the stick again. You'd stopped using it.'

'I always did need it, really,' he said, his face very wry; and in that admission much was revealed.

There were still a few late workers from the boot-factories hurrying home along the high causeways, blackened aprons flung and twisted by the wind; and amongst them were young closers and finishers who were quite exact counterparts to Matt and Lucy as they had been some five years ago, exhibiting the same youthful mixture of hopefulness and disquiet in the pale faces that swiftly passed through the unstable light of the new-lit gas-lamps. That the thought, *we were once as they*, was going through Matt's mind as it was Lucy's, was indicated by his reflective silence; and it was he at last who said, 'Something like walking back into the past, isn't it? I wonder how it will turn out for them!'

No reply that went beyond conversational commonplace was possible to her at that moment, with his physical proximity, and the equally disturbing proximity of poignant memory; but she was saved by their being almost knocked down by a boisterous trio of men who emerged suddenly from an alley close at hand, and who with beery apologies and laughter went roistering on their way.

'Saunds men, I think,' said Matt. 'You heard about them being in the town today? Apparently there was a bit of a scuffle with some Cottesbridge men in the Lord Spencer earlier. I hope both sides will just go home when they've got their jag, and not start one of their free-for-alls.'

They saw several more groups of loungers as they entered the Hole, some glaring ostentatiously at each other across the street in a manner that suggested that the old inter-town rivalry, which had cost Chauncey Middleton more than one bloody nose, was simmering again. They reached Luther's house without incident, however; but the threatening atmosphere seemed to have infected Luther's stepmother, who was reluctant to open the door to them, and only held it ajar a few inches, presenting the same amount of her face to their view, which was indeed as much as anyone could wish to see of it.

'Mrs Benson,' Lucy said, 'it's Mrs Stokes. Is Luther there? I want to see him urgently—'

'Oh, it's *you*,' the old woman snapped. She opened the door a little wider. 'You're the one he pinched the stuff off, I suppose?'

Lucy and Matt exchanged a glance. 'Is he here?'

'He is not. He's where he should be.'

'What do you mean? Has he—'

'He come home early today,' said the old woman, thrusting out her chin and closing her eyes in a very righteous manner, 'and went skulking up to his room wi' summat under his coat. Well, I knew summat was up. He sat up there all afternoon, hiding and brooding, and when I tried to git in he shut the door on me, not before I'd got a look at what was laying there on his bed. And so I went straight out and fetched the police to him. I've had enough trouble from him before, with his slippery ways . . . I've had enough of it, I tell you. I'm a respectable God-fearing woman, and I en't going to put up with it in my house no more. And so I fetched the police to him. He was still sitting there a-brooding when they came; and the funny thing is he just looked up and nodded, and didn't seem at all surprised-like, and went along with 'em as quiet as you like. Huh!' sniffed the old woman, her expression more comprehensively dislikeable than ever. 'There's no understanding him. I've gin up trying. All I know is I've had enough trouble with him, and I can't be bothered no more.'

'Where is he now, then?' Lucy said.

'Why, didn't I tell you? Where he belongs – at the police station. You'd best go along there if you want your jewels back, though why you ever let him git near 'em *I* don't know.'

Lucy and Matt regarded each other mutely for some

moments after the door had been closed.

'Well,' he said at last, 'this is a turn-up . . . It's almost as if he wanted to be found out. Why on earth didn't he cut and run?'

Lucy found she was half smiling. 'We were talking about second chances,' she said. 'And there's such a thing as second thoughts too.'

'I suppose so . . . Yes. I can't see any other explanation. He gave in to the temptation, and then he couldn't stomach what he'd done. But Lucy,' he said, shaking his head sadly at her smile, 'the police have got him now. Red-handed. We came too late—'

'No,' Lucy said. 'It's not too late. Matt, will you come with me to the police station?'

It was his turn to smile now. 'As if you need ask,' he said, giving her his arm.

The wind was whipping itself up almost to a gale as they set off again, and gritty whirls of leather-dust stung their faces; and on the gusts were borne sharp drunken shouts and snatches of belligerent song from the groups of Saunds and Cottesbridge men who could now be seen at every corner and down every alleyway in larger concentrations. There was a tense, dangerous aimlessness about them as they kicked stones or jestingly nudged each other off the kerb or conferred with each other, heads down and hands in pockets, only to step back with a sudden harsh shout of laughter. The police station, with melancholy appositeness, was not far from the Hole; as Matt grimly remarked as they went in, it was the only amenity the place possessed.

'Ah, Mrs Stokes?' the police sergeant said. 'I was going to send a man to your house as soon as we had one free. We're rather short-handed this evening, ma'am, what with this trouble brewing up in town. You've just discovered the theft, I take it, ma'am? Well, you can set your mind at rest straight away. We've got the fellow here now, and your possessions too. I've a fancy they're all there, though of course he may be trying to keep something back, but you'll be able to tell us exactly what was stolen and—'

'Nothing was stolen,' Lucy said.

'I beg pardon, ma'am?'

'Nothing was stolen,' Lucy said, giving the sergeant her sweetest smile. Matt was watching her attentively. 'It's all a mistake. Benson's done nothing wrong.'

'Well, excuse me if I'm a little confused, ma'am, but the fact is Benson had the valuables in his possession when we were called to him and he's told us—'

'I know,' Lucy said. 'I've just come from Mrs Benson's. And it was all a mistake. I'm sorry your time's been wasted.'

'Are you saying that Benson had charge of these articles with your consent?' said the sergeant, frowning.

'Yes. If you like – whatever. But he didn't steal them. He didn't do anything unlawful. It was all a great mix-up and I'm terribly sorry. So . . . could we see him, please?'

The sergeant sighed. 'You certainly can, ma'am. You can keep him, if you'll excuse the expression. We could do without being bothered with the likes of him tonight, with these Saunds men spoiling for a fight, and a lot of broken bones before morning I shouldn't wonder . . . Norris! Fetch Benson here. And bring Mrs Stokes' possessions.'

Luther was brought from the cell, hunched and pale. He gave one glance at Lucy and Matt before lowering his eyes again.

'Mrs Stokes doesn't intend to bring charges, it appears, Benson, so you're free to go,' said the sergeant severely. 'I don't particularly want to see you here again . . . This is what was found with him, Mrs Stokes. I hope it's all there.'

'It's all there,' Lucy said, scooping up the bundle. 'Come on, Luther.'

They left the police station; and Luther walked at their side in the same mute, obedient way as he had with the policeman who had brought him from the cell. It was Matt who spoke first.

'Well, Luther, old shopmate,' he said, 'I just hope you appreciate your luck.' Lucy shook her head at him; but Luther, suddenly fetching a great breath, said emphatically: 'It was Sophie.'

'What?' said Matt.

Luther stood still, his eyes fixed on the ground. 'It was thinking of Sophie, that's what stopped me. Because it was her who showed me the stuff, all innocent-like. And so when I took it . . . I started thinking how I'd used her, in a way. She showed me the pretty things, as she called 'em, in good faith . . . and I went and took 'em. So I'd used a little child. There's a thought for you, Luther. Tekking advantage of a four-year-old child. Why not start robbing children in the street, if that's what you've come to?' He lifted his eyes to

Lucy's, his face gaunt with despair. 'And so that's why I felt sorry, and stopped, and let 'em take me. That's the awful thing, Mrs Stokes. It weren't even through thinking of you, all you've done for me. Even that didn't stop me, though it should have . . . My God, what does that say about me?' He could not look at Lucy any more, and turned to Matt. 'What d'you think, Matt? Any hope for me?'

'Well, you've had your second chance and lost it, as far as I can see . . . But apparently there's such a thing as a third chance,' Matt said, winking at Lucy, 'so maybe there is after all.'

Luther looked from one to the other of them, and seemed to wince at something more than the wind that cuffed his face; but he seemed unable to say anything more, and they went on.

It was Lucy's intention that they should see Luther home, dazed and disorientated as he was; but in her relief and exultation that her trust had not after all been wholly betrayed, she had become forgetful of the disturbed condition of the streets, especially in the Hole, which was one of those doomed places that always form the natural arena for any fights that are going. However, an alarming reminder was forced upon her by their being almost shoved into the gutter by a stream of men running, either in pursuit or flight, with a fearful clatter and sparking of riveted boots and a smell of liquor that was flung in their faces by the capricious wind. Something like that wind was indeed at large in these shadowy streets; something reckless, unpredictable, and frightening.

'The Hole doesn't look the friendliest of places tonight, Luther,' Matt said. 'Why don't you give it a wide berth, and come home with me? I can put you up.'

Luther hesitated. 'Thanks, Matt,' he said. 'But the thing is, there's the old crow at home – my stepmother, I should say. God knows I've nowt much to thank her for, but I wouldn't feel easy leaving her alone tonight.' He gave his first smile. 'Bit late in the day for an attack o' conscience, you're thinking . . . No, you two go home. I'll be all right. And Matt, about that night at your house—'

He did not finish what he was going to say, for at that moment there burst from the alley directly behind them another gang of men; louder, more drunk, and more uncontrollable. It was plain that those who had fled past them a moment ago had been in flight from these; and though Matt swiftly ushered Lucy and Luther into a recessed doorway, they had been seen; and the gang of men, thwarted of their quarry, took an interest in them instead, and had gathered about them in a moment, forming a close ring about the doorway, and cutting off all possibilities of escape.

'Fine folk for these parts,' said one, studying them, and noting Lucy and Matt's clothes; and there was a general grunt of disinterest, for the shoemakers usually sought 'a good stack-up' only with their own kind.

'That's Cottesbridge for you,' said another. The illumination from one of the Hole's few working street-lamps was directly behind the men, making their voices seem to issue from one many-headed black form. 'Nobody'd walk about Saunds at night fligged up like that. Shows you what lilies they are here!'

'We're Saunds men,' came another voice, with a rasp in it. 'Mebbe you've heard on us. Certainly seems like the Cottesbridge men have, 'cos they're all hiding in their burrows!'

Instinctively Matt and Lucy had placed Luther behind them, so that he was as much in shadow as possible; but now a hand reached out from the ring of men and tapped Luther's shoulder. 'What about you, shopmate?' said a voice. 'Where do *you* fit in?'

'Mebbe a Cottesbridge man: just like 'em to hide behint the posh folks!' said another.

'Wait a minute.' One of the men pushed forward until Lucy could feel his vinous breath on her face; but it was Luther he was staring at. 'I know him. Benson. Ah. I know him all right! So do a lot of people, wuss luck for 'em. He's the one who diddled me at Lessington Feast that time – remember I told you about it? Bastard skinned me. There's a real Cottesbridge man for you!'

A raged, baying cheer went up, a cheer that had blood in it, and a host of arms was thrust forward to pluck Luther out from between them; but suddenly the hands shot back with cries of pain and anger, for Matt had lifted his stick and swung it down in a bruising arc.

'Leave him be,' he said quietly.

'Why, what's he to you then?' jeered a voice. 'Your frigging butler?'

'He's a friend of mine,' Matt said, 'and I say leave him be.'

434

Lucy had spent her youth amongst such scenes as th
and was no stranger to the Hole now, and thus far had
no more than a mild alarm; now she was afraid, horril
afraid, and the tightening ring of shadowed faces, the swii
of Matt's stick, the fumes of beer and tobacco, and th
whooping of the wind, were the constituents of a nightmare.

'It en't you we're concerned with,' said one of the voices,
'it's Cottesbridge men we're after—'

'Well, I'm a Cottesbridge man!' Matt cried, bracing his
stick against the side of the doorway so that Lucy and Luther
were fenced behind it; and from his voice and his expression
Lucy knew that some defiance was in him that was not merely
defiance of these bullies, and that this chance event was
acting as a crucible upon mixed feelings. 'Aye, I'm a Cottesbridge man, and proud of it!'

Nightmarish indeed was the confusion of the next few
moments. Someone lunged at Matt: he hit out, but was
grabbed by the collar, and Lucy saw the scars on the knuckles
of the meaty hand that grasped him. Then the hand was
gone as Luther sprang forward and struck the man a swinging
blow in the face; and in the same moment a stertorously
breathing bulk tried to push Lucy aside and with a sharp
reflexive action she drove her elbow into its stomach. Somewhere in those long moments the conviction came upon her
that they were all three going to be killed; and amidst the
grunting and cursing she became aware of her own voice,
shouting, 'No, no, no . . .'

But another sound had supervened – other voices, and the
clatter of approaching boots – and suddenly their assailants
had whirled about to face an oncoming horde of Cottesbridge
men, who came pounding at them from the other end of the
street. The three in the doorway were forgotten as abruptly
as they had been taken up; and there was an almost palpable
shock, like the impact of waves against rocks, as the two
gangs of shoemakers met in the middle of the street. The
mêlée held a moment, then broke – the Saunds men being
greatly outnumbered, and straggling away in a fighting retreat
to new ground.

The shouts and the heavy footsteps faded away into the
next street, the shrilling of a policeman's whistle being heard
somewhere at hand also; and then there was only the blustering of the wind, and Lucy's continued dry sobbing of 'No,
no, no . . .' Again she was hardly conscious of doing so, and

435

the sound of her voice came as a surprise to her own ears; and it was with the same surprise that she found she had her arms round Matt's neck, and was clinging to him as if resolved that they would die together.

XXII

They had parted with Luther at the corner of his street, and
left the Hole without further trouble; the police were out in
force now, and the cells would be full by morning.

'At least old Luther won't be in one,' Matt said. His leg
was very stiff, and their pace was slow.

'I dare say that sergeant thought I was quite mad,' Lucy
said. 'Matt, do you want to stop and rest a moment?'

'Best if I keep moving . . . Are you all right, Lucy? It wasn't
the most savoury of evenings out, was it?'

'I'm all right now,' she said, as much reference as she dared
make to her lapse. 'Do you – do you think I did the right
thing? At the police station, I mean?'

'Oh Lucy, you shouldn't ask me that!' he said, with the
most rueful melancholy.

'Why not?'

He drew a long breath before answering: 'Because I don't
think I've ever once done the right thing in my whole life.'

She was silent a moment; and then said, 'Which of us
has?'

They turned the corner into Lessington Road. White blossoms were visible on the pavement, stirred only a little by
the dying wind.

'Moon's up, look,' Matt said. 'Wind's down now. Must
have blown over.'

The tap of his stick was heavier, and without thought she
put her arm through his.

'But for what it's worth,' he said, 'I think you did the
right thing. What you said about second chances – I've been
thinking a lot about that. I reckon you're right there too, no
doubt about it; but it just makes me wonder . . . If we could
always expect to get a second chance in everything, would
that make us act differently in the first place?'

He looked with anxious expectancy in her face, as if

expecting an answer; but she could not give one. 'I don't understand,' she said.

'Well,' he said, licking his lips, 'take you and me – as we were. If we'd known what was going to happen . . . You see, it seems to me looking back that we expected the world to lay a carpet out for us, just because we . . . because of the way we felt about each other. Or at least, I reckon I expected it. And when it didn't turn out that way, I thought, right, that's it, no good. Bit like a child throwing down a toy and breaking it because he can't make it go. And if someone had talked to me about second chances then, I probably would have scoffed and said, well, in so many words, that I wanted the world on a plate there and then or nothing.'

'We expected too much,' she said simply. 'We expected too much – out of love. You have to stop believing in love like that before . . . before you can . . .' She could not go on: this was too naked, and she could not speak with composure any more; but Matt was nodding vigorously, and his face, drawn and tired, was yet lit with that same animation that she remembered from the derelict mill and the fields and the Feast and all their time together. 'You've thought it all through, you see!' he said with admiration. 'That's what's so wonderful about you, Lucy – and always was. I'd go hopping from one false conclusion to another, and you would think it out—'

'It isn't thinking,' she burst out, unable to bear the regard of those eyes which so disturbingly, treacherously resembled the way he had once looked at her, 'oh, Matt, it isn't thinking. It's feeling. Oh, yes, I do believe what I said about second chances . . . but it's partly because I *want* to believe that, for my own sake.' She stood still: her throat suddenly hurt her, and she feared that she was going to burst into tears in the middle of Lessington Road. 'If I believe there's always a second chance, then I can believe there's a second chance for us. Do you see? And I shouldn't have said it,' she said, turning aside to hide her face, 'I shouldn't have said it.'

'Well, I believe that too,' she heard Matt's voice saying. 'My dear, I believe that too . . . Lucy!'

The final exclamation was soft, hushed, and scarcely audible even in that quiet street; but it fell upon her ears like a shout. The hand that touched her arm was gentle too, but so forcible in its effect upon her that it spun her round and into his embrace in an instant.

At long last they stirred, and walked on together towards her house. It was a clear still night now; the wind had spent itself, the threatened storm having been no more than a gusty fraud. And, just as with passion, the truest thing about it was the peace that followed it.